W9-DGW-967

Books by Lisa Plumley

MAKING OVER MIKE

FALLING FOR APRIL

RECONSIDERING RILEY

PERFECT TOGETHER

PERFECT SWITCH

JOSIE DAY IS COMING HOME

ONCE UPON A CHRISTMAS

MAD ABOUT MAX

SANTA BABY
(anthology with Lisa Jackson,
Elaine Coffman, and Kylie Adams)

I SHAVED MY LEGS FOR THIS?!
(anthology with Theresa Alan,
Holly Chamberlin, and Marcia Evanick)

LET'S MISBEHAVE

HOME FOR THE HOLIDAYS

MY FAVORITE WITCH

HOLIDAY AFFAIR

MELT INTO YOU

Published by Kensington Publishing Corporation

PRAISE FOR THE
NOVELS OF LISA PLUMLEY

HOLIDAY AFFAIR

"Secrets and subterfuge add complexity and zing to this well-crafted, heartwarming story that features a wealth of engaging characters, including five remarkable, memorable children, and great sexual tension. A deliciously satisfying, cocoa-worthy holiday read."

—*Library Journal*

"As is the case with most of Plumley's books, *Holiday Affair* has quirky characters that will make you smile and a fast-paced story that will make you hesitate to slip a book-mark between the pages. *Holiday Affair* is full of Christmas atmosphere and activities, which makes it a great read during the holidays."

—Lezlie Patterson, McClatchy-Tribune News Service

"Lisa Plumley's latest holiday novel delivers. It has warm, gooey holiday moments complete with happy children, Christmas traditions such as caroling and decorating Christmas cookies and, oh yeah, hot and steamy romance. Loaded with fun pop-culture references and witty dialogue, *Holiday Affair* delivers on entertainment!"

—*The Romance Reader* (Five Hearts!)

"A delightful story with utterly charming characters. It brings to life the sounds, smells, and tastes of Christmas as it brings together more than just the two main characters for a joyous holiday season."

—*Romantic Times Book Reviews* (4½ stars)

MY FAVORITE WITCH

"In keeping with Plumley's tradition of lively romantic comedy (*Home for the Holidays*), her first foray into the paranormal-witch-world subgenre is quirky, sexy, creative, and hilarious."

—*Library Journal*

"Humorous adventures and unexpected romance with a sprinkling of heartwarming moments will keep the reader well entertained in this delightful tale, skillfully crafted by the clever Plumley."

—Booklist

"Lisa Plumley delves into paranormal romance, venturing into new territory while keeping her own brand of humor and delivering a delightfully witchy tale in the process."

—Lezlie Patterson, McClatchy-Tribune News Service

HOME FOR THE HOLIDAYS

"Lisa Plumley once again gifts readers with a Yuletide story sure to put you in a holiday mood. This is vintage Plumley. She's created a cast of characters that are a bit eccentric, quirky, and likeable and spun a story that will make you smile."

—Lezlie Patterson, McClatchy-Tribune News Service

"A delightful secondary romance adds to the fun in this upbeat romp that is touching, hilarious, and lightly dusted with seasonal charm."

—Library Journal

LET'S MISBEHAVE

"Once again, Plumley shows her fine flair for comedy as Marisol learns that there is life beyond Rodeo Drive, and the Connelly triplets discover that they can't scare away every nanny. Full of witty dialogue and hilarious situations, this romp with a heart is certain to please readers."

—*Booklist* (starred review; named one of the Top Ten Romances of 2007)

"Plumley not only delivers a fun-filled premise, clever dialogue and a delightfully sexy sports-loving hero, she brings to life a memorable, hilarious and utterly unique heroine readers will adore. This is pure romantic fantasy and an absolutely entertaining novel from start to finish."

—*Romantic Times Book Reviews* (4½ stars; Top Pick!)

Together for Christmas

LISA PLUMLEY

ZEBRA BOOKS
KENSINGTON PUBLISHING CORP.

http://www.kensingtonbooks.com

ZEBRA BOOKS are published by

Kensington Publishing Corp.
119 West 40th Street
New York, NY 10018

All Kensington titles, imprints, and distributed lines are
available at special quantity discounts for bulk purchases
for sales promotion, premiums, fund-raising, educational,
or institutional use.

Special book excerpts or customized printings can also be
created to fit specific needs. For details, write or phone the
office of the Kensington Special Sales Manager: Attn. Special
Sales Department. Kensington Publishing Corp., 119 West
40th Street, New York, NY 10018. Phone: 1-800-221-2647.

Zebra and the Z logo Reg. U.S. Pat. & TM Off.

ISBN-13: 978-1-4201-2212-1
ISBN-10: 1-4201-2212-6

First Printing: October 2012

10 9 8 7 6 5 4 3 2 1

Printed in the United States of America

To John, Kyle, and Ian,
who make all my Christmases merry!

Chapter 1

Kismet, Michigan
T-minus 21 days until Christmas

Babysitting wasn't usually in Casey Jackson's repertoire. Neither was snow.

Taken together, that made it pretty damn confounding that he was currently driving through a blizzard on his way to a babysitting job. But this babysitting job was special. It was, quite literally, a babysitting job he couldn't refuse.

Not if he wanted to stay gainfully employed, at least.

Which he did. It was a matter of necessity. And pride.

Squinting through the windshield of his rented four-wheel-drive Subaru, trying not to become hypnotized by the flurries of snowflakes hitting the glass, Casey reminded himself he could do this. He could babysit. *And* he could drive through a snowstorm.

Hell, he could do anything! He might not typically hang out with rug rats (a very deliberate choice) or grapple with badass subzero weather conditions (or *any* weather conditions, really)—as a top troubleshooter with one of L.A.'s premier talent agencies, he had little need to do either—but he *did* get things done. He got problems sorted, difficult divas placated, and on-set imbroglios smoothed over.

Making things right was Casey's specialty. Handling things that other people couldn't manage was his forte. He was the man who got in, got everyone back on track, and then got out . . . leaving everyone in his wake satisfied, harmonized, and improbably happy to have been "managed" by the best in the business. It was just what he did. He didn't know why he did it so well. He just . . . did.

Until Casey had joined his agency, his job hadn't even existed. One crucial averted crisis later, it had. Thanks to his first major success, now his agency paid him to go wherever necessary to rehab star athletes' dinged public images, settle down wild rockers and rappers, and mollify demanding megastars—megastars like pop sensation Heather Miller, whose over-the-top, over-budget, wildly ambitious *Live! from the Heartland* televised Christmas special had brought him to Kismet in the first place.

His agency didn't usually pay Casey to babysit. But they *did* trust him enough to give him a very long leash. That meant that he was free to deal with crises like this one on his own terms. If Casey wanted to spend the next few weeks making like a muscle-bound, frostbitten, ridiculously over-paid man-nanny while he worked his deal-making magic with Heather Miller and her TV special, he could. So that's what he was going to do.

Even if the thought of doing it while stuck in the tiny, touristy, northwestern Michigan burg of Kismet made him want to bolt for Gerald R. Ford International Airport in Grand Rapids, some fifty miles distant, and forget he'd ever set foot in town.

Seriously. The place was like a freaking Christmas card come to life, Casey realized as the blizzard momentarily eased up. He ran his windshield wipers to push away the snow and then peered outside again, taking in the pictur-esque, snow-piled, lively small-town streets surrounding him. Old-fashioned holiday decorations were plastered over every inch of available space. Holiday music wafted from municipal speakers, penetrating his car's windows as he waited at a stoplight. Shoppers bustled to and fro on the surrounding sidewalks, carrying overstuffed bags and smiling at one another. A few of them even smiled at *him*.

He frowned, momentarily bewildered by their neighborliness. Then he smiled back. He lifted his gloved hand in a brief wave.

The passersby waved back, then kept going. Still flummoxed, Casey watched as they made their way into a nearby sweetshop, stamping their booted feet and adjusting their woolly scarves.

L.A. was friendly enough—hell, just about everyone everywhere was friendly to Casey—but this bucolic, over-the-top holiday jollity was different. It was totally inexplicable.

Somehow, he realized, his newest assignment had taken him to *The Twilight Zone 2.0: The Hallmark Channel Edition*.

Most of the year, as Casey had learned before leaving L.A., Kismet was a resort town full of lakeside B&Bs, busy bait-and-tackle shops, dusty antique stores, and run-down mom-and-pop restaurants. Thanks to in-state day-trippers and out-of-state vacationers who were willing to pay for its kitschy ambiance, the town had done all right for itself, even in a shaky economy.

What Casey *hadn't* uncovered beforehand—what everyone at his agency had undoubtedly hidden from him (with good reason)—was that, in December, the whole damn place turned into Christmas Central. It was, Casey thought as he surveyed the scene anew, like a Norman Rockwell painting crossed with a Bing Crosby song dosed with a big handful of silvery tinsel and hung with candy canes, then broadcast in surround sound and Technicolor. It was idyllic and authentic and damnably jolly.

It smelled like gingerbread, too. *All over town*. He'd

noticed that as he'd gotten out of his car on location to meet Heather Miller. The fragrance still lingered here, miles away. How was that even possible? Who ate gingerbread, anyway? Elves?

The upshot was, Kismet was everything Casey typically avoided. Times ten. Wrapped in a bow. With chaser lights on top and a garland of mistletoe on the side and *way* too much ho-ho-ho-ing going on in the background. Because, to put it bluntly, Casey was not a "Christmas" kind of guy. As a matter of principle, he dodged all things green and red and sparkly and heartwarming. As a matter of necessity, he didn't "do" the holidays. As a matter of fact, he'd never even been tempted to.

Nothing short of a catastrophe on the scale of Heather Miller's problem-plagued, currently in-production holiday special—and the lucrative bonus Casey stood to earn if he brought it in on budget and on time—could have made him spend more than an hour in a town like Kismet: a place that promised candlelit ice-skating sessions, an official Christmas parade, a fanciful holiday-light house tour, sleigh rides with genuine jingle bells, a Santa Claus-lookalike contest (in the town square, right next to the community's fifty-foot decorated Noble fir tree), *and* a weekly cookie-decorating get-together and jamboree.

It was all so flipping wholesome. Casey thought he might be breaking out in freckles and naiveté already. It was possible he felt an "aw-shucks" coming on. He'd only been in town an hour—long enough to meet Heather Miller, hear her initial demands, and start laying the groundwork for the two of them to come to terms. At this rate, he'd morph into Gomer Pyle by lunchtime.

Muttering a swearword, Casey set his Subaru in motion again. He suddenly craved a cigarette, a shot of tequila, and a week's worth of irresponsible behavior—not necessarily in that order.

Boundaries made him itchy. Coziness made him cranky.

And the holidays . . . well, they sent him straight into Scrooge mode.

While Casey realized that that character quirk was part of what made him ideal for this job—because his antipathy toward the holidays gave him a necessary clarity about Heather Miller's TV special and all its escalating complications—he still wasn't ready for . . . *this*.

He hadn't been ready for Heather Miller's opening salvo in their negotiations, either. Probably because she'd caught him off guard.

The problem is my little sister, the pop star had told Casey bluntly and confidentially, giving him an *almost* credible dose of blue-eyed solemnity in the process. *I haven't been back home to Kismet for a while,* Heather had confided, *and frankly, I think she's a little starstruck. I need someone to keep her . . . occupied for a while, so I can focus on performing.*

Casey had been dubious. He'd pushed Heather a little more, relying on his ability to establish an almost instant rapport.

But *People* magazine's pick for "sexiest songstress" had remained adamant. However unlikely her story, she'd stuck to it.

If you can keep Kristen busy for a while, I'm sure I can make fabulous progress on my special! Heather had insisted. She'd tossed back her long, famously blond hair (there was a shade of Garnier hair color named after her), offered him a professionally whitened smile, and added, *Kristen is a great girl. Just a little . . . unsophisticated. She's never left Kismet. She doesn't "get" show business the way you and I do.*

By the time the former *Rolling Stone*, *Vanity Fair*, and *Vogue* cover girl had quit describing her "tomboyish" younger sibling, Casey had formed a pretty clear picture of the braces-wearing, cell phone-toting, gawky girl with Bieber Fever and a wardrobe of Converse sneakers whom he was expected to babysit.

He'd decided to agree to do it, too. To babysit. *Him*.

Or at least, if not technically *babysit*—because Heather hadn't actually used that particular word—then *entertain* the kid long enough to allow Heather to get down to work.

It wouldn't be so bad, Casey figured. He'd probably trail little Kristen Miller to the mall, listen to her squee over the latest *Twilight* movie with her bubblegum-chewing friends, and watch her check in to Facebook a zillion times a day. Maybe he'd help her with her homework or something. Maybe he'd take her to the zoo. If the zoo was open in December. Whatever it took to keep her out of her older sister's way until the TV special was in the can, that's what Casey was prepared to do.

Frankly, he'd agreed to do worse a few times in his life.

As a gambit meant to earn some goodwill with Heather while encouraging her to fulfill her contractual obligations to the network, it wasn't ideal. It was time consuming and inefficient and oblique. He didn't like the idea of keeping the younger Miller sister "out of the way," either. It seemed heartless. As far as Casey was concerned, Heather should have worked out her differences with her kid sister herself, straightforwardly and reasonably, the way a regular person would have done.

But in this scenario, as in all others, Heather was "the talent." That meant she was exempt from normal human behavior and normal human expectations. Casey had logged plenty of hours pacifying performers like her. He knew the score by now. More than likely, Heather's little sister did, too.

If Kristen Miller was wreaking havoc on the TV special, causing delays for America's sweetheart, she'd have to be dealt with. Casey would have to be the one to do it. The sooner, the better. Once he'd assessed the situation more closely, he'd reevaluate things, he promised himself. For now, he planned to meet Kristen, figure out her angle, and see what happened from there. It wasn't a perfect beginning, but it was a start. And Casey believed, above all else, in moving forward.

Because nothing ever lasted forever.

Except maybe fruitcake.

And that persistent gingerbread aroma all over town.

It was actually starting to smell good to him. Spicy and sweet and full of down-home goodness, with just a *hint* of—

Ugh. Screw this, Casey decided as he noticed the unbelievably sappy direction his thoughts had just taken. He was jonesing for old-timey gingerbread, daydreaming about its flavor profile like a wine aficionado anticipating a limited-run Napa Valley merlot, *craving* its Christmassy qualities most of all. *I need a detour from Christmasville before I do something stupid.*

So he wrenched his steering wheel sideways, floored the gas, and pulled into his destination fifteen minutes ahead of schedule. He might not find the Teenaged Terror of TV Specials in the first place Heather had suggested he look, but anything was better than giving in to Christmas . . . and all the syrupy, sentimental, *deceitful* promises that came right along with it.

Chapter 2

When her sister had called her in a panic, warning her about some L.A.-based "hatchet man" who'd come to Kismet to shut down her part-live, part-taped holiday TV special, Kristen Miller hadn't thought much about it. She was used to Heather acting like a drama queen. The whole world was used to Heather acting like a drama queen. After all, Heather had earned multiple accolades, bucketsful of cash, and three People's Choice Awards for her ability to "entertain" people . . . by acting like a drama queen.

Whether the situation called for it or not, Heather was always up for a bravura performance. She'd become famous for singing, but she'd never been limited to that. These days, more often than not, her antics involved fashion shows, dating, or just "being seen" at a fabulous party or gala red carpet.

People *loved* Heather. They loved buying the things she bought, going the places she went, and saying the catch-phrases she said. They loved seeing her, hearing about her, and thinking about her. They loved reading about her. They loved . . . her.

At least most people did. On the phone, Heather was insisting that the "hatchet man" had come to Kismet to destroy her career. So *he* probably did not love her. Very much.

As far as Kristen could tell, he was a minority of one.

"The production company must have hired him," Heather said with an Oscar-worthy tremor in her voice. "He's here to *ruin* me! He's here to torpedo my chances with the network! Forever! If *he's* here, it can't be good. It can't be. Casey Jackson is the industry's hit man! He's a contract killer! You should hear the stories they tell about him! This one time, they say, he—"

"Hold on. Take a deep breath," Kristen interrupted. She ducked into the tiny office space she kept at the back of her diner. It was quieter there, away from the clamor of the kitchen and the din of the front of the house. "I doubt anyone is out to get you *or* to ruin your career. There's probably a reasonable explanation for all of this," she said, because nothing ever went wrong for her famous sibling. "But I'll be on the lookout anyway. Okay? Thanks for the warning. Now, the breakfast rush is still going on and this place is packed, so I've really got to—"

"You've got to do *more* than just be on the lookout!" her sister shrieked. "You've got to *stop* him for me!"

"How am I supposed to do that?"

"Keep him busy. Distract him. Keep him *away* from me, no matter what!" Heather begged. "If Casey Jackson gets his way, I'll *never* get my own reality show. And you know how much I really, *really* want my own reality show."

"I know." Her sister was fanatical about getting her own TV show ("Like the Kardashians, only classier!"). She saw her *Live! from the Heartland* TV special as a crucial first step— as a real-time audition and showcase. She'd talked about little else since blowing back into town. Because despite all her success and popularity, inexplicably, Heather still wasn't satisfied.

"I know you want that," Kristen said gently. "I do. I hope you get it. I really do. But I don't know how I can possibly help with this situation, except to say 'calm down'"—here, she mimed breathing in deeply—"and try to get some perspective."

There was a pause. The sounds of hammering and chattering filtered over the line in the background. Heather was on set, then. Just when Kristen started thinking she'd made a dent . . .

"I know! Feed him some of your pie!" Heather suggested brightly. "Once The Terminator has had some of your pie, he'll—"

"Wait. 'The Terminator'?"

"That's Casey Jackson's nickname in L.A."

Kristen scoffed. "It is not."

"Would I lie to you?"

Hmm. Better not answer that one. Instead, in her most soothing tone, Kristen said, "My pie isn't magical." It *was* her diner's most popular item, though. Hands down. "I can't just feed your Terminator some pie and then have my way with him."

"Yes, you can!" Heather blurted. "Feed him pie! You never know until you try. That stuff is addictive. Once you give The Terminator a few bites, he'll be putty in your hands."

"You are seriously overstating my culinary charms."

"I am not. Just don't be fooled! He'll *seem* nice. He'll *seem* charming," Heather cautioned. "But underneath it all, The Terminator has all the heart and soul of a calculator."

"He can't be that bad."

"Oh yes, he can." Another clatter-filled pause. Then, ominously, Heather added, "He doesn't even like Christmas."

"He doesn't like Christmas?" Kristen froze. The idea didn't compute. "What kind of person *doesn't* like Christmas?"

"The kind of person who comes to shut down another person's Christmas special! That's what I've been telling you!"

"Okay. So you might have a point."

"I know! That's what I've been saying. That's why you have to keep him away from me."

"Right," Kristen said sarcastically. "With magical pie."

"Yes," Heather agreed, completely oblivious to her sarcasm. She could be very single-minded when she wanted something. "Or with . . . whatever else you have available. Sure!"

Kristen sighed. "I'm not going to let you pimp me out to some uptight, permatanned CPA type from La-La Land, Heather."

"Well . . . he's not *quite* a CPA type," her sister hedged, sounding vaguely pensive. "I told you, he's a hit man. But a hit man with charisma. A killer. But with a smile." Possibly sensing that her hyperbolic descriptions weren't helping, Heather tried again. "I guess he's kind of a . . . necromancer. Yeah, that's it. A necromancer! It *sounds* cool, sure, but—"

"A person who communicates with the dead?"

"Oh. No. Is that what that means? Not that, then." The sound of someone else chuckling came over the line. Then a swat. Blithely, Heather regrouped by offering, "He's a magician. A sorcerer. A charmer for hire. The Terminator is like George Clooney in that movie where he goes around and fires people for a living. He's dangerous *and* charismatic. He's—"

"George Clooney, huh? That doesn't sound so bad. Maybe you're overreacting. It wouldn't be the first time."

"—like one of those snakes that hypnotizes you and then bites you. *Poisonously bites you,*" her sister said with blatant melodramatic flair. "He's sneaky. He's smart. You never see him coming. You just see him leaving. I'm lucky I got out alive! Someone tipped me off this morning, otherwise I would have—"

"I'll try to find out why he's here," Kristen broke in, sensing this could go on a while. "I'll see what I can do about keeping him away from your special, too." For instance, *asking* him to stay away might work, she reasoned. Telling him her sister was a temperamental artist who couldn't "create magic" while under stress might work . . . *if* she could pull off calling her own sister an "artist" with a straight face. "Maybe he doesn't even know about your budget over-runs and on-set delays."

Heather snorted. "He knows. He knows *everything*."

"Fine. He knows everything." The easiest way to placate her sister, Kristen had learned through long experience, was to agree with her. "Now can I get back to my customers? The diner is jammed. Some of us have to work for a living, you know."

"Hey! I work for a living."

"Of course you do. Sexy dancing is backbreaking."

"Har har. Just help me, okay?"

"I already said I would." *And I never go back on my word.*

Her sister breathed a relieved sigh. "Thank you."

"Don't thank me yet. I haven't done anything."

"You will. I know you will! You're smart like that."

At that blatant cajolery, Kristen smiled. Living in L.A. had certainly changed her sister. When they were kids, Heather would have tried bullying her into going along with this plan. She wouldn't have bothered with flattery.

"You don't have to sweet-talk me. I already said yes."

"But it's true! You're the smartest person I know!" Heather assured her. "If anyone can successfully distract The Terminator, it's you."

"I'm not going to call him The Terminator."

"Fine. If anyone can successfully distract Casey Jackson, it's you. I mean it, Kristen. He totally arrived here out of the blue! You have *no idea* how disruptive that can be!"

"Hmm. I have some idea." Heather's unexpected return to Kismet had thrown Kristen's entire life into turmoil—and put a serious hitch in her Christmas this year, too. She didn't exactly want her sister to leave town already . . . but she would have preferred *not* having her holidays hijacked by the glam squad. "Don't worry. I'll handle it."

Biting her lip, Kristen considered the tricky logistics of trying to extract information from and/or "distract" a professional career killer and/or sneaky snake like Casey Jackson. It was a good thing Heather was prone to exaggerating—and there probably wasn't a genuine problem here—because Kristen definitely didn't have time for this.

Especially not when . . . "He *really* hates Christmas?"

"Almost as much as he hates children and puppies." A dramatic pause. "That's right: He hates children and puppies."

"Come on."

"Cross my heart and hope to end up on *TMZ* tomorrow."

Uh-oh. This *was* serious. Heather hated trashy tabloids. Especially *TMZ*. Tabloid "news" shows, magazines, paparazzi, and stalkerish celebrity bloggers were her nemeses. Which was ironic, given that gossip media had, arguably, created her fame—and did a lot to keep it stoked, too.

"And *speaking* of *TMZ*," Heather went on in a harassed tone, clearly winding up for a good tirade, "do you know what those bastards think they caught me doing now? *On camera?*"

"Actually, I have to get back to work now. So—"

"Buying toilet paper at Walmart. The economy pack!"

Genuinely mystified, Kristen shrugged. "So?"

"So I have *people* to do that stuff for me! I wouldn't be caught dead doing my own toilet-paper shopping!" Heather's voice dropped meaningfully. More on-set hubbub came over the phone. "*You* wouldn't know anything about that *TMZ* story, would you?"

"Huh? Why would I know anything about that?"

"Just wondering. Okay. Never mind. We'll talk soon! *Ciao!*"

And that, as they said, was that. Thanks to one typically baffling and overwrought phone call, Kristen was stuck running interference between her self-absorbed celebrity sister and the supposedly robotic, number-crunching, child-hating, puppy-kicking, soulless, Grinchy, *charming* bastard who'd just hit town to shut down Heather's TV special.

As if Kristen didn't have enough to deal with right now.

Because as much as she wanted to be on her sister's side—first, last, and always—Kristen knew better than to blindly trust Heather's take on things. Her sister's judgment wasn't the best. Heather's view could be . . . well, seriously skewed.

Her advisors were completely out of touch with reality, too. A person only had to look at the indoor set for her holiday TV special to realize that. There, Heather had four glammed-up Christmas trees, all "sponsored" by various companies, each with a particular "designer" theme: *Vogue* Christmas, "Russian Czar" Christmas, prairie Christmas, "Elvis-in-Vegas" Christmas . . .

And the madness hadn't stopped there, either. Since sweeping into town, Heather's "glam posse" had taken over Kismet, pretty much ruining the holidays in the process. Who knew what other havoc they'd wreak before they were through?

Things had been fine until Heather and her entourage had arrived. Kristen had been content with visiting her sister in L.A. or New York or London. She'd been content with having a long-distance sisterly relationship via phone calls and Facebook and texting. She'd been *perfectly* content with her cozy, happy, regular-gal life in Kismet, her job, her friends, her modest apartment, and her weekly Drunk Yahtzee night. She'd been looking forward to Christmas, too, just the way she did every year. But Heather's invasion had thrown everything into a tizzy.

Now everything that Kristen had worked for, everything she treasured, everything that was good and normal and non-showbizzy and *real* in her life was at serious risk of vanishing.

She was at serious risk of vanishing.

At least it felt that way.

And since even her parents—who were normally caring

and sensible and smart—didn't see the problem, she was on her own.

Except for her friends, of course, Kristen remembered as she pocketed her cell phone and headed back to work.

But her friends had all been inexplicably "busy" ever since Heather had stormed into town, so . . .

So Heather had abandoned Kismet years ago, and this was *her* territory now, Kristen reminded herself resolutely. It was her place to be herself, to live her life . . . and to find out exactly what Casey Jackson wanted before her sister had a full-fledged meltdown. It was the least she could do, right?

Grabbing a full coffeepot, Kristen shook out her hair, put on a smile, and then prepared to save the day, sister-style.

After all . . . how problematic could one "Terminator" really be?

Chapter 3

ANOMIA (uh-NOH-mee-uh) *noun*: the inability to recall names of people or objects

On set in Kismet, Michigan
December 4

Heather Miller hung up her cell phone, then used it to wallop the man standing next to her. "Quit laughing, you dope!"

Alex Taylor only guffawed harder. "You should've seen the look on your face." He adopted a smug, smarty-pants expression—one Heather doubted *she'd* ever sported. "'I guess he's kind of a . . . necromancer,'" he mimicked in a high-pitched voice. "Ha!"

"*You're* the one who got me that Word of the Day calendar."

"I was being thoughtful. You said you left yours in L.A."

"Oh yeah. Right." Uneasily, Heather squirmed. She didn't want to fib to Alex, but she didn't want him to think she was stupid, either. "I guess I was just so happy to have another calendar that I got all overzealous about using it."

"Aha. See there? 'Overzealous' was yesterday's word."

He smiled at her, probably unaware of the high-octane sex

appeal he was unleashing. He seemed unaware of a lot of things. Like, for instance, the massive crush she had on him.

"I know." She hadn't. "I was testing to see if you knew."

"Looks like I did." Another smile. "So . . ."

"So . . ." Dreamily, Heather gazed at him. Alex was *so* smart. And talented. And disciplined. As the construction manager for her holiday TV special, he was responsible for designing and building all the sets she used. He had the muscles to show for all that heavy lifting, too. Not that Alex was just a meathead. He was also a trained architect, a partner in a firm in L.A., *and* the holiday production's unofficial trivia champion.

Ordinarily, Heather didn't go for the brainiac type. But there was something about Alex that really got to her.

Unfortunately, the minute they wrapped production on *Heather Miller: Live! from the Heartland,* she and Alex would go their separate ways, probably never to see each other again.

Heather couldn't let that happen. She just couldn't.

She'd never felt this way before. Not even when she'd signed her first recording contract—and *that* had been a thrill.

"So . . . you really did everything you could to make Casey sound like a serial killer just now." Alex nodded attentively, appearing wry and adorable and clever, as usual. "I thought you wanted to set him up with your sister. On a blind date."

Again, Heather squirmed. She wasn't good at fibbing.

She was good at *performing,* though. She was very good at pleasing people. So she pretended that the cover story she'd concocted—to ensure that The Terminator didn't shut down her TV special before she managed to make Alex fall in love with her—was true, and hoped that it would please Alex, too.

"I *do* want to set her up with him," Heather agreed, wide-eyed. "I think they'll be perfect together. But it has to feel like *her* idea, or it's doomed." She gave a helpless shrug. "What can I say? The worse I make him sound, the more my sister will want him. It's a reverse-psychology thing."

"Wow. I will never understand women."

"I know. We're crazy, right?" Heather heard herself give a hideous giggle and wanted to kick herself. Alex already thought she was a vacuous airhead. He'd practically said so. She didn't have to help along that impression, did she? But something about Alex just obliterated every ounce of her cool. "Kristen is kind of a . . . contrarian when it comes to dating," Heather lied.

"'Contrarian'!" Alex beamed. "That's tomorrow's word."

Heather felt as though she'd scored a million points by using it. Maybe if she learned enough new things, Alex would be impressed. She needed to get more books. Like, yesterday.

Heather had never regretted leaving high school early to take her shot at stardom. After all, she'd succeeded. But now she regretted not knowing more . . . not *being* more than she was.

"You peeked, didn't you?" Alex was saying. Adorably.

"At my calendar?" At his nod, she gave a carefree wave. "Well . . . I'm not very good at waiting. I shake all my Christmas gifts, too. I drive everyone crazy by guessing them."

Alex tsk-tsked. "Naughty girl."

Heather grinned. He had *no* idea the lengths she'd gone to to lock down some time with him. Such as "forgetting" the lyrics to her own songs and slowing down the shooting schedule for the pretaped portions of her TV special. Such as "changing her mind" about the theme for the live performance portion of her special and forcing the sets to be redone, putting them over budget. Such as facing down The Terminator and then purposely misleading him with that crazy story about her "starstruck, disruptive little sister" to get rid of him long enough for her to make one last stand at this.

Heather still didn't know where she'd found the nerve.

Then Alex winked at her, and she remembered.

It was all for a good cause. It was all for love.

Unless Casey Jackson figured out what she'd done and came looking for revenge (an idea that utterly terrified her) or Kristen failed in her assigned mission to "distract" him, Heather figured she was good for another week or two. Given that much time, surely she could convince Alex to at least *look* at her in a way that went beyond friendliness. She *needed* that.

She needed *him*.

Right now, Heather was prepared to do whatever it took to get him . . . even if that meant broadening her vocabulary until she could double as a dictionary, reading until her eyes crossed, and typing all her Tweets with correct spelling and punctuation.

Maybe a pair of intellectual-looking glasses would help. Alex wore glasses. They made *him* look brilliant. Also, sexy.

Then something else occurred to her.

"Hey!" She grabbed Alex. "If you know what tomorrow's Word of the Day word is, that means *you* must have peeked at it, too!"

At the realization, Heather felt tingly with excitement. Because there were two kinds of people in the world, she knew: people who guessed their Christmas gifts beforehand (like her—and Alex!) and people who wanted to be surprised (like Kristen).

But she and Alex were both peekers.

That meant they were *meant* for one another!

In acknowledgment, Alex only smiled. "I never said *I* wasn't naughty, too," he told her. Then he hefted a faux marble column over his shoulder, strode away across the downtown bungalow they were using as a set . . . and left her swooning in his wake.

* * *

Inadvertently, Casey stepped out of the frying pan into the fire. He got out of his car, realized he might seriously freeze to death in the snow, and hauled ass into the Galaxy Diner.

Once inside, he immediately realized his mistake. He wasn't going to avoid Christmas here. It looked as if Santa and his elves had gone on a bender. It looked as if Martha Stewart and Bozo the Clown had teamed up to help them. It looked . . . insane. In an upbeat, idiosyncratic, pass-the-fruitcake kind of way.

From the cartoon Rudolph, the Red-Nosed Reindeer hand-painted on the diner's window to the twinkling lights hung inside to the evergreen garland wrapped around the counters and chairs, the place hadn't missed a single opportunity to get into the holiday spirit. Not that its myriad customers seemed to mind. Bathed in the multicolored glow from the chaser lights overhead, they packed the place to the rafters, chattering in groups while they waited for one of the tables to become available or sitting at one of those tables already.

Inside, it was quirky and warm and in-your-face cheerful, and the moment the strains of a reggae version of "Holly, Jolly Christmas" reached him, Casey seriously considered leaving.

Despite his need to get on with the job he'd come here to do, he did not want to be engulfed in Christmas. But the general hubbub felt weirdly uplifting. And he suddenly caught a savory, delicious (and nongingerbready) smell wafting from the grill. And he realized he was starving at the same time as he realized there were at least two teenagers here who might be Heather's little sister. So he could start babysitting. In Christmas Town.

He had to be crazy. *My Bodyguard* meets *Mary Poppins* meets *Prancer* he *wasn't*. But as a starting point, it would have to do.

Casually, Casey made eye contact with the next person waiting for a table. He kicked off a conversation. Three minutes later, the local man he'd been talking to nodded and said, "Kristen? Yeah, sure. I've seen her. She's right over there."

Casey followed the man's pointing finger. At the end of its imaginary arc, a blond waitress worked the diner's counter.

Casey frowned. "There has to be some mistake."

"Nope. That's Kristen Miller, all right. Only one in town."

It couldn't be. Casey looked again—at the *non*teenaged, *non*braces-wearing, *non*-Bieber Fevered, *non*-Converse-sporting, *non*bratty, *non*tomboyish, one-hundred-percent-grown-up woman he'd been led to believe was terrorizing Heather Miller's TV special.

Something about this situation didn't quite gel.

For one thing, Kristen Miller appeared much too busy to waste time getting in the way of her sister's cheesecake-y, Auto-Tuned, wildly expensive music video-turned-TV special.

For another, Kristen Miller didn't seem the type to be starstruck, disruptive, or prone to petty unruliness . . . although she *was* pretty distracting, at least from where Casey was standing. He could see why a person would have a tough time concentrating while she was around.

But Heather was her *sister*. She wouldn't have been affected by . . . the same things Casey was affected by.

Trying to figure out the disconnect between Heather's description of her "starstruck" little sister and the sensible-seeming, hard-at-work woman he saw at the diner's counter, he considered Kristen Miller more closely.

She was cute. Really cute. She was dressed in a makeshift uniform of a plaid flannel shirt, denim miniskirt, dark tights, and knee-high boots. She'd tied a multipocketed shop apron around her waist to hold her order pad and pen. She was chatting with a customer, looking friendly and knowledge-able and surprisingly down-to-earth for someone who was related to a megalomaniac millionaire megastar with multiple *Billboard* hits.

Overall, Casey thought, she appeared . . . pretty ordinary. And nonthreatening. It couldn't be easy living in Heather Miller's sequin-spangled, paparazzi-filled, much-Twittered-about sisterly shadow. But Kristen Miller seemed to have no problem with it.

Musingly, Casey said, "She looks pretty harmless to me."

"'Harmless,' huh?" The man beside him gave a knowing chuckle. "You're not from around here, are you?"

For the first time, Casey felt a glimmer of uncertainty.

That had never happened to him before. In his line of work, certainty was paramount—followed closely by charisma and trailed by an ability to talk anyone into anything while still staying honest. Because if the people he worked with didn't trust him, he was sunk, Casey knew. So far, he'd never had a problem.

"No, I'm not from around here," he said. "But—"

"Kristen doesn't take any guff from anybody." The man gave her an admiring head shake. "She practically built this place with her bare hands. It was a boarded-up old fifties gas station when she got a hold of it. She turned it around but quick—and woe betide any contractor who tried to drag his feet on the job, too."

"That sounds like the voice of experience talking."

"Yep." His new friend grinned. "I'm a neon contractor. Last one in town. My company restored the old Googie work on the elevated pylon outside." He aimed his chin at the snow-topped GALAXY DINER sign just visible through the window. "I added custom-fabricated LED Channellume to the exterior and did some tube-bending for the neon detail work you see inside, too."

Casey nodded. "Nice job. It's a great-looking place."

It was. He hadn't noticed all the finer points at first—thanks to the overload of sparkly holiday crap threatening to obliterate them—but the Galaxy Diner had character. And style. Its history was evident in the 1950s "bones" of the place, but unlike those ubiquitous "retro-style" restaurants filled with mass-produced "memorabilia," it felt real and modern and fresh.

A metal roll-up service-bay door—an obvious holdover from the property's past—formed one exterior wall. Antique auto lifts made up the bases of three of the tables. Several dinged-up, hand-painted metal FILLING STATION signs hung on the walls beneath the holiday garland and lights. The floor was concrete, the big picture window was edged with steel, and everywhere he looked, it was as if the Galaxy Diner had launched a full-scale Christmas assault on the populace of Kismet, Michigan. Grinchy types like Casey didn't stand a chance against it.

For the second time, he felt a flicker of uncertainty.

Sure, he could deal with a no-nonsense woman who knew how to manage a menagerie of burly contractors. That was easy. But *this* particular woman also seemed obsessed with Christmas. And *that* he couldn't quite figure out how to cope with. A Christmas-crazed woman was pretty much the antithesis of Casey Jackson.

Which was probably just as well, it occurred to him. He couldn't afford to be distracted. Right now, he needed to focus.

"It's definitely a change of pace from what I'm used to," he said, deliberately swerving his attention to Kristen Miller again. She was talking with a customer, oblivious to on-lookers, so he was free to study her. She looked . . . very different from Heather. "It was seventy degrees and sunny when I left L.A."

"L.A.? Is that so?" His newfound confidant looked him up and down. "Well, you're a long way from Hollywood now!" he said with a jovial poke to the ribs. People tended to bond with Casey quickly. Occasional handsiness came with the territory. "At least you're all bundled up. Sometimes tourists come to town wearing the flimsiest, most god-awful winter duds."

"I like to come prepared." But something told him he *wasn't* prepared for Kristen Miller. Which was ridiculous. She was just one ordinary woman. Casey noticed movement across the diner and added, "I see a spot at the counter opening up. You want it?"

"Oh, no, thanks. I'm here with my family. We need a table."

The man gestured at a slightly older woman nearby, who was entertaining two toddlers by playing peekaboo. Seeing them laughing together, Casey felt another pang of uncertainty.

Christmastime meant family. He'd purposely avoided—

"So," the man asked, "how come you're looking for Kristen?"

Dragged from a thought he did not want to be having, Casey forced a smile. "I need some information," he said. "And right now, Kristen is the best person to give it to me."

Then he gave one of the toddlers an exaggerated peekaboo face (provoking a hearty kid-style chuckle in response), offered the mom an offhanded wink (provoking a blush and a giddy wave in response), and headed for the solitary available stool at the end of the diner's vintage Formica counter, ready to work his magic.

Chapter 4

When she'd first come out from the back of the diner, Kristen had wondered, belatedly, how she was supposed to spot Casey Jackson. Heather hadn't offered a physical description of him. Even though it was December—hardly the height of the tourist season in snowy, lakeside Kismet— there were enough unfamiliar people visiting family and friends for the holidays that Kristen couldn't simply button-hole the lone stranger in the crowd and commence "distracting" him.

On the verge of calling back Heather for a more thorough dossier on the habits, habitat, and identifying marks of professional Harbingers of Hollywood Doom once she finished with her current customer, Kristen heard a child laugh. The sound carried over the murmur of customers talking, over the racket of the kitchen staff working, over the sound of the Vandals' "Oi to the World!" blasting over the diner's sound system.

Glancing in the direction of that gleeful laughter, Kristen

spotted a toddler grinning. The inciter of the child's laughter—
a tall, broad-shouldered man making an incongruously playful peekaboo gesture—laughed, too. Then he gave the toddler's
mother a wink. Spotting that, Kristen straightened in anticipation.

She knew that toddler's mother—a no-nonsense type
given to terrorizing her neighbors about untrimmed hedges
and berating the newspaper deliverer for leaving her copy of
the *Kismet Comet* two feet too far from her front porch.
There was no way she'd put up with a stranger peekaboo-
ing her toddler—much less *winking* at her in a flirtatious
fashion. Right next to her husband, too!

Interestedly, Kristen watched the woman's encounter
with the tall, dark stranger. Any second now, she'd smack
him with the latest issue of *Parents* magazine. She'd call him
out on his "inappropriate" behavior. She'd . . . blush and
wave back at him?

Flabbergasted, Kristen blinked. But the tableau didn't
change. If anything, it only became more surreal. Because
not long after the stranger returned the woman's coy wave,
he nodded good-naturedly at her husband . . . and the man
beamed at him in response, as though he'd been blessed by
Diner-Going Jesus.

All that was missing was a heavenly chorus. Or a fanfare
of trumpets. Or maybe a throng of eager groupies. But even
they were represented, Kristen realized, if you counted the
cadre of grandmotherly types nearby. All of them appeared
ready to cook the newcomer some soup, give him some slip-
covers for his sofa, or knit him a scarf, right there on the spot.

Apparently unaware of his fan club, the stranger turned
toward the single available seat at the counter. But everyone
else started talking at once, clearly unwilling to see the party
in the entryway come to an end. And it *was* a party, Kristen
saw. The big urn of coffee and little squares of gingerbread
she offered to waiting customers might as well have been
cocktails and hors d'oeuvre, so festive was the atmosphere

in that cramped space. As the man stepped away, everyone surged nearer to him.

"You try to stay warm now, you hear?" one woman advised him kindly. "This isn't Los Angeles. It's cold outside!"

"If you need any directions or work done on your rental car, just stop by my shop," a local mechanic added eagerly.

"Remember, it's The Big Foot bar," said a second man, who owned a popular hangout a few streets away. "Stop by anytime!"

The stranger promised he would duly bundle up, ask for help if lost or experiencing engine trouble, and grab a beer or two. But the hubbub continued with men and women alike jockeying to offer invitations, all of which were accepted. Kristen had never seen anything like it. That was how she knew, based partly on her sister's overblown hyperbole (and partly on the fact that she overheard someone say his name) that *this* was Casey Jackson.

This was the man who'd come to Kismet on a search-and-destroy mission aimed squarely at *her* sister.

At least he was, if Heather could be believed. That was still debatable. Generally speaking, the more words that came out of Heather's mouth, the less reliable those words were.

Heather had gotten his legendary reputation all wrong, though, Kristen realized. Because *this* particular broad-shouldered, easy-gesturing, über-popular newcomer didn't seem like any "hatchet man" Kristen had ever met. He seemed more like . . . the pied piper of Kismet. Somehow, in the space of two Christmas carols (while she'd been busy delivering a daily special to a nearby table), he'd enchanted all her customers. Now each of them was clamoring to win his approval.

Evidently, they all loved Casey Jackson. At first sight.

Just the way everyone loved Kristen's sister. Unreservedly.

It was as if Heather and Casey Jackson were two peas in a pod. Both were unfairly blessed, unreasonably exempt from normal standards of behavior, and unconditionally adored. No matter how disruptive their behavior might be for everyone around them.

Like, say, *her*.

Paradoxically, the realization made Kristen dig in her heels. Frowning at Casey Jackson, she resolved to find out what he wanted and then—if possible—to get him out of town. Like, *today*. Why stop at distracting him when she could get rid of him? If she was going to have her hero moment, she might as well do it up right. Go big or go home. Wasn't that what they said?

It didn't matter that Casey Jackson was handsome, likable, and (potentially, at least) intelligent. He was the interloper here. He was in town to cause trouble (potentially, at least) for her sister. Sibling loyalty demanded that Kristen retaliate.

As of right now, she decided with an upward tilt of her chin, Casey Jackson was her official archrival.

It didn't matter that he *seemed* charming (as Heather had direly warned her). It didn't matter that everyone in town seemed to think he was some irresistible amalgamation of machismo, guy-next-door affability, hubba-hubba hunkitude, and superhero kiddie-taming mojo. Because Kristen didn't want what everyone else wanted. She was more original than that.

She could think for herself. She didn't need to see flirty Missy Neiman—insurance adjuster and die-hard PTO member—cuddle up to Casey Jackson and suggest he look into "concurrent causation exclusions" to know that *she* would not be getting on this particular Christmas-crush bandwagon.

She was not in the market for hunkitude.

Especially not now, when she couldn't even count on Christmas. She *needed* Christmas, too, Kristen told herself. She needed its sweetness and sentimentality and sense of fun. She needed its reliability. Most of all, she needed its authenticity. Because at Christmastime, people's better, kinder, *truer* selves always shone through. All year long, Kristen lived for that. It *made* Christmas for her.

And what *didn't* make Christmas for her?

Casey Jackson. Here, in her town. In her diner.

Seeming unaware of all the excitement he'd caused—and of Kristen's budding opposition to him—Casey extricated himself from those multiple conversations he'd been having. He shucked his coat. With a carefree air, he hung it on the stand-alone coatrack, almost as though he didn't realize all eyes in the entryway (and some in the dining room) remained fixed on him.

Refocusing *her* attention on him, Kristen wasn't surprised by the general fascination he'd caused. Because, to be fair, Casey Jackson wasn't like anyone else in her tiny, thirty-two seat diner. He stuck out like the Easter Bunny in a Christmas parade. Like a packet of candy corn in a box full of candy canes. Like a polished-looking, square-jawed, dark-haired Adonis with chiseled muscles (she guessed), pouty lips (she noticed), and a knack for wearing a suit and tie (she assessed) as though he had on nothing fancier than a worn-in T-shirt and jeans.

Actually, Casey Jackson was . . . pretty intriguing, she couldn't help thinking. If he was that welcoming in a crowd, how much friendlier would he be on a more *intimate* scale? If he was that comfy in a suit, exactly how relaxed would he be when naked?

Not that *she* needed to find out. Not personally.

But she had to keep those things in mind. Because it was crucial to understand your opponent when trying to distract him. It was important to gauge his capabilities when preparing to oust him from your town. It was critical to know, when going against a professional troubleshooter, exactly how much trouble he might dish out. Say, by flicking his soulful-eyed gaze in your direction—just for an instant—and making your heart skip a beat or two. Which Casey Jackson did in that moment . . .

Those were bedroom eyes, Kristen thought nonsensically. *That's what people meant by that.* And before she could even prepare herself, she was struck by a simultaneous urge to darn Casey Jackson's socks and/or file his taxes and/or kiss him.

She didn't even know what darning socks *meant*.

Irked by her own unexpected susceptibility to Casey's charisma—the same charisma she'd been specifically warned against—Kristen jerked away her gaze. There was no *way* she was falling for some L.A. hotshot's befriend-the-yokels routine.

He probably didn't even mean it. He probably looked at every woman that way—as if he wanted to darn *her* socks, file *her* taxes, and kiss *her* . . . all while whispering sweet nothings in her ear and making her knees go weak with un-fulfilled longing.

Not that Kristen knew anything about unfulfilled longing. She generally took what she wanted, got what she needed, and gave as good as she got. When it came to relationships, she was . . .

Not considering Casey Jackson as a potential relation-ship.

Period.

Although if she *had* been . . .

But she wasn't.

And that's what Kristen staunchly reminded herself of as she watched Casey take the sole available seat at her diner's crowded counter—and watched everyone else at the counter immediately smile and greet him and scoot their things side-ways to make sure he had enough space to peruse the menu. Because she couldn't possibly distract him or banish him from Kismet if she was busy mentally undressing him. Even if she *had* made it all the way past his suit coat and tie so far, and was rapidly . . .

. . . rapidly *stopping* that. Because it was more important to research what she was up against here. For instance, she could notice the way a nearby baby (and the kid's infatuated-looking mother) made goo-goo eyes at Casey. She could observe the way the woman's husband shook hands with him, his face alight with hopes for a budding bromance. And she could caution herself, no matter what else she did, to be careful this time.

Because Casey Jackson was not to be underestimated.

On the plus side, neither was Kristen Miller.

And it would only be fair to find out exactly what Casey really wanted in Kismet before she took action—before she cut him off at the knees and made sure he didn't get it.

So, in the interest of starting off fairly, Kristen put on a smile and decided to offer him a never-fail, always-in-demand, ultra-delicious serving of pie—her specialty, her pièce de résistance, her foodie stand-in. If *she* had been a dessert, she would have been her pie: sweet, tender, and in-your-face good.

Casey Jackson couldn't possibly refuse.

Casey was still considering the possible ramifications of getting stuck in a snowbank on the way back to his hotel when Kristen Miller sashayed over to him, slid something on the counter, and then stepped back with an undeniable flourish.

On her, that aura of bravado was pretty cute. Partly because she appeared about as arrogant as a baby giraffe. And partly because he knew *he* was going to win in this situation.

"Here you go. On the house!" she said. "Sorry about the long wait for a table. It's been crazy busy today, with everyone downtown doing Christmas shopping." Hands on hips, she glanced from him to the object she'd given him: a plate with a napkin at its center, topped by a squat, wide-mouth mason jar full of something sugary-looking, and accompanied by a fork. "It's our specialty: pie-in-a-jar."

"Pie? In a jar?"

She nodded. "Yes. Pie-in-a-jar. The jar makes it easy to take with you," she explained. "It contains all the mess, too. It's really good. What you have there is Dutch apple pie."

"Oh. Thanks, but I'm not much for sweets. That's really kind of you, though." Casey nudged away the plate. "Here. You have it."

"*Me?* What? No. I—" She gawked at him, plainly incredulous. "You're not much for sweets? I've never heard that before."

"It happens." He smiled. "Sorry. I'm sure it's delicious."

She still appeared gob-smacked. "You're not serious."

Casey shrugged. "I just . . . don't like pie."

Her gaze sharpened. "You don't like pie."

"I don't like pie."

"Before you said it was 'sweets' that you didn't like. Now it's pie? Specifically pie? *My* pie?"

"It's not just *your* pie," he hastened to say. "It's—"

"No pie? Ever? What are you, some kind of communist?"

He laughed. "I applaud your passion for your baked goods. But I just—"

"Eat it."

He had to give her points for persistence. Maybe "handling" Heather's little sister wouldn't be so easy after all.

Dubiously, Casey examined the jar of pie. It looked sweet and sparkly from the sugar, with a spicy crumb topping and a neatly crimped crust, all contained in the mason jar. He had to admit it was cute. But he was a grown man. He wasn't interested in cute food. However, if he had to . . . "Do you have any ketchup?"

It was possible her head swiveled around. "For *pie?*"

"Well, if I'm going to have to choke down piecrust, then—"

The thud of an industrial-size ketchup bottle hitting the diner's counter drowned out his explanation. Standing behind it, Kristen Miller eyed him with evident challenge. A hush fell.

"I *dare* you to put ketchup on my pie."

Two stools down, the plumber he'd just met leaned forward to catch Casey's eye. "If I were you, I'd eat that pie."

"Plain," his wife advised. "No ketchup."

"Kristen's got on her angry eyes," someone else said in a knowing tone. "I wouldn't push your luck."

Casey held up his hands in surrender. "I happen to like ketchup!" he told the diner at large, feeling as though he'd confessed to, once in a while, slapping on a pair of kittens and skiing downhill on them. "But I *don't* like pie."

"That's impossible," someone said.

"You'll like *this* pie," someone else added.

Okay. Well, clearly the town was on Kristen Miller's side in this controversy. Casey knew when he was licked.

He picked up his fork. He eyed the mason jar full of pie. Then he shifted his gaze longingly toward the ketchup bottle.

Kristen appeared ready to clobber him with it. Casey almost spoiled his advantage by laughing out loud. He didn't really like ketchup on pie. But the minute he'd seen the expression of certainty on her face, he hadn't been able to resist poking fun.

Other people's convictions had that effect on him.

Casey took a bite. He chewed. Swallowed. "Hmm."

The diner's customers awaited his verdict.

So did Kristen. With her arms folded, she watched him take a second experimental bite. Her eyes were vivid blue, he noticed, and appeared capable of shooting retaliatory laser beams at him if he said the wrong thing.

Doubtfully, he shook his head. He forked up another bite, tasting the flavors of apples and brown sugar and cinnamon, all enrobed in pastry and crumb topping. He quirked his eyebrow, then reached for the ketchup.

A collective gasp rose in the diner. Carelessly, Casey squirted ketchup on his next bite of pie. The people near him reared back in astonishment. Someone snapped a photo with their phone's camera. Blinded by the flash, he chewed.

"Mmm. Better," he announced in an approving tone.

Instantly, another animated murmur swept the place.

"I want ketchup on my pie, too!" someone called out.

Kristen heard. Defiantly, she grabbed the huge, forty-four-ounce ketchup bottle. She shoved it under the counter, where it landed with a crash, then dusted her hands together.

"Okay. That's it. Nobody's getting ketchup with their pie," she announced to the diner as a whole. "It just became Galaxy Diner policy." She narrowed her eyes at Casey. She leaned closer to him in a menacing fashion, propping both palms on the countertop. "Nice going, genius. You just started a dumb trend."

He shrugged. "You're the one who made me eat pie."

"That's right. And I'm not done yet." She sized him up with a glance. "It just became my mission to make you a pie convert."

If she kept on leaning over at him—inadvertently treating him to a glimpse of the lacy red bra she had on underneath her plaid flannel shirt—Casey just might let her convert him.

"Impossible," he said. "It can't be done."

"Now I'm twice as committed."

"Then you don't know when to take 'no' for an answer."

"Something tells me you have the same problem."

She was right. That was interesting. But Casey didn't intend to admit it. "And you can tell that because . . . ?"

"Because my sister warned me about you, Mr. Jackson, and—"

He held up his hands. "Call me Casey. Please."

"—and you're wasting your time in Kismet. All you're going to do is slow down the progress on Heather's TV special." Kristen lifted her chin, seeming to gear up for . . . something. "She's an artist. She can't create magic if she's under stress."

He watched her lips quiver tellingly. He became momentarily sidetracked by noticing that (unlike all the women he knew in L.A.) she wasn't wearing any lipstick or gloopy lip gloss. He found himself musing that the absence of those things would make it feel nicer to kiss her. She would feel . . . *really* good, he bet.

No. He had to concentrate. "That line would go down better," Casey said, "if you weren't laughing while you said it."

"I wasn't laughing!"

"On the outside, you weren't," Casey agreed. "But on the inside . . ." He examined her, heedless of the curious diner customers observing their exchange. "You were cracking up. Nice try at defending your sister's 'artistry,' though. That's very loyal of you. I admire that about you."

"You do?" Wide-eyed, she regarded him. "Aw. That's sweet."

He felt satisfied with that outcome. As usual. Until . . .

"Seriously?" Kristen straightened. Her red bra and pert cleavage vanished from sight. "Do people really fall for that?"

He blinked, dismayed. "Fall for what?"

"Your whole 'I'm so charming' routine."

"I *am* charming." As proof, Casey refrained from pointing out all the new friends he'd already made in the diner. A less charming person would have gloated about that. "So are you, Kristen. Everyone in the world has a certain unique—"

"Blah, blah, blah." Incredibly, she interrupted him by miming a talkative hand puppet at him. Her multiple silver bracelets jangled with the motion. She didn't seem at all surprised that he knew her name. It was possible he'd underestimated her, given that he'd prepped for a sparkly-vampire-obsessed teenager. "You're wasting your time with that 'unique' line, too," she said. "I'm immune to flattery."

Casey swept his gaze over her again. He genuinely did appreciate her straightforwardness, her confidence . . . her matter-of-fact way of confronting him while looking improbably sexy in a lumberjack's shirt and a courtesan's lingerie. The paradoxes inherent in that left him more captivated than he ought to be.

"No one is immune to flattery," he said. "That's a fact."

"Some people are," Kristen disagreed. "Smart people."

Apparently, she had a lot invested in being intelligent. Casey figured he could use that. He needed a shortcut, or he'd be trapped here in Christmasville forever. He glanced across the diner, selected the most immediately brainy-looking person—a man picking up a to-go order nearby—and called out to him.

"Hey, nice choice on the pie-in-a-jar!" Casey offered the guy a nod. "I hear it's really good. You must be an expert."

With a grin, the burly customer raised his to-go bag. "My wife thinks so! Some pregnant women want pickles, but my Rachel is crazy about this cranberry-mincemeat pie. She can't get enough of it."

"You're a wise and thoughtful husband to get it for her."

"Yeah. I guess I am!" Appearing immensely flattered, the man prepared to leave. He saluted. "Thanks, pal!"

Casey lifted his eyebrow and glanced at Kristen. "See? I prove my point. He's certainly smart. *And* easily flattered."

She scoffed. "He's not flattered, and he doesn't look that thrilled with life because of *you*," she disagreed. She gave the man a cheerful wave good-bye. "That's Reno Wright. He got married a couple of years ago, and his new wife is expecting, so—"

"Reno Wright?" Casey goggled. "The former kicker for the Scorpions? The most in-demand, highest-ranked, most popular rookie kicker drafted in the NFL in a decade? *That* Reno Wright?"

Blandly, Kristen said, "You've heard of him, then? He's kind of a local celebrity. A real hometown hero."

Of course Casey had heard of him. Reno Wright had single-handedly won several big games for the Scorpions by kicking spectacular last-second, long-yardage field goals. He'd been unexpectedly tough, too. On kickoff returns, players knew to avoid his quadrant of the field or get brutally tackled.

If he'd recognized him sooner, Casey knew, he'd never have tried making his point about people's susceptibility to flattery by using Reno Wright for an example. But since he had . . .

"My point is, *everyone* can be flattered. Even you. So when I tell you that I admire what you've done with this place—"

"It *is* pretty fabulous. For a money pit."

"—I hope you'll believe me," Casey finished, making a mental note about her apparent money problems. "I heard about some of the renovations you had to do. That must have been tough, trying to update the place while keeping its integrity."

"It was." Her posture eased a fraction, even as the diner racket continued around her. "There were issues bringing the property up to code, plus a whole laundry list of repairs to do and vintage replacement fixtures to find . . ." Abruptly, she quit talking. The sparkle that had entered her eyes while discussing her diner dimmed a fraction. Cannily, she said, "It took longer than I expected, but sometimes things don't go according to plan. Sometimes you have to allow for the unexpected."

He caught her drift. "Like with Heather's TV special."

A nod. "I'm not going to let you cause trouble for my sister. She's working hard. Her special means a lot to her."

"I'm not here to cause trouble. I'm here to help."

Kristen snorted. "Terrifying her isn't helpful."

Reassuringly, Casey grinned. "I'm not terrifying."

"From where I'm standing? No, you're really not."

To emphasize that fact, Kristen looked at him as though

making it plain that she *knew* he'd been transfixed by her lacy red bra a minute ago . . . and had fully intended for him to be.

Uh-oh. How had he missed that? Casey wondered. How had he been gulled so easily? He couldn't afford to make mistakes on this job. He wanted to get out of here as quickly as possible, before Christmas caught up with him.

"But then, I don't scare easily," Kristen was saying matter-of-factly. "From Heather's perspective, things are different. So why don't we just cut to the chase? You tell me why you're here and what it will take to make you leave—"

"I just got here. You want me to leave already?" Grinning anew, Casey clutched his chest. "Ouch. That hurts." Somberly, he said, "You should know I survived a blizzard to get here."

"—and I'll tell you everything you ever wanted to know about turning antique gas stations into diners, if you're really as interested as you seem. Deal?"

He thought about it. "I've never met anyone as direct as you before. Well, except me." It was as if they were destined to be soul mates. Or archrivals. Either way . . . "I like you."

A sigh. "Are you softheaded or something? I was pretty clear earlier. No flattery. No b.s. No flirting—"

"Flirting?" Casey couldn't let that lie. "If you're sensing something between us, maybe it's not coming from *me*."

"—just answers. Okay? Exactly why are you here?"

He wanted to answer her. He really did. But all at once, in that moment, Casey couldn't quite find the brainpower to do so.

He'd never encountered a woman who fascinated him quite as much as Kristen Miller did. She was made up of equal parts devotion, generosity, and toughness . . . all mixed up with long legs and blond hair and a mouth that wanted to smile, but hadn't.

Not yet.

Damn, but he wanted to be the one to make that smile of hers happen. He just knew it was going to be incredible.

"And by the way," Kristen added with a glance outdoors, "that little snow flurry we had a while ago? Not a blizzard."

"I'm from L.A. It was the mother of all blizzards."

"Right. You're very brave." She crossed her arms. "So?"

So she was really busting him here. "The production company hired my agency to get Heather's TV special back on schedule," Casey said. "I'm here to do that, by whatever means possible."

"Are you going to fire people?"

He couldn't lie. "If it's necessary. Usually, it's not."

"Are you going to shut down production?"

"Near as I can tell, it's already pretty much shut down. I'm hoping to put things back on track before Christmas. Way before Christmas. Way, *way* before Christmas."

"I'm sure." Kristen compressed her lips in a telltale gesture. Evidently, she was familiar with the problems on set. That meant he needed more information from her. But first . . .

"Are you going to ruin my sister's career?"

She kept her chin high, but there was an undeniable note of vulnerability in her voice. Hearing it, Casey regarded her with real empathy. He didn't have any brothers or sisters, but the concern in Kristen's face was real. He wanted to reassure her.

"If that homemade sex tape couldn't ruin your sister's career when it came out last year," he said, "I doubt I have a shot at it."

"Really? How sensitive of you, to bring up Heather's most public scandal to augment your case," she said drily. "Are you always this subtle, or is today a special occasion?"

"I don't see the point in tiptoeing around things."

She nodded. Again, Casey had the impression that he and Kristen Miller were on the same wavelength—if not the same side.

"Have you seen it?" she asked.

Casey raised his eyebrows. "Your sister's sex tape?"

She nodded. "It was all over the Internet. She sued to stop the retail DVD version from being released, but it didn't work." Kristen gave him a direct look. "Well?"

Reluctantly, Casey rose. "Maybe I should leave."

"Oh, no." Narrow-eyed, Kristen pointed at him. "You're staying right here, where I can keep an eye on you."

"I can't." With faux helplessness, Casey spread his arms. A Heather Miller holiday song started playing over the diner's sound system, reminding him of his mission. "I have work to do. Set visits to conduct. Phone calls to make. I can't do that here."

"You can if I rent you a booth." With a *gotcha* gleam in her eyes, Kristen jutted her chin toward a corner booth near the cash register. "Two hundred dollars a day."

He widened his eyes. "Two hundred? No, thanks."

"It's cheaper than a commercial space. *If* you could find one. During the holidays, most of the Realtors in town close up shop. Theirs is a summer business, really. Tourist rentals."

"Technically, I don't need a commercial space. I can get everything I need on set, where I can keep an eye on Heather."

Kristen crossed her arms. "You can't get access to me."

"I don't need access to you."

"You do if you want to make any headway with my sister."

Thinking it over, Casey gazed at her. "I doubt it."

"Okay. Fine. Find out the truth the hard way, if you want to." Wearing the most carefree expression he'd seen on her so far, Kristen handed him a menu. "I'll be back for your order. I've neglected my customers too long already."

Then, before Casey could even formulate a new approach, Kristen swept aside his neglected pie-in-a-jar, offered him a cheerful look, and flounced away across her diner . . . leaving him experiencing several contradictory revelations all at once.

First, he was pretty sure she thought (wrongly) that she'd outmaneuvered him, because she was wearing the same ridiculously cocksure look she'd had on while offering him her famous pie.

Second, he didn't think she knew how to negotiate, because she was supposed to have made a counteroffer just now. Duh.

And third . . . well, third was the most damning of them all. Because third, Casey realized that Kristen Miller possessed a curvy derrière that had the power to make a man lose his mind altogether. Most likely, she'd adorned it in red lace, too.

Red lace to match her bra. Red lace to make him wonder . . .

Exactly what other surprises did Kristen Miller have in store for him, if Casey stuck around long enough to uncover them?

Chapter 5

A few minutes later, Kristen looped back around, capably and conscientiously taking an order from another customer.

Casey watched her and felt duly mesmerized. She was feisty, gutsy, and quick on her feet. She was cute, well liked, and respected (even if she *didn't* recognize a full-blown blizzard when one was raging outside her diner). She was . . . interesting.

He felt almost sorry to have already gained the upper hand with her (even if she didn't know it yet). But Casey couldn't go all soppy and sentimental now. He had a job to do.

Despite Kristen's concerns, he didn't expect that job to hurt her sister. Typically, he pulled off his intercessions without upsetting anyone—quite the opposite, in fact. Usually, people were happy to have had Casey involved. Although Heather Miller *did* have some explaining to do about the half-baked story she'd fed him about her problematic "little sister." When Casey talked to Heather again, he intended to clarify matters—and to make it clear that he wanted honesty from her in the future.

Having finished up her stint with her other customer, Kristen passed by again. She trailed her fingertips over the countertop, absently tracing its edge as though reassuring herself it was still there, intact and invulnerable and *hers*.

Casey could relate. "I feel the same way about my watch."

Kristen stopped. She glanced at him quizzically.

"Possessive. And proud." He nodded at her fingers, still resting on the countertop. "Sometimes I can't help checking to make sure it's still there, just like you're doing."

An inexplicable defiance passed over her face. She whisked away her fingers. But she didn't disagree. So he went on.

"It's not that I never owned a watch before." He nodded at its polished face. Its heavy band anchored his wrist with its comforting, familiar weight. "But usually they . . . disappeared."

Her mouth quirked in an almost smile. "Forgetful much?"

"I was being nice. I mean they were stolen."

"Oh. Multiple times?" A frown. "I know you have muggers in the big city, but to be hit over and over again like that—"

Kismet really *was* Mayberry Redux. "I grew up in foster care," Casey told her curtly. He was sorry he'd mentioned this at all. "Things had a way of going missing. All I'm saying is, your diner is pretty great." He grinned, pointedly gesturing at her. "Even if it *is* run by an amateur extortionist who wants way more than market value for a simple booth rental."

But he was too late with his joke. Kristen was already giving him The Look. The gooey-eyed, distressed, pitying look. The sad *foster kid* look. The look that stripped him of who he was and turned him into a latter-day Oliver Twist with a suit, a cell phone, and several years' more experience under his belt.

He hated The Look. It made him feel combative.

"But hey . . . maybe you're just into fondling Formica," Casey joked, wishing he'd never said anything—wishing he'd never felt that weird moment of connectedness with her. "I'm not judging."

To his relief, Kristen grinned. "Don't knock it until you've tried it. I wasn't into it at first. But then I started dating Mr. Clean, and that guy is all about taking care of the Formica." She waggled her brows. "If you know what I mean."

Casey laughed. "Kinky."

"You'd better believe it. Me and Mr. Clean . . . whew! Hot!"

Her gaze met his, full of sass and brashness . . . and also compassion. Damn it. But suddenly Casey didn't mind so much.

Then Kristen leaned over, peered at his watch, and lightly touched her fingertips to his wrist. A jolt went through him.

Stunned, Casey stared at her. But she didn't seem to realize that she'd somehow delivered several volts of . . . *something* to him. Her gaze was fixed on his watch—the most enduring token of his success so far *and* the most difficult for anyone to boost without his noticing—and he had an unencumbered view of her smooth cheeks, straight nose, and downcast eyes. Her mouth was surprisingly lush, he noticed, feeling drawn to it again.

She glanced up. "It's a very nice watch."

He felt stupidly as though she'd approved of *him*. All of him. Absolutely and wholeheartedly. But that was ludicrous. *He* wasn't his watch. Just like *she* wasn't her pie.

All the same, Casey heard himself say, in a rough and gullible voice, "Thanks. I'd like to try more pie-in-a-jar, please." He glanced at the menu. "Pumpkin, this time."

It wasn't breakfast. It wasn't healthy. It wasn't even what he'd intended to order. But Casey couldn't help it.

"Pumpkin?" Her gaze tangled with his. She seemed to hold her breath. "I thought you didn't like my pie."

"Meh." He gave a careless gesture. "It had promise."

His surrender was all in his tone, and you'd better believe she heard it. He would have been disappointed if she hadn't.

She grinned again. Looking at her smile, Casey felt like a hero. *He'd* made that happen. It was his biggest coup today.

"You realize, of course," Kristen said as he was inwardly exulting to himself, "that this means I win."

That's where she was wrong. *So* wrong.

Casey exhaled, feeling the electricity between them zap away. And . . . *gone*. "You had to spoil the moment, didn't you?"

She blinked. "What moment?"

She really *didn't* feel that connection between them, he realized. It was probably just as well. He moved his arm, taking away both his watch and his defenseless wrist with its defenseless nerve endings and its defenseless bare skin.

Kristen Miller had a very arresting way of touching someone. Just now, with him, she hadn't even been trying. How in the world would her touch have felt if she'd been *trying* to make him feel as if he'd die without more of her hands on him?

"You didn't win," Casey pointed out, "because I still didn't agree to rent your outrageously overpriced booth."

"You will," Kristen sang out. "After the pie kicks in."

"We'll see about that." Casey watched her gleefully scratch down *pumpkin pie* on her order pad. Out of lingering curiosity, he asked, "How come you asked if I'd seen Heather's video?"

An enquiring look. "Have you?"

"If I hadn't," he hedged, hoping to keep his options open, "I'd be the only man in this hemisphere who'd resisted."

Kristen's mouth turned downward. She nodded. "Probably."

"So . . . why ask?"

"Oh." Cheerfully, she put the end of her pen in her mouth. She lightly bit down on it, then smiled and took it away. "Well, because I was curious. And because I was considering . . . *you,* and that question happens to be my own personal litmus test."

Casey didn't get it. "Litmus test for . . . ?"

"I thought you were cute," she clarified. "But I make it a policy never to sleep with any man who's seen that sex tape."

And she thought he'd seen it.

Realizing that, Casey wanted to slap his own dumb, purposely misleading mouth. This was what he got for hedging his bets. Sometimes you really couldn't have it both ways.

Not often. But sometimes.

"That seems kind of . . . limiting," he said blithely.

"It's called 'having standards.' You should try it."

"I do. That's why I don't like pie."

"You just ordered pie!"

They were back to this again. "I was trying to be open-minded." *I was feeling empathetic toward you, just like you were toward me.* "But there must be other diners. Other pie—"

"There's no other pie like my pie," Kristen said assuredly. "And there's no other diner with a booth for rent like *my* diner with *my* booth for rent. It's a limited-time offer, too, so . . ."

"I'll take it." He did, after all, have her right where he wanted her. It was a classic reversal. Because he'd threatened to leave earlier, she'd felt compelled to make him stay. That's why Kristen thought she was winning. "But only for one-fifty."

"One seventy-five," she countered, giving him a sneaking suspicion that she *did* know how to negotiate. A little. Maybe he was still underestimating her. "And you agree to eat a jar of pie at that table, in public, every day you're here."

"Hey." With a pseudo frown, he patted his lean midsection. "Are you trying to fatten me up?"

Kristen laughed. "As if. They're small jars."

But there was a flicker of interest in her gaze as she followed his movements. She took in his suit, his shirt . . . and his physique, all in turn. She might as well have had X-ray vision, because that's how exposed he felt under her attentive gaze.

He liked it. He liked confident women, and he liked *her*.

Maybe he wasn't the only one who was interested in something more than a business proposition, Casey reasoned. Or maybe Kristen had intuited the presence of his black boxer briefs and was imagining what they looked like on him, even now.

After all, turnabout was fair play.

"*And* while you're here, you have to do your best to pretend eating pie is a semi-orgasmic experience for you," Kristen added, seeming more like a savvy marketer than a woman who was picturing Casey in his skivvies. Her eyes lit up again. "Like an in-person advertisement for my pie-in-a-jar."

He grinned. "Can I add ketchup?"

"I'm going to pretend I didn't hear that."

"Can I get you to show me around town so I don't get lost?"

She seemed taken aback. She recovered quickly, with an offhanded wave. "If all you want are directions, I noticed about twenty people who were willing to be your own personal Sherpas just now. You don't need me."

"Maybe I want you."

She gave him a forthright look. "If you do, you don't have to pretend you might get lost without me. You can just say so."

"I have a terrible sense of direction."

"I'm not a human compass."

"You're going to feel bad if I get lost in a blizzard."

Her smile dazzled him. "It wasn't a blizzard."

"Says you. I couldn't see my hand in front of my face."

"You just need to get out in the weather some more. Really get acclimated. Try snowshoeing. Or skiing. Or ice-skating. You could even take lessons! After a few hours, you'll—"

"Be a mansicle. I'm not built for cold weather."

She didn't even pause to consider the potential double entendre contained in that sentence, much less crack another smile—the smile Casey suddenly craved. He was really slipping.

"The bottom line is, I've got too much to do to be a babysitter." Kristen turned around, hung his order ticket, then scoured her diner with an assessing look. She returned her gaze to him. "No matter how handsome you look while asking."

He couldn't help preening. "Thanks."

"Or how transparently obvious you are while doing it," she added, dishing out a shrewd look. "I already told you— I'm not going to help you bring down my sister's TV special. If you want to skulk around town digging up dirt on Heather—"

"That's *not* my intention," he said sharply, wondering why his usual charm seemed to malfunction around her. "I—"

"—you'll have to do it with GPS. Or an old-timey map. Because I doubt anyone around here will help you with *that*."

While Casey contemplated that potential setback, a momentary silence fell in the diner. Conversations nearby lapsed. Kristen appeared triumphant. Then, an instant later . . .

"I'll help him," someone said from behind Casey.

Kristen's gaze swiveled to a spot over his shoulder. She spied the person who'd volunteered to offer guide services.

Another Christmas song kicked in over the sound system, reminding Casey that he was dealing with Christmas's number one fan: Kristen. She wasn't his soul mate. She couldn't be. She'd willingly programmed "Last Christmas" by Wham! on her diner's sound system. Any pairing between them was doomed.

But finding true love wasn't his mission in Kismet.

Working his magic on Heather's problematic holiday TV special was.

So, ready to take the next necessary step in this job, Casey swiveled on his chair with his hand outstretched.

"Thanks!" he began, prepared to meet and enchant his new guide-about-town. "I—"

Abruptly, he recognized the person standing there.

The jovial greeting he'd planned stuttered to a stop.

"Aw, hell," Casey grumbled instead. "It's you."

"You who?" Kristen asked, all sweetness and spice.

But Casey didn't want to tell her. Because this Heather Miller job had just gotten one thousand percent more complicated, and he needed to regroup. Not because this job was happening at Christmastime. Not because Casey had a sudden-onset case of the hots for a certain diva pop star's cute younger sister. And not because it was snowing outside.

This job had just gotten more complicated because Casey wasn't the only troubleshooter in town. Apparently, the agency was double-dipping. Because Shane Maresca was in Kismet, too.

"You . . . *you,* apparently. Hi." In lieu of Casey's expected introduction, Kristen offered Shane a handshake. "Welcome to the Galaxy Diner." She shot a puzzled glance at Casey. "I didn't think Casey knew anyone in town. He's lucky you're here."

Lucky. Ha. In the wake of that massive misstatement, Shane Maresca, pro that he was, managed to keep a straight face. Die-hard equanimity was a perennial in his bag of tricks.

"Pleased to meet you, Kristen," he said. "I love your diner. Former fifties gas station, right?"

Kristen widened her eyes. "Yes! How'd you guess?"

"I've always been a big fan of the populuxe aesthetic."

Shane gave a deliberately modest shrug. "But then I'm a helpless retro-futurist at heart when it comes to architecture."

"Me too!" Kristen appeared flattered. Her cheeks turned pink. Her smile broadened. Her voice lowered, full of instant camaraderie. "Most people don't notice the intricacies of the restoration work, but this place was a wreck when I got it."

"Well, it's beautiful now," Shane said. The bastard. He gave her an audacious, approving smile. "Just like its owner."

Kristen tittered. Her blush deepened. "Aw, thanks."

That was it. Casey had had enough. "Never mind about that guide thing, Shane," he said casually. "I was only kidding."

Maresca gave him an "oh, are *you* still here?" glance.

Kristen did, too. That rankled. "What do you mean?" she asked. "You just said you needed a guide in case you got lost."

"Lost?" Shane suppressed a chortle. Sort of. Jackass.

"I never get lost," Casey told her. "And if I did, the last thing I would need is directions from my archrival."

"*Archrival?*" Kristen frowned, glancing from Casey to Shane and back again. "But I thought *I* was your—I mean I—" She broke off, then cleared her throat. "I'll get that pie for you."

Then she took herself across the diner, leaving Casey alone with the only real arch nemesis he'd ever had . . . his one and only former best friend.

Chapter 6

Kristen strode into her diner's office, made a note to order more extra-potent Vietnamese cassia cinnamon for baking pies with, and—on her way out—nearly collided with her friend (and longtime trusted employee) Talia McCoy.

Talia was headed toward her employee locker wearing a purposeful look. Also a flashy ankle-length, leopard-print coat, sunglasses, and her wintertime diner "uniform" of a denim skirt, flannel shirt, tights, and boots. In Talia's case, the whole ensemble was accessorized with several piercings, a couple of tattoos, and something new but not unexpected: long, blond hair.

Talia's wavy hair was usually cropped to earlobe length and colored in a vivid lavender (at least most recently), giving her a vaguely rockabilly Tinkerbell look. But Kristen wouldn't put it past her adventurous friend to try something new.

"Hey! New look?" Kristen asked.

"New . . . what?" Talia blinked. Then she touched her head. "Oh yeah! This!" Laughing, she whipped off her long, blond hair. She opened her locker, stuffed in that headful of fake hair, then shrugged. "Just something I was trying out. But judging by all the catcalls I got on the street on my way here, this look is less 'punk-rock Brigitte Bardot' and more 'daytime hooker.' I think I'll pass for now."

"I dunno. I kind of liked it."

"*You* would. You're a natural blonde."

"So?"

"So you don't understand the travails of the less follicularly blessed." Talia retrieved her nametag. She pinned it on. "Blond hair is automatically eye-catching."

"And lavender hair isn't?"

"Well . . . you've got me there." A businesslike glance. "So, how are things going here? It looks like quite a crush out there."

"Was everyone mobbing a particular tall, dark stranger?" Kristen asked wryly. "Were they letting him crowd surf past all the tables or maybe erecting a monument to his awesomeness?"

"Um, no." Gazing into the employee mirror opposite the time clock, Kristen fluffed her lavender hair. "What's got into you?"

"Nothing. Never mind."

"I'm serious." Via the mirror, Talia cast her a worried glance. "You haven't been yourself since your sister blew back into town. I know it's been hard on you having Heather—and her entourage—back after all this time, especially with all the crazy Christmas stuff they've been doing. So . . . let's have it."

Kristen hesitated. This was going to sound silly, but . . .

"Do you think it's weird to be irked that you're *not* someone's only archrival?" she asked abruptly. "I feel really competitive about this, for some reason, and I—"

"Wait." Talia froze with her arm in the air, caught in the midst of straightening her eyebrow ring. "*You're* someone's archrival?"

"Well, I *thought* I was," Kristen said in a disgruntled tone she couldn't help (or believe). "But now I'm not so sure."

Talia put her hands on her hips. "Whose archrival?"

"This . . . new guy." Vaguely, Kristen waved. "The crowd surfer."

"There was nobody crowd surfing when I got here." Talia came forward. Concernedly, she urged Kristen to take a seat on the employee break table, then she held her hands. "You're not making sense. What are you talking about?" Apparently struck by a possible explanation, she gave a chary look. "Did one of those paparazzos get in here? Is that it? Did they upset you and threaten to torpedo your Christmas again? Because if they did, I'm not above a little necessary ass-kicking."

Warmed by her pugnacious tone, Kristen smiled. She really did have great friends—friends who would defend her fiercely.

"No. Heather made a deal with the paparazzi, remember? She let them take 'candid' on-set photos of her in exchange for them leaving me and my diner alone. I'm safe here."

"Mmm." Noncommittally, Talia made a face. "Yeah. For now."

"For good. Heather promised."

"Mmm-hmm. So, about this supposed crowd-surfing archrival—"

"It's nothing. He's—" *Surprising. Annoying. H-O-T: hot.* "He's a troubleshooter who's come to fix Heather's TV special. He says he won't fire anybody—"

"The corporate types always do."

"—and he promises to be out by Christmas—"

"Efficiency freak. Gotcha."

"—but I'm still not sure what to make of him," Kristen admitted. "Heather asked me to try to 'distract' him for her—to keep him away from the set and away from her while she tries to sort things out herself—"

"Fat chance. She's about as capable as a bag of bricks."

"—and I promised I would do it—"

"Oh, Kristen." Talia shook her head. "Big mistake."

"—and I'm doing *great* so far." Warming up to her news now, Kristen scooted across the table, making room for her friend. She patted the table. Talia joined her. "I couldn't very well leave the diner for hours at a time to tail this guy, so I maneuvered him into agreeing to set up shop here."

"Here? But what if he's a spy?" Talia narrowed her eyes. "What if he's an undercover reporter for *Us Weekly*? What if he's trying to get some dirt on Heather and her 'humble' background?"

"He's not. You're even more cynical than I am."

"He might be. And yes, I am."

"You haven't even heard the best part yet." Kristen gave a canny smile. "He's agreed to pay one hundred and seventy-five dollars—*per day*—for the privilege of renting our corner booth. Right where I can keep an eye on him, near the cash register."

Talia's mouth dropped open. "The booth with the squeaky seat cushion?" At Kristen's nod, she gawked anew. "Okay. I'm impressed. That must have taken some mad negotiating skills."

"Not really." A pause. "I think he likes me."

"Of course he likes you!" Talia said faithfully.

"No, I mean . . . he *likes* me," Kristen said, remembering the way Casey had looked at her . . . the way he'd reacted when she'd touched his wrist, even just briefly. She hadn't been able to contain a jolt herself. Fortunately, she'd used her studious examination of his watch as a clever cover for her own reaction. "And *I*—"

"Who wouldn't like you?" Gareth Richards—one of her line cooks and another close friend—sailed into the break room. "You're totally lovable." Fondly, Gareth hugged Kristen. When he leaned back, he eyed Talia. "Everyone tells me this guy is superhot. I wouldn't know. I've been turning out burgers all day. But he's all anyone can talk about out front."

Kristen confirmed as much. "That's part of the reason I'm back here. I needed a chance to breathe." *And to think about why Casey had seemed so bugged to have run into Shane Maresca—whoever he was—in Kismet.* "I could barely move out there for all the people stopping me to ask about 'the new guy.'"

Gareth and Talia exchanged knowing glances.

"Well, I've got to see this earth-shattering superstud corporate flunky for myself, then." Talia hopped down from the table. She headed for the entryway to the back room, through which the sounds of clanking dishware, Christmas carols, and chattering diners could be heard. "What's he look like?"

Kristen resisted an urge to describe her own mental image of Casey Jackson. Her version of him involved far too many sexy smiles and imaginary darned socks to admit. Also, she wanted to play it cool. Her friends were already protective enough of her. They didn't need any reason to think she might already be smitten with the enemy. Or at least with her sister's enemy.

Or at least with her sister's potential enemy.

Besides, being *smitten* was the province of Jane Austen heroines. Not sensible, forward-thinking, modern women.

So, sensibly, Kristen said, "He's dark-haired. Polite. *Really* good-looking, but with this air of vulnerability that catches you off guard. You know? He's surprisingly kind. And confident. And intelligent, too. But he's not arrogant about it. In fact, just when you're not expecting him to, he—"

She became aware that her friends were staring at her, apparently befuddled by her rhapsodic description of Casey.

"He's the one in the suit," Gareth advised Talia wryly.

"A *suit?* Then he *is* some corporate drone?" Talia shook her head. "You know how I feel about soulless businessy types."

"He's not soulless," Kristen said in Casey's defense, uncomfortably remembering herself saying something similar to Heather about the "permatanned CPA type" she'd be expected to disarm and distract. She lifted her chin. "He's an orphan."

They both gawked at her with twice as much disbelief.

"Or a foster child, at least," Kristen amended, feeling a fresh tug of empathy for him. The look on Casey's face when he'd told her about his watch being stolen had really struck her. She didn't think he'd meant to tell her about it. "When he mentioned it, I got the sense that he didn't like to talk about it much."

Just like *she* didn't like to talk about her attachment to her diner very much. But Kristen did identify with her work there. She was proud that she'd made something out of nearly nothing—even if she had almost gone broke while doing it. She was proud that she'd done something—anything—that Heather hadn't done first, to more resounding applause, and better.

"Right." Talia crossed her arms. "Tragedy. Very slick."

"A difficult childhood isn't 'slick'!" Kristen protested.

"He's probably not even telling the truth."

"Talia!"

But her friend only poked her head into the passage to the dining room and looked around. "Hmm. It's tough to single out 'vulnerability' in a crowd." With a droll grin, she motioned for Gareth to join her. She pointed. "There. Is that him?"

Gareth held up his hands. "I don't want to be in the middle of this. When you two fight, it makes me want my blankie."

"Very funny." Talia dragged him closer. "Just look!"

"I'm on Kristen's side," Gareth insisted.

Talia sighed. "Fine. I'll just go ask him myself." She tied on her apron, stuck her order pad in her pocket, then squared her shoulders. "One dreamboat, on the house, coming up."

"No!" Gareth grabbed her. "You'll blow Kristen's chances."

"What chances?" Kristen glanced up from the break table.

Gareth looked guilty. Then, airily . . . "Nothing. Never mind."

But it was too late. By then, Kristen had already realized what he was up to. "*Don't* try to set me up with him," she warned. "I told you before, if I want a date, I'll get one."

"No, what *you* always get is a dirty, sordid fling."

Kristen grinned. "That's the best kind."

"It's the most meaningless kind," Gareth said. "You deserve more. You deserve *love*. And happiness!"

"Believe me, the kind of love I get makes me very happy," Kristen joked. "Especially when it's done right."

Talia backed him up. "You know what we mean! The second a guy seems like he might actually be nice and things might be going somewhere between you two, you drop him like a rock."

"Right." Skeptically, Kristen gazed at her friends. "So that's why you want to fix me up with a mysterious troubleshooting former orphan who'll only be in town until Christmas. Hmm. Sounds like perfect long-term romance material to me! What could possibly go wrong?"

"He," Talia said meticulously, "was a foster kid."

"He might be long-term romance material," Gareth added, a familiar matchmaking gleam in his eye already. "We don't know."

Kristen only laughed. "It doesn't matter anyway. Sure, I like him. But I already gave him my litmus test—"

At that, her friends both groaned in unison.

"Do you *want* to die old and alone?" Talia asked.

"That stupid test is a guaranteed hookup-breaker," Gareth said.

"—and he failed. Okay?" Kristen slid down from the break table, then straightened her apron. "Even if I wanted to sleep with Casey, I would have to resist. It's my policy."

"It's dumb," Gareth said. "Bordering on destructive."

"You *have* to separate yourself from your sister some other way," Talia put in. "Because that method is doomed to fail."

"It's working pretty well so far." The idea of getting hot and heavy with someone who'd seen Heather "performing" was beyond creepy. "I'm going to stick with it." *Even if it does mean I'll never get to experience Casey's flat abs, taut biceps, and broad, strong shoulders for myself.* If he had them, of course. Technically, she'd only imagined those physical details.

Along with his make-believe tight black boxer briefs. *Mmm.*

"As a strategy, it's only going to fail *more* as time goes by, too," Gareth said in a knowledgeable tone. "Because it's not as though people get bored with porn or anything. I mean, that video of Tommy Lee and Pamela Anderson is a bona fide classic. It's right up there with *Lesbian Spank Inferno* in total views."

Kristen sighed. "I wish it was different. I really do."

She did, too. Because she bet Casey would be *spectacular* in bed. He had the eyes for it. His eyes stayed focused on you, full of attentiveness and admiration and not-at-all concealed attraction. He had the hands for it. His hands moved nimbly and surely and capably, just the way she enjoyed the most. Most especially, Casey had the mouth for it, Kristen mused, because his lips looked soft and full and firm and kissable and . . .

"Hey, Kristen. Heads-up!" Her pastry chef, Walden Farr, strode into the break room wearing his cranberry-compote-smudged chef's whites. His linebacker-size body, beard stubble, tattoos, and long, dark dreadlocked hair combined to make him an imposing presence—but his chocolaty brown eyes turned him into a teddy bear. "That asshat from the bank is out front."

"Again?" Kristen groaned. "He's not supposed to be here! I've been over this and over this with the bank. They were supposed to be looking into the situation."

"Yeah." Walden nodded. "They're 'looking into it' by harassing you. My guess is, they think if they hound you enough, you'll just buckle and let them repossess the place."

"Ha! They don't know you very well then," Gareth said.

Concernedly, he and Talia frowned at her. The whole gang knew about her travails with the bank. Somehow, during a recent bank merger, her mortgage documents for the diner had gotten mixed up with a bunch of repossessions paperwork. The bank's threats to close her diner hadn't exactly made Kristen's Christmas season, but she couldn't afford to hire a lawyer to rebut their claims on a more informed and official basis.

Maybe after the holidays, she'd be in a better financial position to deal with all of it. But Kristen couldn't help hoping that if she could just dodge the bank rep for another few weeks, the bank would sort out its paperwork, let her off the hook, and save her all those attorney's fees in the process.

"I heard Avery tell him you're not here." Walden nodded toward the front, where the waitress in question, Avery, was working. "I'd suggest you make that a true statement."

Gareth and Talia nodded. "I'll cover for you," Talia told her, offering a shooing motion. "Don't worry about a thing."

"Don't even worry about coming back to close later," Gareth added. "We'll handle everything."

Kristen hesitated. It wasn't like her to skip out early, but it *was* only a few hours until closing time. The Galaxy Diner was a breakfast-and-lunch joint only, open until 3:00 P.M. most days. She had hopes of expanding into dinner service someday, but until she bolstered her finances somehow, this was it.

She'd already sunk all of her personal resources into the diner. Every dime of profit went to covering operating costs and repaying her debts. She couldn't give any more.

"Okay." She handed her keys to Gareth, gave Walden a grateful nod, then outlined a few last-minute instructions to Talia. She shrugged into her coat. "Hey, thanks, you guys.

You're the best. I'll have my cell phone if you need anything."

"We won't need anything."

"But if you do—"

"Get out of here!" all three of them shouted at once.

Practically pushed outside by the force of her friends' insistence, Kristen grabbed her purse. She slung it over her shoulder, offered another grateful smile, then bolted for the back door. She only hoped she could make it to her apartment—tucked upstairs above a shoe store-turned-coffee shop a few blocks away downtown—before the bank rep caught up with her.

Chapter 7

She couldn't do it, Kristen realized a block and a half away. Because although she'd successfully ditched the bank rep who'd come to her diner, there was an unfamiliar car parked outside the coffee shop . . . and the suit-wearing guy loitering conspicuously next to it with his eagle-eyed gaze trained on the stairs leading to her apartment didn't look like any espresso aficionado she'd ever met. He hadn't even bothered to bolster his cover by buying a peppermint mocha to go. The two bank reps were very, *very* obviously working in tandem to flush her out.

Why? *Why?* Kristen couldn't help wailing to herself as she spied her theoretical banker/stalker. Why couldn't the bank at least wait until after the holidays to hound her for her supposedly overdue mortgage payments? Especially since they weren't even overdue?

Caught, she wheeled to a stop, unsure what to do next.

People passed by her on the sidewalk, most of them still out Christmas shopping and all of them bundled against the wintery weather. A few snowflakes drifted down from the steely skies, lightly piling up on the holiday lights strung across the streets and on the municipal gold and silver decorations affixed to the old-fashioned lampposts. The city's official holiday music soundtrack—which included several Christmas songs from Heather's new CD—filtered vaguely into Kristen's hearing, but most of her attention was fixed on that menacing banker.

She couldn't go home. Not right now.

She couldn't stay near the bustling shops and other restaurants, either. It was only a matter of time before someone recognized her and called attention to her position.

Kristen imagined someone calling out her name, pictured the Repo Man/Banker swiveling his head toward her like evil Agent Smith in *The Matrix,* saw herself trying to run away and instead being caught. Maybe even handcuffed and hauled into custody.

She didn't know if it was a crime to evade bankers. But if she couldn't afford a lawyer to defend her record of spotless (if difficult-to-make) mortgage payments, she *definitely* couldn't afford a lawyer to bail her out of jail.

Decisively, Kristen turned. Clutching her purse, she strode in the opposite direction. For now, she just had to get away.

A dark-colored Subaru pulled up beside her with its engine idling. Kristen darted a glance at it, then walked faster.

The Subaru's window rolled down with an electronic hum.

"Hey!" a man shouted. "Kristen!"

Oh God. There were *three* of them! How had *she* made the bank's most-wanted list? She was just a girl-next-door turned struggling diner owner! She wasn't exactly a criminal.

The car crept forward, keeping pace with her. "Stop!"

She couldn't. Robotically, she kept walking. Maybe if she pretended to be engrossed in window shopping . . .

"I don't want a Sherpa. I want you!" the man called out.

A Sherpa? Struck by that, Kristen stopped.

Disbelievingly, she glanced to the side.

Casey Jackson sat behind the wheel of that Subaru, idling beside a festive, candy-cane-style decorated fire hydrant, staring through the open passenger-side window at her.

When he saw her looking back at him, he grinned.

Idiotically, that grin of his felt completely comforting.

"You look like you're in a hurry," he observed.

She gestured up the street. "Sort of."

Another too-observant glance. "Is something wrong?"

Yes. On the verge of admitting it, she gazed across the distance separating them. She caught the expression of concern on his face and longed to spill everything. Which was very unlike her. Sure, Casey was nonsensically appealing. Yes, being near him gave her the remarkable feeling that everything would work out okay in the end. Somehow. But she would have to be a lunatic to own up to any of that. Especially on the street.

"Nope," Kristen lied. "I'm just busy."

"Are you too busy to help me find my hotel?"

"Are you *that* easily lost? Get an atlas."

"I just changed hotels. So how about it?"

She hesitated. "You don't give up easily, do you?"

"No. And I'm sort of in a hurry, too. Get in."

"For all I know, you're some kind of homicidal maniac."

"A homicidal maniac who drives a Subaru?"

"Maybe." She jerked up her chin. "It takes all kinds."

Casey gave a carefree laugh. "Come on. It'll be fun. Who knows? You might even wind up enjoying yourself."

". . . said the guy who's here to make my sister unemployed."

Without responding to that, Casey leaned over. He opened the passenger-side door, then gave it a shove. It swung ajar. Invitingly, he said, "If you're going to impugn my character, you might as well do it in here, where it's warm and dry."

Apprehensively, Kristen shot a glance at the Repo Man waiting outside the coffee shop. At the same moment, he started to turn his head. Any second now, he'd spot her standing there.

She couldn't bolt fast enough. Like a shot, she dived into Casey's staid, responsible, rented Subaru. She slammed shut the door.

He only grinned at her with both hands on the wheel.

"Well? Gun it, why don't you?" she urged. "Let's go!"

Casey shot a curious glance over his shoulder. Down the block, the bank rep *had* to still be lurking there.

"What about your friend?" Casey asked mildly.

She probably shouldn't have been surprised that he'd noticed her shadow, but she was. His perspicacity was annoying.

Not as annoying as his ability to make her feel over-heated when it was a brisk twenty-three degrees outside, but still . . .

Kristen waved. "He's probably a paparazzo. I've been getting hounded by them ever since Heather arrived in town."

That was *technically* partly true, so she didn't feel too bad about misleading him. Besides . . . "Will you just *move* already?"

Obligingly, Casey did. Ten seconds later, the bank rep dropped out of sight. *Whew.* Feeling relieved and slightly felonious, Kristen slunk a little lower in the passenger seat.

They drove without incident past the Galaxy Diner, where the other bank rep was probably still lying in wait for her.

"Just keep going," she improvised with a don't-stop wave. "We'll have a tour of Kismet first. You know, see the sights."

With an agreeable nod, Casey expertly took a corner. They were traveling out of downtown now, headed roughly in the direction of the lake. Casey might like to pretend he was permanently lost, but he seemed to have a pretty unerring sense of direction, especially for a newcomer. He was driving right toward the most picturesque parts of Kismet.

He appeared unimpressed by his own accidental tourism expertise, though. Or unaware of it. Possibly, Casey was so good at everything that he couldn't be bothered to crow about specific examples.

"So the way I see it," he said, "you owe me."

Kristen scoffed. "How do you figure that?"

"I rescued you from that 'paparazzo' back there."

He angled his head toward the area of Kismet they'd just left, drawing her attention to his close-cropped dark hair. In the snow-shrouded daylight, Kristen couldn't tell if his hair was dark brown, as she'd initially thought, or brown shot through with hints of auburn, which better matched his emerging beard stubble. She also couldn't tell if he believed her about her stalkerish paparazzo. His tone was decidedly ambiguous.

This would be a good time to augment her cover story, Kristen decided. "Like I said, those media buzzards have been hounding me ever since Heather came back to town," she explained. "I don't know why they're so interested in *me*—"

"*I'm* interested in you. You're interesting."

"—but they wouldn't leave me alone until Heather struck a deal with them. My diner and my apartment are official safe zones now, but—"

"Until today."

"Huh?"

"Your apartment was a safe zone until today, you mean. It was safe until that 'paparazzo' violated the agreement?"

Oh yeah. "Right. Anyway, I'm just glad you happened along when you did. I'm not half as photogenic as my sister."

Unlike everyone else she knew, he didn't accept that joke at face value. Casey's lips quirked. "I bet you hold your own."

"Sure, I do. I'm not exactly hideous to look at. Children don't run bawling from me or anything." At his expression, she laughed. "I'm not saying I'm crippled by self-doubt or anything. I'm a pretty awesome person. But next to Heather, well . . ."

"Anybody would look a little ordinary?"

She didn't want him to understand. But apparently he did.

"Let's just say I do my best not to compete." Kristen gazed out at the Subaru's window as the town's lake flashed by, fully frozen over and dotted with ice-fishing shanties. A couple of them sported multicolored Christmas lights. "I thought the days of people expecting me to compete with Heather were behind me."

"But they're not?"

No, Kristen thought. *They're back with a vengeance.*

She frowned. "Are you always this curious?"

"About people I'm interested in?" Casey shot her an appreciative sideways glance. "Yes." He stopped at the next intersection, peered at the rural businesses and snow-covered evergreen trees bordering it, then shivered. "You're your own person. You shouldn't have to compete with Heather."

Kristen gave a sardonic grin. "Try telling that to the rest of the world. Including my parents." She couldn't believe she was confiding in him, but Casey Jackson had a way of listening that created a sort of instant solidarity. Somehow, she felt he was on her side. "My mom and dad have a serious case of Celebrity Spawn Syndrome. Last week, they were interviewed by E! for an upcoming TV special. This week, they've already chatted on camera with *Extra*, *Entertainment Tonight*, and *Access Hollywood*. They've even been sending out regular updates on their new @Heather_Hotline Twitter account. They got over a million followers the first week alone." She cast a wry glance at Casey. "The whole thing has made them rock stars among their friends. I mean, how much more public evidence of your stellar parenting skills do you get than raising a megastar?"

"I know some parents of megastars who'd disagree," Casey mused. "Sometimes it's not easy having children who basically outrun you in the race of life."

Kristen had never thought of it that way. Her mom was a part-time clerk at Reno Wright's sporting-goods store. Her dad was a retired long-haul trucker. *Could* they be bothered that their daughter had succeeded beyond their own wildest dreams?

"Maybe they're overcompensating for that," Casey suggested. "Or maybe they're just genuinely proud of Heather." He shrugged. "I hear it happens—parents being proud of their children."

Despite his nonchalant tone, Kristen couldn't help feeling a momentary pang on his behalf. Had Casey really never known what it was like to have parents who were proud of his accomplishments? To have parents who were proud of *him?*

That was rough. Kristen's own parents had always seemed over-the-moon pleased with Heather's achievements: that homebrew sex tape, a *Hot Buns* workout DVD, a line of shoes and "club clothes," and a guest-judging stint on *Project Runway,* included.

Oh, and several wildly successful music CDs and tours, too.

A Nobel Laureate Heather was *not*. But she was lovable.

Her mom and dad were *definitely* proud of Heather. Kristen knew it was true, because they let her know about it all the time. They'd gushed about Heather and her success for years.

Unfortunately, they hadn't done the same for Kristen. But she didn't need any cheerleading anyway. She was her own person. Her own sense of pride and accomplishment were enough for her.

They would *have* to be enough, wouldn't they? Because she wasn't expecting anything else.

"That doesn't explain my customers who've morphed into junior paparazzi themselves," Kristen said, sidestepping that thorny issue altogether. "When Heather first showed up at the diner, totally out of the blue"—*eight days ago (and counting)*—"one of my regulars took a cell phone snap of the two of us reuniting."

"That was nice of him."

"It wasn't for us," she clarified. "He later sold it to a tabloid for five thousand dollars."

"I think I see a way out of your money problems."

Kristen sharpened her gaze. "What money problems?"

Another shrug. "You said your diner was a money pit."

Oh. *Whew.* Maybe Casey Jackson wasn't as clairvoyant as he seemed, despite his knack for bailing her out of trouble at exactly the right moment—and despite his ability to make her want to confide in him. It just . . . made her feel better to do so.

If she hadn't had so many friends, she would have thought she was starved for someone just to *listen* to her for a change.

"Since then," Kristen went on, hoping to evade the issue of her finances, "people have been hanging out at the Galaxy Diner double-time, hoping they'll score a big payday, too."

"At least that's good for business."

"*If* they order anything," Kristen agreed, admiring—despite her intention not to—the way Casey handled that stolid vehicle. In his hands, that four-wheel-drive Subaru cut through traffic like a Ferrari. "I've had to be pretty tough on a few loiterers. And that doesn't even count the way my friends have been behaving ever since Heather came back! We used to have lots of time to hang out together, but now that my superstar sister is in town, people are 'too busy' to spend time with me. They'd rather go watch her performing or filming, I guess."

All she could *do* was guess. She hadn't been able to bring herself to ask outright. Although she had overheard Gareth and Avery discussing the TV taping they'd attended a few days ago. The possibility that her own friends (and her parents) might be choosing Heather over her was too hurtful. Kristen didn't want her suspicions confirmed. Ever.

Casey gave a commiserating frown. "That's tough."

His empathic tone only egged her on. "I can't really blame them. I mean, for other people, spending time with a celebrity is a thrill. But to me, Heather is just my sister. I love her. I do. But I don't want to be thought of as Heather's Mini-Me."

"If it's any help, I've never thought of you that way."

". . . and *that's* why you're famously charming. Because of audacious lines like that one." With a jolt, Kristen snapped back to reality. She couldn't let herself get carried away with trusting The Terminator, she reminded herself. It was his job to get people to talk. As proof, she'd just basically copped to the truth: that she'd felt invisible (again) ever since Heather had blown back into town. "So, which hotel are you staying at?"

"Very subtle redirection."

"Well, I don't see the point in tiptoeing around things."

"Touché." Casey frowned at the modest houses they drove past next, as though resenting their light-and-icicle-bedecked eaves and holiday yard decorations. "I was staying at the Riverside Hotel, but now I'm moving to The Christmas House B&B."

"Ooh! The Christmas House! Good choice." Kristen approved. "I love the atmosphere there!"

"You would." Grimly, he kept driving. "I expect not to, given the name and the likely shtick that goes with it."

"Oh, that's right, Scrooge. You hate Christmas."

"I guess my reputation preceded me?"

"More than you know." Kristen examined his suddenly tense posture. Beneath his coat and suit, his whole body appeared taut. As Casey drove onward, his thigh flexed, calling her attention to the well-developed muscles there, making her wonder about things she had no intention of exploring any further. Instead, she said, "If the idea of a B&B devoted to the ultimate Christmas experience is such a nightmare for you—"

He made a face. "Tell me it's not really that bad."

"—then why are you doing it?"

"Because Shane Maresca is staying there, and I can't let him get the jump on me. I have to know what he's up to."

"I see. Competitive much?"

Casey's jaw flexed. "You don't understand."

"Then make me understand. I spilled my guts to you."

"That was different."

"Why?"

"Because it was *you*."

"Aha. You don't like to be vulnerable." Kristen watched his profile, fascinated by the way his easygoingness had just ebbed away. His features were solid. Friendly-looking. He hovered just this side of *too* handsome to be tolerated. "I get it."

"I doubt it." Casey rubbed his thumb over his wristwatch in an undoubtedly unconscious—and undoubtedly comforting—gesture. As though suddenly realizing what he was doing, he glanced down. "Hey, time's wasting. How about those directions?"

Agreeably, Kristen gave them. She could wait a while to find out about Shane Maresca. After all, Casey would be spending a lot of time at her diner. She could pump him for information there. Or, since it was likely that Shane would come back to the Galaxy Diner—because he was such a fan—she could simply ask him.

Within minutes, she and Casey were zipping around the other edge of the lake, traveling through the snowy, tree-dotted terrain that led to The Christmas House.

"You realize this place is *renowned* for its holiday atmosphere," she told Casey as they neared it. "The owners, the Sullivans, are even more crazy about Christmas than I am."

"There must be something in the water around here."

"It's really nice! They provide an all-inclusive holiday experience and a wonderful Christmas ambiance for their guests, all for a reasonable price and with a personal touch. If I remember correctly, they have multiple Christmas trees, a holiday-shopping concierge, gift wrapping assistance, a cookie-baking-and-decorating party, sleigh rides with jingle bells—"

"I think I'm breaking out in a rash."

"—Christmas-caroling outings, *amazing* gourmet meals three times a day, homemade eggnog, a special Fun Zone with activities for the kids, an evening happy hour with mulled cider—"

"I hope *that's* happening early today. How much of a buzz do you think you can get from mulled cider?"

"—and a resident mascot, Digby the dachshund, who wears the most adorable holiday-themed sweaters. He is too cute."

"Christmas sweaters? For a dog?" Casey gave her an appalled look. "You're making that up."

"I am not." Playfully, Kristen hugged herself. "There's nothing I love more than a dog in a sweater."

"Ugh."

"Unless it's *two* dogs in *two* sweaters."

"That's it. We can't be friends anymore."

"Or a sleepy kitten in a teacup," she mused with mock dreaminess. "There's nothing cuter than that."

"What? A kitten in a—" Casey stopped. "What? *Why?*"

"Haven't you ever visited cuteoverload.com?"

He shuddered. "Not in this lifetime."

Kristen stifled a smile. "You'll see. Once you've spent a night at The Christmas House, you'll be converted, just like me. As soon as the Sullivans get their hands on you, that's it. You're done. Betty and Robert own the place, but their niece, Vanessa, handles most of the day-to-day stuff. You know . . . transforming Grinchy types like you into candy-cane-loving, Santa-hat-sporting, ho-ho-ho-ing true believers."

That did it. Inadvertently, she pushed things too far.

"You're trying to make me panic." Casey shook his head, still driving. "It won't work. I'm immune to Christmas."

"*Nobody's* immune to Christmas."

"I'm immune to all the bullshit that goes with it, too."

"That's not possible."

Casey gave her a look that said it wasn't only possible—it was inarguable. "Christmas might have meant something once. But these days, it's just a bunch of greedy corporations playing on the sentiments of lonely, distracted people. They leverage our collective memories to make a buck, and we gleefully buy in."

"Except you."

A stony nod. "Except me."

Stunned by his cynicism, Kristen touched his arm. "You get all that from a few lights and wreaths and bayberry candles?"

No wonder he'd been giving the stink-eye to the holiday decorations they'd passed on the way. He *really* disliked Christmas.

At least that meant she didn't have to feel *too* sorry about Casey failing her official litmus test. It wasn't as if she'd be missing out on sleeping with her soul mate or anything. She couldn't possibly be destined to fall for Scrooge Redux.

Unaware of her musings, Casey pulled the car to a stop beside a long rolling yard filled with fresh snow and sparkly holiday decorations. At its far end, near its hilly crest, stood the B&B: a big white house, a bona fide barn, and several additional outbuildings. The house's wide front porch was fully decked out in lights, ribbons, and the aforementioned wreaths. Next to the car was a hand-painted sign with a familiar holly-wreath logo and the words *The Christmas House* in fancy script.

"If you think you can change my mind," Casey said as he turned off the car's ignition, "you're welcome to have at it."

But Kristen was too wary—and maybe too cynical herself, by now—to fall for that. At least from him. "You'd like that, wouldn't you?" she asked astutely. "If I'm busy trying to show you the wonders of Christmas, I won't even notice what you're doing to sabotage Heather's holiday TV special."

"I told you, I'm *not* going to sabotage—" In midsentence, Casey gave up. "Look, you'll see. I have ways of handling problems like your sister's TV special. It's my specialty. And as for all the Christmas stuff, usually I'd be in Mexico by now, kicking back with some buddies. So if you can make missing out on my winter vacation more tolerable, I'm all for it."

"Oh. Really? But what about—" *Your family,* she started to ask. *Whoops.* She'd already realized that was a sensitive subject with him. Awkwardly, Kristen regrouped. "*Really?*" she asked brightly. "You go on vacation this time of year?"

A nod. "Typically I go someplace sunny for the holidays—Cozumel, Anguilla, Kauai—and get as drunk as possible."

Kristen gave him an empathetic look. "How's the mulled cider in Anguilla? Pretty tasty?"

"I wouldn't know. I drink beer."

"Do the places you go to have Christmas trees and lights and holiday music? Do they have gifts and fudge and mistletoe?"

"You don't get it. I'm trying to get *away* from that stuff."

She really *didn't* get it. The very idea was beyond comprehension. "How about stockings? Gingerbread? Sugar cookies? Yule logs? They *must* have Yule logs. Maybe on the beach? Like a beach bonfire? A Yule log beach bonfire?"

"I wouldn't recognize a Yule log if you smacked me with one."

"That's the saddest thing I've ever heard."

"You think *you're* sad. I'm the one getting walloped."

"No, I mean your understanding of Christmas is sad."

"Not as sad as a kitten in a teacup. *That's* messed up."

"You seem," Kristen said, realizing how right Heather had been about this, "*completely* deficient in Christmas cheer."

She wished the realization didn't make her feel so sorry for him. She didn't want to feel sorry for her archrival.

It was going to make things pretty damn inconvenient.

Patiently, Casey pocketed his car keys. He gazed at her,

seeming willing to stay in the car and discuss this with her all day, if necessary. It was a weirdly seductive quality of his.

"I never had any Christmas cheer," he told her succinctly. "I never wanted it. That's never going to change."

The challenge inherent in that statement was almost enough to make Kristen offer a plan to the contrary, just because he thought she couldn't. But at the last second, she quit admiring Casey's big, talented-looking hands, stopped trying to decide if his shadowy beard stubble qualified as auburn or chestnut, and managed to rein in her intrinsic compassion.

She gave an offhanded wave. "Okay. Have it your way."

After all, maybe Casey just had a bad attitude. Maybe he *hadn't* had a disadvantaged youth; plenty of people wound up thriving in the foster-care system, Kristen knew, having been sheltered by loving and kindhearted foster parents. Casey's upbringing didn't have to equal fear and loathing of Christmas.

No matter how full of self-protective curmudgeonliness he seemed to be when it came to discussing the holidays.

Casey took her turndown in stride. "You're probably the wrong person to ask for help anyway," he said carelessly. "I mean, how much do you really know about enjoying Christmas, if yours can be thrown off so easily by Heather's arrival in town?"

To Kristen, those were fighting words.

She intended to react appropriately, too. But first . . .

"Who said Heather's homecoming wrecked my Christmas?"

Casey only looked at her. "That's got to be especially tough for someone like you. Someone who *loves* the holidays."

It had been tough. It still was, in fact. Just last week, her mom had canceled their annual mother-daughter pre-Christmas shopping trip so she could pick up her *Heather Miller Live! from the Heartland* souvenir T-shirt order and distribute the shirts to the members of her knitting club. But

Kristen hadn't told Casey that. *How* had he gotten to be so freakishly perceptive?

Dumbfounded, Kristen couldn't guess. All she knew was that Casey's overt sympathy—served up with another helping of bedroom eyes for a starter and a hint of potential make-out session for dessert—made most of her remaining resistance to him crumple.

"Heather and her glam posse brought in *animatronic reindeer,*" Kristen told him. Surely, once Casey knew the facts, he would be on her side. "*Multiple* animatronic reindeer, to use around town while filming on location. Then, as a pièce de résistance, they dressed the reindeer in couture harnesses."

"You must have loved that. Like dogs with sweaters!"

"Uh, no." Kristen made a face. "The French designer who made the harnesses was feeling 'inspired' by vintage Parisian S&M gear. Those reindeer look like animatronic refugees from Disneyland's 'It's a Small Sadomasochistic World' ride."

"Hmm. Bondage reindeer. Interesting choice."

"Dasher, Prancer . . . and *Vixen!* They're all over town now," Kristen explained, "just like that 'Cows on Parade' exhibit in Chicago. It's *disturbing*. And it's *not* Christmassy." She considered it. "Those harnesses don't even have jingle bells!"

". . . because *that's* the biggest problem with whips-and-chains robo-reindeer." Casey made a sardonic face. "You're being circumspect, but I bet I can guess which designer it was. I've done some troubleshooting at Fashion Week, and I—"

"They blew in huge piles of fake snowdrifts outside, too, on top of the real snow," Kristen rushed on, lest he get sidetracked before she made her point, "because the authentic stuff didn't 'read well' on camera. They made all the local extras in the 'audience' get spray-on tans, because they looked too pale and 'sickly' to be Heather Miller fans. They said they didn't look 'aspirational' enough for TV viewers."

Casey nodded, unfazed. "That sounds about right."

She couldn't believe he couldn't see how wrong all those things were. "They're perverting the idea of Christmas, just for the sake of having a bigger, better, *faker* Christmas for TV. There's more, too. Personal things. I can't begin to tell you—"

"You know," Casey mused with a shrewd expression, "if I can get them to move up the live-performance part of the show and wrap the rest of the production early, all that craziness will come to an end." He gave Kristen a direct look. "If you help me get Heather on track, you can have your Christmas back." A pause. "You can have your life back."

Clearly, she'd given away too much already, if Casey had any inkling how much she wanted *that*. He definitely seemed to.

Kristen shook her head, wishing she'd never spoken up. This situation wasn't as cut and dried as Casey wanted it to be. "My sister is more important to me than any Christmas tradition. I want her to be here, *really* at home for the holidays."

He gave her a puzzled look. "Heather doesn't have to leave town when she's done with her TV special. In fact, afterward she'll be *more* free to spend time with you and your parents. There just won't be any Robo-Rudolphs, SnoFoam, Snowcel, acrylic icicles, or Mystic-Tan-spackled Michiganders around."

But Kristen knew different. This was the first holiday season in years that Heather had been home. That was partly why her parents had jumped so hard on the Heather Miller bandwagon.

"She'll leave," Kristen told him. "Without an excuse to stay in Kismet, Heather will borrow someone's private Learjet and head back to her real life. My mom and dad will be devastated. I can't let that happen." Turning away from that sobering thought, Kristen mustered a grin. "But hey, maybe you'll see Heather in Cozumel sometime!"

"So you're sacrificing *your* Christmas happiness for the sake of ensuring a big, cozy, family holiday for your folks?"

She hadn't thought about it that way, Kristen realized. But that was about the size of it. She just wanted a little harmony.

"You don't have to sound so befuddled by that."

"I'm not. I'm not *befuddled* by family loyalty." Casey didn't sound completely convinced. "So tell me: What makes a perfect Christmas for you?"

She snorted. "As if *you* want to know, Mr. Grinch."

"I mean it. Just because I don't want one for myself, that doesn't mean I can't appreciate all the necessary elements. But it's a personal thing, right? So when it comes to *you . . .*"

"All right," Kristen said, deciding to play along. "I like having family and friends nearby, first of all. Which is at the crux of my problem with Heather's Christmas invasion, actually, since she's *here,* which is good, yet she's ruining everything, which is bad. I like doing all the traditional things, too—decorating, baking cookies, exchanging gifts, going to parties."

"Mmm-hmm." Appearing deeply engrossed in what she was saying—while also deeply, irrevocably averse to everything she was talking about—Casey nodded. "That sounds nice for you."

"I have to say, you seem as though you'd rather eat rocks than immerse yourself in Christmas." Kristen angled her head toward the B&B outside. "Are you sure you want to do this?"

Now Casey appeared grimly determined. "I can take it."

"Right. So you can keep an eye on Shane Maresca."

"What's more," he went on, ignoring her leading statement, "I can make sure *you* have the Christmas you want this year."

"Are you trying to bribe me or something? Because if you are—" *It might help me feel better about "distracting" you.* She couldn't say that, so she tried something else. "It won't work."

"Consider it a favor. Just because I like you."

Suspiciously, Kristen regarded him. She couldn't help wanting that to be true. Because, despite everything, *she* liked *him,* too. "Really?"

"Yes." Casey glanced out the window next, as though girding himself against the B&B's festive façade. "Now. Will you come inside and help me survive this Christmas gauntlet?"

"Around here, we like to call it 'checking in.' It's easy."

"It's not going to be easy." Casey shook his head. "It's going to be a big slice of tinsel-covered disaster pie."

"Whoa." Kristen held up her hands. "First of all, don't malign the world of pie. Second of all, I'm your conscripted Sherpa, not your therapist. I'm not here to hold your hand."

Casey's warmhearted gaze suggested he'd like that . . . and more.

Probably, so would she. Better not think about that.

Heather's sex tape. Heather's sex tape. He'd seen it!

Whatever else she did, Kristen remembered, she could not cave in and sleep with Casey. No matter how fun it sounded . . .

"I'm asking for your company," he said, not seeming at all like a guy who watched grainy pornography. "For an afternoon."

"I didn't agree to that, either."

"It was kind of implied when you rocketed into my car to escape your 'paparazzo.'" He gave her a casual, all-too-knowing glance. "Or are you ready to tell me the truth about what that guy was really doing lurking outside your apartment?"

She'd been planning to tell Casey she intended to call a taxi from outside The Christmas House and then take her chances sneaking back into her aforementioned apartment. Or, failing that, retreating to Talia's place for the night. But now . . .

Argh. "How did you know it was my apartment?"

Casey only observed her. Patiently. And confidently.

Damn it. She couldn't lie outright. "They should call you the Ninja Stalker," Kristen grumbled, "not The Terminator."

His gaze intensified. "Who calls me The Terminator?"

"Um, *everyone?* In L.A., at least. That's what I heard."

He pursed his lips. Then he nodded. Was it only her imagination, or did Casey seem a little . . . *hurt* by that nickname?

Before she could start feeling *too* sorry for him, he gazed through the frosty windshield. He frowned at the B&B's sign.

"That's how Heather got you to agree to pump me for information," he surmised in a rough voice. "By scaring you with stories of the big baddie who'd come to cause her trouble."

He was too close for comfort. Kristen squirmed, unwilling to admit it. "Hey, I don't scare easily, remember?"

"Maybe not," Casey agreed, "but you *do* seem to have a mile-wide loyalty streak. Obviously, Heather . . . doesn't. She was willing to do whatever she had to do—even exploit your sense of sisterly solidarity—to keep me away from the set today. The question is, why? What exactly is going on down there?"

"Technically, that's two questions."

Decisively, Casey glanced at the B&B. "I'm going inside for a supersize dose of Christmas cheer. It'll probably be lethal." With a beguiling grin, he beckoned her. "Are you coming?"

She boggled. "Aren't you going to the set of Heather's TV special instead? A second ago, you said you wanted to know what's going on down there."

He'd also said that Heather had *exploited* her. That didn't sit well with Kristen. She crossed her arms and waited.

But Casey merely smiled at her. "I'm not going to go down there and start raising hell right this minute, no. If that's what you're expecting," he said. "That's not how I work."

His cryptic tone only piqued her interest. "How do you work, then?"

But Casey only squinted more attentively at the B&B. "I think I see that sweater-wearing dachshund you were telling me about. That's a nice Christmas tree in the window, too. See it?"

Pointedly, Kristen didn't look. But she felt the tug of those seasonal accoutrements, all the same.

"Seriously," she insisted. "How do you work?"

"Stick close to me. Maybe you'll find out."

Casey flashed her a tempting grin. Then, before she could reply, he got out of the car. The driver's-side door slammed shut in his wake. He tromped toward The Christmas House's homespun sign. He put his hands on his hips. Then he grinned at the sign—almost as if he truly, genuinely *liked* it.

She didn't get him. That's partly why he was so disarming.

Also, *she* liked that sign, too. A local artist had painted it. There was something irrevocably unpretentious and welcoming about it. Which was probably why Casey was calling her attention to it, rather than simply trudging uphill to his Christmas doom.

He wanted her to *want* to come with him. Willingly.

"I didn't agree to this!" Kristen said from inside the car. She pantomimed reluctance to make her message clear. "You're still trying to pit me against my sister. It won't work."

"Am I?" Casey held up his cell phone. "Will you take a picture of me beside this sign? It'll blow my friends' minds."

If she got out of the car, Kristen knew, she was sunk. From there, it would be that much easier to heed the lure of eggnog and peppermint bark and evergreen garland and simply accompany Casey inside The Christmas House. There, she'd be twice as susceptible to his charms. Christmastime weakened her resolve.

Christmastime might even be capable of overriding the *off* switch she typically employed when it came to her libido—and men who failed her litmus test. Men like Casey Jackson.

Oblivious to her mental battles, Casey waggled his phone. He gave an enticing little smile, too, just to sweeten the deal.

Although that's not *precisely* what tipped the scales in his favor, Kristen suspected she'd look back later and curse his relentless boyish charm. So far, it was proving to be her undoing. She couldn't seem to *not* trust him, no matter how hard she tried. But Kristen did have the presence of mind—and the pride—not to make her (temporary) surrender look easy.

She cracked open the passenger-side door, then offered him a scowl from within the resulting gap. "If I spend the afternoon with you," Kristen specified, "I want dinner, too."

"Fine. It'll be my treat."

His instant acquiescence told her she should have asked for more. But Kristen was committed now. She got out, then tromped over to him. "Excellent! They serve an incredible buffet at the B&B, full of every single Christmas specialty you can think of."

"Sounds nightmarish."

"Just smile for the camera."

Then Kristen snapped a photo of Casey beside the B&B's holly-wreath-decorated sign, thereby sealing into posterity the moment when she stopped being officially skeptical of him . . . and started being willing to go along with him (at least partway) instead.

Chapter 8

When Walden Farr emerged from the Galaxy Diner's walk-in at the end of his shift, he wasn't thinking about Christmas wishes. He was thinking, more or less, about the batch of spritz cookies he was chilling, the chocolate ganache he was planning for service tomorrow, and the likely improbability of anyone from his hometown, roughly three thousand miles distant, coming to see him at Christmastime.

It wasn't because his family didn't care. They did. But they couldn't afford airfare for holiday vacations. They also couldn't afford the time off from work (or the gas) needed to make a multistate road trip. At this point, although he had a good job, neither could he. That was just the way it was.

This year, like most years, Walden and his far-flung family would be having a very Skype-y Christmas. Video calling had its advantages, though. For one, if the Internet connection was sluggish enough—and he tied back his dreads—his mom might forget to nag him about getting a haircut. So that was a plus.

Walden believed in looking on the bright side. Most of the time, he was pretty good at it. That's why, when Talia invited him to participate in the scheme she and Gareth were pulling off, Walden decided to go along with it. Because he knew they meant well. He knew they would probably succeed. And he—as the new guy in town—wanted to be in on the action when they did.

Also, he wanted to be near Talia.

He'd never met anyone cooler than Talia. She was mouthy and sarcastic and freaking *unconquerable,* and just being around her made him feel as though someone had cranked the dial to ten. He loved her energy and her loyalty and her weird purple hair. He was pretty sure she thought of him as a spatula-wielding, cake-baking freak of nature, but on the off chance she didn't . . .

"Hey, Talia." Offhandedly, Walden nodded at her as he entered the break room and glimpsed her there. "How's it going?"

She turned to look at him, giving him a dizzying dose of big blue eyes and brainy intimidation. "*You!* You're *perfect!*"

At her exclamation, her eyes got even bluer (if that was possible). Her excitement at seeing him crackled clear across the room. Her coolness touched him, too. And *that* was the moment when Walden starting thinking about Christmas wishes—thinking that he wished he could have *Talia* for Christmas. Because even though Talia's statement was an unmistakable non sequitur, it segued so well with his dreams that Walden didn't care.

You! You're perfect!

How many times had he fantasized about Talia looking at him, really *seeing* him, and then saying something like that?

Well, lots of times. More than he wanted to count.

"Perfect for what?" he asked, striving to keep his cool.

"For *this*." Excitedly, Talia brandished a box.

He looked at it. "A home pregnancy test?" He shrugged. "Okay. If you're *that* ready to get pregnant, I'm your guy."

Wishing he *was* her guy, Walden started unbuttoning his double-breasted chef's jacket. He gave his hips a burlesque-style wiggle in a maneuver designed to make the most of his checkered-pants-clad bottom half. He grinned, then continued his bump and grind. "Get ready, future baby mama! Here I come."

At his semiseductive warning growl, Talia guffawed.

"No, silly!" Grinning, she smacked him in the belly. She seemed to be caught by surprise when her fist *didn't* encounter acres of doughy pastry chef flesh. She gave his abs a curious poke. "Hey, you're kind of, um . . . *cut,* aren't you? I mean, you're really—" Her gaze lifted to mingle interestedly with his. Then she waggled the pregnancy-test kit. "*This* is for our scheme."

Aha. He quit unbuttoning, leaving his chef's whites open atop his *The Strokes* T-shirt. "Our scheme to help Kristen?"

"No," she deadpanned. "Our scheme to save the whales."

"Ha ha."

"Our scheme to make beer pong an Olympic event."

"Very funny."

But Talia was on a roll now. "Our scheme to take over the world!" she elaborated theatrically, her eyes sparkling. "Just like—"

"Just like we try to do every night. I hear you, Brain."

Her eyes widened. Walden wasn't sure why.

"But the pregnancy kit is for . . . what, exactly?" he asked patiently. "If you don't want volunteers to get you pregnant—"

"That's not what I came here for, Pinky."

"Then what's it for?" And why am I perfect for it?

Talia wasn't ready to tell him. Instead, she went on gazing at him inquisitively. "Wait. You really got that reference?"

"To *Pinky and the Brain*? The cartoon?" Walden nodded. "I'm a grown man who makes a living frosting cupcakes. So . . . yeah."

Her admiring gaze swept over him. Of all the things to have finally impressed her with, his connoisseurship of a 1990s animated TV show about a genius laboratory mouse and his feebleminded sidekick mouse had to be the most unlikely.

"Really?" Cagily, Talia asked, "What did you think of Wang Film Productions' work on *A Pinky and the Brain Christmas*?"

Walden scoffed. "I think Tokyo Movie Shinsha did the animation on that one. What are you, some kind of amateur?"

Talia laughed. "An amateur who owns all twelve discs from the DVD box sets. *And* the graphic novels. *And* the Game Boy game."

"Wow." This time, it was Walden's turn to give her an admiring look. "I think you're my dream girl." *I know you are*.

She nodded. Probably, Talia was used to being someone's dream girl by now and was totally unfazed by the concept.

"We should get together and watch it sometime," she said.

Walden wanted to say yes. Gazing into her shining, cobalt-colored eyes, standing close enough to touch her, he wanted nothing more. A *Pinky and the Brain*-a-thon with Talia? Hell, yeah! But something kept niggling at him. Something like . . .

Like maybe Talia was already pregnant. With someone else.

Oh yeah. Forcibly, he dragged his attention to that damn box in her hand. "Do I have to overthrow your baby's daddy first? Or is he cool with you having guys over? Because I'm a pretty wicked arm wrestler, so—" He offered her a comical tough-guy look, then shook his head. "I wouldn't want to hurt him."

"You're not 'a guy.' You're my friend! It's fine."

Ugh. The Friend Zone. The Chinese handcuffs of man-woman relationships. Didn't she know how crushing that statement was?

"Look," Walden said. "Do you have a boyfriend or not?"

"Oh." Talia looked surprised. She glanced down at her

pregnancy test, then looked up at him again . . . lingering on his midsection. "Is *that* what you're asking? Because I thought—"

"That I was seriously looking for an arm-wrestling match?"

She bit her lip. He wanted to do the same. To her. Gently.

"Well," she prevaricated, "you *are* the new guy in town. It's anybody's guess what kind of kinky stuff you're into."

That was the Talia he knew and loved. "If there's anything you want to know about me," Walden said stoutly, "just ask."

Her forehead wrinkled adorably. Not surprisingly, she did ask him something. "Okay. Do you like popcorn and cranberries?"

"Together? No. I'm not one of those molecular gastronomy guys. I mean, I learned how to do all that crazy stuff in culinary school"—technically, he'd aced all his classes and gotten A-pluses across the board—"but I'm not interested in subverting culinary expectations and deconstructing what it means to dine. I don't serve 'tasting' menus printed on edible paper with fruit inks. I don't want to juggle liquid nitrogen or offer 'meat foam' as an entrée. I *really* don't think it's satisfying to serve 'essence of' anything just to smell. You can't eat a smell! Give me a good piece of pie instead."

Talia look amused by his rant. "Oh. I see. Well, I'm only asking because I'm having a popcorn-and-cranberry stringing party tonight at my place, and I want to know if you'll come."

Walden was still confused. He didn't want to step on any toes here. Was Talia asking him out on a date? Or was she just trying to leverage him into popcorn-and-cranberry slave labor?

He never would have pegged her for an old-school type who made popcorn-and-cranberry garlands for her Christmas tree in the first place. He would have guessed she was more of a retro-fake-silver-tree type.

Well, he liked a woman who surprised him, Walden decided.

But not if that surprise involved another man's baby.

"But what about your pregnancy test?" he asked.

Gareth chose that moment to come along and pluck the box from her hands. Gleefully, he said, "*That's* for me!"

"Huh?"

"I'm going to plant this pregnancy test in Heather Miller's Dumpster." Gareth shifted a satisfied look in Talia's direction. "You know, the trash collection unit that the tabloid people are always digging through looking for gossip fodder?"

"If they think Heather's pregnant," Talia explained, "the resulting 'baby bump watch' will occupy a *lot* of time."

"Time they *won't* spend pestering Kristen?" Walden guessed.

"Exactly." Gareth ripped open the box, crumpled up the instruction sheet, stuffed it back inside, then opened one of the testers, too. "Once I make sure this thing looks good and used, we'll be all set. You've got to make it believable," he added as he caught Walden's aghast look. "I'm not going to pee on a stick *myself*, but if I toss a pristine, unopened pregnancy-test kit in Heather's trash, it's going to look like a setup."

"It *is* a setup," Walden reminded them.

"Yep. It sure is!" Gareth said, his bearded face alight.

He and Talia exchanged cheerfully devious looks.

"'Baby bump watches' are a fixture in tabloids," Talia said. "If a starlet eats a big lunch, suddenly she's gestating."

Walden nodded. "And when Heather denies being pregnant—as she inevitably will—it will only create more 'news' about her."

"Which is exactly what we need right now," Talia agreed.

"So the press will be too busy going ape shit about this"—Gareth held up the freshly mangled pregnancy-test kit—"to harass Kristen."

"I hope so." Remembering all his friend had gone through recently, Walden sobered. "I thought Kristen was actually going to cry when her mom canceled their Christmas shopping trip."

"That just about broke my heart," Talia agreed, making him love her even more for her compassion. "The day before that, Kristen told me the press invaded the traditional Miller family holiday ice-skating-and-cocoa trip. They wrecked *everything*. Poor Grandma Miller couldn't even slap on a skate without some fuckwit screaming her name. When they wouldn't 'play along,' the paparazzi assaulted them all with flash photography anyway."

Walden shuddered. He'd been on duty when the paparazzi had first overrun the Galaxy Diner, looking for any scoop they could get on Kristen's famous sister. Among the pack of them, the cheap bastards hadn't even ponied up a tip for their harassed waitress. He and Talia and Gareth had sneaked a tip for Avery onto the table themselves so she wouldn't be stiffed.

"Not to mention how those jackals have affected business here at the diner," Gareth said, practically reading Walden's mind. He shuddered too. "Some of the regulars can't even get in anymore—and that's *with* Heather's supposed ban in place."

They all knew that Heather's unexpected and over-the-top arrival in Kismet—and her "down-home" holiday TV special—had thrown a monkey wrench into Kristen's holiday this year. Kristen was way too nice to say so, but she'd been struggling. So together, Talia, Gareth, and Walden had decided to help her out.

Their first step had been to try getting the press officially banned from the Galaxy Diner. That hadn't worked. Next, they'd approached Heather and asked her, up front, to do something about the situation. That strategy had resulted in the cease-fire/safety-zone deal that was supposed to keep the media away from Kristen's business and her apartment. None of them (except Kristen) was naïve enough to expect it to last long.

Sometimes, Kristen had way too much faith in her sister.

Sometimes, friends had to step in to help friends, too. Even if that meant going a little above and beyond. But Kristen was worth it. They all loved her. They wanted her to be happy.

"There's only one problem," Walden mused, considering how best to accomplish that goal. He pointed at the soon-to-be-planted "evidence" of the pregnancy test. "How's Heather supposed to be believably pregnant when she hasn't been seen publicly dating anyone since her split from that hockey player?"

Gareth frowned. "You have a point."

"I already thought of that! The only solution is for *our* Heather to have a new boyfriend." Talia looked pointedly at Walden. Again. Excitedly. Just the way she had earlier. Maybe even more so. "A really hot-and-heavy boyfriend. You know, the kind of guy who can practically knock up a girl just by giving her a sexy look? A man's man. A macho man. A studly stud."

Walden and Gareth gazed at her in perplexity. "You can't tell any of that by just looking at a guy," Gareth protested.

Walden was too busy fighting an urge to bump and grind his way into Talia's heart to join his friend in manly concord.

Talia gave them a pitying look. "That's where you're wrong! You can tell a lot about a guy just by looking at him—*if* you're packing enough imagination, that is." She tossed another heady, overtly suggestive glance at Walden. "Anyway, since *I'm* the best Heather impersonator of the three of us—"

"You've already proven that you're the *only* plausible Heather impersonator of the three of us," Gareth cut in, eyeing the leopard-print coat, huge sunglasses, and sexy blond wig still visible in Talia's employee locker. "You've been doing a great job with that, too, by the way. Kudos."

"Yeah. I thought Kristen almost caught on when she saw me earlier today," Talia confessed in an aside. "But she was too engrossed in that troubleshooter guy showing up." She glanced approvingly at Gareth, then added, "Way to think on your feet with that 'matchmaking' plan of yours. Now if Kristen notices anything suspicious about what we're up to, she'll just chalk it up to our supposedly secret 'matchmaking' activities."

"Exactly my plan," Gareth agreed, tapping his temple.

"You *do* make an excellent 'Heather' decoy," Walden added, coming in late with his compliment but wanting in on the action all the same. "Even if I do prefer your real purple hair."

Talia smiled at his compliment. His heart almost stopped.

Then, "Speaking of which . . . back to our scheme! I say *I* should get to decide who's going to portray my superhot boy toy. Right? Right." Wearing a mischievous look, Talia put her fingertips to her chin. She glanced at Gareth. Then at the break room. Finally her gaze fell on Walden . . . then roamed all over his body. "*Hmm* . . ."

Her contemplative, potentially naughty tone should have scared the bejeezus out of him. But it didn't. Walden was an adventurer at heart. He wanted to do his adventuring with Talia.

"Pinky," she said, "are you pondering what I'm pondering?"

There was no *way* he was missing his cue. "I think so, Brain," Walden said in his best cartoon-mouse voice, "but . . ."

"*You* are going to be 'Heather's' new baby daddy. It's set!" Smugly, Talia crossed her arms. "Unless you don't feel *potent* enough, of course." She raised her eyebrow at him. "How about it, stud? Do you feel like impersonating a pop star with me?"

Walden still wasn't sure if the popcorn-and-cranberry thing was a date or a ruse to force him into indentured Christmas-decorating servitude. He wasn't sure if Talia saw *him* or a piece of biscuit-baking beefcake when she eyeballed him. And he wasn't sure if Talia was ultra-determined to help

Kristen because of their longtime friendship or if she just wanted an excuse to wear a leopard-print coat and make out with someone in public.

Just then, he didn't care. He was willing to risk it.

"You don't know me that well yet, or you'd already know that I never miss a chance to feel potent," Walden told Talia with a grin. He rubbed his hands together. "That means you're about to get all the hot and heavy action you can handle."

Talia looked intrigued. "That sounds like a promise."

"That's because it is. Bring on the baby-making!"

At that, Talia balked. "Wait. You know I'm not interested in making this a real thing between us, right?" She touched her grape-Pixy-Stix-colored hair. "I mean, I'm not exactly prime motherhood material. I think that's obvious to everyone."

Walden didn't think anything about Talia was obvious. Except that he really, really liked her. "It's Christmas," he said coolly. "Let's just take things as they come."

"Booya! That's good enough for me!" Gareth crowed. He put on his army jacket and knit trapper cap, then brandished the pregnancy-test kit. "I'm off to plant this in the most devious, incriminating, tabloid-baiting way possible." At the door, he paused. "Then I'm going to take my nieces to see Santa Claus at the mall. Later, all!"

Left alone with Talia, Walden smiled. He'd just struck holiday gold, and he hadn't even been trying. How much more amazing could things get if he put in a little effort?

The only way to find out was to do it. He gave Talia a cocky look, held out his hand, then nodded. "Ready?"

Talia inhaled. She looked at his hand. She took it.

"Before we do this public Heather make-out thing," she astonished Walden by saying, "we'd better practice."

He blinked. "Practice making out?"

She gave a demure nod. "We want to be believable, right?"

"Absolutely," he agreed. "Let's do this. For Kristen."

They were actually going to do this. For Kristen.

And him.

It was possible, Walden thought dazedly, that he should have wished for even bigger things for Christmas this year. Because as long as a few of his dreams were coming true . . .

But then Talia tugged him closer and got straight down to business by kissing him, hard and fast and then sweet and slow and then everything in between, and Walden realized the truth.

Nothing was bigger than this. Nothing was better than being with Talia. For however long it lasted . . .

Chapter 9

The Christmas House B&B, Kismet, Michigan
T-minus 20.25 days until Christmas

Casey didn't plan to spend his first full afternoon in Kismet making gingerbread houses at The Christmas House B&B. But, since that's what he spied Shane Maresca doing as he came in from the indoor-outdoor tour of the property that Vanessa Sullivan had given him and Kristen after he'd checked in . . .

Well, that was it. Gingerbread houses crowded their way onto his schedule and didn't let go. End of story.

Standing in the B&B's cozy, wood-smoke-and-pine-scented common room, surrounded by *two* Christmas trees piled high with wrapped gifts and an array of garland, wreaths, and candles, Casey turned to Kristen. He'd been planning to share the property tour with her, feed her dinner, and then drive her back to downtown Kismet so she could get on with her day. After all, she didn't owe him an afternoon's entertainment. And he usually worked best on his own, when he could be quick on his feet.

But something about Kristen's expression, as she gazed in wonderment at the B&B's holiday decorations, made Casey reconsider. She looked so . . . *enthralled*. So *hopeful*. And since her reaction was obviously a response to the Christmas overkill surrounding them, he couldn't quite bring himself to end it.

"Hey." Casey nudged her. He nodded through the entryway to the B&B's adjoining room, where tables had been arranged with slabs of prebaked gingerbread "walls" and "roofs" in a sort of gingerbread-village assembly line. Bowls of various toppings and icings and decorations were arrayed along the centers of the tables, along with individual foil-lined trays designed to hold the guests' unique creations. "I'm game if you are."

Kristen looked surprised. "To make a gingerbread house?"

"Why not?" He couldn't see Shane Maresca inside that room—not at that precise moment—but he'd been there a second ago. He couldn't have gotten away already. "Maybe it'll be fun."

Now she looked skeptical. "And *you're* all about the fun."

"Hey." Casey pulled a chastising face. "Even we 'Terminators' like a few red and green sprinkles sometimes."

Even if they didn't necessary like being called "Terminators." That was one he'd never heard applied to himself before. Probably, Heather had made it up on the spot. But that didn't mean the nickname didn't pack a sting. A *tiny* sting.

Casey knew he was much too invulnerable to be truly hurt.

All the same, Kristen's gaze softened. "Come on. I'm sorry I said that. I didn't know you were sensitive about it."

Casey forced a chuckle. "Sensitive? Me? People can call me whatever they want—as long as they also say I get the job done."

"Right." She didn't appear persuaded—but she *did* appear interested in that impromptu gingerbread-house construction project. She bit her lip. "There are little kids in there too, you know. And Christmas carols. And probably Digby the dachs-hund. You *really* want to make a gingerbread house?"

"It's a *construction project*." The idea appealed to him on a macho level. "It's *architecture*. Besides, I figure there's probably some kind of B&B record to be broken here."

"A gingerbread-house-building record?"

Casey nodded. With relish, he rubbed his hands together. Kristen laughed. "Okay, hotshot. Let's do it. But I've worked with icing and cookie dough before. You haven't. So don't come crying to me when your Casey Jackson Mega Tower crumbles."

He widened his eyes. "Who said I was making a mega tower?"

She only gave him a knowing look. "Aren't you?"

Actually, Casey *had* been wondering exactly how high he could stack the layers of gingerbread to make something really impressive. But just at that moment, he spotted Shane Maresca mingling with the guests and children in the next room, and there wasn't time to strategize anymore. He just had to *do*.

"Look, you're making it really hard to do something nice and Christmassy for you, you know that?" he asked Kristen.

"Is *that* what this is? Nice Christmassyness?"

"I told you I could do it. This is how it starts."

With an impish grin, she put her hands on her hips. "If you have to tell me the fun's already started," Kristen said, "then I've got news for you: It hasn't actually started."

Her dancing eyes and audacious expression drew him in in a way that cookie dough never could have. Transfixed by her knack for making him feel . . . *energized,* Casey arched his eyebrow.

"Why don't you come over here and say that?" he asked.

She accepted his challenge by taking one step closer. Her upturned face swam in his vision, pert and daring. "Say what?"

"Say you're not having fun yet."

"I'm not having fun yet."

"Closer," Casey urged. "You're still too far away."

Kristen obliged. Now her toes almost touched his. Her cheeks turned pink and her smile broadened and her plaid flannel shirt, so prosaic and lumberjack-like, chose exactly that moment to gape in the front, revealing another glimpse of her red lacy bra. Kristen really ought to work on that, he thought. Her clothes seemed to want her to be undressed; they were staging a mutiny to accomplish it. Her red lacy bra was the ringleader.

Shifting his gaze away from that alluring sight, Casey felt his heartbeat kick up a notch. Incongruously, given that there were hordes of children and B&B guests *and* his arch nemesis just a few feet away, he had the sense that he and Kristen were the only two people in the world. The Christmas music fell away. So did the multicolored lights, the smell of cinnamon potpourri, and the lingering knowledge that he really ought to be working.

Just then, Casey didn't care about working.

If that made him a bad Terminator . . . so be it.

Kristen tilted her face toward his. "How's this? Close enough for you yet?" Her voice hitched. "I told you, I'm not scared of you. And I'm pretty sure I'm not having fun yet."

"You," Casey replied assuredly, "are a terrible liar."

She swallowed tellingly. "Who says I'm lying?"

"Me." Suddenly, it seemed crucial that he breathe in the sweet, vaguely pumpkin-pie-spiced scent of her hair. It seemed critical that he examine the creamy pale skin at the vee of her shirt . . . that he lower his hand to touch her hand. When he did, Kristen jumped. He smiled. "If you weren't having fun yet, you wouldn't be all sparkly-eyed and breathless. You wouldn't be leaning toward me. You wouldn't be here at all."

He expected her—in order—to close her eyes, hold her breath, lever herself backward, and leave, just to be contrary.

Instead, to Casey's indescribable relief (which he refused to contemplate any further), Kristen only smiled at him.

"Takes one to know one. You're doing the same thing."

He was? Taken aback, Casey glanced down at himself. He'd thought *he* was the one controlling this encounter. It wasn't like him to lose the upper hand in a situation like this one and not even grasp it. The realization was startling.

More startling still, he couldn't bring himself to care.

Not when Kristen stood only inches away from him, giving him that Christmas-crazed come-hither look of hers. Not when she stroked her fingers over his hand, making all his nerve endings go on red alert. Not when she puckered up, leaned in closer . . .

. . . then gave him a big, fat, jokingly passionate "Mm-mmwhaa!" of a kiss. A *parody kiss*. To *him!* No woman had *ever*—

"Quit stalling." Kristen gestured toward the other room. "I'm ready to kick your ass in gingerbread-house building."

Still gob-smacked, Casey stared at her. "Oh yeah?"

"Before I'm done, you're going to beg for mercy."

Casey sort of already wanted to. *Please just give me a real kiss,* he wanted to plead. *You know we'll both enjoy it.*

He still couldn't believe she'd been so close, had appeared so captivated, so *into him* . . . and then she'd broken the spell. Effortlessly. *Hell.* Why didn't Kristen Miller want him?

Stymied by the question, Casey looked at her. She seemed like a regular woman—a woman without a genius intellect, a world-famous derrière, or a golden singing voice. She seemed *ordinary*. Average. Yet he felt endlessly intrigued by her.

"I'm *never* going to beg for mercy," he told Kristen, mustering as much bravado as he could. Most likely, Casey knew, he wasn't performing at his peak after a cross-country plane ride, a blizzard, a potential babysitting quest, *and* a Christmas-themed B&B tour, all back to back. "You might have forgotten who you're dealing with here," he boasted, "but *I'm*—"

Too late, Casey realized she wasn't even listening. Instead, she was gazing raptly at the gingerbread and goodies.

What the hell was the appeal of Christmas? He didn't get it. He never had. Decorations and baked goods shouldn't have mesmerized a woman more than *he* could mesmerize a woman. So why—

Suddenly, Casey spied Shane Maresca in the crowd. He followed the path of Kristen's gaze straight toward that bastard and realized the truth: Kristen was interested in Maresca!

That's why she'd tuned out his "no mercy" blustering.

That's why she'd ended their toe-to-toe almost-kiss, too.

Casey couldn't let this happen. It was an affront to his manhood—to his very *essence*. *He* was the man who made things happen, who fixed the unfixable, who left everyone satisfied.

Shane Maresca wasn't. But at that moment, he *was* the man who raised his big, stupid, conventionally "handsome" head, spotted Kristen gawking at him, and broke out in a daffy grin.

"Hey, Kristen!" Maresca waved. "How are you, beautiful?"

Ugh. Casey rolled his eyes. There was no way a smart and independent and interesting woman like Kristen was falling for Maresca's smarmy "hey, beautiful!" shtick. She was too good for the likes of him. She was too kind. Too assertive. Too clever.

Casey turned to Kristen to congratulate her on that.

Unfortunately, she was already almost pushing him out of the way to get to Shane Maresca. "Hey, handsome!" she called.

Amid the gingerbread and giggling children and upbeat Christmas music, the two of them met. They embraced. While Casey watched in disbelief, Kristen laughed at something Shane said. He couldn't fathom how they'd developed such instant rapport. That was *Casey's* specialty. Kristen was *Casey's* guest here.

On the verge of charging over there to remind them both of that irrefutable fact, Casey realized he was clenching his fists. Ouch. He raised his hands. He gawked at them. He forced them open, wondered why he'd gotten so worked up about a woman—especially a woman he'd only met because it was part of his job.

He inhaled. He had to lighten up. He had to screw his head on straight before he endangered this damn Heather Miller job. It was important. It was high profile. If he screwed up—

Well, he couldn't screw up. That was that.

When Casey looked toward Shane and Kristen again, he saw that Maresca was pointing at something dangling over his head. In response, Kristen sent her gaze upward. So did Casey.

He spotted the freaking bunch of mistletoe hung from the freaking doorjamb a millisecond before Kristen did.

Oh no. Not this. Not this obvious, insulting, dumbass maneuver. Kristen wouldn't fall for it. But she did. To Casey's disbelief, she smiled cheerfully at Shane. She put her hands on his big, stupid, conventionally "broad" shoulders. Saying something intimate and hilarious (by the looks of it, at least), she raised herself on tiptoe. Not even noticing that Shane had brought his arms to her waist to steady her, she got ready to plant a big, stupid, Christmas mistletoe kiss on him.

This was wrong. It was all wrong. It was so, so wrong.

Noooo, Casey wanted to scream. *Stooop!* he wanted to yell while running in agonized slo-mo toward them both.

Instead, in the instant before their lips met, Casey found himself frozen in place. At the same time, Shane turned his gaze toward Casey. He saw him looking. He gave him a galling wink.

He knew exactly what he was doing, Casey realized. He was doing it to annoy Casey. And it was damn well working.

Kristen's lips met Maresca's cheek. Shane closed his eyes in apparent ecstasy. Casey could have sworn he heard moaning.

That was it. Somehow, he had to put a stop to this.

Hurtling himself purposefully into the next room, Casey wrenched off his suit coat. He yanked loose his tie. He rolled up his shirtsleeves. He eyeballed the most promising pile of cookie slabs he could find, then beelined straight for it.

He was going to create the biggest, best, most badass gingerbread skyscraper anyone had ever seen, Casey vowed. He was going to beat Shane Maresca at everything they did—including the Heather Miller job—or he was going to die trying. Kristen would be there to see it, thanks to his diner-booth-rental deal, and she had to see him at his best. Because all at once, Casey felt unreasonably certain that if Kristen didn't kiss him sometime soon . . . he wasn't going to survive Christmas at all this year.

Two hours later, Kristen completed construction on her foot-high gingerbread bungalow. It sported Craftsman-style front porch beams made of stacked cookies, a pitched peppermint-patty roof accented with buttercream "snow," melted hard-candy "glass" windows . . . and a next-door neighbor who excelled at glowering.

Right now, the target of Casey's disdain was sloping dangerously to the right, threatening to crumple under the weight of too much royal icing and too many gingerbread stories.

"I warned you that was too much icing," she said, putting aside her piping bag to examine his gingerbread high-rise. "All that excess icing is making your structure lose its integrity. More isn't always better, you know. Sometimes, less is more."

"'Less is more'?" Casey scoffed, looking endearingly determined. He seemed ready to go for the Olympic gold at gingerbread-house building. Or maybe die trying. "Have you been sniffing glue? That doesn't even make sense."

"Yes, it does," Kristen insisted. "Your building proves it. Less would definitely have been more with that . . . thing you made."

In the midst of prayerfully holding up an interior load-bearing wall, Casey stilled. He transferred his gaze from his gingerbread creation—if it had been on fire, *towering inferno* would have been the most apt term for it—to her face.

"I can make it work," he said. "I always do."

"But you don't have to 'make it work'!" Surprised at his unyielding demeanor, Kristen softened her tone. She nudged his shoulder. "Hey. It's supposed to be fun, remember? It's Christmas! It's jolly! The fate of the world isn't riding on the success or failure of your gingerbread house."

His renewed glower told her Casey wasn't convinced. She wondered if every aspect of Christmas made him feel this way—as though, if it didn't succeed, *he* was somehow to blame for it.

If it did, no wonder he didn't like Christmas.

"It won't be a failure." He tightened his jaw as though hoping to strengthen his tottering gingerbread house through force of will alone. "I refuse to let it be a failure."

"I see. And how's that working out for you?"

He transferred his tight-jawed look to her. "It's great."

Yikes. She blanched, belatedly realizing that he really meant it. Something about this project was genuinely getting to him. "Okay! Sorry! I keep forgetting you've never done this before." After all, Casey had volunteered to build gingerbread houses for *her* sake. She couldn't very well give him a hard time about it now, when he'd only been being nice. "Let me help you."

"I don't need any help."

She pointed at his building's roof. "I beg to differ. *Casa*

Jackson is sliding into the ocean." She indicated the "sea" of crushed wild-blue-raspberry candies he'd used as a base. "See?"

"I don't need help," Casey insisted. "I'm the one who does the helping, not the one being helped. I'm the troubleshooter, not the trouble." Stubbornly, he propped up his gingerbread house's sloping exterior wall with his forearm. "Check it out. That makes *three stories* of gingerbread. This building *rocks*."

"Yep." Kristen gave him a commiserating look. "All you have to do now is stay here, frozen in that position, all night long, until the four inches of icing you used dries out."

He nodded. "No problem. I'm a human pretzel. I have infinite patience, too." Not demonstrating it at that moment, he peered at his structure. "Whoa!" Catching another imminent icing avalanche, Casey stuck out his elbow, too. Now he was truly contorted. But he looked at her with perfect nonchalance. "There. See what I mean? I have a knack. It's easy-peasy."

She stifled a grin. "You're a quick study at this."

"That's right. I can go all night, baby."

She laughed outright. "I'd like to see you try."

"Stay here," Casey said, "and you will."

Tempted by that, Kristen hesitated. She'd only planned to accompany Casey to the B&B's famous Christmas buffet, then return to town to deal with her own problems. Surely she'd already "distracted" Casey as much as she'd promised Heather she would for one day. Besides, he hadn't even been interested in visiting Heather on set. Not yet, at least. So Kristen had been officially off the hook, dealing-with-The-Terminator-wise.

But then Casey had touched her hand near The Christmas House's twin decorated Noble fir trees, and he'd invited her to make gingerbread houses with him, and he'd appeared so charming and eager and *hopeful* that Kristen hadn't been able to resist.

She almost hadn't been able to resist kissing him, either. Fortunately, Shane Maresca had come along at exactly the right moment to give her a convenient excuse to bail. Otherwise, Kristen knew, she would have been locking lips with Casey like there was no tomorrow, in full view of everyone at the B&B.

She might be open-minded about sex (and she was). She might be willing to go for the gusto when it came to the sensual give-and-take involved (naturally enough). But she *wasn't* usually this easy when it came to men (seriously). Despite Talia and Gareth's cynical take on her love life, Kristen was not typically overinvested in go-nowhere relationships.

At least she didn't think she was . . .

Was she?

Nah, she assured herself as she watched Casey perform a few semiacrobatic maneuvers to one-handedly add candy-cane trim to his spicy gingerbread skyscraper. She simply hadn't met anyone who made her *want* to take things more seriously yet. She couldn't help that. She couldn't help liking the adventure and excitement and breeziness of a fast-and-casual relationship.

Most of all, Kristen realized, she couldn't help liking Casey. *In spite* of the fact that any relationship between them would be (necessarily) casual. Not *because* of that.

It didn't seem to matter that they'd only just met. Kristen *liked* him. She liked the way he looked, the way he sounded . . . even the way he smelled, like soapy studliness and fresh air rolled into one. It was a heady mix, especially when combined with his promise to make sure she had a nice Christmas this year.

That was already impossible, of course, but still . . .

"So . . ." Cheering up, Casey gazed at her. "Having fun?"

"Well, you *did* arrange some cookie decorating for me," Kristen mused, "which was one of the things on my list of official Christmas favorites. So . . . yes." A nod. "I am having fun."

He beamed. Then he leaned sideways as far as he could without endangering the structural integrity of his sky-scraper.

"Hear that, Maresca?" he asked. "She's having *fun*."

On Kristen's other side, Shane Maresca leaned past her.

"Yeah, I heard. I'm really glad." He offered Casey's wobbly structure a pitying look. "Too bad about your ginger-bread hut, though, dude. I think it's going to have to be con-demned."

For a nanosecond, a wounded expression flashed across Casey's face. Without thinking, Kristen reached out to him.

"I think it's charming!" she insisted.

But she was too late. The two men were already off.

"Ha," Casey shot back. "Your *face* should be con-demned."

"Really?" Shane offered in a blasé tone. "If you think you're man enough to do it, have at it, punk."

"Good idea." Casey scowled threateningly, still holding up his gingerbread walls. "I'll use your face as a wrecking ball."

Shane sneered. "You'd have to let go of your 'creation' to do that. It won't stay up without your stupid elbows."

"You'd know about stupid, with your big, stupid face."

At that, Kristen shook her head. She ought to break up this potential showdown, she knew, but their over-the-top machismo was actually kind of entertaining. She had enough guy friends to know that sometimes men related to one an-other strangely.

On the other hand, although most people had decamped to other Christmas activities by now, there were still a few children present at the gingerbread house table. They prob-ably didn't need to hear two grown men taking potshots at each other.

"At least *I* know how to get my 'big, stupid face' under the mistletoe at the right moment," Shane was boasting when she tuned back in. "Unlike *you*, Jackson, I know how to take advantage of an opportunity."

Galvanized by his words, Kristen momentarily lost the ability to play referee. Shane *had* to be talking about the harmless Christmas kiss they'd shared under the mistletoe—and he was using it to goad Casey. Judging by the thunderclouds darkening Casey's expression, Shane's jab had hit its mark, too.

That was . . . surprising, she thought. By anyone's standards, it had been a pretty harmless kiss. It had been on the cheek. It hadn't involved tongue (which—on the cheek—would have been both gross *and* weird). And it had been a simple by-product of Christmas cheer. That made it officially harmless.

Apparently, Casey and Shane didn't see it that way.

"Hey." Kristen rose. "I'm *right here,*" she told Shane. "And I'm not some kind of prize to be won with Christmas kissing."

Shane relented. He spread his hands. "Kristen, I didn't mean it like that. I'm sorry. Of course you're not a prize."

He cast a chastising scowl in Casey's direction. "Even if *some people* want to behave as though you are. *I* won't do it."

Kristen sighed. "You just did! You did it again."

Casey scowled anew. "Do you want me to smack him for you?"

At his pugnacious, bloodthirsty expression, Kristen almost laughed. Whatever had happened between these two, it must have been a doozy. Because while she fancied herself a newly minted archrival, Shane and Casey really *were* sworn enemies.

Which was strange, given how curiously alike they were . . .

"No, thank you, Casey," she said politely.

"It's no trouble," he insisted. "I'd be happy to do it."

"I said I can handle it," Kristen told him, not bothering

to elaborate. If Casey had really done as much reconnaissance on her as he seemed to have done, he already knew she was self-sufficient and capable. She didn't need a man to fight for her.

"I can smack him myself," she added. Then she did.

Her playful wallop to Shane's shoulder was more gratifying than it ought to have been. Especially since Shane played along by yelping and exaggeratedly grabbing his shoulder. "Hey!"

"There," Kristen said with a self-satisfied grin, dusting off her hands. "Now we're square."

"*I* would have done that," Casey grumbled.

"*She* did it better than you would have," Shane goaded.

But this time, Casey didn't take the bait. Instead, his gaze swerved from Shane to a spot someplace over his shoulder. He squinted, his attention momentarily diverted to . . . something.

Probably to something imaginary. Something that would get Shane to look, too. Kristen used to play this game with Heather when they were kids. They called it the "made you look!" game.

"*And* my gingerbread house is bigger than yours," Shane added. He nudged Kristen. "Did you see my chocolate terrace?"

"Do you ask all the ladies that question, or just me?"

Shane laughed. "Just you. You're special."

Briefly, he shifted his gaze to Casey, who was still looking outside. In the yard, a light snow had begun to fall. Some of the B&B guests were assembling for an activity.

But Casey missed his chance to catch Shane looking, so Shane handily returned his attention to her. "Hey, don't leave me hanging here, gorgeous. Go on. Take a look."

Obligingly, Kristen leaned toward his gingerbread house. It was about the same size as Casey's, but . . . "Wow. You've got yourself a regular gingerbread pied-à-terre there."

"It's a model of my summer apartment building in the

16th arrondissement," Shane told her proudly. "Near the Trocadéro."

"In *Paris?*" Impressed, Kristen looked more closely. Now that she knew its origins, she could spy the candy architectural details that gave Shane's creation a Parisian feel. "I've always wanted to visit Paris. Do you go there every summer?"

"I try," Shane said. "I have a lot of friends in the area."

Kristen smiled at him. "Lucky you."

"Honestly? I feel luckier to be here right now, with you." Shane fleetingly touched her hand, then moved his fingers away. "Who needs a bunch of French diplomats and designers to pal around with? Give me a nice, down-home Christmas and I'm happy."

"Me too." Kristen nodded, reminded all over again that Shane had a talent for conversation that was very much like Casey's. For whatever reason, though, Shane's banter didn't affect her the same way Casey's did. Neither did his touch. Which was probably for the best. Her life was already complicated enough. "At this point, I'm kind of pinning my hopes on next year's Christmas, though," she confessed.

"Really?" Shane looked concerned. "Why?"

"Well . . ." Hesitant to confide in yet another newcomer about her Heather-related holiday travails, Kristen shrugged. "It's complicated. Forget I said anything."

"Is it because of that lunkhead over there? Is he spoiling your Christmas already?" Shane joked, nodding toward Casey. "He's a verifiable Grinch. Has been since he was just a kid."

That perked up Kristen. "You knew Casey when he was a kid?"

That would give the two of them more history together than she'd originally thought. Lots of things could have happened between them to cause the rift they were experiencing.

"Since I was twelve," Casey broke in curtly from the other side of her. He aimed a censorious look at Shane—a look that held a confusing amount of what looked like . . . *fondness?* It vanished before she could be sure. "We were in the same foster home for a while, raising hell and stirring up trouble."

"Really? That makes you an odd choice to become a troubleshooter," Kristen said, picturing the two of them as rowdy preteens. It was an entertaining—and surprisingly heart-tugging—image. She turned to the man on her right. "But I don't even know what you do for a living yet, Shane. What—"

"Another time." With a fleeting smile, Shane stood, too. He squeezed her hand, then leaned in to brush his lips against her temple. It was a very European gesture. "I just saw someone I know. I want to go say hello before they get away."

"Oh, sure," Kristen began. "Go ahead. I—"

But Shane had already grabbed his coat, leaving her standing there with her arm in the air in a casual wave.

Puzzled, Kristen watched as Shane hightailed it across the room—but not before tossing a triumphant look at his gingerbread pied-à-terre. Obviously, he'd thought he'd won.

She looked at Casey. He was watching Shane, too.

"Go ahead," she told Casey after Shane had left, giving his shoulder a poke. "You know you want to follow him."

"Follow him? What for?"

"Because otherwise he'll get the jump on you. You won't know what he's up to. You switched hotels to keep up with him!"

Casey smiled. "I told you, I don't work that way."

"I mean it," Kristen urged. It was ridiculous, but she wanted Casey to win . . . in whatever preposterous, macho contest the two of them were having. "I'll even babysit your gingerbread skyscraper for you until the icing-glue dries."

"Not necessary. I dismantled it."

"It wasn't *that* bad!"

"It was pretty good for a first attempt. I never would have even tried it without you." Seeming surprisingly . . . *surprised* (and a little pleased) by that, Casey caught her hand again. He pulled her down to sit next to him. "What I mean is, while you were talking to Maresca, I took apart my gingerbread house and gave away my supplies. I never would have had the patience to wait for all that icing to dry anyway."

"I thought you said you had patience to spare."

"I also have the ability to prioritize." Casey eyed her. "Maybe I'm saving my patience for the things that deserve it."

Like waiting for a real kiss, Kristen imagined he was thinking, based on the suggestive glimmer in his eyes . . . and the memory of his shocked—but instantly determined— expression when she'd delivered him that silly "Mmmmwhaa!" of a kiss earlier.

"You could still win," she felt compelled to say. "Shane's gingerbread house isn't *that* cool. Now's your chance! If you add another layer to yours while Shane is outside, you'll beat him."

"I told you, it's gone. I dismantled it," Casey said. "And Shane's free to go wherever he wants. I'm not his keeper."

"But you were looking out the window so intently before," Kristen insisted, noticing at that moment that Shane had gone to the yard where the B&B guests were assembling. Undoubtedly, Casey saw where he'd gone as well. Maybe Casey *hadn't* been playing the "made you look" game. Maybe he'd actually spied something intriguing outside. Because Shane sure had—he hadn't wasted a nanosecond getting to it. "You wanted to go, too. *You* were interested in whatever Shane is interested in, so—"

She fell silent, belatedly noticing that the silver foil-lined tray in front of Casey held nothing but gingerbread crumbs and icing smears, plus a thick layer of crushed wild-blue-raspberry candies. Oookay. He'd dismantled it. And then what?

Confused, Kristen looked around. Her gaze eventually lit on a nearby pigtailed girl, about six years old, sitting across the table from them a few chairs down. She was gleefully mashing together some very familiar-looking, overfrosted chunks of gingerbread to assemble her own gingerbread house.

Seeing where Kristen's gaze was directed, Casey shrugged.

"She didn't want the crushed-candy 'sea,'" he said. "She said it looked like Barney the Dinosaur pooped on my tray."

Kristen guffawed. Once again, she found herself not understanding Grinchy Casey Jackson in the least . . . but very much wanting to.

It had seemed to mean a lot to him that he construct his gingerbread skyscraper correctly (and impressively enough to beat Shane), yet he'd surrendered it to a little girl without a qualm. It had seemed vital to him that he go outside to join the other B&B guests in their new activity, yet he'd stayed there beside Kristen while Shane ostensibly gave him the slip.

"But she was all over my gingerbread and icing," Casey went on, nudging his chin toward the dwindling supplies left on the table. "At this point, pretty much everything else is gone."

"Except *Shane's* gingerbread house," Kristen pointed out with a meaningful glance at his archrival's abandoned creation. "You could have given her *Shane's* house and won for sure."

Casey seemed as though that idea honestly hadn't occurred to him. Maybe Kristen was the only devious one here.

"That wouldn't be winning. It would be cheating."

"But . . ." Kristen gestured at the engraved gold trophy standing in a place of honor on the mantel nearby. Casey had been right—there really *was* a record for gingerbread-house building at the B&B. A photograph of the previously winning house stood near the prize. "All's fair in love and war, right?"

"If you're doing it correctly, you don't have to cheat."

She shook her head. "You are *not* a very good Terminator."

His eyes flickered. "Not today, I guess."

Then maybe he was on other days? Kristen wasn't sure.

"I'm finding it hard to picture you as a rebellious preteen troublemaker right now." She scrutinized him again. Still no dice. "Are you *sure* you and Shane were hell-raisers together?"

Casey gave her a shuttered look—a belligerent, semi-dangerous-looking look. Suddenly, Kristen had second thoughts.

"Do you really want to talk about this?" Intently, he listened. Then, "They're playing your favorite Christmas carol."

At his obvious attempt at misdirection, Kristen shook her head. "That's not my—" She listened. "Oh, wait. It is!"

His smile made her want to smile back. All night long.

"You couldn't *possibly* know my favorite Christmas song!"

"You're right," Casey said nonchalantly. "I couldn't."

Yet he did. Shaking her head again, Kristen examined him.

"You're a confusing man to read, you know that?" she asked.

"Yes, I do. That's exactly the way I like it."

"Ooh, *mysterious!*" Kristen laughed, miming a scarier version of jazz hands at him. Casey laughed, too. For a moment, a cozy sense of harmony enveloped them, right there amid the sugar overload and the gingerbread crumbs and the sounds of Bing Crosby's "Christmas Is A-Comin'" playing on the sound system.

"You know," she mused further, losing herself in his smoky eyes, "maybe this Christmas isn't going to be so bad after all."

"Maybe not," Casey agreed, his voice low and intimate and seemingly just for her. "It all depends on how you define it."

She couldn't help smiling. She felt pretty sure she leaned toward him again, too. She just wanted to be . . . *closer* to him.

"I already defined it!" Kristen reminded him. "Back in your 'blizzard'-crushing killer Subaru mobile. Remember?"

"Hmm. Remind me, then . . ." Hastily, Casey whipped his gaze toward the other room, then back to her face again. His calm, intimate tone didn't even waver. "Did your definition of the perfect Christmas include a holiday-lights house tour?"

Kristen couldn't believe this. "The famous Kismet holiday light show in the Glenrosen neighborhood? I *love* that tour!"

"Good. Because I'm pretty sure Vanessa Sullivan is on her way over here to shanghai us into participating."

Kristen craned her neck to see. It was true. The B&B's acting manager was headed their way with her cousin, Reid, and his adorable new family in tow. There were six of them all together: the two Sullivans, plus Reid's new wife, Karina, and her three children—Olivia, Josh, and Michael. Reid had relocated to California after having met Karina at The Christmas House, Kristen had heard, but they always came home for the holidays every year. Robert and Betty Sullivan wouldn't have had it any other way. By the looks of them, neither would the children.

Vanessa saw Kristen and Casey. A familiar matchmaking gleam came into her eyes. "Hey, you two! You're looking pretty cozy!"

Guiltily, Kristen jumped apart from Casey. She didn't know why, but she suddenly wasn't wild about letting people know she was attracted to him. Which was silly, honestly.

What difference did it make if people knew she liked him?

Heather would assume Kristen was doing a whiz-bang job of "distracting" Casey. So she would be happy. Talia and the gang at the diner would assume Kristen was having a no-holds-barred, sexapaloosa romp with Casey. So they would be happy—or at least they would be spared the matchmaking they'd seemed intent on doing (especially in Gareth's case). And everyone else in town . . .

Well, everyone else in town would continue to glimpse Kristen on the street or in the store or at The Big Foot bar, assume she was Heather (because everyone had "fabulous!" Heather on the brain, now that she was back in town, and the two sisters *did* look a little bit alike, according to most people), and get all excited to be meeting someone special . . . only to realize (with obvious and demoralizing disappointment) that Kristen was only *herself.* Only regular-gal Kristen Miller and not ultrafamous pop star Heather Miller, loved and adored by everyone.

Kristen frowned. She looked up at Vanessa and her family, still good-naturedly bearing down on them. She would have liked to have gone on the Glenrosen holiday-lights house tour. But if doing that meant letting everyone know she was into Casey . . .

She just couldn't do it. She didn't know why.

"I just remembered—I've got to run!" Kristen leaped to her feet. Hastily, she wound her knit scarf around her neck. She pulled on her gloves, then whipped on the quilted coat she'd slung over the back of her chair. Properly outfitted for the mounting snowfall outside, she smiled at The Christmas House's managerial entourage. "Nice to see you all. Later!"

Looking confused, Casey got to his feet, too. "Wait. I'll drive you." He grabbed his suit coat, then looked around for his warmer winter overcoat and gloves. "Just let me grab these—"

"No need! I'll call a cab. You enjoy the house tour!"

Casey gave Vanessa, Reid, Karina, and the others an apologetic smile. Then he turned to Kristen again. "We didn't even have dinner yet. You were looking forward to the buffet."

"I can have eggnog and fruitcake another time. Bye!"

And just like that, Kristen made her escape . . . trying not to notice that in addition to looking perplexed, Casey also looked a little bit sorry to see her go. But that couldn't be, she reminded herself. Because Casey was in Kismet to do a job, and to him, Kristen was only a means to an end—a means to finding out more about Heather and learning what was going wrong with her holiday TV special, so he could "troubleshoot" it. Period.

The last thing Kristen needed to do was forget that.

Chapter 10

Kismet, Michigan
T-minus 20.25 days until Christmas

It took him a while, but Casey finally managed to extricate himself from the Glenrosen holiday-lights house tour.

Vanessa Sullivan was understandably baffled by Casey's refusal to attend along with the other B&B guests. That was because Casey had privately arranged for Vanessa to "impulsively" show up during the gingerbread-house-building session and "spontaneously" invite him and Kristen to go along.

"But why don't you just ask Kristen yourself?" Vanessa had originally asked him when he'd approached her. "I mean, look at you." A flirtatious up-and-down wave. "I think she'd say yes."

"Maybe." Just then, hard on the heels of the Shane Maresca mistletoe-kiss incident, Casey hadn't been so sure. "But I'm looking for a little boost. A little insurance, so to speak."

"I can't imagine why you'd need it."

"Then you've never fallen for someone who's out of your league." Whereas *Casey* maybe (just possibly) just had.

Vanessa had blinked. "You're kidding, right?"

"About what?"

"You honestly think Kristen Miller is out of your league?"

Casey had considered what he knew about Kristen so far . . . versus what he knew about himself. *Yeah.* "Will you do it?"

Looking astounded—and delighted—Vanessa had agreed.

But all his maneuverings had been for nothing. Because at Vanessa's approach, Kristen had bolted from The Christmas House as though her delectable ass was on fire, leaving Casey looking exactly like the love-struck sucker he feared he might be becoming when it came to Kristen Miller.

He didn't know how it had happened, but he liked her. He *really* liked her. And not just because she could fill in the missing pieces about Heather's holiday TV special, either. He liked her attitude and her smile and her slightly husky voice. He liked her kick-ass boots and her miniskirt and her lacy red bra. He liked her straightforward way of relating to people.

Except, of course, when she was bailing out on those people under blatantly false pretenses, like she had today.

I just remembered—I've got to run!

Right. Narrowing his eyes, Casey watched as Vanessa finally left him behind and instead herded her guests toward the B&B's designated vans for the holiday-lights house tour. He still didn't understand why Kristen had ducked out on it. He didn't believe there was anything in the world she wanted to do more than soak up some hackneyed, gooshy Christmas atmosphere.

Except maybe mack on Shane Maresca some more, he was reminded when his archrival suddenly appeared in the foyer on Casey's way out. Stopping short, Casey gave him an even look.

"Something wrong?" he asked. "I thought you'd be headed out for the holiday-lights hoo-ha tour along with everyone else."

Shane shook his head. "You didn't really think I'd fall for that patented 'subtle misdirection' thing you do, did you?"

"I dunno. You certainly *seemed* to fall for it."

"Maybe at first. It's been a while since I've—"

Seen you hung in the air between them, unvoiced but no less damning in its implications. It *had* been a while, Casey knew. It had been a while since Shane had decided to turn to the dark side and work against everything Casey stood for. It had been a while since he'd last hoped they could patch things up somehow.

So far, Shane Maresca was the only person Casey couldn't "fix"—the only person he'd ever failed to come to terms with.

"—since I've encountered a blatant bullshit artist like you," his former best friend went on. He gave an acknowledging wave. "I'll admit it: I did go for it at first. You were pretty convincing. You wound me up with all that competitiveness—"

That part had been real, Casey knew. But he didn't say so.

"—then you got transfixed by all the people outside, which meant *I* had to know who was so fascinating out there." Shaking his head, Shane chuckled. "You've been pulling that trick since we were young enough to still believe in happy endings, bro."

"You know as well as I do—there aren't any happy endings."

Shane arched his brow. "Even with your new lady friend?"

Casey didn't want to talk about Kristen. Especially not with Shane. He compressed his lips, then looked outside.

He swore. "Another blizzard is on its way."

Shane laughed. "Jesus, you're ham-fisted today. Am I supposed to actually bite on that? The *weather?*"

Most people would have, Casey knew. Maybe he'd forgotten how long it had been since he'd seen Shane, too.

Maybe he'd forgotten how well Shane knew him.

That didn't exactly bode well for the job at hand.

It was a long shot, but . . . "Tell me you're not here for the Heather Miller job," Casey said. "Because if you're not—"

"If I'm not, then we can be friends?" Shane's laid-back look turned a few degrees sharper. "Nice try. I don't buy it."

Casey shrugged. He could accept that. He'd learned a long time ago not to get too close to people. There was no reason Shane should be the exception. Or Kristen, for that matter.

"How's La Vieuville?" Casey asked. "Did you see him last time you were in Paris? You're still neighbors, right?"

"Jacques is doing well."

"Still working on those S&M-themed designs he loves?" Shane's wary look was as good as a yes, Casey figured.

"If you get a chance, you should check out the animatronic reindeer displays around town. I hear they're . . . unique." Casey pulled out his car keys. "You'll like the bondage elements."

For a few seconds, Casey waited. But Shane knew better than to tip his hand straightaway. When he'd been bragging to Kristen about his Paris pied-à-terre and the "diplomats and designers" who were his neighbors, he probably hadn't expected Casey to be familiar with his association with Jacques La Vieuville.

Then Casey got lucky. Or Shane got sloppy. Either way . . .

"If you're suggesting my friendship with Jacques had something to do with his involvement in—let's be honest here—the fucked-up costume design for Heather Miller's TV special . . ." Shane spread his hands in sham innocence. "You're barking up the wrong tree. I wasn't even on the job when that decision was made."

"Right. And it would be *so* unlike you to hedge your bets," Casey said acerbically, "just in case you got called in later."

"Totally." Shane turned jovial again. "We're all hoping Heather Miller's special goes off without a hitch. Right?"

"Yeah." Frowning anew, Casey held up his hand in a curt good-bye. Then he reconsidered. "Just do me a favor, okay?"

With even more guardedness than before, Shane waited.

For a heartbeat, Casey had the impression Shane was hoping that his "favor" would mean . . . what, exactly? That he was asking for a détente? A cease-fire? A *reconciliation?*

The way he saw it, they'd lost that chance long ago.

"Stay away from Kristen," Casey said. "She's not used to people like you."

Shane shook his head. "People like *us,* you mean."

Maybe. But Casey didn't want to say so. "Just do it."

To his surprise, Shane conceded. Partway. "I'll think about it." He glanced around the B&B's foyer, filled with twinkling lights and mini fir trees and enough evergreen garland to reach from Kismet to L.A., if laid end to end. "I can't believe I'm going to say this," Shane said quietly, "but . . . Merry Christmas."

For a second, Casey believed he meant it. He remembered everything they'd shared, everything they'd confided in one another, everything they'd been through as "difficult to place" kids in a tumultuous foster care system. Then he remembered that, once upon a time, Shane Maresca had taken everything Casey had ever wanted for Christmas, and he'd taken it for good.

That memory still hurt. Every time Casey heard a Christmas carol, every time he saw a Christmas tree, every time he smelled a rum-soaked glacéed fruitcake, it knifed him all over again.

"Yeah." Casey nodded. "I can't believe you're saying that, either," he said. Then he opened the door and stepped out of the past and into his future—starting with a surprise visit to the set of Heather Miller's troubled holiday TV special.

For the first time in her life, Heather Miller felt like a verifiable *genius*. Because although her plan to sic Casey on

Kristen (temporarily) while Heather tried to woo Alex Taylor into falling in love with her had been an admittedly spur-of-the-moment thing, it seemed to be working out *wonderfully*.

It had been three days now since The Terminator had shown up unexpectedly on set. Since then, Heather had been through sixteen more vocab words on her Word of the Day calendar (because she had to stay ahead of Alex, of course). She'd endured five more outrageous rumors about her private life (thanks to those loser paparazzis). And she'd wrangled several more delays on the pretaped portions of her "live" holiday TV special (with the end result of seeing *lots* of Alex). But she'd heard not a peep from Kristen about the potential problems she'd unleashed on her in the form of Casey Jackson. And while that wasn't typical of her straight-talking, take-no-guff younger sister, it wasn't like Heather to look a gift favor in the mouth, either.

Casey, of course, had been back. Heather's assistant had told her that Casey had made a surprise visit on the evening of day one, just as everyone was wrapping things up after another day of (purposely) failing to make their shooting targets. But, according to her assistant's (besotted-sounding) coverage of that visit, all Casey had wanted was to "say hi" to everyone.

After that, supposedly, he planned to leave them alone.

And okay, so *first* he'd mentioned to the production crew—and the backup dancers and the makeup artists and the hairstylists and the PAs and the few lingering, allegedly infatuated-with-him extras—that he'd be working from a rented booth at the Galaxy Diner, Heather recalled her assistant saying. And he'd assured everyone that they could find him there, if they had problems to confide, and he'd do his best to help them. But that was it.

And *that's* where Casey Jackson had tripped up, too.

Because now Heather knew Casey's M.O.: his *modus operandi* (thank you, Word of the Day from two weeks into the future!), and even better than that, she knew it wasn't going to work.

Because everybody *already* went to the Galaxy Diner on a daily basis. They didn't *need* to go there to see *Casey*. Duh.

He'd accomplished exactly *zero* with his "cunning" plan.

Remembering it now, Heather had to conclude that fate was conspiring to help her. How else to explain that Kristen had conveniently refused to hand-deliver her top-secret-recipe, extra-delicious pies-in-a-jar and other goodies (like mushroom veggie burgers and homemade potato tots, yum!) to the crew on set? Kristen had claimed that she didn't have the time or the resources to do deliveries. She'd also added that she didn't intend to give her own sister "the diva treatment."

But to Heather, that had been all right. Because she'd already known by then that she was desperate to make Alex Taylor notice her. Having the crew scamper several blocks away for "coffee breaks" on a moment's notice only helped her cause of delaying production while she enchanted Alex and tried to get him to look at her more closely through his sexy, nerdy, cutie-pie glasses.

Not that Casey Jackson knew that. That's where the fate part came in. Casey didn't know anything about Kristen's pledge to treat Heather like a regular person (which was kind of endearing but ultimately doomed, of course). He probably thought he'd outwitted Heather and separated her from her staff so they could rat her out. But that only proved Heather's theory. Because anyone who was really trying to do his job of cold-heartedly shutting down her holiday TV special would have done the necessary research and come up with a better strategy.

It was almost, Heather thought as she peered into her dressing room mirror, as if Casey Jackson was one of those people who was just marking time. A clock puncher. A slacker.

A *malingerer*. That was a funny one. She smiled as she

thought of it. Sometimes she was pretty sure her Word of the Day calendar was making up new words. There was no other way to explain a goofy-sounding, so-called word like *malingerer.*

"Maaaaliiiingerererer," Heather said into her mirror.

"I'm three minutes late! You don't have to call me names."

She turned at that sound . . . and Alex was there, smiling at her. *Yay.* He'd maintained his businesslike cover by bringing some new set-design plans to their "meeting." He'd dressed the part of a hardworking crew member by wearing a sweatshirt, gloves, and his pair of broken-in jeans with the busted-out knees that hugged his backside to perfection. But Heather knew that he knew that she knew that they weren't *really* there to discuss the set.

"Sorry! Just practicing one of my Words of the Day!"

"No problem." Alex paused, looking charmingly concerned and polite and seductive. "Should we have our meeting later?"

Okay. Maybe he *didn't* realize what they were there for.

But she knew he was brilliant enough to get it, if she made things clearer. So Heather rose from her seat. She sashayed her way toward him, using her best girl-on-the-prowl walk (the one she'd used in her last music video). Then she gave him a smile.

"No, stay," she purred. "Right now is perfect for me."

You're perfect for me, she longed to say, but didn't.

Because she couldn't afford to overplay her hand. Not now. Not when she was close. Not when she'd already—

Rats! She'd already forgotten her prop: her book of poetry.

Hastily, Heather grabbed it. She opened it at random, squinted at the pages, then nodded. "Yes, it's a perfect time." She peered at Alex. "I was just doing a little light reading."

"Are those new glasses you're wearing?"

"Hmm? These old things?" *Special ordered. With rush delivery.* A nonchalant shrug. "I wear them sometimes."

He looked at the spine of her book. "'. . . and this is the wonder that's keeping the stars apart,'" Alex said in a dreamy-sounding voice. "'i carry your heart (I carry it in my heart).'"

Heather gawked. That was *beautiful*. But . . . "Huh?"

"Your book." Alex raised his brows. "E.E. Cummings?"

She looked at the spine. She laughed. "Oh yeah. Right!" God. She *really* had to start actually *reading* this stuff.

"I love his work." Alex gestured. "Can I see it?"

Heather shoved the book at him. "Keep it! It's yours!"

"I can afford books, princess. I just want to see if one of my favorite poems is in this volume, so I can show it to you. I think you'll like it. 'My father moved through dooms of love'?"

"My father moved through the use of the air horn and the interstate highway system. He was a long-haul trucker."

"No, that's the first line of the poem." Alex shot her an inquisitive look. "You haven't heard of it, I guess? It's one of his best-known works. It was originally published in *50 Poems*."

This was getting out of hand. Heather laughed. "Actually, I've had my nose stuck in the tabloids lately. I didn't want to admit it, but . . ." She paused for dramatic effect, knowing her next revelation would definitely get Alex's attention. "Now they think I'm pregnant!" she cried. "They think I've been running around all over town with some sexy bohemian boy toy!"

At that, Alex's frown deepened.

Heather's heart raced. *It was working*. It was really working. Alex's reaction was worth all the aggravation and trauma she'd been through over those vicious rumors.

For about two minutes, she'd seriously wondered if *Kristen* was pregnant, and the paps had somehow confused the two of them. Kristen insisted that sometimes happened to her, even though it *never* happened (in reverse) to Heather. But no. There was definitely something more nefarious going on. Because the tabloids actually had *pictures* of "Heather" making out with her "boy toy" all over town. They had snaps of her "baby bump," too.

Heather was starting to wonder if Kristen was *purposely* causing those rumors to spread somehow, out of petty envy or competitiveness or spite or . . . something else that was mean.

Granted, that kind of behavior wouldn't be typical of Kristen. At all. But those photos were pretty damning evidence. There weren't that many people who resembled Heather—complete with leopard-print coat, blond hair, and huge sunglasses—and she couldn't think of another explanation for it. Unless she'd been experiencing short-term amnesia. And then forgotten it.

"You shouldn't worry about it, though," she assured Alex, gently stroking his muscular arm to reassure him. "It's not me. I'm pretty sure there's a crazy 'Heather Miller' impostor in town who's pretending to be me. Probably someone I went to high school with, who's envious of my success. That happens a lot."

Privately, Heather congratulated herself for *not* revealing her semi-suspicions that her own sister might be involved. Even for Alex's sake, she refused to throw Kristen under the bus.

However, those suspicions *did* make Heather feel a lot better about sending The Terminator to babysit her sister three days ago. If she'd known then that Kristen might be actively trying to sabotage her reputation (instead of vaguely suspecting it, based on that gross toilet-paper-shopping "story" that had *also* hit the tabloids), she could have spared herself a few days' worth of a guilty conscience.

Not that Kristen couldn't handle herself, even in the face of Casey Jackson and his scary tactics. Kristen was, after all, famously poised. Their parents couldn't quit raving (to Heather's irritation) about Kristen's composure, talent, work ethic, and dependability. In fact, their rampant parental pride—*in Kristen!*—went pretty far to explain why Heather didn't return to Kismet very often. She couldn't take knowing she would always come in second . . . to an ordinary, not-especially-charismatic, lovable girl-next-door type like Kristen. Forever.

But that was enough sibling angst for right now, Heather decided. Because despite her *herculean* efforts (thank you, Word of the Day from yesterday!) to make Alex fall insanely in love with her, he was still frowning at her instead. Heather was starting to believe it *wasn't* because he was jealous.

Then Alex smiled. Handsomely. "I know it's not you."

"Why not?" she asked perversely. "I could have a boy toy!"

His chuckle did not help. At her quelling look, Alex sobered up enough to explain. "You don't have attached earlobes. Your impostor *does*. So when I saw those pictures . . ." He shrugged. "All I needed was the necessary attention to detail."

Heather frowned. She touched her earlobes. "Huh?"

"Your earlobes are detached, like mine." Helpfully, Alex came closer. When he stood near enough to make her almost hyperventilate from his sex appeal, he gently grasped her earlobe. He waggled it. "Otherwise, I couldn't do this."

Heather's knees felt weak. She lifted her gaze to his. "You've never touched me like that before. I—" *Love it.*

Alex winced. "Yeah, I probably shouldn't have done it just then, either. Only you looked so worried, that I—" He broke off. Tragically, he released her tingly earlobe. "Sorry about that."

"No! I—" *I want you to touch me.* Wishing he'd do it again, Heather touched her ears. Marveling at him, she said, "You've really looked closely enough at me to notice my *earlobes?*"

Alex's cheeks colored. He cleared his throat. "Uh. Yeah."

Thrilled, she hugged herself to keep from dancing.

"Like I said," Alex went on in a quashing tone, "I probably shouldn't have touched you at all. Because the reason I was frowning at you before, the reason I was staring at you—"

"Yes?" *This was it*. Ohmigod, ohmigod, ohmigod. "Go on."

"—is because I'm pretty sure you have the chicken pox. You have a papular vesicular rash, right . . . *there*." Alex pointed at her nose. "And there. And I think it's spreading to . . . there."

Helpfully, he indicated her cheek. Her neck. Her arm.

She scratched. "You've got to be joking. The chicken pox?"

"I'm afraid so." Sorrowfully, Alex nodded. "I hate to be the bearer of bad tidings, but looks as though my favorite star has been infected with the varicella zoster virus."

Wow, he was smart. He'd said she was his favorite star, too!

"God, I love it when you talk like that," she breathed.

"I'm serious. You should go to the doctor—and probably be quarantined from the rest of the production crew, too."

"What?" Quarantined from him? That was unthinkable. "I refuse to accept that," Heather said. "Besides, kids get chicken pox. I'm an adult."

"Adults can get chicken pox, too. My girlfriend had it last year." Alex's expression took on a faraway look. "I nursed her through it. It's a good thing you're *not* pregnant, because—"

But Heather couldn't hear the rest of what he said. She was too busy hearing *my girlfriend, my girlfriend* gonging through her ears. Maybe chicken pox caused auditory hallucinations?

"You have a girlfriend?" she asked, hoping for the best.

". . . so I'll probably have to be quarantined with you," Alex was saying, casting a speculative look around her dressing room.

They stopped. They stared at each other.

"That might not be so bad," Heather said cheerfully.

And that's how, six hours and one doctor's visit later, Heather wound up sequestered in blissful privacy with Alex, exactly the way she'd wanted . . . leaving, in their absences, her *Live! from the Heartland* holiday TV special to fend for itself.

Chapter 11

On the morning of his fourth day in Kismet, Casey dodged two bell-ringing sidewalk Santas. On purpose.

He ignored one battalion of schoolchildren—adorably dressed up as green-suited elves—singing Christmas carols in the snowy town square. He declined the coffee shop's sidewalk-sale offer of a sample-size "Christmassy" peppermint hot chocolate with a candy cane stirrer. He scarcely noticed the way the residents went overboard with decorations and yard ornaments or the way local businesses decked out their storefronts with lights and their windows with seasonal art. He even came face-to-face with the ultimate holiday cuteness test—a baby wearing a tiny, Santa Claus-inspired, red-and-white hooded onesie—and didn't so much as coo at the kid. That meant it was official.

He'd beaten Christmas at its own fakery-filled game.

He didn't even enjoy the persistent gingerbread smell that lingered all over town very much anymore, Casey noticed. He was going to be all right. This wasn't going to get to him.

Christmas wasn't going to get to him. Not even here in Kismet, in the ho-ho-ho epicenter of the universe.

Feeling positively bulletproof (at least as far as the holiday onslaught was concerned), Casey hefted his laptop case from his Subaru's seat. He burrowed more warmly into his coat, then strode past the piled-up snowbanks into the Galaxy Diner.

Inside, a whole new level of Christmas cheer assaulted him. One of Heather's Christmas songs played on the sound system. Lights and garland abounded everywhere. Two charity Christmas trees overflowed with paper angel-shaped ornaments designating Kismet residents as "be an angel" gift givers, proving that the holiday spirit of generosity still thrived in town.

Casey strode blithely past it all, able to acknowledge it and then immediately put it behind him. He wasn't the sentimental type, prone to going all gooey at every little kindness or trapping of the season. He was, officially, over it.

Then he reached his rented corner booth. He saw the hand-written RESERVED sign waiting on the tabletop in exactly the same place it had been every morning so far. And his inner stoicism crumpled like so much tossed-away wrapping paper on Boxing Day.

Damn that sign. It still got to him.

Hoping to downplay his reaction, Casey scowled at it.

It didn't help. That ordinary piece of paper—taped onto an injection-molded plastic table tent typically used to promote specials at the diner—warmed his heart. It made him feel a *part* of things at the Galaxy Diner. *That* was a sensation he didn't experience very often. It made him feel . . . more guarded than usual.

Not that his inherent wariness helped him much. Not when, an instant later, Talia wandered over with a jolly smile and a cup of coffee—black with one sugar, just the way he liked it—and set down a folded copy of the *Kismet Comet* newspaper for him.

"We keep an employee copy on hand," Talia said. "I thought I'd save you the trouble of getting a paper from the machine outside, the way you do every morning. It's cold out there."

"Thanks," Casey said in an easygoing tone. "That's nice. I didn't think anyone noticed my morning newspaper pilgrimage."

But what he really meant was, *I didn't think anyone cared.* Realizing that painful truth, he couldn't help frowning anew.

Yes, he ponied up fifty cents for a *Kismet Comet* every day. Yes, he did so after setting up his rented booth with his laptop, coffee, notepad, pens, and cell phone at the ready for a day's worth of troubleshooting. Yes, he was a guy who liked routine. So what?

"Your fan club noticed." Grinning, Talia nodded toward the cadre of regulars seated at the end of the counter.

As one, the group of women and men waved to him. "'Morning, Casey!"

"We don't want you getting frostbitten just because you want to keep up with current affairs." Talia set down a half-pint wide-mouth mason jar filled with homemade Concord grape jam. She'd noticed Casey's preference for grape versus the usual strawberry, then. Argh. She looked straight at him. "You might as well face it, Mr. Big. You're one of us now."

Double argh. That mishmash of teasing and kindheartedness—unique to Talia and to the diner—didn't help either.

Neither did the arrival of Walden, the wild-and-woolyhaired pastry chef, a moment later. He brandished a doilycovered plate, tossed Talia a peculiarly intimate look (at which she blushed feverishly), then set the plate in front of Casey.

"Voilà! You're the first taste tester of Kristen's newest creation," Walden told him. "It's a cinnamon-bun crescent. See? It's shaped like a croissant, but it's made of *brioche vendéenne* instead of *pâte feuilletée,* then rolled up with cinnamon-sugar-and-brown-butter filling for an upscale meets down-home spin. Kristen said you mentioned liking cinnamon rolls as a kid—"

Cagily, Casey nodded. Vaguely, he remembered having accidentally copped to a weakness for those refrigerated cinnamon rolls—the cheap kind that came in a pop-open cardboard container and were frosted after baking with a miserly amount of prefab frosting from a tiny plastic tub. As a kid, he'd *loved* those things.

". . . and you know Kristen," Walden was saying. "She never misses a detail, and she can never leave well enough alone, either. She's creative like that. She *loves* special projects, too. So she rolled up her sleeves and made these just for you."

Casey eyed the crescent roll. It smelled buttery and spicy. Its sugary crust sparkled. It made his nose practically twitch with nostalgia. It smelled . . . exactly like Christmassy goodness.

Oh hell. Had he *really* just had that sappy thought?

Gareth's arrival saved him from considering it further—but not for long. Because somehow, Gareth managed to entrench him even more deeply in the damn sense of *belonging* Casey felt whenever he arrived at the Galaxy Diner and saw everyone there.

"Oh no, you don't, you pastry freak!" Aiming a warning glance at Walden, Gareth slid a plate full of the current breakfast special—a scrambled egg platter with chestnut-sage stuffing and cranberry compote on the side, served with black pepper brioche toast—in front of Casey, then stood back proudly. "Casey's not having any goodies until he gets a proper meal. He needs vitamins and vegetables, not just butter and sugar."

"You sound like somebody's mother, Gareth," Talia quipped.

But Casey could overlook that, just this once. Appreciatively, he inhaled. Everything smelled delicious . . . even if it *was* a little too holiday inspired. "Thanks, Gareth. This looks great," he said. "I didn't even order yet, though."

"I know." Gareth nodded. "But this is what you've had the past three days, so we figured it was your favorite."

"We renamed it 'the Casey Kick-Starter' on the menu." As proof, Talia brandished the latest edition of the handwritten menu. "It's even more popular since the renaming."

Waiting for the punch line, Casey stared at them.

Nada. What the hell? Were these people actually for real?

In his world, at least, *nobody* was this kind, this genuine, or this welcoming. Not even a ragtag bunch of foodie misfits with purple hair, nose rings, piercings, dreadlocks, hipster clothes, an uncanny ability to overlook blizzards, and an excess of Christmas spirit.

"I've never been an eponymous breakfast eater," Casey joked. He *almost* nailed it. "But I'll try anything once."

"We've never named a menu item for anyone before." Walden shrugged, stepping nearer to Talia. He gazed with perfect forthrightness at Casey. "We made an exception for you."

Casey shook his head. *That* kind of special treatment didn't help either. At this rate, he wouldn't survive the morning. He would take up permanent residence at the Galaxy Diner and never, ever leave. He would . . . wonder what the hell was wrong with him.

He'd befriended a lot of people over the course of a lot of troubleshooting assignments. He liked people. They liked him. So what made the Galaxy Diner, its crew, and its owner so special?

Well, Casey knew what made Kristen so special to him. It was her ability to help with Heather's TV special, he reminded himself ruthlessly. She could give him inside access to Heather—access no one else could. He had to remember that. All the same . . .

All the same, he was behaving like an idiot. He was tougher than this. He was smarter and sharper and more hard-nosed than this. He was (according to some) The Terminator! Casey Jackson couldn't be undone with a few small-town Christmas kindnesses.

"You know, you might as well just come in an hour earlier, before we open," Gareth said, "and join us for the family meal."

Casey sharpened his gaze. "I'm not family."

"Well, you're *practically* family," Gareth hedged. "I mean, you're here every single day. You're always one of the first ones in the door. You're paying for the privilege with that booth rental, and we all know you now. So you're actually—"

"I'm. Not. Family," Casey bit out.

"Oh! No! You thought—" Gareth broke off with a sense of enlightenment brightening his face. He looked anxious—probably because Casey undoubtedly appeared ready to clobber him with a coatrack. "Sorry. I meant the 'family meal' in the restaurant sense," Gareth explained belatedly. "It's the meal we all share before service starts. In this case, predawn and precoffee, which leads to some pretty hairy moments. Kinda . . . like this one."

"I know what you meant," Casey said. "The answer's no."

They all seemed perplexed. *It's just a meal, lame ass,* Talia's expression said. *Dude, lighten up,* Gareth's added.

Mmm. Talia looks fantastic today, Walden's finished.

"Hold on!" Avery hustled over, wearing her usual waitress's uniform of a denim miniskirt, plaid flannel shirt, tights, boots, an apron . . . and a hokey red-and-white felt Santa hat, too. She plunked down a bottle of ketchup. "Don't forget this!"

That capped it. Avery had remembered Casey's condiment of choice. Gareth had remembered Casey's favorite (so far) breakfast special of the day and renamed it after him. Walden had hand-delivered Casey a specialty baked good. Kristen had *hand-created* that baked good. And Talia had saved Casey from frostbite, delivered him a newspaper, and brought custom-prepared coffee to his exact specifications with a smile.

What's more, they all seemed *delighted* to do it.

What were they trying to do? Disarm him completely?

This had to be some sort of trick. Some sort of small-town seasonal gamesmanship. A pretense of some sort—a maneuver with a specific end game in sight. Casey just didn't know what it was.

In his experience, most people had an agenda. At least in the business circles he ran in, they did. That's just the way it was. He hadn't excelled in his line of work all these years just to be defeated by a bunch of amateurs now, when it counted most.

Were they all trying to protect Heather Miller? Casey wondered intently. Were they trying to lull him into not *caring* that Heather was torpedoing her TV special and then giving up his work in town? Were they making fun of his cluelessness about Christmas? Or were they all just that gosh-darn *nice?*

While Casey tried to decide which absurd scenario was more probable, all four of the Galaxy Diner crew stood beaming at him, oblivious to his confusion. A few more regulars entered the diner. They waved at him. Casey knew all their names by now, it occurred to him. He knew where they worked and how many children they had and whether they were Michigan natives. He knew *them.*

None of this was part of his assignment here.

Realizing that, Casey took another deep breath. He tried to fortify himself against Talia, Gareth, Walden, and Avery's unique blend of friendliness, helpfulness, and conviviality. He tried to look past the welcoming attitudes of the Kismet Elks Club members, the warmth of the knitting-circle grandmas he'd met, and the "hey, what's up?" geniality of the on-winter-break college students who usually occupied the next booth over.

It wasn't working. He swore. Maybe he needed coffee first.

As Casey hastily slurped some java, his desperate gaze fell on Kristen. She was serving a plate of gingerbread waffles to a trucker sporting grizzled gray beard stubble and a knit cap.

These weren't his kind of people, Casey reminded himself. They were bundled against the wintery, blizzardy, Christmas-time-redolent weather he abhorred. They were unfashionably dressed, untanned, and unaware of the latest "It" nightclub. They were willing to make friends with strangers—with people like him.

Yeah. That was working. Feeling a fraction more normal, Casey swallowed more coffee. He let his gaze linger on Kristen, taking in her long blond ponytail, her energetic stance, and her wide smile. Yeah. None of this was affecting him anymore. *Whew.*

Then Kristen turned that smile of hers directly on *him,* and just like that, Casey was lost. The Christmas music crashed back into his consciousness, the gingerbread smell of Kismet's whole-town holiday-air-freshener routine returned, and he couldn't quit seeing ornamental sparkle every damn place he looked.

The worst part was, he liked it. He liked all of it. He felt part of it. He felt, for one instant, as though he *belonged* there. Or at least as though he *could* belong there, if he wanted to.

At the edge of his overpriced rental booth, the foursome of Walden, Avery, Gareth, and Talia smiled at him all over again.

"That's more like it. Now you're waking up," Walden said roughly, nodding in a way that sent his dark dreadlocks flapping against his chef's whites. "Eat that cinnamon-bun crescent, too! And don't forget to tell Kristen what you think of it. We're always testing new ideas in the pastry department."

"We're always testing savory stuff, too," Gareth said enthusiastically, his wiry arms waving. "It's all seasonal. We do this fantastic asparagus omelet with green garlic, smoked mushrooms, and thyme-roasted new potatoes in the springtime—"

"I won't be here in the spring," Casey interrupted.

Gareth exchanged a glance with Talia. She shrugged.

"Okay. Whatever you need to tell yourself, cranky." Knowingly, Talia nodded at his coffee. "You'd better swallow some more joe before making any more predictions about your future whereabouts. Usually you need about a quart before you really start sounding coherent in the morning, I've noticed."

Pointedly, Casey set down his coffee cup.

The four of them only chortled. Avery shook her head. "You don't fool us, Casey. We all know how grumpy you are before the coffee kicks in." She peered at his breakfast. "Aw, look! The kitchen staff gave you one of our special holiday-themed plates today! Usually we don't break out the holiday-themed tableware until the week before Christmas. You know, to keep it special. The back-of-house staff must really like you."

Casey frowned at his plate. Its porcelain edge was gilded with Christmassy stars, then bordered in miniature Christmas trees strung together with winding red and green ribbons.

Feeling provoked, Casey glanced toward the back of the diner. Lingering in the passageway, the busboy and dishwasher gave him a united, "Hey, Casey! How's it going, bro?"

Their merry grins only served to put the capper on Casey's morning. So much for his immunity to this emotional stuff.

"I'm not paying extra for this special treatment," Casey warned the staff at large. "This booth rental is exorbitant enough as it is. So if you're all angling for bigger tips—"

Looking wounded, they all frowned at him. Avery's lower lip trembled. Gareth stroked his hipster beard. Talia rolled her eyes . . . then yelped and swatted Walden. With a sheepish, semi-naughty grin, Walden moved his hand from its place on her ass.

Hmm. Despite his current bad mood, Casey couldn't help noticing the flirtatious chemistry between them. That was new.

"We're not after bigger tips, you nitwit," Talia broke in, hands on hips. "We like you. We take care of people we like."

"Yeah!" Defiantly, Avery sniffled. "That's what people do."

Walden nodded. But Gareth only went on gazing in thought at Casey. "Not everybody does that, guys," he said quietly.

His gaze met Casey's. Something . . . *bleak* passed between them.

A second later, it was gone.

"But all the cool kids do it," Gareth amended. "They also pick up their friends at the airport when needed, let them play 'Everybody Hurts' on repeat a gazillion times after a breakup"—he aimed a meaningful glance at Talia—"even when their friend hates REM with a seething passion, *and* they come along with them to help serve punch and cookies at the senior center tomorrow."

Brightly, Gareth waggled his eyebrows. A variety of exclamations and grumbles met his thinly veiled hint/invitation.

But before the gang could get down to making or breaking plans to spend the evening throwing a holiday gala for seniors . . .

"Look. I'm here to get to the bottom of what's going on with Heather Miller's TV special," Casey told them. "Once I do, I'm going to fix it. So if any of you can help me, please do."

Suddenly, Gareth grew immensely interested in the assortment of vintage Christmas-tree toppers hanging on wires from the diner's ceiling. Avery decided she needed to deal with another customer. Walden muttered something about needing to finish some pear-almond tarts for afternoon service. And Talia . . .

Talia looked right at Casey. "If we thought helping you would save Kristen's Christmas this year," she said, "we might do that. But I'm not at all sure it would. So . . . nice try, but no. We've already got everything under control ourselves."

Then she turned and went to deal with her customers, leaving Casey with the interesting realization that Kristen's friends weren't exactly fans of Heather's glam invasion, either. They obviously blamed Heather for upending Kristen's Christmas. They didn't seem to like that much.

The only questions now were: Would Kristen's pals be willing to do anything about it? If so, how far would they go?

Because judging by their unusual reactions to Casey's request for help—and by Talia's claim that they had things "under control"—Gareth, Talia, Avery, and Walden had already done *something* to improve Kristen's Christmas. They *definitely* had something to hide. Casey was sure of it.

Now he just had to find out what it was.

Chapter 12

Galaxy Diner
Christmas Takeover: Day 12½

During the brief lull between lunch service and closing time, Kristen finally did what she'd been trying not to do all day: slide into Casey's booth. Once there, she couldn't help smiling at him, too, exactly the way she'd known she would.

That was a problem. Given how *alive* she felt when in Casey's presence, Kristen didn't doubt her infatuation with him was written all over her face. Her smile was like the Goodyear blimp of Christmas crushes, advertising her feelings as surely as lunging across the table and kissing him would have done.

Maybe even more. Since kissing was only physical . . . and the way she felt when she was near Casey went way beyond that.

Forcing herself to focus on something more material than the shape of Casey's lips, the breadth of his shoulders, and the endearing crease that developed between his eyebrows whenever he concentrated on working, Kristen lounged in the booth.

"I figured it out," she announced. "I know how you do it."

Casey looked up, temporarily short-circuiting her ability to think straight. Geez, he was fun to look at. His jaw was rock solid, his eyes were the color of almost-caramelized sugar, and his dark hair made her want to run her fingers through it.

He set aside his cell phone. "Do what?"

"Troubleshoot the problems you're assigned to. I know how you do it. I've been watching you for the past few days. It's taken me a while, but I finally got a grip on your method."

A playful smile edged onto his face. "If you wanted to get a grip on my 'method,'" Casey said, "all you had to do was ask."

"I didn't know there was an open invitation."

"For you? I'm an in-person Evite. Anytime, day or night."

"Mmm-hmm." Wanting to take him up on that—but knowing better than to do so—Kristen gave him a wily look. "This is part of it, you know. This"—she twirled her finger between them, indicating them both—"*thing* you do. This misdirection, or whatever you want to call it. I'm close, and you're worried, and that's why you're trying to distract me with innuendo."

"If you want some 'innuendo' from me, just ask."

"See?" She laughed. "It's a knee-jerk reaction from you."

"I do see." Casey nodded. "What do you think that means?"

"About you?"

Another nod. He seemed genuinely interested in her take on things. His cell phone went off, but Casey didn't so much as blink. Kristen couldn't help being impressed. Most people didn't have that kind of focusing ability. They responded to their phones like Pavlov's dogs, lunging for them instantly.

"I think it means you're still doing it," she said. "You're hoping I'll forget what I've figured out about your methods. But I won't. Because here's the thing—I'm still supposed to be keeping an eye on you. I made a promise. So I'm keeping it."

"That's the least you can do for your poor sick sister," Casey agreed. "I'll bet she really appreciates it."

Kristen considered the few short phone calls she'd had from Heather recently. She hadn't sounded particularly appreciative, but she *had* sounded pretty chipper for someone with chicken pox.

Because Heather had been quarantined, Kristen had eased up on her no-diva policy. She'd arranged a daily delivery of food and goodies to Heather's room at Lagniappe at the Lakeshore, the five-star country inn she'd been staying at across the lake from The Christmas House B&B. It had been necessary to deliver enough food for two people each day, because of Heather's unnamed "co-quarantinee"—probably her long-suffering assistant.

"Yes, I think she does appreciate it." Kristen watched as Casey gave a friendly nod to one of the grips from the set of *Live! from the Heartland,* who'd arrived to pick up a to-go order . . . which reminded her why she was here. "But we were talking about *you,*" she said, "and your troubleshooting ability."

Caught, Casey smiled at her. "I'm only trying to help."

"Right. Which you do by *listening* to people!"

At the *aha* note in her tone, Casey quirked his mouth. "A heinous technique, I know. But sometimes it's necessary."

"It's integral to your method," Kristen agreed, "because without it, you couldn't do the next part: suggest a solution."

He shrugged. "Sounds pretty innocuous so far."

"That's just it! That's the brilliant part of it. Because of the way you do it, everyone winds up thinking *your* idea is *their* idea. That makes them extra motivated to make it happen."

Casey remained silent . . . then he reached out to touch her hand. Kristen jerked, feeling that same electric connection pass between them. She whipped up her gaze, wondering for the umpteenth time if he'd felt it too . . . then realized that Casey was merely tapping her hand so she'd lift it and allow him to retrieve the paperwork she'd accidentally put her hand atop.

He tapped his papers on the table to square them, then slid them into his laptop case. Near it, his computer hummed. His pens and notepad stood at the ready. His cell phone buzzed again. Again, he didn't acknowledge it. "Interesting theory."

"*Correct* theory," Kristen pressed. "You don't have to go down to the set, full of Terminator-style sound and fury, and force everyone to do your bidding. Because you make sure they *want* to do what you want them to do. Which is probably what the network or the production company wants them to do. It's—"

"Ingenious?" Casey supplied with a devilish eyebrow raise.

"—insidious," Kristen countered. "Because nobody knows what's happening. Yet I've seen it work over and over again this week. During the course of a conversation with someone from Heather's TV special, you subtly slide in a solution to whatever problem is at hand—delays, disasters, disorganization—and then you simply . . . wait a while. Before long, the person you're talking with inevitably comes up with *exactly* the same idea you had!"

"Hmm." His smoldering gaze lifted to hers, compelling and attentive and mesmeric. "That's quite a trick."

"Yes, it is!"

"But it's just that—a trick. I do don't tricks."

Undaunted, Kristen went on. "It's the only way you can achieve the unprecedented success you've achieved—"

"Have you been checking up on me?"

"—because if you tried to strong-arm people into going along with your solutions, they would resist. Inevitably. It's just human nature *not* to do what you're told, if you can possibly help it," Kristen told him. "If you barged onto the set and started issuing orders, people would argue with you."

"Right. But since I'm somehow hypnotizing them . . . ?"

"It's not hypnosis. It's . . . skill. And it's smart."

She wished she could think of a better explanation for it, but that's what it boiled down to. Casey possessed an unprecedented skill for understanding what people needed and then giving it to them, almost entirely imperceptibly. Unlike most people, Casey didn't let his ego get in the way. He was willing to give other people credit—even for his own ideas. Once he'd succeeded, he wasn't interested in crowing about it, either. "It's . . . kind of remarkable," she said.

"It's troubleshooting." He shrugged, full of apparent matter-of-factness. "Part of the job is leaving people happy when you're done. Anyone can come in and be a hatchet man—"

"Like Heather accused *you* of being."

"—but not everyone can devise real solutions."

"Is that what Shane Maresca would say you're doing?" Kristen pushed, reaching for the only reasonable counter-comparison she could make. "Devising real solutions?"

A frown. "He would say I'm getting in his way. I hope."

"Still bloodthirsty, then?"

"Still winning." Uneasily, Casey shifted. "I hope."

Kristen shook her head. "What *is* it between you two, anyway? You were clearly close once. What happened?"

Casey frowned at his cranberry-pecan pie-in-a-jar with cinnamon whipped cream and streusel crumble. True to his word, he'd downed an entire mini pie every single day . . . and had nearly incited riots with his almost pornographic appreciation of it.

She'd say one thing for Casey: He delivered.

"Shane got what I wanted for Christmas one year," Casey told her curtly. "I had a hard time getting over it."

"Shane got the Tonka truck you wanted, and you didn't?"

His jaw flexed. "Something like that."

"No. That can't be it. I don't buy it."

Casey lifted his gaze, dark and unfathomable, to hers. "Whether you do or not . . . that's not my problem."

The bleakness in his eyes made her sad. Impulsively, Kristen reached for his hand. She squeezed it. "Go on. Make it my problem. Tell me about it! Maybe you'll feel better."

He actually appeared to consider it. Then . . .

"You'd do better staying away from Shane Maresca. Tell Heather to stay away from him, too. She won't take my calls, and I can't get anywhere near her in person," Casey said, "thanks to her very convenient quarantine."

"'Convenient'? You don't think it's real?"

"I know it's real. That doesn't mean it's not convenient."

"Well, either way, it doesn't matter," Kristen said. "Heather's never even heard of Shane Maresca. I asked her."

Casey frowned. "Then it's worse than I thought."

But before Kristen could ask what he meant, another member of Heather's TV special production crew wandered in. She picked up a cup of coffee and a mincemeat pie-in-a-jar to go, spied Casey, then trundled over to his table with her bag in hand.

"Hey, Casey," she said. "I just wanted to let you know that I *did* talk to Maggie about rigging the lights the way I knew they ought to be. We were able to come to terms with it."

"That's good news." Casey smiled at her. "So you win!"

"Yep!" They high-fived. "Anyway, thanks for listening yesterday. That was a really enlightening conversation. Bye!"

Looking pleased, the crew member left the diner. Kristen watched Casey as he watched her leave. Then she pounced.

"Let me guess," she said. "You talked to Maggie, too? And she happened to come to the same conclusion about the lighting?"

"Something like that." Casey gazed at her. "What difference does it make? It's a good thing when problems are solved."

"It's deceptive."

"Maybe that's just what I *want* you to think. Maybe my spellbinding troubleshooter mojo is getting to you, too."

"Joke all you want. I'm onto you."

"Does that mean you're done interrogating me?" Adorably, Casey feigned disappointment. "I was just getting into it."

"No, I'm not done yet." Considering him, Kristen leaned more cozily into the booth. Around them, the usual hubbub of customers and crew went about their business, with their days brightened by Christmas carols and eggnog French toast. "I still want to know more about Shane. When I told you Heather hasn't heard of him, why did you say it's worse than you thought?"

With clear reluctance, Casey sobered. He wrapped his hands around his coffee cup—nearly succeeding in side-tracking her with thoughts of how skilled and manly and mesmerizing his hands looked—then squinted at the nearest of the diner's two charity Christmas trees. She was surprised it didn't burst into flames.

"Shane is an anti-fixer," Casey finally explained, his tone wry but unswerving. "Since Heather's TV special is already in trouble, he's here to derail it completely."

That was unexpected. "Why would he do that?"

"For the insurance money. The production company takes out insurance on every project—every movie, every TV show, every awards show or made-for-TV docudrama . . . and every holiday special," Casey said. "Rather than sink unrecoverable cash into an already troubled production, sometimes the company would rather cut their losses and collect the insurance."

"You really mean this?"

A nod. "The fact that Heather hasn't even met Shane yet—that she probably doesn't even know he's here in Kismet—suggests he's succeeding, too. From behind the scenes, where people like him work best."

"I dunno," Kristen mused, considering everything she knew so far. "That sounds a lot like what you're doing."

Casey's gaze darkened. "Shane is here to ruin things. It's

what he does best. He just does it with a smile, that's all. Sometimes, he starts early—doubling his chances of being hired by creating on-set dissent where it doesn't already exist."

"But . . . an *anti-fixer?*" Kristen almost laughed. "That sounds so preposterous! That can't be a real thing, can it? Come on. I might be a small-town girl, but I'm not *that* gullible."

"If it helps, think of him as a consultant," Casey suggested. "I don't know if he's working for Heather's network or a rival network or another production company with a similar show in the works. He could have been hired by more than one entity. He could have laid a lot of groundwork by now, too. I promise you, Shane Maresca is real. And he means trouble."

"Uh-huh." She remained doubtful. "Whereas *you* mean . . . ?"

"Trouble." Casey flashed her his most affecting, most flirtatious, most *irresistible* smile yet. "I never claimed to be harmless myself. I have a long and glorious history of causing trouble. The difference between me and Shane is that I've been spending my time making up for all the trouble I've caused."

Skeptically, Kristen eyed him. It was tricky business. Mostly because that latest smile of his gave her a serious case of the want-mores. As in, *I want more of that smile. I want more of that rumbly, husky, bad-to-the-bone timbre to your voice. I want more of this conversation between us . . . and I want it to be personal, too.* It was making it difficult to concentrate.

Probably, Casey knew it, too. That's why he'd chosen that particular moment to smile at her—to charm her into not asking any more questions. But Kristen needed to know the truth about what was going on . . . for Heather's sake, if nothing else.

Defiantly, Kristen straightened her spine.

"Maybe Shane is just misunderstood," she said staunchly. "Maybe he's not 'trouble' at all. He seems nice to me."

Casey merely shook his head. "He probably does," he said casually. "But one of the advantages of growing up in a lot of different households is that you learn how to read people pretty quickly. You have to. Otherwise, you don't survive long."

"I see. Do you also learn how to manipulate people?"

He arched his eyebrow at her, not saying anything.

That's how Kristen knew she'd struck a nerve.

Because Casey *always* had something to say. Usually (unlike her) he had the *right* thing to say, at exactly the right moment.

But Kristen couldn't back down now. The words were already out there. The only thing that might possibly help was . . .

"I'm sorry," she said. "That was insensitive."

"No, it was a reasonable question," Casey disagreed. "I respect you for not tiptoeing around me. I'm not made of glass."

"As far as I can tell, you're made of machismo and dick jokes, with a big dose of charisma and pie love thrown in."

"'Pie love'? Is that what you're calling it now?"

"You skipped 'dick jokes' to focus on 'pie love'?"

Casey laughed, leaving her feeling immensely relieved that he wasn't hurt by her off-the-cuff comment. *Whew.* That meant things were okay between them. Their camaraderie was intact.

Kristen didn't want to risk dinging it again. Not even, she realized with a start, for the sake of getting to the bottom of Casey's plans for Heather's TV special. Because over the past few days, she'd gotten to know Casey much better. They'd hung out, they'd talked, and once—memorably—they'd even shot a few games of decidedly *non*-Christmassy pool at The Big Foot bar.

Being around him had been fun. They'd taken their instant

bond to a whole new level. In fact, if Casey hadn't already failed her usual "should I sleep with him?" litmus test . . .

Maybe, Kristen thought, he deserved another shot at it.

Or maybe she should just forget about her test altogether.

"What can I say?" he asked, obviously referring to his *very* convincing enjoyment of today's pie-in-a-jar. "That walnut-caramel pie of yours is growing on me. Someday I might even like it."

"My diner customers think you want to *marry* it," Kristen joked, "after yesterday's show-stopping performance."

"Or at least take it out a few more times . . . show it a good time." Casey pulled a funny face. Then, with abrupt seriousness, he said, "I don't manipulate people. That's not what I'm doing."

"No. You're just making them want what *you* want," Kristen said. "If that's not manipulation, I don't know what is."

Casey gave her another smile. This one reached all the way to her toes and made them curl up with tingly excitement inside her boots. How was it that she'd made a terrible conversational blunder, stepped all over his difficult childhood, and basically interrogated him since she'd sat down . . . and Casey somehow made her feel as if she was the most remarkable woman alive?

Going toe-to-toe with him this way was . . . invigorating. He made her feel unique. Fascinating. Brave. *Necessary.*

All the things she believed she was, deep down . . . but still longed, on the inside, to have confirmed by someone else.

"It's called seduction, Pollyanna." Casey pinned her with another knowing look. "It helps make the world go around."

"Maybe for you, it does. I prefer the truth."

Casey seemed taken aback by that. "Just because I might have made you want it doesn't mean you don't *really* want it. In the end, *you're* still the one who's feeling the desire."

"Wait a minute." Kristen blinked, feeling confused. "Are we still talking about fixing things? Or *not* fixing things?"

"I'm talking about manipulation, now that you've brought it up," Casey said. "And the truth is, if you think you're immune to being seduced, a hundred times a day, by the things around you and the people you meet . . . well, you're just kidding yourself." He relaxed in his side of the booth, visibly comfortable with the topic at hand. "But that's all right. You're in good company. Most people like to think they're in control—"

"I *am* in control!"

"—when really they're just operating on autopilot. That's not living. That's existing. And it's prone to being nudged, with just the subtlest push, in any direction that comes along."

"So *that's* how you do what you do!" Victoriously, Kristen pointed at Casey. "You push people when they're not looking."

"Gee whiz. That makes me sound pretty gosh-darn awful."

At his aw-shucks routine, she couldn't help grinning. It was a *really* poor fit for him. "If the shoe fits . . ."

Appearing vaguely wounded, Casey shook his head at her. "Is that really what you think of me? That I'm *manipulative?*"

Kristen couldn't deny it. "If the evidence is there . . ."

Before she could press him further, a PA from *Live! from the Heartland* dropped by his table. "Sorry to interrupt, you guys! But Casey"—here, she turned to him with grateful, shining eyes—"I had to tell you how glad I am that we talked yesterday. Like I told you, I was convinced the reason the director was such a bitch to me—pardon my French—was because I sucked at my job. I just knew she was about to fire me! But I decided to talk to her after I saw you yesterday, just because I was feeling so strong and pumped up, and you'll never guess what happened?"

"What happened?" Again, Casey ignored his buzzing phone.

"She's getting a divorce!" the PA confided. "She'd been feeling really alone and sad about it, too. So we went for drinks at The Big Foot after yesterday's pickups were done, and you know what? We're getting along *so* much better now."

Casey nodded. "I'm glad. That was really smart of you."

"I know! Who knew?" The PA brightened. "Maybe I *will* have a career in showbiz after all. I seem to have a knack for it!"

After a few words to Kristen about her "fab pie!" and other "awesome" menu items—including a request for one of Kristen's top-secret recipes—the PA headed outside into the snow.

"All right. That's a nice outcome," Kristen told Casey. "But I still don't see how creating harmony among the production crew is supposed to put Heather's show back on track."

"How else would I do it?" Casey looked truly mystified.

"I don't know . . . make them work harder?"

He laughed. "Is that what you do here at the diner? You just crack the whip and expect everyone to fall in line?"

This time, it was Kristen's turn to laugh. "Not exactly."

"Problems don't exist in a vacuum. Neither do solutions."

"Neither do 'fixers,'" Kristen pointed out. "Or anti-fixers. Even if Shane Maresca is as bad as you say he is"—and she still had her doubts—"he's probably not working alone," she reasoned. "After all, *you're* not. Not technically. You have me, and your new Galaxy Diner fan club, and all my friends. You're not alone. Everyone is falling all over themselves to help you—"

Casey only frowned, looking peculiarly fearsome.

"—including everyone on the set of Heather's holiday TV special. Unless . . ." Kristen went motionless as something else occurred to her. "What if it's *not* Shane at all—"

"You really have a thing for him, don't you?" Casey grumbled. "I promise you, he's not worth your goodwill."

"—and someone on the *production* is sabotaging things?"

"That wouldn't make you feel better about it."

"It would make me feel better about liking Shane."

Heaving a sigh, Casey shook his head. "You're really going to make me do this, aren't you?"

"Do what?"

"Defend Maresca. On purpose."

"You have to consider all the options, don't you?"

"Once I saw that jerkface, the options narrowed considerably."

Kristen smiled. "Says you."

"These problems didn't start out of the blue," Casey argued. "Someone has been deliberately causing trouble on set for a while now. The trouble began with location and wardrobe issues and is continuing now with interpersonal conflicts and oddball delays. Whoever's at fault, they've been doing a pretty effective job of exploiting typical onset problems."

"Making mountains out of molehills?"

"Exactly. Just like Shane would do, as someone who's intimately familiar with these things. Turning small problems—like that PA's lack of confidence or her boss's sloppy divorce or the rigging crew's ongoing lighting dispute—into big ones is the no-brainer way to create a believable disruption."

"Or to turn a promising holiday TV special into a troubled one," Kristen surmised, worried now that if Casey *didn't* help her sister, Heather's TV special would be history for sure. "All it would take," she went on, "are a few well-placed rumors and a detailed knowledge of the people involved to stir up trouble."

"The kind of trouble that would lead to the production being canceled and the company collecting the insurance money."

But Kristen wasn't ready to go with that theory. "Shane wouldn't have enough knowledge of the people involved to *really* stir up trouble," she guessed. "Not at first, at least—"

"You'd be surprised how quickly we can get up to speed."

"But an *insider* would know all those things. Right?"

At Casey's reluctant nod, Kristen felt a total rush.

She was right! Maybe. No wonder Casey liked his job. Figuring out problems this way was surprisingly engaging.

Feeling like Watson to his sexy Sherlock, Kristen asked, "But why wreck the special? These are people's jobs! Surely whoever's at fault doesn't want to risk winding up unemployed."

Casey made a face. Maybe he'd spotted another sidewalk Santa. "Evidently, someone feels their job isn't at risk."

"Well, the only person who fits that description—"

Is Heather, Kristen realized with a jolt. Her brainstorming fun came to an abrupt end as she realized it was true. Her sister probably *was* the only person on the entire *Live! from the Heartland* set whose job was immune from being cut. She was the only one who was essential to the holiday special's success.

Suddenly, Kristen wished she hadn't leaped to Shane Maresca's defense. No matter how friendly he'd been. She hadn't expected her alternate theory to point straight at her sister.

"—must already know that *you're* in town now, ready to raise hell and take names," she prevaricated, unwilling to reveal her potential suspicions of Heather. They were still sisters. Kristen owed her that much loyalty, at least. But, all of a sudden, Heather's "quarantine" *did* seem twice as convenient.

"Are you sure everyone you've dealt with is one hundred percent susceptible to your manipulation technique?" Kristen asked, suddenly hoping they *were*. "Because otherwise—"

"It's *not* a 'manipulation technique'!" Casey broke in, looking aggrieved. "You have got to stop calling it that."

"Hey, I like to call a spade a spade."

"And you look damn sexy while doing it," he agreed roughly. "But you're killing me here. *I'm* not the bad guy."

She shrugged. "I like to come to my own conclusions."

"And you've already decided the worst about me?"

On the verge of admitting that *of course* she hadn't decided anything about Casey (because honestly, who could have?) except that she wanted very much to know if he slept in the nude, if he preferred Guinness or Budweiser, if he liked her as much as she liked him, and if there was any chance he *hadn't* seen Heather's sex tape, Kristen hesitated. Why did Casey seem so upset? Just because she'd said he manipulated people? He was The Terminator!

This couldn't be the first time he'd come face-to-face with his own dubious conciliation techniques—but it *was* the first time Kristen had seen him looking so troubled. Granted, the major signs of his distress were a single ticking muscle in his jaw and a certain hard-edged glimmer to his eyes, but still . . .

"At least give me a chance to change your mind," he said.

Kristen considered it. "How?"

Cheering up, Casey angled his head toward the back of the diner. "Let's go in your office," he suggested. "I'll try to 'manipulate' you, and you tell me how you feel about it."

"Why can't you do that out here?" she wanted to know.

"Because I can't," Casey said vaguely. "But if you still think I'm a Machiavellian jerk afterward, I won't complain."

She examined him. "This sounds like a trap."

"Only if you're worried about being too easily led."

The very idea was ludicrous. "*I'm* not worried. *I* know my own mind," Kristen said. "I have the advantage of knowing what you're doing, too, so I don't see how—"

"You're stalling." His too-astute gaze challenged her.

Unfortunately, being challenged was catnip to an independent-minded person like her. "You're goading me. It won't work."

"It's already worked."

Darn it. He was right. "Fine," Kristen said. "Let's do it."

They both slid out of the booth. Casey left his things; she took a quick glance around the diner to make sure everything was still under control. It was, but her reflex to make sure only reminded her of what Casey had said earlier.

Most people like to think they're in control . . .

Well, she *was* in control, Kristen told herself. Especially here, in her own diner, her unofficial home away from home.

Partway to her office, she realized she ought to try to prepare herself—just in case Casey really *was* as dangerous as Heather seemed to think. After all, she'd seen him convince people of some pretty unlikely things over the past few days.

What if he manipulated her into thinking that changing her menu was a good idea? Or becoming convinced that the only thing standing between her and the Tour de France was a better grade of Schwinn than her existing vintage cruiser? Or believing (like him) that Christmas was an overcommercialized waste of time?

"Hey." Kristen tapped him. "What are you going to try—" *Manipulating me into?* No, she couldn't say that. Otherwise they'd be stuck arguing semantics all day. "Convincing me of?"

"That's easy." Cheerfully, Casey glanced over his shoulder at her. "I'm going to persuade you to abandon your litmus test."

At that, Kristen stopped. "My litmus test?"

"Yeah. The one that dictates who you're interested in sleeping with." Casey gave her a faux innocent look. "Or do you have more than one? Because that's the one I'm targeting."

Oh boy. "Nope. Just the one!" Kristen said.

Then she edged in front of Casey and took the lead. Because while her own big, fat mouth might have gotten her into this fix, she was determined that Casey wasn't going to get her out of it. Not on his terms, at least. Not today.

Chapter 13

Galaxy Diner
17 mixing, piping, cookie-spritzing, chocolate-dipped days until Christmas

Walden first realized that he might be getting serious about Talia when he started having withdrawal symptoms.

After several exhilarating days of sneaking around Kismet, dressed as Heather Miller and her boyfriend du jour, and making out everyplace they were likely to be spotted and photographed, Talia and he had been forced—because of Heather's chicken-pox quarantine—to cool it. After all, not even divalicious pop stars could be in two places at once. And everyone knew, thanks to an overconfiding *In Touch* cover story, that Heather was communicably ill. So Walden had, grudgingly, agreed to put a hold on his new favorite off-hours activity: being with Talia.

It wasn't easy, though. Especially since they still worked together. Being near Talia and not being able to touch her was like starving while sitting atop an uncrackable vault full of caramel pecan pie and bourbon whipped cream. It was giving him the shakes. It was making him antsy and needy and distracted.

The worst part was, it wasn't the making out that Walden

missed most. It was *her*. It was Talia. He missed her smile
and her laugh and her smart-mouthed comments. He missed
her cute little wiggly walk when she sneaked around a corner
to pinpoint a paparazzo. He missed her touch—and not just
her sexy touch, either. He missed her tender touch, too . . .
like when she fixed his collar or tugged his dreads to tease
him or held his hand.

Walden didn't know how he was supposed to survive
losing that. Every day, he saw Talia doing something endearing and sexy, like delivering maple syrup to table three or
reaching into the rotating pie case for a jar of peppermint
chocolate mousse pie with candy cane sprinkles. Or—as was
the case just then—innocently stepping into the diner's walk-
in refrigerator at the same time Walden was there to bring out
some eggs.

"Oh! Walden! Hi!" Talia turned her cerulean gaze on him.
Skittishly, she took a step forward. "Um, how's it going?"

"Better now." Walden stepped forward, too. It had been
hours since they'd last touched one another. He could think of
little else. He couldn't remember what he'd come into the
walk-in for. He could only gawk at her. Yearningly. "I miss
you."

"You don't have to say that." Talia picked up a stainless
steel tub full of prepped sage-garlic butter. She hugged it to
her middle like a shield. "There aren't any cameras here."

"You look great," he said. "I like your skirt."

"*Everyone* wears this skirt," she protested in her usual
wry tone. "It's identical to the ones that Kristen and Avery
wear."

"And those boots. Those boots are sexy."

"Again." Talia rolled her eyes . . . but her cheeks took on
a pretty pink glow. "They're the same boots everyone else
has."

"Maybe. They look different on you."

"Only because you're myopic." She seemed to forget the

compound butter in her arms. "Did you forget your contact lenses today? Because you're looking at me kind of cross-eyed."

That was probably true. "I'm imagining you in my arms."

"Oh." A winsome smile spread over Talia's face. "It's too bad we agreed not to do any more 'practicing' here at work."

Avery had nearly caught them during their first make-out session. They'd decided, since then, to limit their Heather/boy toy run-throughs to other locales. Just to be circumspect.

"I'm imagining you," Walden went on as if she hadn't spoken, hearing a certain husky tone roughen his voice, "wearing those boots and that skirt while I make love to you standing up, right here in the walk-in. It's pretty cold in here, but *that* would definitely warm us up."

"What about my tights?" Talia inquired. "And my panties? They'd be in the way," she pointed out practically, "so you couldn't technically warm up either of us without more effort."

He stifled a grin, loving—despite everything—that she'd chosen that moment to be contrary. It was just like . . . *her*.

"It's a fantasy," he said. "Try to roll with it."

"Aha." At that, she brightened, getting in sync with him instantly. "On the other hand, this *is* a pretty private place. And we *could* be quick about it. And we *could* use the practice." Decisively, Talia set the container of sage-garlic butter on the shelf. "Just hang on. I'll go get the wig."

He thought they'd been over this. "You don't need the wig!"

I want you as you, Walden thought. *Not as pretend Heather.*

But Talia didn't even slow down. He didn't know why—the timing of their "fling," maybe, or the fact that it had taken him so long to let Talia know he liked her—but she seemed under the impression he *only* wanted her now that she was "Heather."

Walden wasn't even sure she heard him. By the time he said anything, Talia was already ducking out of the walk-in, clearly on a mission to enable their spur-of-the-moment quickie. It was almost as if she'd come there on purpose, Walden realized, looking for *him*. Wouldn't that have been great?

But he didn't know if Talia wanted him . . . or a "boy toy," either. After all, she hadn't liked him until their Heather ruse had started. Maybe she just wanted to be thoroughly practiced up for whenever Heather finally got out of chicken-pox quarantine.

A minute later, Talia was back, sporting her long blond Heather wig. At the sight of it, Walden felt an obvious pang. He liked her real lavender hair. He liked *her*.

"I really care about you, Talia." Earnestly, he reached for her wig, dying to take it off. "To me, this is more than just—"

A fling, he wanted to say.

But she interrupted before he could.

"Shut up and kiss me." Intently, Talia grabbed his chef's whites in both hands. She hauled him closer. Their bodies crashed together. "Before Gareth realizes I'm gone."

"But I wasn't suggesting a quickie!" Walden said. "It just popped into my head and straight out my mouth. I couldn't help it. I'm impulsive like that. But I was only having fun."

"What do you think I'm doing?" Talia kissed him. Eagerly, she rubbed against him. "Solving trigonometry problems?"

Uhhh. Just then, she was driving him crazy.

"I didn't mean we should get busy right here next to the mustard-seed aioli," he managed to say between breaths. "It's not very romantic."

"Romance is overrated." She unbuttoned his chef's jacket. Her hands delved beneath his T-shirt underneath it, then flexed against his bare chest. "But *you're* not overrated," she purred. "You're even better than I expected. Who knew you were so *hot?*"

"Not in here, I'm not hot. Brr," Walden joked, trying desperately to slow down the Nookie Express before he forgot how to speak altogether. "It's just that I've realized some really major things lately. About us. When I saw you just now, I'd missed you *so* much, and I knew that could only mean—"

"Prove it." Determinedly, Talia unzipped his pants. She delved her hand inside. "Prove you missed me. I want you to, Walden," she urged. "Come on. Be my bohemian boy toy."

Helplessly, Walden groaned. He wanted to communicate to Talia that he needed to be *more* than that to her. That he wanted this to be *real* between them. That they should probably have a serious conversation. Soon. But with her tongue in his mouth and her hand zeroing in on his own personal sweet spot, he could barely think, much less speak coherently about relationships.

Valiantly, he tried again. "I love . . ."

You, Walden wanted to say. Instead, he only panted.

Talia chose to interpret that as an invitation to caress him. Suspended between pleasure and tender emotion, he closed his eyes, trying to find enough fortitude to poetically profess his love for her without simultaneously dry humping her. That wouldn't have had the necessary gravitas. The necessary *love*.

But it wasn't working. Talia was just that good. Her touch took every lucid thought he had and scattered it to the wind.

Giving up, Walden opened his eyes. When he did, he focused on Talia's sweet face—and for a heartbeat, he *knew* he glimpsed comprehension there . . . and a certain reciprocal feeling, too.

Was it possible? Did Talia love him, too?

"*This,*" she finished for him, breathlessly. She kissed his neck. His mouth. His neck again. "Me too! I love this, too."

Transfixed by what he'd seen, Walden went still.

Talia loved him. It was everything he'd ever wanted.

Then she flung her long, blond, fake tresses over her shoulder, reminding him of her insistence on wearing that

damn Heather wig, and Walden knew it was more complicated than just loving him. *Talia* was more complicated than
just loving him.

Otherwise, they wouldn't have been getting it on in a
superchilly walk-in refrigerator, surrounded by plastic-
wrapped foodstuffs, all for the sake of not being caught
together.

At the realization, he shuddered. He had to change this.

"Are you still cold?" Talia felt his tremor and completely
misinterpreted it. She winked. "I know how to warm you up."

Then she tossed down her apron for an impromptu cushion. She gave him a uniquely tenderhearted smile. Then she
dropped to her knees and quickly made Walden forget everything he knew about . . .

Well, pretty much *everything* in the universe that didn't
involve her mouth, his body, and the wonderful things that
happened when the two of them came together.

With a sense of steely resolve, Casey followed Kristen
into her tiny office in the back of her gas-station-turned-
diner.

He watched her march with swivel-hipped, tomboyish
élan through the Christmassy chaos in the front of the house,
usher him inside her private sanctuary, and then close the
door behind them. He watched her prop her hip on the edge
of her desk. He watched her cross her arms, take a deep
breath, then nod at him.

"All right. I'm ready," she said. "Take your best shot. Make
me abandon my litmus test. *If* you really think you can."

Uh-oh, Casey realized. It was even worse than he'd
thought.

Kristen seemed convinced he was exactly the kind of manipulative, semishady con man she'd accused him of being a
few minutes ago. Judging by her uplifted chin and I-dare-

you expression, it wouldn't be easy to change her mind, either.

But that's how Casey knew he had to try. Because with that single gesture, Kristen communicated to him something he'd already begun to suspect . . . but hadn't wanted to acknowledge.

Kristen was *perfect* for him. Despite all the Christmas brouhaha. Despite the inconvenience factor of her pop-star sister. Despite the fact that she came as a matched set with an unnerving diner-based family of lovable nonconformists. Despite all those things, Casey couldn't stop thinking about her.

He needed her. He wanted her. He might even . . .

Well, he couldn't say he *loved* her. He wasn't completely sure what that meant. He didn't know what it felt like.

If love felt like finding it captivating when Kristen tried on stuffed-felt reindeer antlers and modeled them for the regulars . . . Casey had it.

If love felt like seeing a goofy, spangled, made-in-China piece of craptastic "holiday décor," thinking that Kristen might like it, and then secretly buying it for her . . . Casey had it.

(He might also have had some sort of psychological break while experiencing that one, because he'd actually touched a Christmas ornament, *on purpose*, then paid for it.)

But he had to move on.

Because if love meant hearing a song and wishing Kristen could hear it too, because it described his feelings for her in a lyrical-but-impossible-to-say way . . . Casey had it. He had it bad.

And he was starting to fear that Kristen didn't.

Worse, that she never would.

Because he was him, and she was her, and the two of them, together . . . Well, the two of them together would be fantastic, if only they could get over a few of the hurdles first. And the first and most daunting of those hurdles was Kristen herself.

Frankly, Casey had seen plastic mannequins at the department store look more malleable than she did just then.

Not cutting him any slack—and thereby proving herself his perfect woman *again*—Kristen arched her eyebrow. "Can't do it?"

"Oh, I can do it," Casey assured her. But his usual mojo didn't seem to be working. With her, it sometimes didn't.

Damn it.

All those years of moving from home to home, of struggling to understand his new environment and somehow ingratiate himself within it, of working his ass off to be the best possible kid—they all felt like wasted time right now. Sure, they'd paid dividends in Casey's ability to go anywhere and get along with anyone at the drop of a hat. But with Kristen, things were different. They were more important. They were essential.

Why hadn't she been able to see the real him? Casey wondered as he took another look at her, still feeling vaguely upset by what she'd said about him. Why hadn't she been able to look past what he did for a living to who he was on the inside?

The fact that she hadn't had hurt. It still did.

So far, Christmas in Kismet was one big carnival of pain.

Because of that, Casey wanted to leave. Instead, he stepped closer to Kristen. Because sometimes, he knew, the only way to get out was to go through. Sometimes the things that scared you most were exactly the things you needed. And Casey Jackson was nothing if not brave. His entire life had taught him to be.

"You can 'do it,' huh?" Kristen asked, breaking into his thoughts. She glanced at the wall clock. "If you'd quit with the double entendres, we might get somewhere with this."

Except it hadn't been a double entendre, Casey knew. It had been a heartfelt expression of his most fervent and most closely held wish.

Oh, I can do it. I can make you want me, Casey had wanted to tell her.

But he hadn't. Not outright. And *that's* when he realized the truth. It nearly bowled him over, too. Kristen had never seen the real him because he'd never shown her the real him. He'd limited their conversations to innuendo and flirtatious banter and quests for information about Heather's TV special.

He'd treated Kristen, he realized, just like everyone else.

When she couldn't have been more different. From everyone.

So, dredging up every ounce of bravado he had, Casey showed her the real him instead. He hoped like hell she'd approve.

He started by gazing at her. "I like you," he said.

As though he'd announced that he liked to spend his spare time training monkeys to juggle, she gave a cautious nod.

"I like you, too."

"You're unlike anyone I've ever known," he added earnestly.

"I'll assume that's a good thing," she countered, "since you're trying to seduce me into sleeping with you right now."

Casey blinked. "Is that what you think? That all I want to do is sleep with you?"

"That's what you implied a few minutes ago," she reminded him. "Why else would you mess with my litmus test?"

"Well," he hedged, "I *do* want to sleep with you—"

But there's so much more to it than that. He just didn't know how to explain it. He'd never had to try before. Usually, if he'd been alone with a woman for this long, one or both of them would have been ripping off each other's clothes already.

"Wow. You do?" At his helplessly deliberative tone, Kristen gave him a sardonic grin. "Hold me back."

Geez. She was going to make this hard for him, Casey thought. Didn't she know he was new at this stuff? He was new at being sincere, new at being emotional, new at *needing* someone the way he needed her. But just when he'd braced himself for a tough fight, Kristen made things unexpectedly easy on him.

She got up from her desk, then gave him a deliberately provocative once-over. "Seriously. Hold me back."

"Huh?"

"I've been dying to kiss you for days."

Casey's head spun. This wasn't what he'd expected.

"You can stop pretending to be nervous now." Smiling, she took a step closer. "You did it. You made me want you."

He hadn't been pretending. He really was nervous—nervous because he'd just realized this *meant* something.

"I didn't do anything yet," Casey protested.

"*Exactly*. You didn't have to."

"You're not making sense."

She shrugged. "That must be the lust talking."

No, no. This was all going off the rails. Casey wanted to explain to Kristen how much he cared about her. He couldn't get sidetracked with lust. No matter how tempting the idea was.

"Right," he said. "About that lust thing—"

"My litmus test is overrated," Kristen interrupted, surrendering faster than he'd ever dreamed, coming close enough to trail her fingers seductively down his chest. "I think we should go for it right here, in my office. My desk is free."

"Actually, I have something more romantic planned," Casey told her, backpedaling now, trying not to envision both of them naked and panting atop her paperwork, beside her logoed Galaxy Diner mug. "So—"

"So that can wait until later, right?" Smiling up at him, she toyed with the crewneck of his cable-knit sweater as though considering whether to strip it off him or just make it unravel on its own to suit her seduction plan. Her miniskirt-clad hips swayed suggestively nearer to his hips, scrambling his thoughts.

"Right," Casey parroted. "It can wait until later."

Wait. What was he doing? Besides getting incredibly over-heated in the thick sweater, button-down shirt, thermal underlayer, and warm wool pants he'd put on as protection against the freezing, finger-numbing Kismet winter weather?

"No, it can't wait," he tried again. He caught hold of Kristen's wrists, then held them close against his chest. It wasn't easy. Her kittenish pout made him want to set her loose immediately to touch him however and wherever and for as long as she wanted to. "I need to tell you something."

"If it's anything besides 'take off your clothes,' save it for later."

"Something important."

"Is it 'I'm taking off *my* clothes'?" She sent her gaze roving over him again. "Because I'd like that, too."

Spotting the wicked gleam in her eyes, Casey didn't doubt it. He looked down at her impish face, her restive hands, her arresting mouth . . . and loved them all. There was one thing he could say for Kristen: he didn't have to wonder what she was thinking. Every opinion she had came trotting out, sooner or later, to fascinate him or befuddle him or make him want to know more.

He was glad she was more than equal to keeping up with him. He respected and admired her for that. Brainstorming the potential causes of the issues with Heather's holiday TV special with Kristen had been invigorating. Casey wished, just then, he had her with him to help on all his jobs.

But that was work . . . and this most definitely was pleasure.

Or at least it would be, once he'd set things right.

"I don't want our first time together to be here in your office," he told her gruffly, "next to an industrial kitchen supplies catalog."

Kristen swept the offending catalog off her desk. Wearing a smart-alecky grin, she lounged near the place where it had been.

"All better now." She kicked away the catalog for good measure, sending it sliding under a chair. "So how about it?"

"I don't want it to be where someone could walk in on us, either."

She locked her office door. Pertly, she faced him. "There. All fixed."

"I think you have a future as a troubleshooter."

"Really? You do?" She flashed a knowing grin. "That's a pretty lame effort in the 'manipulation' department, I've got to say. Complimenting me on locking a door?" She strolled nearer, waggling her hands. "Whoopee! I have opposable thumbs. Is that all you've got? Because so far, I think I'm winning."

"You're not winning."

"Oh no? Because from where I'm standing, I'm winning."

"You're not winning," Casey insisted, "because I'm not done playing."

Talking wasn't working. Being responsible wasn't working.

Kristen was expecting another bout of "manipulation" from him. The only thing that would work, he decided, was action.

So he hauled in a deep breath, strode over to where Kristen stood, then took a long, deliberate, undoubtedly smitten look at her. He cupped her face in his palms. He stroked his thumbs over her cheeks, savoring the softness of her skin, the unique arrangement of her features, the wonderful *her-ness* of her face.

"Pay attention," Casey said, "because I'm only going to do this once."

He saw the smart-ass rebuttal leap to her mind. He saw the additional thought—as Kristen looked more carefully at him—that shut it down. He saw her breathe in . . . then nod.

"Okay," she said. "Do it."

He smiled. "If I could only do one more thing in my life," he said, "this would be it."

Then he brought his mouth nearer to hers, inhaled another

breath, and just . . . *felt* her. He felt her tension and her eagerness. He felt her sweetness and her needfulness. He felt her body lean toward his, felt her warmth reach out to meet him, felt her breath flow out to meet his.

It wasn't a kiss. Not yet.

But it was everything else Casey needed. It was Kristen, with him. It was her face in his hands and her heart within reach. It was nearness and possibility and wild, heady desire.

Questioningly, Kristen angled her head the merest inch upward. Her hands grasped fistfuls of his sweater; her booted feet crowded against his. It was close and not close enough. It was more than he'd ever dreamed, and he meant to take even more.

"I can't wait to be with you," Casey said, finally bringing his mouth near enough. He brushed his lips against hers.

Gratifyingly, Kristen gasped. So he did it again.

"I need you to know that," he added, keeping his mouth against hers as he spoke. The texture of her mouth made him dizzy; the warmth of their mingling breath made him lean closer.

"I need you like apple pie needs à la mode," he went on, grinning at his own daffy analogy but liking it anyway. It was more apt than she knew. He *loved* her baked goods. But that was his own secret to keep—just one of many. Bringing his mouth to hers again, he closed his eyes and offered another slow, luxurious glide across her lips. "You feel . . . *so* good."

With an incoherent sound, Kristen crowded closer, but Casey resisted the urge to deepen their kiss. It wasn't time for that. Not yet. First he needed to show her that he meant this.

So he bided his time by gently biting her lip, by giving her another slow, soft kiss . . . by tracing his tongue just over the seam of her lips. The sensation made him feel drunk with need.

"Casey—" Kristen gasped, but he wasn't done yet.

"I thought nothing could come close to the way I imagined

this moment," he said, flexing his fingers against her jaw to hold her steady for his next tender kiss. Kristen wiggled a lot, he noticed, when he flicked his tongue to meet hers. She panted and clutched his clothes and did everything except climb on top of him. All because he truly delighted in kissing her. "But you're everything I've ever wanted and more. You're amazing."

"Mmm." She wriggled enticingly again. Impatiently, she grabbed his head. "*You're* the amazing one. Are your lips drugged or something? Because I've *got* to have more."

Kristen levered upward and pressed her mouth to his, taking charge of their kiss herself. This time, Casey was the one who gasped. He abandoned his hold on her jaw to wrap his arms around her waist. He pulled her against him, then deepened their next kiss. With gratifying eagerness, Kristen pressed both hands to the back of his head and held him there. She moaned while their mouths came together again. Again. *Again*.

Kissing her felt like the key to the universe, like the answer to every question Casey had ever had, and if she hadn't kissed him back, he felt pretty sure he would have stopped existing altogether. Because this was necessary. It was now. It was mouths and tongues and heat and wetness, and he didn't care that her desk jabbed him in the ass and that cornball Christmas music kept playing outside, vaguely filtering through her office door, and that the location was neither romantic nor ideal for making an impressive seductive move. Because he wasn't trying to seduce her. He was trying to tell her, with words and kisses and the most hard-to-control touching he'd engaged in for years, that he needed her and wanted her and cared for her.

Wide-eyed, Kristen leaned back. Her pupils were huge, her expression thrilled and surprised at once. "Yeah. Like that."

"It's good," Casey agreed in a husky voice. "*So* good." He twined her hands in his. He gave her a squeeze. "Which is why it has to end here. Because I don't know how much more I can take—"

"I can think of a good way to find out."

"—and you mean too much to me to go on this way."

She gave him a puzzled look. "Huh?"

With tremendous effort, Casey pulled away. The few inches of fresh air he placed between them felt almost impossible to achieve, but he did it. "I have to leave now."

"You're not serious." Kristen gawked. "*Now?* But I locked the door. I kicked away the catalog. I—" She frowned, then crossed her arms. "This doesn't usually happen to me. Usually I'm *really* good at spur-of-the-moment casual encounters."

Casey couldn't help smiling at her. "Then that's where the problem lies," he said, letting himself reach up to caress her cheek one more time. "Because this *isn't* a casual encounter."

He leaned in for a final kiss, hauled in a deep breath for fortitude . . . then unlocked her office door and walked back into the Christmasville diner, hoping like hell he wasn't making a huge mistake by leaving Kristen behind in the process.

Chapter 14

It took Kristen almost fifteen minutes to pull herself together after Casey left her in her office at the diner. She needed another hour or so before she quit remembering his kisses and breaking out in spontaneous goose bumps. But despite all that, by the time she arrived at the Kismet Senior Center that evening for their annual Christmas Disco Night, she still hadn't been able to get Casey's parting words out of her mind.

Then that's where the problem lies, he'd said with absolute conviction. *Because this isn't a casual encounter.*

But it *had* to be a casual encounter, Kristen knew. That's why she'd decided, spontaneously, to abandon her litmus test.

Because there couldn't be anything else between her and Casey except a casual encounter. She still didn't know if she could trust him. She still wasn't sure if Casey was only using her to get to Heather. And she still didn't want to get close to somebody from her sister's glammed-up showbiz world, either.

Because if she did, inevitably, the comparisons would

start. Then the disappointment would set in. Eventually, things would end badly. It was the only way the scenario could play out.

After all, *her own parents* couldn't seem to see Kristen whenever Heather's overwhelming, glittery shadow got in the way, Kristen reminded herself. Their canceled Christmas plans with her, multiple media interviews about Heather, and time spent on their @Heather_Hotline Twitter account—when they were *supposed* to have been (traditionally) Christmas shopping and cookie baking and wrapping gifts with Kristen—were proof enough of that.

Could Kristen realistically expect Casey to spot her, *Where's Waldo?*-style, and then to stick with her, when he'd encountered her showier, more celebrated sister first?

No, Kristen reminded herself as she skirted a snowbank, opened the evergreen-wreath-festooned double glass doors of the Kismet Senior Center building, and stepped inside. *She couldn't expect that. Not from Casey or anyone.* She followed the sounds of kitschy 1970s Christmas music down the corridor toward the rec center, knowing that while she might be a fantastic person in her own right—and she *was*, damn it—to anyone who'd met Heather first, Kristen was an also-ran. End of story.

She'd come to terms with that a long time ago. There was no point mulling over the roads not taken on her own personal Google map of life now. All she could do was go forward.

The only mistake she'd made with Casey, Kristen decided further, had been underestimating him. When they'd headed into her office together, she'd actually thought she could beat him at his own game. She wouldn't be making that same mistake again.

But she *would* be getting more than a few mind-bending kisses from him tonight. She could guarantee that. Because she hadn't thrown over her litmus test for nothing. She wanted more. More more more. And she wanted to prove to herself that this *was* a casual encounter between them. Not that it wouldn't also be good, Kristen knew. It would be good and steamy and hot hot hot. Because if there was one thing she was drop-dead certain about when it came to Casey, it was that he . . .

. . . was a *Boogie Nights*-caliber disco dancer?

Boggling at the unexpected sight before her, Kristen stopped inside the rec room's doorway. Beyond it, a disco ball spun from the ceiling, splashing multicolored shards of light on the garland-swagged walls and light-festooned crown molding. In one corner stood a tall, fancifully decorated Christmas tree; in another, a handmade crèche held a place of prominence. In between them, people crowded in groups of fours and fives. They clustered at the refreshments table. They grooved on the dance floor. They chatted near the makeshift DJ booth where Gareth was currently bopping his headphone-adorned head, making the long strings on his Nordic knit trapper hat wave to and fro.

But Kristen noticed all those details only in the most subliminal way. Because in the middle of everything, surrounded by smiling, dance-happy seniors and the seniors' family members and several regulars and staff from the Galaxy Diner, was Casey.

Seeing him there, unselfconsciously making like John Travolta in *Saturday Night Fever* with two laughing, gray-haired septuagenarian ladies for partners, Kristen just . . . *melted*. Those were not the actions of a Terminator. Casey didn't have a single thing to gain by charming two elderly senior center residents. He was simply . . . *generous,* Kristen realized. He might not want to admit it—and in fact, he'd probably actively deny it—but she couldn't think of another word to describe it. Casey was . . . *nice*.

He was dancing to a deep cut from a disco-era holiday novelty album. He was laughing and doing that goofy pointing gesture. And he seemed to be enjoying himself while doing it.

If that wasn't nice, Kristen didn't know what was.

And sure, so it was also *improbable*. Especially from him. But that's why she found herself feeling so enthralled while she watched him. Casey didn't care if he looked silly. Because of that, he *didn't* look silly. He looked . . . completely endearing.

Smiling helplessly, Kristen went on watching him. She watched as he carefully spun around one of the spry senior ladies, then adroitly dipped the other. They both beamed.

"*This* is the single greatest Kismet Senior Center Christmas Disco Night ever," Avery enthused, coming to stand beside Kristen with a paper cup of eggnog in her hand. She nodded at Casey. "Did you see Casey out there? He's got some moves!"

Kristen nodded. Now several of the other ladies were dancing nearer to him, energetically waving their wrinkled and bejeweled hands, evidently deciding to share him, en masse, as a partner for anyone who was dancing. Given the ratio of female to male senior-center residents, that was a sound strategy. Faces alight with enjoyment, they all gave in to holiday disco fever.

In the center of the crowd, Casey executed a spin move. Spontaneous applause broke out. Hammily, Casey did it again.

Kristen laughed, feeling her heart expand even further. *This* Casey was more than a man who kissed her senseless. He touched her on a deeper level than that. He made her want . . .

More. More than she usually dared to reach for.

Because while her ordinary-girl life was pretty great, it was sometimes lacking a few things. Like a more intimate connection with someone who didn't work with her, hadn't had desk sex with her, and had actually woken up beside her, bedhead and all (rather than being unceremoniously ushered out the night before on the pretense of her needing a good night's sleep).

Maybe, Kristen thought, her mania for Christmas was really an undercover desire to inject some specialness into her life—a tactic she tried exactly once every year, then quit pursuing for the other eleven months that remained.

But with Casey, she mused, maybe she could have more.

Maybe she could have something as wonderful as Christmas on a regular basis. Maybe she could have . . . *love?* Did she dare try?

It was a lot to ask. Usually, Kristen didn't even let herself feel the loneliness that sneaked into her life, making it feel a little rough around the edges. Instead, she stayed busy with work and pie and Drunk Yahtzee night. She stayed *her*.

Defiantly her. *Not* Heather her.

Just . . . *her,* for better or worse.

"*And* Talia and Walden," Avery went on, breaking into Kristen's thoughts as she nodded toward them. "Have you seen them? I mean, it's totally obvious they're knocking boots."

Shocked out of her musings, Kristen stared. "Huh?"

"Talia and Walden." Avery gestured toward their position on the dance floor, where they bumped and grinded amid the seniors. "It's practically *Dirty Dancing* out there. I'm afraid if Gareth plays a slow song, they'll be doing a full-on Lambada."

"The forbidden dance?" Kristen joked in a pseudo Caribbean accent, swiveling her hips. "Walden and Talia? Come on. They're just having fun! I doubt the two of them are really—"

An item, she meant to say, but then she took another look—just as Walden gazed deeply and longingly into Talia's eyes—and Kristen was stunned into silence. Because next Talia smiled at her big, dreadlocked, grizzly bear of a partner . . . and her smile all but outshined the glittery holiday decorations and tinsel. It was just that starry-eyed and special and unmistakable.

It was, it occurred to Kristen, a lot like the smile she imagined *herself* sporting whenever she looked at Casey.

Whoa. This night held too many bombshells already.

Deciding to duck out on them all while she got a grip on herself, Kristen wielded her white baker's-box of goodies.

"I've got to deliver these mini pies to the refreshments table," she told Avery. "I'll talk to you later, okay?"

"Okay," her friend said in a hesitant tone, "but don't you want to dish about Walden and Talia? I mean, it's not every day that love dive-bombs into Kismet and hits our best friends!"

You don't know the half of it, Kristen thought. But by then she was already smiling and offering an apologetic wave, making her escape from everything she wasn't yet ready to deal with.

Moments later, Kristen found herself surrounded by lively senior-center residents, making conversation and discussing Christmas plans and doing what she usually did when serving people her baked goods: refusing requests to share her recipes.

"But I just can't figure out the secret ingredient!" one of the residents said, waving her fork. "You have to tell me."

"No, tell *me,*" someone else urged. "I'm a better baker."

"All I need is a good recipe," another resident added, "and I'll be able to bake my way into the heart of Mr. Room 22."

All the ladies *oohed* at that. "Good idea, Rose!"

Energized by their approval, Rose asked again for Kristen's recipe for milk chocolate French silk pie with crème anglaise and hazelnut-caramel crunch. Around them, the general clamor only increased as more residents pushed for her recipes. Kristen felt sorry to turn down everyone, but the plain truth was . . .

"My business depends on those secret recipes," she explained. "If I give them away, nobody will want to come to the Galaxy Diner. And if nobody wants to come to the Galaxy Diner—"

"The world will be a sadder place," someone broke in.

Surprised to hear a more youthful-sounding male voice amid the din, Kristen turned. Shane Maresca stood there, dressed in a soft-looking cashmere sweater, collared shirt, and pinstriped pants, looking as if he'd just stepped out of an ad for festive Christmas menswear. Even with his requisite beard stubble, tousled hair, and devil-may-care attitude, he didn't *seem* unscrupulous, Kristen thought. He seemed respectable. Polite. And possibly on the verge of making several elderly women swoon.

Evidently, Shane really *was* Casey's doppelganger. Because so far, the only other person who'd caused this much excitement among the residents of the Kismet Senior Center was Casey.

Who, she noticed, was still doing the hustle on the dance floor. Which left *her* free to deal with Shane on her own terms.

Which she fully intended to do—provided she could escape from the Betty Crocker Brigade and its recipe inquisition first, of course. Conveniently, Shane provided her the perfect excuse.

"Ladies, I'm afraid I'm going to have to steal away your favorite baking genius." Chivalrously, Shane caught hold of Kristen's elbow. He winked at her. "We have some business to discuss, and it just can't wait."

Amid the disappointed outcry his announcement caused, Shane swept her away. Christmas lights blinked around them. Gareth's holiday music kept up a hectic rhythm. Residents and friends waved and shouted hellos to Kristen as she passed by.

When they'd reached a more isolated corner, she turned to Shane, ready to drop their pretense of having "business" to conduct. "Thanks! Given another few minutes, I think they would have broken out some advanced grandma interrogation techniques, and then I would have *had* to have given them my recipes."

"I'm happy to help. You seemed in a bit of a bind." Shane gave a self-deprecating smile. "And there I was, looking for a damsel in distress to save. Besides, I totally get your wanting to protect your business. The Galaxy Diner is fantastic."

"Thanks! That's nice of you." And here she'd been—after her conversation with Casey—thinking Shane was evil, Kristen recalled guiltily. Taken aback by his obvious kindness, she nodded at him. "I'm a pushover for people who like my diner."

"Then you can add me to your fan club," Shane said with a twinkle in his eyes. "I hope you will. Because I'm a big fan."

Oh. He was *flirting* with her, Kristen realized belatedly. It figured. Just when she'd gotten her heart set on one probably unattainable guy, men were coming out of the woodwork to be with her. But she *wasn't* looking for a chance to chitchat with anyone just then, including handsome "anti-fixers" like Shane.

She'd come to the party—the way she did every year—to support Gareth and have a good time. Gareth's nana had been a resident at the senior center; over the years they'd been coming there to visit her, Kristen and Gareth and Talia and Avery (and lately, Walden) had become very fond of all the residents. Every year after Thanksgiving, they also hosted a get-together between the seniors and the kids from one of Kismet's elementary schools. It, like Christmas Disco Night, was a big hit.

"Thanks. And now that my top secret recipes are safe for the night," Kristen told Shane, opting for a get-out-fast approach, "I'm going to have to say good-bye. I have some people to see"—*before I sneak away with Casey to finish what we started in my office*—"and not much time to do it in."

"Wait." Compellingly, Shane touched her arm to stop her. "Before you go—has it occurred to you that if you license your baked goods and set up good distribution, you can reach millions more people than will ever visit your diner in person?"

Oh. Maybe Shane *wasn't* flirting with her. Maybe he was on-the-spot proselytizing her, with the bible of capitalism at his elbow. "Merry Christmas to you, too. It's a party, remember?"

He smiled. "I know. I shouldn't be talking business. But I'm an idea man at heart, and the idea I had when I heard your conversation with those women was too good not to share."

"You mean the licensing and distributing idea?"

Shane nodded. "If you play your cards right, *you* could be the *second* big success story to come out of this little burg."

"With the first being Heather, I'm assuming?"

Seeming on the verge of agreeing, Shane hesitated. He must have caught the sarcasm in her voice, because he changed tactics instantly. He seemed pretty confused, though.

You mean you don't want to morph into Heather Miller 2.0? his incredulous expression asked.

As if being an imitation *anyone* would be better than being the authentic *her*. Despite her faults, Kristen wanted to be *her*.

Why was that so difficult for everyone to understand? Did the *non-Kim* Kardashian sisters face this problem? Or just her?

"You could be the next Mrs. Fields," Shane tried again. "Of Mrs. Fields cookies fame? There's not a mall in America that doesn't have a Mrs. Fields cookie counter."

"Thanks," Kristen said, "but I'm not interested."

Her diner was *her* thing—her one thing that her famous sister wasn't part of. Kristen didn't want to give that up.

"Come on," Shane coaxed with an ingratiating smile— one that made several passersby swoon. "You haven't even thought about it yet! There's already been a gourmet cookie craze. A cinnamon roll fad. A fro-yo frenzy. A mania for cupcakes that went viral overnight. Who's to say your pies won't be the next big thing?"

"Technically?" Kristen crossed her arms. "I am."

His smile begged her to reconsider. Dazzlingly.

"You're a serious businesswoman," Shane said. "I respect that. Which is why I'm coming to you with this idea first."

"Who else would you come to?" Kristen wanted to know. "It's *my* baked goods you want to license and distribute."

Another grin. "Aha. You're a smart cookie."

"So I'm told."

"But you're not ready to sign on to this deal yet?"

At his cheerful doggedness, Kristen couldn't help smiling. She'd say one thing for Shane Maresca: he didn't quit easily.

"If I'm ever ready, you'll be the first to know. Okay?"

Shane nodded. "That's good enough for me. For now."

"It won't be anytime soon," she warned. "Maybe never."

"I've heard that before. Sometimes 'never' really means 'tomorrow, when conditions are right.' I promise you, I've got the connections to make this happen." Shane's confident demeanor almost made her a believer on the spot. "You just need the right incentive to bring you on board," he predicted. "Someday you'll be glad we had this conversation. I'm willing to bet on it."

"Oh yeah?" His certainty roused her natural sense of perversity. She just couldn't help it. Impulsively, Kristen eyed his outstretched hand. "I'll take that bet."

They shook on it. As their hands met, Kristen waited for lightning to strike, for the earth to move, for her heartbeat to jack up into the red zone the way it did when Casey touched her.

Nada. Interestedly, she released Shane's hand.

"Now I have a question for you," Kristen said. "What do you think of Heather's Christmas special?"

"I think it's going to be fabulous."

"Even given all its delays?"

Shane looked puzzled. "Every production experiences

delays. It's part of the business. Most production schedules build in a certain amount of wiggle room, expressly for that reason." He considered it a bit more. "As long as Heather's back on her feet in time to shoot the live performance sequences before Christmas Eve, I'd say things should be fine."

"Wow! You sound like an expert!" Kristen gushed. She gave him her most winning smile. "You know, it just occurred to me that you never told me exactly what your job is."

"I'm a consultant, like Casey," Shane said without hesitation. "I'm in town to bring *Live! from the Heartland* up to speed and across the finish line. I'm good at working with people, so—"

So that was exactly what Casey had told her, Kristen realized. But if his "anti-fixer" theory was correct, at least one of them wasn't telling the truth. She owed it to Heather to find out which one. *Not Casey, not Casey, not Casey.*

"Someone told me you're here to derail the production."

Shane frowned. "I'm guessing that 'someone' was Casey?"

Well, she'd never claimed to be skilled at subterfuge, Kristen told herself. Shane had seen right through her attempts to get more information. Caught, she glanced toward the dance floor. But she could no longer see Casey discoing in its center.

Surprised, she scrutinized the rec center. The party was in full swing now, with gifts being piled beneath the Christmas tree, music pumping from Gareth's speakers (currently, "Run, Run, Rudolph"), and more seniors cutting a rug.

Deliberately and determinedly, she looked back at Shane. "It doesn't matter who told me. I'm asking *you* face-to-face. Are you going to ruin my sister's TV special? Because it really means a lot to her. She's put in a lot of work already. And if everyone would just step off for a second and let her focus—"

Shane's smile broke into her dedicated defense. "If I were in town to cause trouble for Heather, would I be here hanging out with you? Wouldn't I be stirring up trouble on set instead?"

"You can't. Everyone's probably gone home by now."

He laughed. "You haven't spent much time down there, have you? Making a TV show is not necessarily a nine-to-five gig."

Kristen had no defense for that. She *hadn't* spent much time on the set of Heather's holiday TV special. "All the same—"

"All the same, you have nothing to worry about." Shane gave her a flattering look. "I admire your loyalty to your sister, Kristen, but you're looking in the wrong direction. I'm not the enemy." He scoured the rec center with a telling glance—a glance that suggested *Casey* was the enemy, not him. "Give some thought to that licensing deal, okay? I promise I'll be in touch."

Then, before Kristen could remind Shane that she wasn't interested—now or later—in his promises or in his licensing deal, he ducked into the crowd and disappeared from sight.

Chapter 15

It took all the forbearance Casey possessed not to stalk over to where Shane Maresca was looming smarmily over Kristen, drag him forcibly away from her, and then punch him in the face.

He figured his former best friend would look pretty good laid out on the rec-center floor with a black eye forming and maybe a tooth or two missing. It would only be poetic justice. Because Shane had caused a lot of trouble for a lot of people over the last decade or two of his life. It would be only fair if he experienced some of the pain he dished out for himself.

But then Casey saw Kristen shake hands with him. He saw her smile up at him. And he realized that, now more than ever, he could not resort to brute thuggery to get what he wanted. His days of using his fists to solve problems were behind him. He had to remember that . . . even if, somewhere in his caveman brain, he wanted to grab Kristen by her hair and haul her off someplace where they would finally be alone together long enough to enjoy . . . *everything* there was to enjoy about being alone together.

Before he could think about that, though, he had to deal with Shane. Because the only thing worse than having Shane in his face in full anti-fixer mode was having Shane lurking behind the scenes in stealth anti-fixer mode. Casey needed to get to Shane before he went underground—before he set in motion whatever underhanded schemes he'd arranged to derail Heather's TV special and then disappeared the way he always did.

So Casey waited until he saw Shane make his move. He tailed him through the jolly crowd of shimmying seniors. And he caught up with him outside, just as Shane was pulling out a pack of cigarettes. Shane tapped out a smoke, pulled out a lighter . . .

. . . and then found himself smacked against the fake garland and twinkling lights that adorned the senior center's exterior cinderblock fence. His body made a satisfying thud when it hit, too.

Okay. So maybe Casey *wasn't* quite over the brute force approach yet. He wasn't perfect. Or anywhere close to it.

"Hey!" Belligerently, Shane shoved him back. "Watch it."

Casey stumbled a few steps backward. He made fists.

Then Shane saw that it was Casey who'd followed him outside. His pugilistic attitude softened. He even grinned.

"Jesus, Casey! Lighten up with the bro-hugs, dude. You almost made me drop my cigarette." Shane raised that slender cylinder in demonstration, then propped it between his lips. His lighter flared. A few practiced motions later, his cigarette burned brightly, sending up tobacco smoke. "What's up?"

"That *wasn't* a 'bro-hug,'" Casey informed him, shoulders tense. "In case you hadn't noticed, we're not friends anymore."

"Yeah. It's hard to stay friends with someone who wants to kick your ass. Although God knows I've tried." Through a haze of cigarette smoke, Shane eyed him. He squinted, plucked a stray bit of tobacco off his lip, then flicked it toward the senior center's sidewalk. "About that 'friends' thing. I think we should—"

But Casey didn't want to hear it. He wished Shane had never brought it up. "I thought I told you to stay away from Kristen."

"You did." A shrug. "I said I'd think about it."

"Think harder," Casey advised.

His former friend's smile flashed at him. "Hey, girls like me. I can't help it. Am I supposed to hurt her feelings?"

"Am I supposed to believe *she* came on to *you?*"

"It's not beyond the realm of possibility." Shane drew deeply on his cigarette. He examined its glowing tip. "But since it's Christmastime and all, I'll do the generous thing—"

Casey chortled. As if Shane could ever be generous.

"—and let you know, before your inner Hulk comes out again, that Kristen and I were talking business. That's all."

"What kind of business?" Casey asked suspiciously.

"Personal business."

A growl forced its way from Casey's throat. He started. Since when had he become some sort of club-wielding Neanderthal?

Oh yeah. Since Kristen. Since he maybe-fell-in-love with Kristen. Since he started thinking they could have a future.

"Oh, calm down, He-Man." Shane laughed at Casey's undoubtedly murderous expression. He spread his arms in an ostensible show of harmless goodwill. "Your lady friend wants to set up a licensing deal to distribute and sell her baked goods nationwide. I guess she thought I could help with that somehow."

"Why would she think that?"

A shrug. "Maybe I look smart. Or connected. Or both."

"*I'm* smart. And connected." Too late, Casey heard the

aggrieved tone in his voice. Viciously, he tamped it down. Smoothly, he asked, "What did you tell her?"

"About the licensing and distribution deal?"

"No, about the true meaning of Christmas."

Another laugh. "Look, we both know I'm the wrong guy to try to put a deal *together*," Shane told him. "That's hardly my specialty." It was the closest he'd ever come to acknowledging his shady business practices. "All I can say is that Kristen seemed pretty keen to get in on something soon. Especially if—"

Abruptly, he quit talking. Casey glared at him. "If what?"

"Nah. I shouldn't say." In the multicolored glow of the damn twinkly holiday lights, Shane waved his cigarette. He took another deep drag. The smell of tobacco *almost* overpowered the ever-present Kismet-specialty gingerbread aroma that Casey had come (against his will) to enjoy all over town. *Almost*.

"I should get back inside," Shane said. "I promised one of those old coots I'd take a turn at calling Christmas bingo."

Casey narrowed his eyes. "Screw bingo," he said . . . only in much cruder terms. There was no need for subtlety between them.

"Fine." Shane rolled his eyes. Seeming resigned, he hunched against the cold. "If you're going to drag it out of me—"

"I could beat it out of you," Casey offered good-naturedly. He cracked his knuckles to prove it. "I'm pretty sure I have some lingering frustrations that need expressing."

Shane clucked in disapproval. "You should get some therapy for those anger issues, dude. Seriously. What's done is done. It was a long time ago!" He gazed toward the town surrounding them, examining the houses with their frosty Christmas-light-strung eaves and their windows shining with togetherness. "I already told you I was sorry. I don't know what else I can do."

Sorry could never replace what Casey had lost. He knew

that. He couldn't believe Shane didn't. That meant he had to be twisting the knife on purpose. Or he was impossibly kludgy—to the point of being unable to function in society. Since *that* was obviously not true . . . Barely able to speak, Casey settled for delivering Shane a killing look. His former friend seemed to realize he was treading on thin ice. He sighed theatrically.

"Kristen didn't say it outright," Shane relented, "but I got the impression she'd be especially interested in a licensing deal that involved her sister somehow. She and Heather are really tight." He tossed down his cigarette, then ground it out beneath his boot. He frowned at Casey. "Consider that piece of intel a peace offering, from me to you. Again . . . Merry Christmas."

Then Shane held up his hand and turned into the night, leaving Casey alone to wonder . . . Could he trust Shane? Ever again?

Could it be possible that he really wanted to mend things between them and was trying a stupidly ham-fisted way to do it? Or was he trying to keep Casey busy while he pursued Kristen?

It would be just like Shane to do whatever he had to do to impress a woman—even one who would never be his.

Even one like Kristen.

Either way, Casey decided, he couldn't afford to overlook whatever information came his way—however specious its origin.

After all, Shane had been right about one thing: Kristen and Heather really were close. He knew that was true. Probably the rest of what Shane had said was true, too, and Kristen *did* want a licensing and distribution deal that involved her sister.

Casey had to beat Shane to making that deal happen. Because even though he couldn't claim credit for this Christmas party (one of the must-have items on Kristen's wish list, he remembered), he *could* try to arrange a very special gift for her this year. A gift that would bring her closer to Heather, solve her financial problems, *and* change her life forever.

As far as Casey could see, there was no downside to that.

Just like Shane, *he* had connections, Casey reminded himself, feeling combative all over again. In fact, he probably had *more* connections—in higher places—than Shane Maresca ever thought of having.

Casey had smart ideas. He had marketing expertise. He had—when he decided to take advantage of it—the kind of unfettered access to Heather Miller that Shane could only dream of. And he had persuasive ability to spare. All that remained now was using those qualities. For Kristen's sake. To make her happy.

Because that's what people in love did. Right?

Casey wasn't one hundred percent sure. He'd never been in love before. Not like this. But he did know of *one* surefire way to make Kristen feel very, *very* happy . . . and it didn't involve marketing or networking or on-the-job expertise. All it involved was him, her . . . and about sixteen days' worth of getting-to-know-you time. All compressed into a single mind-blowing night.

Galvanized by the thought, Casey swiveled on his heel. The motion brought him face-to-face with the Kismet Senior Center's modest sided exterior, extravagantly strung Christmas lights, and overall aura of hominess. It smelled like gingerbread and evergreens and medicinal arthritis ointment. It sounded like the holidays had gotten wedged inside, circa 1976, and couldn't get out. It swelled with laughing residents and generous workers and friends and families and locals who'd just stopped by to boogie.

And Casey would be damned if he didn't kind of like it.

He especially liked it at Christmastime, just like this.

Shuddering at that traitorous thought, he shrugged more

deeply into his suit jacket, then deliberately crunched down some snow on his way back inside. He was going to find Kristen and make her his . . . but there was no way in hell Casey Jackson was going to fall in love with Christmas while he was doing it.

Despite her determination to grab Casey and duck out of the Christmas Disco Night party early (for once) for the sake of enjoying some long-awaited private time with him, in the end, Kristen discovered that she just couldn't do it.

It wasn't because she couldn't find Casey; she did, shortly after her talk with Shane. It wasn't because she changed her mind; she *really* didn't do that. After all the kissing she and Casey had done in her office, Kristen felt more ready to go than ever. And it wasn't because Casey didn't provide the necessary ingredients to keep her motor running; he really did, in spades.

In fact, in his well-fitted wool suit, shiny oxfords, and pristine button-up shirt, Casey provide all the inspiration a girl could have asked for—and more. Which was to say that he looked *fine*. Like an amalgamation of James Bond and an action-movie hero, with a dash of outdoorsiness and a lot of friendly approachability thrown in. Just looking at him as she laughingly crossed the dance floor to join him in her own version of the hustle made Kristen feel all *fluttery* inside. It was as though, if she didn't get Casey alone soon, she might have to relax her policy on getting lucky within earshot of all her friends and neighbors and just try out a vacant room. Since she'd already tossed aside her famous litmus test for him (at least preemptively), she had to retain some standards.

Not that it was going to be easy . . .

In the end, the only reason Kristen couldn't simply bash Casey over the head with a Yule log and drag him home to her den of disrepute was a simple one. Because, as they finished dancing and meandered down the senior center's central corridor to find a quieter place to take a breather (and maybe discuss ditching the party altogether), Kristen unexpectedly heard Casey say something that surprised her.

"Are those paper snowflakes?" he asked.

She looked. "Looks like it. So, about this party—"

And leaving it, she was about to say, but then she realized that Casey had stopped cold near the senior center's glass-windowed sunroom, while she'd already been motoring past it. He was staring at the hand-cut scraps of lacy-looking office-bond white paper adorning the windows in homemade holiday style. Against the dark night outside, they looked stark and bright and old-fashioned, reminding Kristen of the umpteen paper snowflakes she'd created as a kid during those long—and sometimes boring—days of Christmas vacation from elementary school.

Looking transfixed, Casey strode inside the sunroom. He was already at the nearest window, holding out his hand to touch the closest paper snowflake, when she caught up with him. The look of wonder on his face was as astonishing as it was moving.

"I've never seen them up close like this before," he said. "They really look like gigantic snowflakes, don't they?"

And *that's* when Kristen realized that she couldn't simply shanghai Casey into a night of between-the-sheets passion. At least not right away. Because she had to consider who she was dealing with here. And it was very obvious, all of a sudden, that she was dealing with a seriously Christmas-deprived man.

Casey hadn't even encountered in-person paper snowflakes before? No wonder he was so grumpy sometimes.

But Kristen knew she could change all that. Just for him.

"We should make some ourselves!" With an eager air, she went to the sunroom's coffee table. Someone had left a partial ream of paper, a cup full of safely stowed scissors, and a trash can full of scraps at the ready. "Come on. It'll be fun."

Casey snatched away his hand. "I was just looking."

"And soon you'll be doing." Kristen patted the sofa beside her. Party sounds still filtered down the hallway from the rec room. Bayberry potpourri scented the air. "Grab some scissors."

"No. We shouldn't be here."

"Right." Poker-faced, she nodded at him. "And *you're* a total rule follower." She laughed. "You'll like it. It's easy."

Casey lifted his chin. "I didn't say I couldn't do it."

As it turned out, he didn't have to. Because it was evident, from the clueless way Casey folded his paper, snipped huge, aggressive chunks out of it, then frowned in bewilderment as it fell apart in pieces instead of unfolding into a graceful paper snowflake shape that he (literally) couldn't do it.

As unlikely as it was, Kristen found that endearing, too.

Casey couldn't construct a gingerbread house to save his life, she realized. He couldn't fashion a paper snowflake. He probably didn't know how to make construction-paper garland. Or an orange-clove pomander. Or a wooden-clothespin Rudolph, the Red-Nosed Reindeer with googly eyes. Or a tissue paper red poinsettia. He probably had never pulled taffy, enjoyed a horse-drawn sleigh ride, or gone caroling with all his friends. In an otherwise perfect world, that did not make Casey her dream man.

But in *this* world . . . all Kristen wanted to do was help him.

She wanted to give Casey everything he'd been missing—and more. Because she cared about him. Because she was (let's face it) a little bit crazy about him. Because he was just so . . .

. . . determined to mangle his latest sheet of paper. Yikes.

"Try behaving *less* as though you're trying to show the paper who's boss," Kristen suggested, "and just go with it."

Casey tried glaring his paper into submission instead.

"Whoa. The goal *isn't* to light it on fire, you know."

He set down his scissors. "Are you *sure* you want to do this?" Invitingly, he angled his head toward the door. "We could be at my B&B in twenty minutes." A meaningful pause. "Alone."

As she glanced in the direction Casey had indicated, Kristen could have sworn—for an instant—that she saw *Heather* passing by in the senior center's hallway. She clearly caught a glimpse of long, blond hair, oversize sunglasses, and a flashy leopard-print winter coat. But then she changed her mind.

This was one time when she *definitely* didn't want the subject of her superglam sister to come up and spoil the mood.

"We're alone right now," she told Casey. "We couldn't be any more alone than this at your B&B."

"Oh, yes, we could. We could be *nakedly* alone."

Hmm. That sounded good. Really good. Momentarily diverted, Kristen considered the idea of Casey in the altogether. She bet he would look *incredible,* with tawny California-guy skin and sleek muscles and a dazzling smile that would entice her into getting naked, too, so they could kiss some more and touch each other some more and find out—in explicit detail—exactly what felt the best when their bodies came together, skin on skin . . .

Ahem. So far, she was a terrible Christmastime tutor.

"I know you can do this." As encouragingly as she could, Kristen scooted closer on the sofa. Her hip encountered Casey's hip. Their thighs touched. Their breath combined. The instant intimacy of it reminded her again of the amazing kisses they'd shared earlier and nearly changed her mind. But then she remembered that Casey was practically the Dickensian poster child of Christmas deprivation. It was her mission to change all that. "Look." She picked up her scissors. "Just watch me."

"I have been watching you. That's why I want to leave."

"Huh?" Busily scissoring, Kristen didn't look up.

"You look incredible tonight," Casey clarified. His voice took on a low, husky tone—a tone meant to seduce her into doing whatever he wanted. It was predictably effective. "You make cutting out snowflakes look really, *really* sexy," he said.

"Thanks. You're not getting out of this that easily."

His groan of frustration almost made her laugh. But it was this part of being with Casey that made Kristen feel so happy—this sense of connectedness and understanding and fun.

Casey accepted her wholeheartedly. He gave her the freedom to be herself. *And* he might have been the only person who'd never once acted as though he wished she was more like her famous sister. That made Casey unique. The least Kristen could do, she reasoned, was give something back. Something like Christmas. Or at the very least, an appreciation for Christmas.

And paper snowflakes. Lots and lots of paper snowflakes.

Feeling overcome with affection for Casey despite his Grinchy ways, Kristen snuggled a little closer. Trying to ignore the appreciative (if over-the-top) glances he tossed her simple red sweater dress and boots and cardigan—because her go-to wintertime festive-but-not-sexy party ensemble did *not* deserve that much admiration, even in a perfect world— she snipped and turned and cut and frowned and unfolded. A few minutes later . . .

"Voilà!" She displayed a rudimentary paper snowflake. Then she handed Casey another piece of paper. "Now you go."

"If I do," he grumbled, "will you quit pestering me?"

"Just get scissoring, sexy."

So, handily enough (and with an adorably telltale blush at her nickname for him), Casey did. Apparently he was a quick study, because after having watched her intently for several minutes, he managed to cut out a very acceptable snowflake.

Kristen could tell as much even before he unfolded it. But Casey, as a surprising newbie to this most elementary holiday activity (something Kristen had mastered in fourth grade) could not. With bomb-defusing-worthy concentration, he unfolded the first edge of his cut-out paper. Then the next edge. Then the next. Finally, obviously expecting disaster, he opened it.

When it *didn't* fall apart, the look of wonderment on his face was everything Kristen could have asked for. And more.

"I did it!" Casey blurted, gawking in amazement. "Look!"

He proudly held out his paper snowflake for her to see, and she almost burst into tears at the sight. What kind of childhood had Casey had, Kristen couldn't help wondering, if *this* ordinary activity came as such a revelation to him?

"It's beautiful," she said. And she meant it, too. It could have been the crookedest, lamest, most hacked-up paper snowflake in the whole universe of paper snowflakes, and she would have thought it was the best one ever. "You did a good job."

Looking abashed now, Casey swerved his gaze from his first-ever paper Christmas snowflake to her face. "I could make a bigger one." He set his jaw in a mulish line. "A *lot* bigger one."

His determination and rawness only made her love him more.

"Maybe later," Kristen said. "I have more to show you."

But Casey wouldn't be dissuaded. He reached for another sheet of paper. "I'll make it quick. And humungous. For you."

He folded and creased, snipped away, folded again, peered at his creation, cut some more . . . and then something else seemed to occur to him. He looked up at her with an intimidating frown.

Hastily, Kristen tried not to seem head-over-heels infatuated with him. She seriously doubted she succeeded. But Casey appeared far too intent on saying something to notice.

"If you tell anyone about this," he said in an extremely fierce tone, "I'll only deny it."

"I wouldn't dream of telling a soul."

"No one would believe you if you did," he warned, deepening his frown, "so you might as well save your breath."

"I hardly ever speak as it is," she fibbed, deadpan.

At her joke, he gave her a long look. "I know what you're trying to do, you know. I'm not an idiot." Casey nodded at his in-progress paper snowflake. Roughly, he said, "So . . . thanks."

Kristen brightened. "There's more where that came from!"

"God help me." He scissored some more. Scowled anew.

"Don't try to pretend you don't want more."

"I don't want more," he said convincingly. "You can't make me like Christmas," Casey informed her. "It's not happening."

"It's already happening."

"Don't you know how to take 'no' for an answer?"

"If I ever hear you say it convincingly, I will."

"I said 'no' fifteen minutes ago, when you suggested sneaking in here to make sneaky paper snowflakes!"

"That was different," Kristen hedged. "I could see in your eyes that you were *dying* to make some snowflakes yourself."

"Oh, so now you're psychic?"

"I don't have to be psychic to know what you want."

"Oh yeah?" Undoubtedly prompted by her semi-smug tone, Casey eyed her. He let his gaze rove from her tights-covered knees to her messily upswept hair to her face. Intently, he looked into her eyes. "Tell me then: what do I want right now?"

"Right now? What do you want right now?" Feeling pleased with herself—and full of certainty—Kristen prepared to tell him.

She inhaled a deep breath. She met Casey's steadfast gaze with a straightforward look of her own. She considered all the potential options, one by one. Maybe Casey fancied a glass of mulled cider. Or a walk around the Glenrosen neighborhood to see the famous Christmas lights all the residents put up. Or a session of making funky chenille garland out of red and green pipe cleaner loops strung together to make a festal decoration.

Then . . . *no,* Kristen realized. Casey didn't want any of those things. What he wanted just then, she discovered as she gazed more intently at his dark eyes and smoldering expression, was *her.* Casey wanted *her.* He wanted her in ways that had nothing to do with holiday handicrafts or seasonal activities or mulled apple cider. In fact, if pressed, she'd have had to say . . .

"You want me," she said in an awestruck tone.

"Right here," Casey confirmed. "Right now."

Compared with an invitation like that—and it *was* an invitation, Kristen realized while gazing raptly at him—the idea of sharing wholesome Christmastime activities with Casey simply couldn't compete. Not when he was right there beside her, giving her bedroom eyes and letting her know—with an intense increase in the amount of heat crackling between them—that he meant it.

She ought to resist, Kristen knew. For the sake of Casey's continuing Christmas education, she ought to hold firm to her higher ideals. Maybe she should take him ice-skating at the Kismet rink, which was decorated and outfitted for candlelight skating on wintertime nights like this one. Maybe she should teach Casey how to make gift tags from leftover greeting cards or create fancy gift bows from spools of ribbon and a little ingenuity. Maybe she should . . . slide a little closer and kiss him.

With an impressive amount of fortitude, she didn't.

"*That* would stun the senior-center residents," Kristen joked instead. "Us, getting busy in here amid the paper scraps and the back issues of *Reader's Digest.* I mean, seriously, we'd hit the *Kismet Comet* for sure." With an unsteady grin, she held up her hands to span an imaginary newspaper headline. "Sexed-up snowflake bandits strike again!" she said. "Authorities are baffled by what appear to be breaking and entering sexcapades—"

"It's more than that between us," Casey said quietly, echoing his earlier statement. "And you know it."

She did. Maybe that's what scared her the most.

But because Kristen Miller didn't admit defeat easily, and because she was proud of her higher ideals and her new impulse to help Casey experience the best Christmas season of his life, she actually managed to try again. "I think I saw a gargantuan roll of paper in the senior-center office on the way here." She gestured vaguely toward the hallway. "With that, you could make the world's biggest, most awe-inspiring paper snowflake!"

She nodded at him, expecting to see the usual competitive fire she often saw in his expression. But, apparently, Casey's desire to conquer the world of paper snowflake construction had already been satisfied. Or it was taking a backseat to his much greater desire to conquer *her* . . . lustily, sweetly, and completely. Because all he did was carefully set down his scissors.

Then he stood. He held out his hand to her. "Coming?"

She was dying to make a joke of that—to unleash the most salacious double entendre of all time and defuse the tension that suddenly existed between them. Because Casey's overt interest in being with her was making her knees feel like jelly and her heart feel like it wanted to jump out of her chest and her breath feel stuck in her throat. Heat leaped from his gaze to hers. Need and desire swept between them. And just when Kristen thought she might still be able to connect with her more noble Christmas impulses . . . Casey *smiled* at her, and she was lost.

He knew precisely the moment when she surrendered, too.

"We can be at The Christmas House B&B in twenty minutes," he reminded her, his voice husky and intent in the quiet room.

He waggled his fingers, urging her to her feet. Helpless to resist any longer, Kristen rose. She took his hand.

She nodded. But since she was still her—a woman who knew what she wanted and wasn't afraid to say so—she also smiled.

"We can be at my place in ten," she said. "If we hurry."

Casey knew exactly how valuable shaving off ten minutes' driving time could be. His cocksure grin told her so. "Then I think I'm about to set a Subaru land-speed record," he said.

And just like that, they were on their way. But not before Kristen scooped up Casey's first-ever paper snowflake—the one he had proudly shown her and had nearly brought her to tears with. Surreptitiously, she slid that paper snowflake into her purse for safekeeping, then she patted it in place with a smile.

Someday Casey might want it, she figured.

Once they were both thinking straight again, they might want something to remember this night by . . . just in case the love and lovemaking and—oh yeah—*love* (if they were lucky) weren't enough to spark up the proper nostalgia all on their own.

Then Kristen caught another look at Casey's intent face as he pulled her toward the senior center's coatroom, and she felt the sizzle that started at their joined hands and whipped all the way through her body, and she understood the truth.

There was no way either of them was forgetting this night. No matter what. Because this *was* more than a casual encounter between them, and Kristen was about to discover exactly what experiencing more (more, more, *more!*) with Casey really felt like.

Chapter 16

MOUNTEBANK (MOUN-tuh-bangk) *noun*: an unscrupulous pretender

Lagniappe at the Lakeshore B&B
December 8

Curled up on her suite's plush king-size bed, wearing cozy flannel pajama pants and watching a cheesy pay-per-view holiday movie while munching through a bowl of popcorn, Heather Miller caught an unexpected glimpse of herself in the mirror on the opposite wall. What she saw nearly made her heart stop.

It was *her*, the pop diva superstar of the moment, as no one had ever seen her before. Along with her pajama pants, she was dressed in sweat socks and a saggy old T-shirt from her beginning showbiz days on the Disney Channel. She'd piled her hair on top of her head in a haphazard ponytail-bun hybrid—not a cute, stylishly disheveled ponytail-bun hybrid, either, like you might see in *Vogue* with some sequins and a full face of make-up. No, this was full-on sloppy, unwashed, not-fit-for-Pilates-class hair, with a skunky streak of roots where blond hair should have been. Her face was bare. She might have been developing a zit on her chin. And her cheeks bulged with the latest handful of her high-carb (*all* carb?), *non*-detoxing, salty, bloat-inducing popcorn.

This was her? Slovenly and zit-faced with a bad dye job?

Gripped by shock and nausea, Heather tried to stop and think things through. After all, thanks to Alex's influence, that was what she did these days—stop and think things through before reacting. So she deliberately swerved her appalled gaze away from the mirror, tried to calm her hammering heart, then looked at the bowl of popcorn in her lap. Objectively.

This wasn't just popcorn, Heather tried to tell herself. It was a singular room-service delicacy prepared especially for her by the chef at Lagniappe at the Lakeshore. It sported imported Piedmont truffle oil *and* fancy fleur de sel de Guérande. It came in a silver bowl lined with a designer napkin and accompanied by another designer napkin, both linens printed in a cheerful holiday pattern. This popcorn was supposed to lift her spirits, because being quarantined with chicken pox was boooring, and there were only so many pies in a jar one person could eat before going crazy and beginning to crave *other* foods in a jar.

Macaroni and cheese in a jar, she'd raved to Alex in a fever of inspiration. *Meat loaf in a jar. Prime rib in a jar!*

He *hadn't* thought her ideas were as brilliant as Heather had. Even though she'd already texted several of those brainstorms to Kristen (because her sister was obviously missing the boat at the Galaxy Diner), Alex hadn't been impressed. He'd only hugged Heather, then told her that her idea for various foods in a jar already existed ("it's called baby food"). After that, he'd brought her more calamine lotion and tucked her in so she could get some more (apparently muchneeded) sleep.

It had really been very thoughtful of him. If Alex hadn't been dotted with pink calamine lotion himself at that moment, she might have been tempted to take things to the next level between them. That would have been fun. Really, really fun . . .

Back to the popcorn, Heather commanded herself. *Focus*. The popcorn. Hmm. It was . . . cottony. Roundish. Cold (now). Stuck for another objective observation, Heather hesitated. For inspiration, she inhaled the popcorn's delicious salty/truffley aroma. She looked at its fluffy kernels. She ate more of it.

Strictly as research, of course. But that didn't help. None of this helped. Popcorn was the enemy, and Heather had been (literally) in bed with the enemy. She had to stop this somehow.

Setting aside her fancy popcorn bowl with a clatter, Heather scrambled upright. Salt sprinkled off her pajama pants and fell onto the deluxe, gazillion-thread-count, five-star comforter, but she barely noticed. All she could see in that mirror, now and maybe forever, was her own pale, unmade-up face, her own ballooning belly, and her own (ugh) gullibility.

People thought Heather Miller was dumb. She'd just proved them right. She'd let down her guard, and look what happened!

All her hard work to remain performance-ready had gone down the tubes. In a matter of days. If people could see her now . . .

Taking in the usual array of tabloids and glossy weekly magazines spread across the coffee table and the floor and the end table and the foyer table (geez, maybe she had a problem!), Heather couldn't help wishing she really *was* pregnant, like they were still claiming. That would be preferable to sporting a supersize popcorn-baby like the one she had now. That would be . . .

Nice. Wistfully, Heather considered it. A baby would be *really* nice. She was nurturing. Alex was wonderful. The two of them could start a little family together. They could be happy.

Except they couldn't. Not while she looked like this!

She'd actually believed that Alex—who was only there in the first place because he'd been quarantined with Heather by force in her suite at the Midwest's most luxuriously rustic lakeside B&B—would want to stay here with her after she was well again. But that wasn't going to happen. Because Alex had seen her, Heather realized with a powerful sense of foreboding, like *this*.

Unadorned. Unprotected. Unlovely.

Vulnerable.

Panicked, Heather leaped to her feet. But there was no place she could go. The worst of her chicken pox had cleared up. She was no longer itchy. But she wasn't seeing the doctor again until tomorrow, and until she received a green light from him . . .

Well, until then, *Alex* would be nearby to see her, 24/7.

Maybe, she thought in a dither, Alex had been *hoping* to see her like this. Maybe he'd been photographing her while she slept—all drooling and spotted—or videotaping her while she pounded popcorn by the fistful. It could happen. God knew, she'd had boyfriends who'd turned pretty devious the minute they got her alone with a recording device in their hands.

That stupid sex tape, for instance, still haunted her.

Heather had never wanted to make it at all. She'd thought she'd sneaked over to the video camera and slyly switched it off before all the action had started. But she'd never been very skilled with technology (her parents often joked that Kristen had inherited all the "tech savvy" in the family— along with an unfair share of "the smarts"). So all Heather had accomplished by fiddling with the video camera was capturing herself in an even *more* unflattering and embarrassing angle.

For the whole entire video-streaming world to see.

Mortified all over again at the memory, Heather paced across her hotel suite. From the bathroom came the sounds of Alex showering. But where once it had given her a cozy feeling to be sharing the mundane details of life with her crazy-for-him crush, now Heather saw the true danger she'd put herself in.

Because Alex could hurt her, too. Just like her other so-called boyfriends had in the past. Alex could take advantage of her vulnerability. He could photograph her or video her or spill his guts to the "news journalists" about his relationship with her. *Alex could betray her*. Heather didn't need a Word of the Day calendar to realize that. He could hurt her. A lot.

For all she knew, Heather thought crazily, Alex didn't even have the chicken pox! She hadn't technically seen any spots on him that *hadn't* been covered with opaque pink calamine lotion. Even those could have been faked. Especially if he was working in cahoots with one of the make-up artists. Heather knew darn well what those people could achieve. With a few brushes and some concealer and blush, they could work miracles! They could probably create authentic-looking chicken pox spots, too.

She should have scrutinized Alex more closely, Heather realized too late. For her own protection. But she wasn't a devious person by nature. She was pretty trusting most of the time. Besides, she hadn't had a chance to get *that* close to Alex. Not physically. Because although she'd wanted to get naked with him (and he with her), they'd both felt too feverish and unwell to start getting seriously frisky with one another.

They'd shared a few very sweet kisses, sure. They'd done a little over-the-pajama pants, under-the-mangy-T-shirt cuddling, yes. But they'd been waiting for the go-ahead, all-clear sign from the doctor before indulging in the anticipated main event.

Alex had said he wanted their first time together to be memorable. He'd said he wanted it to be *non*fevered and during a time when they wouldn't have to stop to scratch. At the time, Heather had thought that was very sweet of him. But now . . .

Now she wasn't so sure she could believe him. In fact, Heather assured herself, she *didn't* believe him. Narrowing her eyes, she marched to her suite's peninsula, where Alex had left his watch and keys and cell phone. With her heart pounding, she picked up his cell phone. Stealthily, she keyed through the menus. She pulled up his photos. She peered at the first one.

It was a hideously unflattering candid shot of *her*.

So was the next photo. And the next. And the next!

Every last photo formed a horrifying collage of career-killing unattractiveness. Taken together, they were all the proof Heather needed to know that Alex really *did* have ulterior motives. She saw herself, wan and speckled, weeping over *It's a Wonderful Life*. She saw herself, greasy-haired and shabbily dressed, guffawing over *A Christmas Story*. She saw bad angles, awful lighting, weird poses, and bizarre expressions. She saw red-eye, zits, and how manic she looked like when pursuing a reluctant "patient" (Alex) with pain reliever and Evian water, playing nurse to someone she cared about. Under other circumstances, Heather would have had these photos incinerated.

There could be only one reason Alex had them, she knew—one reason he'd taken those photos, one after another, all while assuring her his cell phone was "off" and he was only joking around to cheer her up.

Alex planned to sell her out, Heather realized with dawning horror. And *she'd* bought in! He planned to turn a fast buck, even if she got hurt in the process.

But Heather hadn't even come to terms with that before the usually beloved sound of Alex's voice interrupted her spying.

"Hey! What's up, hot stuff?" he asked cheerfully.

Heather almost jumped a foot. Sneakily, she hid Alex's cell phone behind her voluminous pajama pants, then turned to him.

Uh-oh. At the unexpected sight that greeted her, Heather almost lost her burgeoning sense of outrage. Because Alex, lingering in the bathroom doorway, was dressed only in a towel and his own water-beaded skin, and he looked *great*. Really great. Until tonight, he'd gotten dressed before coming out of the bathroom. Ordinarily, Heather would have taken his newfound comfort level as a positive sign that they were becoming closer.

But now, in the wake of her newly awakened suspicions, she only felt . . . even more suspicious.

"Hi!" She gave him a stiff-feeling hello wave with her non-cell-phone-holding hand, wishing she'd tried harder at the acting lessons the network had insisted on. "You, uh, usually don't run around nearly naked."

"Yeah." Alex gestured sheepishly at himself. "You'd think I was a little self-conscious about my chicken pox spots, huh?"

"Yeah. Maybe." *Or maybe he was lying!* Trying to get into the right mind-set for scoping out the truth, Heather paced, Columbo-style. "Except you don't have any chicken pox spots!" she pointed out in her most accusatory *aha!* tone. "Why is that, Alex? Huh? Why don't you have any spots?"

He gave her a confused look. "Because I'm better now?"

Right. Deftly, Heather sneaked his cell phone into her pajama pants pocket, where it would remain out of sight until she could examine it in more detail later. "Mmm-hmm. Lucky you."

Another baffled frown. "Is something up with you?"

"I could ask *you* the same question! Couldn't I?"

"All right. Hold on. There is definitely something going on here." Alex grabbed his glasses. Then, patiently, he sent his concerned gaze around their shared suite. He noticed Heather's cast-off popcorn bowl. The TV with its muted pay-per-view holiday movie still playing. *Her*. As though taking inventory of the suite's contents, he moved to the sitting area and then the peninsula, where his watch and wallet were— where his cell phone conspicuously *wasn't*. "Did something happen while I was in the shower? Did someone visit, or—"

Realizing that he was going to notice his missing phone

any second now—and *then* she'd really have some 'splaining to do—Heather abandoned her impromptu interrogation in favor of a hastily fabricated excuse. The first thing that came to mind was . . . "I'm upset. Because *you* hardly have any spots at all, while *I* have been *ravaged* by the chicken pox! It's just not fair."

He grinned. "Ravaged. Word of the Day from last week."

Ordinarily, she'd have beamed beneath his proud, approving expression. She'd have been thrilled by their shared word-geek camaraderie. But tonight, Heather only narrowed her eyes.

"I look *awful!*" she moaned theatrically, hoping to keep up her cover. If she could get Alex to go into the other room and get dressed (she couldn't believe she was actively campaigning for him to put *on* clothes), she could finish thumbing through his cell phone photos and find out exactly what kind of perfidy her shoulda-been, wasn't-gonna-be boyfriend had been up to.

Perfidy. That was a Word of the Day from next month. Now Heather was smarter—the way Alex had inspired her to be, against her will—and it was all for naught. No, for *nothing*. Argh.

She was shredding that dumb Word of the Day calendar the first chance she got. But until then . . . "My hair is all stringy!" Heather complained further, hoping to explain away her moodiness. "My clothes are all gross, and my face is naked—"

"Soon we'll have to get the rest of you naked, too."

At Alex's devilish eyebrow waggle, Heather nearly lost the will to go on with this. His potential treachery had sapped her strength and broken her heart. She'd thought he was special.

She'd thought he was The One. The One for her.

"—and I've got a huge bloated belly," she pushed relentlessly onward, starting to get invested in what suddenly felt less like a cover story and more like the truth—more like a desperate plea for Alex to disagree with her. The way anyone else in her entourage would have. (*No, you look fab, Heather!*) "And I'm pretty sure my pedicure is completely shot, too."

Alex only smiled at her. "I'm pretty sure it is."

She gawked. "You're criticizing my *toes?*"

"I'm agreeing with you. Isn't that what you want?"

"Of course not!" Didn't he know anything? Didn't he know you weren't supposed to agree with a woman who was kvetching about her appearance? It just wasn't done. "I'm really upset!"

Because I think you're a traitor. And I trusted you!

"I can see that. I'm sorry. Let's start over." Sobering, Alex came nearer. "All I mean is, the fact that you're noticing what you look like is a good sign. It means you're getting better. It means you're feeling like yourself again."

"How's that? Superficial?" she demanded to know.

Another smile. If she hadn't known better, she'd have believed Alex meant it. "When you're sick as a dog with chicken pox," he said, "you usually don't care if you look like hell—"

"I looked like *hell?*" Even though Heather knew it was true—objectively—it still hurt to hear him say it out loud.

"—but when you're on the mend," Alex continued patiently, holding out his hands to ward off a potential freak-out, "you start to notice that you haven't combed your hair or showered."

"Are you saying I stink?" Indignantly, she crossed her arms over her chest—a pose that had the advantage of isolating any supposed BO. She just got stealthier and stealthier. It wasn't a quality she cherished in herself. "Are you? Just say it!"

"Okay. You stink. A little." Evidently not bothered by that, Alex came a little nearer. He really did look supercute in his towel. He even had nice-looking legs. And his chest was—

"I *stink?*" With effort, Heather made herself quit ogling

him. She had to have some self-respect here. She couldn't get distracted. "Gee, Alex. You really know how to seduce a girl."

"I really do," he assured her. With the same tranquility he always displayed, Alex gently unfolded her arms, making room to put his arms around her waist. He gazed meaningfully into her eyes. "I think I'm recovered enough to show you, too."

At the unmistakable sexiness in his expression, she balked. He couldn't mean . . . "Show me? You mean you really want to—"

"I really, *really* want to. With you."

No. She couldn't fall for this. "Even though I'm—"

Ugly? Lazy? Awkward? She couldn't say those things aloud. But they dogged her thoughts and made her feel scared. Of this.

Especially now, when she knew she couldn't trust him.

"Even though . . . *everything.*" Tenderly, Alex kissed her. "I'm not here for glamazon Heather. I'm here for real Heather."

"'Real Heather'?" Deliberately, she scoffed. "That's aiming pretty low, isn't it? I mean, why settle for ordinary Heather, when you could wait for me to pull myself together and have—"

"*People* magazine's 'sexiest songstress'?"

"Well . . . yeah." That's what everyone wanted from her.

With a thoughtful, semiamused look, Alex gazed at her. He actually looked as though he . . . *treasured* her or something. Wow.

He *definitely* had to be scamming her somehow.

"That stuff is what you *do,*" he said. "Not who you *are.*"

Heather disagreed. "They're the same thing."

"Not to me, they're not." Alex touched her grungy T-shirt. He lay his palm over her heart. "I like *you.* I like who you are when you're alone with me, just hanging out. I like who you are when you think I'm not looking, and you sneak French fries from my Galaxy Diner delivery. I like who you are . . . no matter what."

Oh, boy. This was really weakening her. "You do?"

Alex nodded. "We've been through a few things together over the past several days. I think I know who you are. *Really.*"

Feeling herself begin to relax, inch by inch, into his arms, Heather tried once more to resist. "The members of my Facebook fan club think they know me, too. But they don't."

"They haven't duct taped mittens to your wrists to keep you from scratching your chicken pox spots, now have they?"

"Argh!" Heather guffawed. "Don't remind me of that!"

"Hey, it made you laugh. It was worth every minute."

At the sappy look Alex gave her then, Heather was a goner.

Maybe he was secretly planning to betray her. Maybe he had only pretended to have chicken pox as part of some nefarious scheme. But right now, Alex seemed so sweet and real and sexy . . .

Well, right now, the possibility of sabotage felt very far away. Because Alex had his lanky arms around her. He was giving her the kind of love-struck look ordinarily only found in Nicholas Sparks novels and Pepé Le Pew cartoons. He had said he liked *her,* the real her, and Heather knew that that was an unusual quality for anyone to have . . . because no one, in her experience, had ever had it. Including her own parents, who seemed to appreciate their eldest daughter primarily because her fame brought them bragging rights and comped tickets and nice vacations to far-away places that were *not* like Podunk Kismet.

Frankly, it hurt that they valued Kristen for who she *was*—smart, practical, determined, kind—and Heather for what she *did*.

"You *have* taken good care of me," Heather admitted, setting aside those painful family dynamics for now. She gazed curiously at Alex. "Not many people would have done that."

"Any one of your staff would have done it," he said, poo-poohing her skepticism. "Your loyal hangers-on would have purposely infected themselves with the varicella zoster virus, dabbed calamine lotion on you, *and* done that taped-on mittens trick. They would walk through fire for you."

"Maybe." Heather snuggled closer. She gave Alex a kiss that made him quit arguing and made her forget the uncomfortable revelation she'd had. "But they wouldn't have done *that*."

His eyes turned even dreamier. "They might have."

"Really?" She caressed his bare chest. "How about this?"

He swallowed hard. Nodded. "Probably."

"You make it sound as if I have a bunch of first-aid-trained, low-self-esteem prostitutes on staff." Smiling, Heather trailed her hands down Alex's chest to his towel. She was dying to pull it off. But first . . . "When really, all I have are a few well-paid sycophants and a couple of genuine friends."

Alex's bedazzled gaze met hers. "Sycophants. Word of—"

Heather cut him off with another kiss, not wanting to be reminded of the linguistic bond they used to share. "Enough talking."

He nodded. Heat leaped between them. At the thought of what was to come—what she'd yearned for all this time—Heather nearly squealed with excitement. She was finally going to be with Alex!

They were going to kiss and hug and get naked. They were going to be sexy and playful and intimate. They were going to take their relationship to the next, most necessary level.

She'd never wanted anything more. Not even a Grammy.

"Yes, ma'am," Alex said in a wiseass tone she loved. In an admirable show of post-chicken-pox strength, he hoisted her in his arms. "No more talking. Just a lot of loving. Coming up."

He was so romantic! With a sigh, Heather laid her head on his shoulder, waiting for Alex to carry her to the nearby king-size bed, honeymoon-style, and then make love to her. She could hardly wait. Any man who could *want* to get busy with her while she was wearing a tatty old Disney T-shirt was a keeper for sure. She loved Alex. She just *loved* him! He was so *perfect*.

Well, except for that potential photo-related sabotage he might possibly (almost assuredly) be planning. But maybe Heather was wrong about that, she rationalized. In the face of immediate temptation, she'd developed a very accomplished ability to rationalize. That's what working in show-biz did to a person.

"Here we go." Manfully, Alex adjusted his grip on her, headed for that cushy bed. Tenderly, his arms cradled her. Adroitly, his fingers flexed against her flannel-covered thighs.

He stopped moving. An unusual expression crossed his face.

Oh God. "Am I too heavy?" Heather blurted, knowing it was true. "I am, aren't I? I should never have had so much popcorn!"

But Alex hadn't stopped because she was too heavy for him. After all, he routinely hoisted heavy beams while constructing sets, she recalled belatedly. But he did set her down anyway.

Confused, Heather righted herself, only to see Alex peering down at his hand—where he now held his formerly contraband cell phone. She recognized it instantly. Had it fallen out of her pocket? Had he felt an unusual lump in her pajama pants pocket and effectively pickpocketed her to find out what it was?

"This is my phone." His gaze sharpened. "What are you doing with this?"

Oh no. Not this. Not now. "Um, making . . . a call?"

"Your phone is right there on the nightstand."

"Yours is . . . cooler?" Heather tried.

That *almost* worked. Flattering Alex's guy-centered gadget sense almost bought Heather enough time to regroup—enough time to get them back to romantic gestures and sweet words and love.

Alex tightened his jaw. "You were spying on me."

Heather's heart dropped to her unpedicured feet. This wasn't the way she'd wanted things to go. She'd thought she was in the clear. In fact, she'd sort of *forgiven* Alex, generously ahead of time, for the treachery he was going to enact on her.

How *dare* he act like the offended party here?

"No, *you* were spying on *me!*" Heather huffed.

His betrayed gaze seared into her. She knew she'd never forget it. "Is that really what you think?" Alex asked.

"It looks that way, doesn't it?" she said cryptically.

"Yes," he said. "It does. And I'm sorry for it."

With a sigh, he turned away. For a heartbeat, Heather wondered if she'd made a mistake. Could Alex be innocent?

Standing with his back to her, still nearly naked and rippled with lean muscle, Alex bowed his head. "Most of all, I'm sorry for you, Heather. Because if you can't trust me . . . this can't happen between us. And I was really hoping it would happen."

That sounded sort of heartfelt. And intelligent. And mature, too. But Heather felt too wounded and baffled to listen anymore. This was all happening much too fast for her.

"Oh yeah? Well, don't feel sorry for *me!*" she said, jerking up her chin in a dramatic way. "Because *I* can have anyone I want." *Except you,* her poor naïve heart insisted on whispering. Ignoring it, Heather stomped across the suite. "And there's no reason I'd want a glorified carpenter for a boyfriend!"

Alex flinched. His troubled sidelong gaze met hers. His

shoulders slumped another fraction of an inch. But he didn't argue with her assessment of him. Heather decided that meant she was right about him. He really had been planning to hurt her.

Who was she kidding? He'd already hurt her. A million times over. He'd allowed her to hope things could be different.

That was the worst thing anyone could do to someone else.

"Yeah," Alex said. "That's what I figured. That you wouldn't want someone like me for your boyfriend."

Heather wanted to disagree. After all, she'd spoken hastily and (admittedly) untruthfully. She loved his expertise at his job. She loved him, too. She didn't care that Alex was neither famous nor sophisticated. But she had too much pride to give in. She had too much pragmatism (now that Alex had demonstrated how to practice critical thinking) to simply accept him at his word. Especially not when there was damning evidence right at hand.

Those cell phone photos of her had been *awful*. Furthermore, Alex did not, after all, have any chicken pox spots. Heather could see that for herself now, plain as day, after his shower.

He'd been faking. He'd been pretending about . . . everything.

Maybe he'd even been the one feeding the tabloids those bogus stories about Heather and her supposed bohemian boy toy.

Four minutes later, Alex had dressed. Thirty seconds after that, he was at their suite's door. There, he stopped.

He's going to say he didn't mean it, Heather prayed. Then she could say *she* hadn't meant it, either. Everything would be fine between them. That was the way arguments worked, wasn't it?

That was the way, in her experience, relationships worked.

"If you ever decide to get real," Alex said, "look me up."

"Ha!" Heather burst out, feeling as though her heart might be splintering somehow. "As if *that* will ever happen."

That I'll call you, I mean, she thought. *Not that I'll get* "*real.*" But by then it was too late. She was terrible at this.

Alex cast her a final glance over his shoulder. "I hope it does happen. You deserve it, Heather. You deserve . . . everything."

His measured tone only made her want to shriek. *Don't go!* was what she, specifically, wanted to howl. But she didn't.

"I *already* have everything," Heather said smugly.

Alex's nod seemed to confirm it. But his eyes disagreed.

So did her heart. Because she didn't have *him*. She didn't have love. And above everything else, Heather wanted that most.

Why couldn't she just say so? Why couldn't she fix this?

Was she just that dumb, that the obvious solution escaped her?

With a woeful look, Alex raised his palm in a good-bye gesture. It felt like the last thing she would ever see him do.

"You can't go out there!" Heather blurted, unable to resist a last-ditch effort to make him stay. "You're contagious!"

Alex hesitated. Her heart performed a somersault.

If he stayed, it would be a bona fide Christmas miracle. Reminded of that, Heather got even more desperate.

"And it's almost Christmas. Stay until Christmas!"

It was as close to begging as she was willing to come.

It almost seemed to work, too. Alex actually turned around. He gave her the ghost of a smile, making her heart lurch. "You really *don't* pay attention to anyone except yourself, do you?"

That stung. It confused her, too. What did paying attention to people have to do with Alex enjoying a few sugar cookies, some gifts, and maybe a karaoke Christmas carol or two?

Willing, now that it was crunch time, to swallow her pride a tiny bit, Heather smiled. "Please stay for Christmas."

Alex shook his head. "I'm Jewish. I told you that."

Uh-oh. Vaguely, Heather remembered that. "I . . . forgot?"

But before she could concoct a more reasonable excuse for not paying attention to something as important as his heritage and personal beliefs, Alex opened the door . . . and left their suite.

Stuck on her own with her troubling thoughts, Heather scowled at the empty doorway. "I don't have to remember!" she yelled after him in her haughtiest tone. "*I'm* Heather Miller!"

But for the first time in her life, that didn't help.

Because all at once, being Heather Miller was anything but fabulous . . . and facing down the rest of the night alone was going to leave her with far too much time to think about that.

Chapter 17

After Casey hastily parked his car downstairs near the coffee shop, he and Kristen hurried hand in hand toward her apartment. A light snowfall blanketed the quiet downtown Kismet streets, squeaking under their boots and diffusing the light from the garland-wrapped wrought-iron streetlamps. They reached an obscure door, just to the left of the coffee shop's decorated plate-glass window, and turned-off-for-the-night neon sign.

"It's just in here." With gloved hands, Kristen fumbled through her purse. She extracted a jangling set of keys, her breath frosty on the night air. "Down the hall, up the stairs—"

"Sounds too far to go," Casey said, and kissed her.

Their mouths met in the semidarkness, open and hot and seeking more, and kissing Kristen felt exactly as good to Casey then as it had just moments ago, when he'd kissed her in the car. Within seconds of making his move, he'd been crushed against the driver's side door as Kristen had all but pole-vaulted over the center console to meet him (more than) halfway.

Panting and kissing and touching, unwilling to wait a second longer, they'd fogged up the car's windows and tried to get closer. They'd nearly succeeded, too—until a late-night dog walker had happened past with a jingle-bell-wearing schnauzer on a leash and inadvertently broken the spell between them.

Now though, there was nothing except Casey and Kristen and a handy exterior doorway where they were partly sheltered from the chilly night air. Bringing his hand to her head, cradling her cozy knit cap in his palm, Casey pulled her nearer.

He opened his mouth at a new angle, teased her with his tongue, and felt a heady sense of gratification when Kristen moaned beneath his kiss and grabbed him right back. Because they were both so bundled against the cold, all she caught hold of were his quilted coat and long woolly muffler, and Casey cursed the stupid wintery Michigan weather all the more as he realized how much more *naked* they both could have been in California. Or Cozumel. Or Anguilla. Or Kauai. Or anyplace else where freezing subzero temperatures didn't reign supreme every December.

Briefly, Casey wondered if Kristen would like going away with him at Christmastime. If she'd like margaritas on the beach and sand between her toes and sunshine and surf and sex. It was possible, he thought as he kissed her again, that he could have his usual escape-from-Christmas getaway *and* have love, too.

Surely those two things could coexist. Couldn't they?

But then Kristen whipped him against the building's exterior door, using his shoulders *and* his daydreaming as leverage, and then she took control of their kiss herself, and Casey forgot all about . . . everything else. If it wasn't Kristen's mouth or her warm minty breath or her impatient gloved hands roving all over him, he couldn't feel it. Or think about it.

All he knew was her warmth. All he wanted was her

touch. All he felt was *her,* lithe and eager in his arms, and he knew, in that moment, that he didn't need anything else ever again.

Except maybe more. More more *more.* The only way that was happening, Casey realized dimly, was if they made it inside. Because while going on as they were—all but ripping off each other's multiple layers of coats and scarves and clothes beneath the municipal banners announcing the annual Kismet Christmas Parade and Holiday Light Show—was definitely *fun,* doing so while inside Kristen's apartment would be even better. And hotter.

In every sense of the word.

"We should go inside," Casey murmured, caught up in kissing her neck. Her jaw. Her mouth. Her ear. Essentially everyplace that was exposed. "I don't want you to get too cold."

Kristen laughed. "There's zero chance of *that* happening. Not with all *this* going on between us."

The amusement in her tone intrigued him. So did the flirty invitation she'd offered by slipping her arms deftly between his overcoat and suit jacket. Clearly more versed than he was with cold-weather gear, Kristen squeezed him closer. Then she did everything except stand on his feet to reach his mouth again—including holding his jaw steady for her next kiss.

"Mmm," she moaned. "I like it right here, just like this."

Honestly, Casey did, too. Dizzy with wanting her, he gave in to their next kiss. And then the next. And the next. Tendrils of her hair tickled his fingertips; exhalations of her breath warmed his neck as she kissed him. She wriggled with apparent delight, then did it again. Casey was pretty sure Kristen might be capable of making him forget himself enough to risk indecent exposure *and* frostbite, all for the sake of feeling her hands on him everywhere, without the impediments of all his clothes.

But there was something invigorating about feeling the cold air against his overheated, exposed skin—about knowing that he and Kristen couldn't *quite* forget themselves as long as they were still kissing in a doorway like a pair of insatiable long-lost lovers.

The chill of that door penetrated through the back of Casey's coat, but Kristen's body heat seared him from its front, and as he kissed her again, he realized that she was the only woman he'd ever known who'd actually thrown him against a door and kissed him as though she couldn't get enough of his mouth, of his body, of *him*—all the way through—and he realized that he liked that a lot, and he further realized that Kristen's gloved hand was sliding purposefully downward, over his shoulder, past his chest, over his belly, lower and lower, until . . .

Whoa. Another few inches and he wouldn't care anymore that they were in public.

Deliberately, Casey caught hold of Kristen's wrist. Their gazes met. In the evening shadows, Kristen's eyes sparkled up at him. Her mouth curved in a smile that looked far too audacious for its own good, promising him she was up to no good. Her smile all but guaranteed that—if left to her own devices—Kristen would make him lose control in a heartbeat, right there on the deserted Kismet street, with snow falling on his head and his body headed straight for hypothermia.

"On the other hand," she told him, "I can't touch you the way I want to out here on the sidewalk. We'd better go inside."

As far as Casey was concerned, she could have anything she wanted, as long as it involved her and him and nakedness.

"Since I can't feel my toes anymore," he said, "inside sounds *great.* I think I might be getting frostbite."

Kristen laughed. "That's not frostbite. All your blood has rushed elsewhere." She gave him a cheeky look. "I think I know where, too. I'll make it a point to double-check in a second."

"Anything that's mine is yours," Casey promised.

Kristen wasted no time in making her move, but it still took much too long to reach her second-floor apartment. After all, there was the exterior building door to unlock, then the hallway to navigate, then the stairs to ascend . . .

By the time they reached the landing that led directly to Kristen's apartment, Casey thought he might be losing his mind.

Could unfulfilled lust do that to a person? Just then, it felt as though it could—and as though the only way to stop it was to grab Kristen's arm, pull her close, and kiss her again.

Gratifyingly, she melted against him in response, her keys jingling as she brought up both hands to his chest. Completely inflamed now, Casey caught her head in his palms and kissed her with a sense of purpose that kept him rooted in place, even as snowflakes melted and turned to wet spots on his coat and his head and even his face and his eyelashes, and he knew he'd *definitely* never kissed anyone who made him feel the way Kristen did, which was why it suddenly seemed imperative that they get inside her apartment and get on with things, because if these mushy, sentimental feelings kept welling up inside him, Casey wasn't sure what would happen. It made him feel a little crazy and a lot uncertain, and since he didn't like uncertainty . . .

"Is it this one?" He took her keys and, at Kristen's wide-eyed nod, unlocked the only door on that floor. A few seconds later, they'd practically dived inside her apartment together. Without looking around, Casey found the first available empty space: the wall beside her front door. "Aha. Home at last."

As a sort of *welcome home* maneuver, he kissed Kristen against that wall, then caged her in with his arms and kissed her again. She felt *so* good and *so* right, and as she glanced up at him between kisses, wearing a smile that was as uniquely *her* as it was ridiculously alluring, stroking his face with her gloved palm as though she cherished him and needed him and *wanted* him beyond all else, Casey felt another glimmer of that schmaltzy feeling that had blind-sided him a minute ago, and he knew that he had to get things going between them in a more purposeful and sexual way, or else he might start feeling . . .

Well, God only knew what he'd feel. He wasn't sure he wanted to find out.

"It took *forever* to drive here, didn't it?" Kristen said breathlessly. The teasing way she said it thrilled him. So did the eager way she tugged off his knit cap and then went for his muffler. "I could barely walk upstairs. All that kissing made my legs feel too wobbly. You've got quite a knack for kissing me."

"That's not all I've got," Casey promised. "I've got—"

Love, he was about to say, but Kristen cut him off before he could. Thank God. He was obviously drunk on senior center holiday punch and too much fruitcake for any sensible person.

"Way too many clothes on," she complained, tossing his muffler to the side. In the dark, Casey couldn't see where it landed. So far, his sense of Kristen's apartment was limited to catching vague glimpses of the outlines of her furniture, smelling the combined fragrances of cinnamon and pine tree in the air, and sensing that, if he moved the merest inch to the right, he could swing the door all the way shut with his foot.

Chivalrously, he did so. The motion effectively sealed them alone together, with no barriers to *being* together, for the first time ever. Overwhelmed by the realization, Casey went still. Suddenly it seemed that he could have *everything* he'd ever wanted. With Kristen to share it with. It seemed that he could know what it felt like *not* to be secretly yearning for more on a level he scarcely acknowledged, even to himself. That he could be together with her, now and maybe later, too, and—

"Were you expecting to be attacked by grizzlies on your way to Christmas Disco Night?" Kristen grumbled, struggling to unfasten the buttons on his overcoat. Exasperated, she gave a yank. "You're wearing so many clothes you're practically armored. Who needs Kevlar when you have this much wool?"

Looking at her downturned face and frisky expression, Casey felt flooded with tenderness. That's how he knew he had to get her naked. Quickly. Before this attack of mushiness got to him.

Before it made him do something he'd regret.

Because while love was fine *in theory*—say, while planning a Christmas surprise for Kristen or agreeing to cut out paper snowflakes with her at the senior center—actually *feeling* love, in practice, was something else altogether. It was . . . not for him.

"Where's your bedroom?" he asked, peering into the gloom.

Momentarily diverted, Kristen pointed. "Through there."

Casey wasted no time following her directions. He was going to strip them both to bare skin, find the nearest soft surface—if that was Kristen's mattress, so much the better, but if not, he could work with that, too—and then make them one. Over and over again. And if he did it right, he figured, this weird feeling of connectedness would be forgotten about like so many abandoned curbside Christmas trees on New Year's Eve morning.

They reached her bedroom. Inside, it smelled like clean sheets and girly grooming products, all mingled together in a mélange of let's-get-busy atmosphere. Or maybe that last part was mostly in his mind. Just then, Casey decided not to worry about it. Basically, just being there let him enjoy the private side of Kristen, and that was the biggest aphrodisiac of all.

If he could have, he would have bottled the essence of her bedroom to take with him after he left. Because nothing this good could ever last. He knew he would miss it. He knew he would never forget it. But there was no way in hell Casey was admitting to a thought as sappy as that one. So, instead of letting her know exactly how deep his newfound sense of Hallmark-worthy mushiness went, he pulled her into his arms.

"Nice bedroom." He gave her a Lambada-style hip swivel, bringing them into even closer contact. Then another kiss. "I like it."

His growled approval only made her laugh. Kristen waved her arm. "It's too dark! You haven't even seen it properly yet."

She pulled away before he could assure her he had. Left alone in the semidarkness, Casey waited for her to come back.

An instant later, Kristen flicked a switch. Then, "Tada!"

Holiday lights glowed to life around them, illuminating her bedroom with their miniature, nonblinking pinpoints of radiance. Christmas light strings followed the lines of her ceiling, eliminating the need for a lamp. They wound around her bed's headboard, making its piled-up pillows and chenille spread look twice as appealing. They brightened Kristen's face, letting him see how beautiful and how excited and how earnest she looked.

It occurred to Casey that *she* might be feeling all mushy toward *him,* too. But that wasn't what this night was all about. This night was about them coming together, raw and urgent and unstoppable, until they erased all the sentimentality and sweetness and were left with just feeling and being and doing.

"It's really Christmassy," he said. "It's very you."

He realized, as he said it, that he *liked* that about this room. He liked that Kristen's bedroom was unabashedly full of holiday cheer—that it glowed with celebratory lights and brimmed with plush surfaces and cushy, holiday-themed pillows. Because that's what made it *hers*. Kristen truly loved Christmas, and she would probably never want to go to Anguilla in December (because then she would miss all this corny holiday stuff), and the thought of that made Casey feel unexpectedly sad. So he took a step forward and squashed that unwanted feeling by kissing her.

"Mmm." Delving his tongue against hers, he moaned and then kissed her again. Her knit cap was in the way of his roving hands, so Casey pulled it off and dropped it. He made short work of her plaid scarf, her coat, and her gloves, too. With his hands, he tugged her hair gently loose from its knot, letting more tendrils wind around his fingers. "You feel . . . so good."

"Yeah, I do. Especially now that my hands are free." With a devilish grin that told him she *did* feel good—and was likely feeling better all the time, as they went on kissing—Kristen clutched at his overcoat. She wrenched it off him, then hurled it toward a waiting upholstered armchair. She grabbed his suit jacket lapels next. "You're going to be so sorry you made me wait all this time," she assured him. "Because right now, after all this buildup, I'm feeling pretty insatiable."

"Me too," Casey rumbled. "Bring it on."

"Oh, I'm going to." Panting, Kristen wrestled off his suit coat. She frowned at his vest and shirt and pants. "By the time I get all this off you, I'll have earned a reward of some kind."

"I have just the thing in mind," Casey promised.

He could not get her naked quickly enough. Not quickly enough to stanch all those caring feelings of his. But that didn't mean he skimped on the effort. After a few more kisses, Kristen's soft cardigan joined his overcoat on the armchair.

Both items looked weirdly right together, Casey thought fancifully. It was almost as if he and Kristen were *meant* to be a couple, living and laughing and loving in her apartment. It was almost as if even their clothes were comfortable together.

Then he realized the nonsense he was thinking and pulled himself together. Clearly, being around this much Christmas paraphernalia was doing something damaging to his sense of self. Or his brain. Mostly his brain. Because . . . What the hell?

The rest was psychobabble. And Casey Jackson didn't do psychobabble. He got in, got things done, and then got out, leaving everyone in his wake feeling satisfied that he'd been there. That was his raison d'être. It was *him* in a nutshell.

To prove it, Casey steered Kristen toward the bed. In a giddy backward tango, they made it there, kissing all the while. Together, they tipped headlong into the glow of the sparkly lights. They landed on the mattress, but somehow Kristen wound up on top of him. She looked right at home there, too.

"Now I've got you where I want you," she announced, straddling him with a suggestiveness that made Casey's head spin. Her thighs flexed against his hips. Her boots rubbed against his pants, their myriad buckles clanging out a triumphant rhythm. Her red sweater dress rode up, making Casey yearn to pull it off her completely. Kristen gave him a look. "And you thought *you* were in charge of this between us."

Chapter 18

"I am," Casey said, then he tilted his hips sideways.

Kristen tottered, then fell with a squeal, surprised by his sudden move. Casey was there to catch her, though, rolling them both against the mattress until those damn holiday lights blurred in his vision. All that remained was him, and her, and the anticipation of getting them both fully naked.

"And don't you forget it," he warned, then he kissed her to make sure she didn't. But Casey's fierceness was all for show, he realized, because when he raised his head at last, Kristen was gazing intently at him with the reflections of those tiny holiday lights in her eyes, making her look all dreamy and full of longing. He felt a tug of protectiveness toward her then—as though he wanted to make sure he didn't hurt her feelings or break her heart or something else in between—and Casey knew he had to extinguish that burgeoning sentimentality of his before it got out of hand. Because Kristen probably didn't know the difference between wanting and needing and not having—not in the way that Casey did—and there was only one way to handle this.

By ignoring it. Because he didn't want it. He wanted *her*.

Confidently, Casey kissed Kristen again. Urgently, he roamed his hands over her body, feeling all the curves that she seemed passionately insistent on pressing against him. And he was pretty sure he was hearing things, because he thought that, as he stroked Kristen over her sweater dress, she spoke to him and said something that was pretty much unimaginable.

"I want you, Casey," she whispered, kissing his jaw, his neck, his cheekbone, his mouth. She stroked him all over, to mind-bending effect, making him shake in her arms. "I do. I want you *so* much. And not just because you're hot and sexy and outrageously good at kissing, but also because—"

"Hey, give a guy a chance to earn all those accolades," he interrupted before she could go too far and break *his* heart by changing her mind later. He knew people sometimes changed their minds about him—and not necessarily for the better. Otherwise, he wouldn't have switched foster homes so much as a kid. "We've only just gotten started."

"Yeah, but I can tell it's going to be good already."

Casey could, too. But still . . . "You're not even halfway naked," he pointed out. It felt like a condemnation of his own damn failure to stay on track and quit thinking about her in all those syrupy, overemotional ways. "I thought by now I'd have your boots off, at least. Although, as a California native, I'm inexperienced with heavy winter boots like those, so—"

"So I can fix that." With a grin, Kristen shucked her boots. They clunked to the rug covering the hardwood floor. She wriggled atop the mattress with her back to him for a few more seconds, then she tossed aside something else. "And a bonus for you, too, just to help you out as a wintertime novice."

Grinning, she launched herself at him again. They collided on the bed in an impassioned tangle of arms and legs and heart-pounding middles, and Casey realized in a daze that it had been her tights that Kristen had sent sailing across the bedroom. Which meant her legs were bare now, bare and silky beneath his hands, and it occurred to him that she might have slipped off her panties, too, in which case there would be no stopping them.

Riveted by the thought, Casey felt himself grow twice as engorged, twice as hard, twice as ready. If he didn't get his pants off soon, he might as well kiss the zipper good-bye. Because there was no way a measly few inches of metallic fastener could contain . . . well, *everything* he felt for Kristen.

Flatteringly, she noticed. Before he could fully explore her potential under-the-dress nudity, she wriggled sideways, took a good, long look at the bulge in his pants, then drew in a deep breath. Her dark-eyed gaze lifted to his.

"Yes, please," Kristen said with a seductive eyebrow raise. "I'd like *all* of that. As quickly as possible, too."

Casey almost groaned aloud. "I can't wait to give it to you."

She smiled. "I'd like to point out that you're *already* waiting. Seeing as how you're still wearing all those clothes."

"Well, in the interest of fair play . . ."

Casey whipped off his suit vest, unbuttoned his shirt, and did his best not to pant too loudly. He'd never felt so driven, so desperate, so full of desire and need and . . . *tenderness?* Again?

No, it couldn't be that. Because they were only here to have a good time. Yes, he'd assured Kristen that there was more between them than just a deskbound quickie, but there were miles of wiggle room between that and what he *might* be feeling now.

Even if he loved her, it would be a mistake to let her know. Being vulnerable could only lead to trouble. Casey knew that. He knew that the same way he knew how it felt to breathe.

Which he *almost* forgot to do just then. Because while he'd been wrestling with his demons and the many buttons of his shirt, Kristen had been busy working her magic on his zipper.

Biting her lip in anticipation, clearly reveling in her erotic victory over his pants, she trailed her fingers over his crotch. This time, Casey *did* groan. He couldn't help it. He levered his hips upward, all thoughts emptying from his head like the unnecessary complications they were. There was nothing in the world better than Kristen touching him. There was nothing better than her looking at him, devouring him with her eyes, letting him know that she wanted this, wanted him, wanted *more*.

In fact, if all Casey ever had was this moment, this feeling between them, this first-night, last-night togetherness . . .

Well, it might have to be enough. He knew that, too.

"Mmm." With a seductive purr, Kristen slipped her hand into his open fly. She caressed him, making his boxer briefs feel tighter and more of an unwanted barrier than ever before. "I can't tell you how many times I've thought about touching you this way." Her gaze lifted to his, even as she went on stroking him—even as she made him tremble. "It was a pretty good fantasy, but I have to say, reality is even better. You feel . . . *amazing*."

He felt *constricted*. Also, yearning and urgent and sorry he hadn't yet tugged off her dress. Mindlessly, Casey lowered his hands to its knitted hem, intending to do exactly that. But then he got distracted—between Kristen's caresses and his own discovery that if he slid his palms up her thighs, savoring the sleek curves and soft skin he found there, it made Kristen moan in a very satisfying way—and he forgot to undress her at all.

Instead, Casey swept his hands higher, to her hips, feeling her shake now beneath his touch, and he kissed her again, even as they rolled over on the bed once more, and he didn't want her to stop touching him, except that if she didn't stop, he would forget his gentlemanly share-and-share-alike impulses completely. With a groan of sheer desire, Casey broke off from their next kiss and panted against her neck.

"You're driving me crazy," he murmured, helpless to resist cradling her breasts in both hands now, feeling her nipples peak beneath her dress's cozy knit. "I've got to have more."

Slyly, she arched her brows. "More than this?"

As she said it, she caressed him again, bringing him to an even greater sense of urgency. Casey realized, hazily, that if he didn't speak now, he might lose the ability to do so for . . . oh, several hours more. He gritted his teeth, then nodded.

"Yes," he managed to say. "A lot more than that."

She kissed him, then delicately trailed her fingertips along the turgid length of him. "More than this?"

Casey shuddered. He closed his eyes. He nodded. "Yes."

This time, coming up with additional words was beyond him. As though sensing that, Kristen moved languorously nearer. Her breasts pressed against his chest; her mouth met his, then delivered a naughty bite to his lower lip. "More than . . . this?"

She straddled him again, pushed him to the mattress, then slowly slid herself down his body. Her tumbledown hair dragged sensuously over him as she kissed his neck, his chest, his taut belly. With a needful gesture, Kristen wrenched apart his unbuttoned shirt. She stroked him, slid a little lower, then brought her lips to the bare skin just visible at the junction of his open fly. She kissed him there. Casey nearly levitated.

Her intentions were plain. She was going to kiss him . . . *everywhere*. His mouth. His chest. His belly. His cock.

At the thought, Casey moaned again. He hadn't even taken off his own clothes the way he'd planned, much less gotten Kristen naked. How had she taken control of things between them?

He didn't know. But he did know how to get it back.

So Casey thrust his hands in her hair, tilted her face to his, then gave her a brilliant smile. "I have a better idea."

Kristen smiled back. Then she looked directly—and admiringly—at him. "Better than this?" She chuckled, then made her point by caressing him again. "I don't think so."

"I do." Another gasp. "I'd like a chance to prove it."

"Mmm?" Still seeming engrossed by the contents of his black boxer briefs, Kristen went on looking at him. With apparent effort, she finally raised her gaze from his cock. "Prove what?"

"I'll show you," Casey assured her. Then he did, starting with a heady, tongue-sweet kiss—and ending with Kristen pulling off her sweater dress . . . exactly the way he'd hoped she would.

Or maybe even better than the way he'd hoped she would. Because she scrambled up from the bed with a provocative gleam in her eyes, then sent her dress and bra sailing off to join the rest of their cast-off clothes without a second's hesitation.

Casey nearly applauded. He'd never seen a woman undress with quite the same élan as Kristen did, it occurred to him. Because where some women got naked nervously, and a few got naked proudly, Kristen got naked while exuding an unmistakable sense of keen anticipation. It was as though she knew that only good things could come from baring herself completely to him.

The idea was as alien to Casey as pie-in-a-jar had been.

In that moment, though, Kristen possessed exactly what he needed and wanted, and she exulted in that knowledge. She was womanly and openhearted. She was sweet and indomitable. She was real and imperfect and completely at ease with that, and although they had never been together before, she was ready to give and receive and take all the pleasure they could share, and as Casey watched her turn to face him, it was all he could do not to gawk in wonder. Because where he definitely appreciated her pert derrière and graceful back and poised arms—and where he absolutely loved her hips and thighs and waist and shoulders and lovely rounded breasts, too—what he truly enjoyed seeing most was the promise in her eyes as Kristen looked at him.

"I'm going to make you *so* happy you're here," she said.

Shaken, Casey swallowed hard. "I'm already happy."

"Oh, you have no idea." Smiling, Kristen came a little closer. She trailed her hand over her naked thigh. Then her hip. Then higher, to her breast. Her budded pink nipple pushed against her fingers. "You can get *much* happier than that."

To demonstrate that, she came closer. She took off his shirt in one certain motion, a full-service striptease that left Casey glad to be shirtless for her. Her bare breasts bobbed enticingly in front of his face, just out of reach, as Kristen leaned back again, still standing near the bed, to examine him.

When she nodded, Casey felt as though he'd won . . . *everything*.

"You look *great,*" she told him. "Even better than I imagined." Her big-eyed gaze confirmed that it was true. Her attention roved approvingly from his shoulders to his arms, from his chest to his abs, then lower still. She smiled. "You belong someplace where you can be shirtless all the time. You're hiding your light under a bushel."

He wanted to make a joke of that. He wanted to remain unaffected by that cornball Midwestern saying of hers and *not* feel pleased that Kristen liked the way he looked. He wanted to remind her that ordinarily he *would* have been shirtless on a beach somewhere at this time of year. But Casey just couldn't do it. Transfixed by her easy nudity— by the tantalizing nearness of her hips, her thighs, the blond triangle of curls at their apex, and all the glorious rest of her—he could only nod.

Then he realized . . . Kristen had done it again! She'd beaten him at his own game. She'd taken control of their tryst.

If he wasn't careful, she'd take control of his heart, too, Casey knew. Or at least she would have done that, if his heart had been available for the taking. As it was . . .

As it was, he was thinking and feeling, when he should have been doing. So he reached out and took Kristen's hand. He pulled her nearer to him. He inhaled the intoxicating scent of her—that dizzying amalgamation of cinnamon and sugar and femaleness—and he brought his other hand to her back to hold her close to him, and in the moment when Casey finally brought his mouth to her breast and heard her moan, he realized something else.

All he wanted was Kristen's pleasure. All he needed was to make her feel . . . *everything*. So Casey pulled her down to meet him. He kissed her with a hunger and a hardness that surprised even him. And he lost himself in the feel of her warm, soft skin, her incredible feminine shape, her sweet, spicy scent and her hot, wet warmth and her cries of enjoyment and her bedazzled, head-tossing looks of wonder as he went on loving her.

Because that's what he was doing, whether she knew it or not, Casey realized as he drew Kristen back onto the bed and into his arms. During those long, intimate moments, he lavished her with all the love he possessed and all the skill he could muster, and as her breathy cries filled the room, he knew he would never forget the way Kristen looked as he drove her on and on, as she clutched the Christmassy printed sheets, as she shuddered in ecstasy, as she came undone, screaming in his arms, with the glow of the holiday lights all around them both.

She'd never been more open to him. Or more beautiful. But Casey had little time to think about that. Because even as his ears still rang with the husky sounds of Kristen's pleasure, she opened her eyes. She angled her flushed, radiant face toward him. Then she trailed her fingers down his chest to his cock.

"I think we've already established that I want this, too," she murmured with a wicked gleam in her eyes. "Please."

"Well, since you're being so polite . . ." Giddily, Casey

smiled at her, feeling almost overcome with gladness at being with her this way. "I'll see what I can do about that."

Moaning, Kristen clenched the sheets again. "Hurry up."

"Bossy, aren't you?" Secretly loving that, he kissed her again. He situated himself between her thighs, where she felt exactly as hot and wet and ready as he'd dreamed. Then he teased them both by entering her . . . just barely. "Mmm. How's that?"

"More." Kristen tossed her head. "Please."

"Ah. Yes. More." With an impatient shudder of his own, Casey pushed further. Bliss enveloped him, making him groan. Somehow, he managed to hold back an urge to thrust harder. "How about now?" he inquired in a raspy tone. "Better?"

Kristen's incoherent response counted as a no, he figured. Especially since she clutched at his back, his hips, his ass, trying to bring him closer to her. "Please, Casey. I want—"

"Yes?"

"*You,*" she finally said, opening her eyes with an adoring look he knew he would always treasure, no matter how unwise it was to do so. "I want *you,* Casey," she said. "Please—"

"You've got me," he assured her roughly, partly to stop her from saying anything more. Because Casey couldn't believe in anything more. Not then. Not for him. Not even with her.

A heartbeat later, he pushed that knowledge from his mind and finally made Kristen his. He united them both in the best possible way. Hot, pulsing, grinding together, they made real every fantasy, and it was everything Casey had ever imagined.

Again and again he thrust inside her; again and again she met him with an exuberance and a passion that humbled him. With Kristen, he wanted more and more . . . and he got it, too, with a thundering, heart-pounding, headboard rattling climax that left Casey shouting her name. He'd never felt anything like it.

But then, he'd never known anyone like her.

Spent and replete afterward, Casey lolled on the mattress with Kristen wrapped in his arms. It was possible he'd just had an out-of-body experience. It was also possible that Kristen had come again, just before him, with another shout and a series of sweet convulsions that had tipped him right over the edge.

Wearing a beaming grin, Kristen gazed at the ceiling. Her hair flowed across the pillows. Her hand clasped his. Her profile appeared both enchanting and enchantingly familiar to him. Because now that they'd shared . . . well, *everything* with each other, Casey had the sense that they were forever changed by the experience. No one else would ever know Kristen in exactly the way he did. No one else would ever know *him* the way she did.

Suddenly alarmed by the thought, Casey went still. He felt freakishly vulnerable and foolishly happy, all at the same time. It occurred to him that maybe those two states went hand in hand somehow, and that was why he'd never experienced them in this way before. Because he was *never* vulnerable, not anymore, and he was rarely—if he was truly honest with himself—completely happy.

Did that mean he couldn't be happy without being vulnerable? *If so, screw that,* Casey thought with a burst of belligerence. Because not even happiness was worth opening up like an idiot. That was just asking to be kicked in the teeth.

But then Kristen sighed and hugged him close, and Casey forgot about being introspective. Because the here and now was all he'd ever been able to count on. That hadn't changed just because he'd had mind-blowing sex. He had to remember that.

"Wow," Kristen breathed, looking starry-eyed. "That was . . ."

"Earth-shattering," Casey supplied.

"Yeah." Her quixotic tone made him happy. So did the way she snuggled even closer, then put her head on his shoulder. "Unless we had a rare Michigan earthquake just now, I think there's only one explanation for what happened here tonight."

Grinning over her teasing, Casey stroked her hair. He could have spent all night this way—with frequent breaks for more erotic activities thrown in, of course. "Mmm? What's that?"

"Christmas came early this year," Kristen told him with a smile in her voice. "That's what happened. I got just what I wanted, too."

"Good. No coal in your stocking, then?"

"Hey. If that's a euphemism—"

"It's not." Warding off the idea with his palm outstretched toward her holiday lights, Casey laughed. "Cut me some slack. I'm a Christmas newbie. I don't know what the protocol is."

"Not for long, you won't be a newbie," Kristen assured him with a kiss. "Speaking of which . . . I have big plans for you."

Casey hoped those plans included more romps between her snowman-printed flannel sheets. He was seriously never going to be able to look at novelty Christmas sheets without getting a hard-on. If *that's* what she meant . . . "I'm yours to command."

But Kristen missed his suggestive tone. Instead, she pursed her lips, clearly still considering her "big plans" for him.

"First, I'm going to take you candlelight ice-skating at the Kismet rink," she announced. "Then maybe afterward—"

"Will you be wearing one of those short, flippy little ice-skating skirts? Because that has some promise." Grinning anew, Casey pictured it. "Maybe I'll agree, if I get to see that."

"Then some Christmas caroling," Kristen went on, disappointingly neither confirming nor denying her intentions to wear a sexy skating skirt for him. "I know Talia and Walden and Gareth and Avery will want to come along for that. After that—"

"Is there a sexy outfit for Christmas caroling, too?" Casey wanted to know. "Because if you're going to be carrying an old-timey candle and wearing one of those long monk robes—"

"They're called choir robes."

"—then I don't know if I'm on board with caroling."

"You will be, once I get through with you."

"Oh yeah?" Unreasonably intrigued by Kristen's cocksure tone, Casey rolled over. Nude and happy, he propped his head in his hand so he could better enjoy the sight of *her* looking nude and happy. "Are you going to brainwash me? Convert me? Drug me?"

"In a manner of speaking. I'm going to persuade you with sex to do whatever I want. No matter how Christmassy it is."

"You're going to persuade me *with sex?*" That sounded good to him. But Casey didn't want to let on how easily he might be gulled by such a tactic, even by her. Doing so went against everything he was an expert in. "That's a devious plan."

"Fine. I'm going to persuade you with love and kindness to do whatever I want. No matter how Christmassy it is."

Love and kindness? *Love?* Did she mean that?

With his mind suddenly racing, Casey went motionless. He couldn't remember having blurted out an *I love you* a while ago (which might have prompted Kristen's casual mention of *love* now), but that didn't mean it hadn't happened. He *had* been feeling that weird, unstoppable romantic tenderness toward her . . .

Anything could have happened. No matter how crazy that would be. While overcome with his feelings for Kristen, Casey knew, he might have said anything.

That would be bad. So bad. Why couldn't he just be happy with what he had for once? Why couldn't he stop grabbing for more? By now, he knew better than to expect to get it.

Right then, Casey vowed not to say anything else that might get him in over his head with her. No matter what. It wouldn't be fair to Kristen to let her believe he might be capable of more than he could give. Like forever. Or even next week.

He wasn't good at commitment. He refused to let her believe he was. Hell, he didn't even know what commitment looked like.

"Hey." She nudged him. "Are you okay? Where'd you go?"

Casey blinked. Feeling his heart pounding, he looked at Kristen. Slowly, her concerned face came into focus.

Her expression reminded him that she was more than capable of being kind and loving *without* being head-over-heels crazy for someone. Especially him. What they had was casual, right? Her remark about love and kindness probably didn't mean anything.

"I was only kidding," she went on, inadvertently confirming as much. "If you don't want to do that Christmassy stuff, we don't have to. I mean, I have ways of making you want to"—here, Kristen broke off to deliver him a saucy look—"but I'm not in the business of forcing people to wassail."

Casey was afraid to ask what that meant. "Sounds kinky."

"I know, right?" Apparently satisfied, Kristen snuggled up to him again. "Don't worry. If I do my job right, you'll be *dying* to go wassailing in no time. Believe me, once you open yourself up to Christmas in Kismet, it definitely gets to you."

"Yeah. That's what I'm afraid of."

"Hmm?"

"Nothing. Hey, how big is your shower?"

Instantly alert, Kristen eyed him. "It's . . . shower sized."

"Smartass." But Casey couldn't help loving that about her. Kristen's sense of humor was one of the many things he liked about her. He also liked that she wasn't afraid to give him a hard time—and that she *didn't* buckle under his supposedly hypnotic troubleshooter routine. She was too smart to be easily led. She was also too straightforward to pretend otherwise. Casey appreciated that. "Is your shower big enough for two?"

"Hmm." Kristen bit her lip. Then she threw back the covers and leaped from the bed. "There's only one way to find out."

Stark naked and magnificently vivacious, she jerked the covers off Casey, too. Then she gave a comical eyebrow waggle.

"Race you to the shower. Last one there buys breakfast!"

Kristen took off running, bare-assed, toward the unknown location of her bathroom, before Casey could even react to her challenge. "Hey! Does that mean I'm staying for breakfast?"

He really hoped (foolishly and helplessly) that he was staying for breakfast.

From down the hallway, Kristen popped back into the bedroom. Her breasts bobbed invitingly. Her waist nipped in alluringly. Her wild blond hair and unique cocky stance and bright-eyed, pink-cheeked face drew in Casey in ways he didn't even want to contemplate. Kristen was . . . perfect. Perfect for him.

"You can stay all month, if you want. It's up to you." She lifted her shoulder in an elegant shrug. "My apartment can't beat The Christmas House for ambiance, but it has its charms."

"I'll say," Casey told her. "Because *you* come with it."

"Aw." Another flirty look. "That's nice. But flattery *won't* help you win the who-pays-for-breakfast shower race."

Then Kristen took off again, leaving Casey behind to realize that, not only was he in imminent danger of losing his first-ever shower race . . . but he was also alarmingly *disappointed* to know that Kristen *hadn't* been saying she loved him before.

Because, perversely, he'd wanted her to. He'd wanted her to love him, and he'd wanted her to want him to stay with her, too. *Non*casually. For a night or a week or a month or forever.

He was *really* in over his head with her.

So what, exactly, was he supposed to do now?

Chapter 19

Kismet, Michigan
Christmas Takeover: Day . . . oh, who cares?

Actually *racing* Casey to her shower was the second-dorkiest thing Kristen had done that night, she realized as she reached her bathroom. The first had been practically shouting from the rooftops that she was planning to love him. *Love him!*

As if someone like Casey was going to go for that.

He didn't even want to be in Kismet! He had other options, other plans, other tropical getaways to escape to— probably with other nonsnowbound, bikini-wearing women to accompany him. Kristen knew that. She'd always known that. So why had she let a single night of astounding sex set her off-kilter so much?

Kristen didn't know what was wrong with her. Wrenching on the shower taps didn't enlighten her. Neither did watching the water cascade from her showerhead, predictably and ordinarily, just as though this night was like any other night.

Kristen knew differently. This was the night when she'd officially fallen in love with Casey, and that made it special forever. Even if he didn't return her feelings. Even if he'd be returning home to Los Angeles in a matter of weeks. Even if . . .

Even if he'd only met her because he wanted to keep an eye on everyone connected with Heather and her holiday TV special.

Oh yeah. If meeting her dream man via her divalicious sister wasn't the pinnacle of irony, Kristen didn't know what was. Because Heather typically torpedoed Kristen's chances at love, just by being herself. Kristen had lost count, over the years, of how many of her "boyfriends" had revealed that they'd secretly been seeing her as a means to get closer to Heather. That kind of amateur subterfuge wasn't anything she needed to worry about with Casey, but he presented unique challenges all his own—challenges Kristen didn't normally have to deal with.

Usually I'm really good at spur-of-the moment casual encounters, she'd told him. And with just as much certainty, Casey had set her straight. This isn't a casual encounter.

And that was the crux of the problem, wasn't it? Still. And maybe forever. Because until Kristen knew if she could trust Casey, she couldn't give him anything more. At least not openly.

She had her heart to think about, after all. She liked it whole and unbroken, ready to give to someone who deserved it. She wanted that someone to be Casey. But until she knew more . . .

Well, until she knew more, Kristen reminded herself as she closed her eyes, leaned against the bathroom wall, and listened to the water cascading in the shower as it warmed up, she would just have to be careful. Or she would have to find a way to suss out Casey's true intentions. Maybe, while showing him the Christmas adventure of a lifetime, she could do exactly that.

Or maybe she could just take a chance and give in. Because that's what she really wanted to do. No matter how dumb it was.

"Hey," came Casey's deep, affectionate-sounding voice. "Here you are."

As usual, his arrival made Kristen melt. She opened her eyes to see him lounging naked in her bathroom doorway with one shoulder against the jamb, tousle-haired and mouth-wateringly sexy, looking at her as though he knew everything she needed.

More than likely, he did. And he wanted to give it to her.

"Yeah," she said, rousing herself. "I win!"

At her victorious, both-arms-up gesture, Casey smiled sexily. "Well, then," he said. "Let me offer you your prize."

Feeling herself go all loose-limbed and breathless, simply at his approach, Kristen knew that her supposed love-him, don't-love-him quandary was really a nonstarter after all. She could no more stop herself loving Casey than she could make it be ninety degrees and sunny in Kismet on Christmas this year.

She smiled at him, then stepped naked into his arms. His eyes sparkled down at her, his strong body cradled her, and all she could think was that Casey was . . . perfect. Perfect for her.

"I begin to think you weren't even trying to win the race," Kristen accused in a lighthearted tone. "You slacker."

"Guilty." Not the least bit abashed to have come in second in their challenge, Casey kissed her. "I decided I'd enjoy congratulating you a lot more than I'd enjoy winning."

"But you're supercompetitive! Just look at you and Shane—"

"I'd rather look at you." Giving her a dazzling grin, Casey kissed her again. He cradled her jaw in his hand, let his gaze roam over her face, then nodded. "Yep. You're worth losing for."

"Wow," Kristen cracked, unable to resist a joke. Because Casey was too close to making her believe him, and she didn't want that. "That's what every woman dreams of hearing."

"You're worth fighting for and dying for," Casey amended seriously, locking his gaze on hers. "You're worth everything."

At that, Kristen couldn't hold out any longer. She could resist Casey's sexiness (up to a point). She could withstand his flirtatiousness (sometimes). She could even hold the line against his charm (occasionally). But his sincerity?

His sincerity left her disarmed.

Giving in completely at last, Kristen kissed him back.

"I'm really going to love that free breakfast tomorrow morning." With a wink, she pulled away. She drew aside the plastic curtain, then nodded toward her steamy shower. "This looks big enough for both of us to me. What do you say?"

"I say," Casey informed her as he took her hand, "that you're going to have a hard time getting me out of here."

They both stepped into the spray. Laughing as its warmth hit her, Kristen turned. Casey raised his big, soapy, extra-talented hands, then approached her with a purposeful look.

"Hey, don't look so wary," he teased, flexing his lathered-up fingers. "I only have the best intentions at heart."

Offered another chance to trust him, even in a tiny way, Kristen nodded. She opened her wet arms to the sides, baring herself entirely to Casey. "Go ahead," she said. "I dare you."

Because the only way to get anything in life, she remembered in the few fleeting seconds before Casey's soapy hands caressed her and made her quit thinking altogether, was to be completely open to it—to just let go and let it all in.

Here I am, Kristen thought. *Yours, for now or forever.*

But since she was still her—and she couldn't possibly be passive about something as important as this and still respect herself in the morning—she just had to raise the stakes.

"Because I think I love you, Casey," Kristen said bravely, touching his face as the shower rained down on them. She blinked as the warm water struck her face. "I really, really do."

Looking down at her, Casey blinked, too. He grinned. "Hmm?"

He hadn't heard her. Oh. Well, maybe that was a sign.

Maybe in situations like this, being bold and assertive was overrated.

Maybe declaring her feelings for him didn't have to happen yet.

"Hand over the soap," Kristen said loudly instead, gesturing toward it. "I want a turn at soaping you, too."

Casey angled his head, looking at her more closely, and for a second Kristen had the impression he *had* heard her the first time.

Then he shook his head. He gave her another rascally grin. He lowered both wet hands to her breasts. "Not this time," Casey vowed hoarsely. "This time, I'm having things my way first."

Kristen meant to disagree. Honestly, she did. But there was something intrinsically magical about the way Casey touched her . . . and as he went on stroking her, adroitly and sensuously and with a clear sense of manly enjoyment, she found she simply didn't have the will to resist him. It turned out, she realized, that when it came to her and Casey together . . . he won every time.

"Heather? Hi!" Speaking via cell phone to her sister's voice mail account, Kristen paced across her bedroom wearing a short robe. The thin light of another wintery December morning penetrated her curtains, then fell on the discarded clothes she and Casey had left on the bureau and chair and floor the night before. Even after an entire long weekend spent together—beginning on the evening of Christmas Disco Night and continuing during the past two days—they still hadn't bothered dealing with the hilarious amounts of cast-off clothing they generated by getting dressed and undressed. "I just wanted to find out how you're doing," Kristen said into her phone to Heather. "I was wondering how your doctor's visit went the other day, and, um . . ."

Breaking off, Kristen scooped up Casey's shirt. Feeling

sentimental, she inhaled the distinctly masculine scent that clung to its starched folds. She hugged it to her chest. Just holding it reminded her of everything she and Casey had shared.

Kristen never wanted to forget it. She doubted she ever would. No matter what happened between them next, now that their romantic, sex-filled, amazing lost weekend was coming to an end.

". . . wondering whether you're out of quarantine yet," Kristen went on to her sister, "and I wanted to let you know that I *have* been receiving all your texts with your food-in-a-jar ideas."

There had been, literally, at least a dozen texts from Heather over the past several days—so many that Casey had taken to teasing Kristen about her "consultant" sister and their budding "partnership" involving the Galaxy Diner and its food.

"And thank you for thinking of me," Kristen added, "but that's probably all the new-item ideas I need for right now . . ."

Or for forever, her more prideful side suggested, unwilling to admit that Heather—as a pop star and *not* a baker-turned-diner owner—had actually proposed a few useful suggestions, scattered among the obviously hallucinatory food-in-a-jar concepts.

". . . and um, well, usually you answer your phone," Kristen told Heather, still hugging Casey's shirt, "so I'm sorry I missed you, but I guess maybe the doctor is there with you or something. I'll try again later, okay? I hope you're feeling better."

With a shake of her head for her typically flaky sister, Kristen disconnected the call. She might not have reached Heather, but at least she hadn't been shunted automatically to a member of Heather's entourage via the "personal number" (actually an assistant's phone) that her sister usually gave out.

Kristen was one of the chosen few who had Heather's real

phone number. Heather had ordered her to guard it with her life—even though, as far as Kristen knew, her sister still wasn't feeling well and would hardly be expecting a gazillion calls.

It was possible that Heather was being extracautious now though because, deprived of oddball sightings of their favorite pop-star diva during her chicken-pox quarantine, the press had gotten more desperate than ever to get the scoop on her.

In Heather's absence, they'd started speculating that her quarantine was only a publicity stunt. They'd begun hanging around her holiday TV-special set with new fervor, printing rumors, and pressing "close friends" of Heather's to confide in them about what Heather was "really" up to in her "hideaway" at Lagniappe at the Lakeshore. Gareth had been approached for gossip; so had a couple of Kristen's regulars at the diner.

Kristen hadn't been approached. Not yet. But until Heather emerged from quarantine and (A) proved she had *not* been hiding in a "love nest," (B) was *not* pregnant, and (C) was *not* dating a "bohemian boy toy," those shenanigans would probably continue. Because evidently, where the paparazzi were concerned, "friends" were merely "unnamed sources" and "quarantine" *had* to be code for "astonishing secret that should be published immediately!"

Not for the first time, Kristen felt glad not to have her sister's "charmed life" for her own. Because despite her occasional protests, Heather (mostly) lived for the attention. Everyone knew Heather loved getting special treatment. It was like oxygen to her. She wanted it, demanded it, and got it.

Whereas Kristen got . . . well, she got a variety of sore muscles in unusual places after a long weekend spent doing some *very* imaginative things with Casey, she remembered with a private grin. That man was definitely creative. He had stamina to spare, too. Kristen had the pleasantly achy inner thighs, twinge-y shoulder muscles, and (possible) minor neck strain to prove it.

She really ought to try to behave with a little *less* abandon sometimes, Kristen told herself as she headed for the other room. But when it came to Casey, control was very hard to find.

So was perspective, Kristen learned as she entered her kitchen and found Casey sitting at her built-in peninsula, chowing through a mini mason jar full of chocolate-cherry Black Forest pie with mocha whipped cream and bittersweet chocolate shavings and almond brittle. Because the downright *blissful* look on Casey's face left Kristen with no perspective at all.

He was fantastic. And sweet. The end.

He was also, Kristen observed, making roughly the same kinds of pleasure-filled sounds he'd made last night while making love to her. With each new forkful, Casey's ecstatic expression grew. His eyes fell closed. Another moan burst from him. He even gave a burly shoulder shimmy. Evidently, despite his frequent and enduring protestations to the contrary, Casey did *not* "hate" her pie, after all.

"Hey, there." Filled with simultaneous amusement and affection, Kristen stopped on the other side of the counter. She eyed Casey's expression of almost illicit pleasure. She grinned. "It looks as though you found a way to tolerate my pie."

At her poker-faced observation, Casey snapped open his eyes. Caught in the midst of actively cradling his pie-in-a-jar in one hand while fisting a whipped-cream-festooned forkful in the other, he gave her a guilty grin. "I was starving."

"Mmm-hmm."

"And I, um, couldn't find the ketchup in your fridge."

Kristen marched to her refrigerator. She opened the door. She pointed to the ketchup bottle. "It's right here." A meaningful pause. "Next to all the remaining pies in jars. You know—the pies that are identical to the one you're eating."

"Oh. I must have missed it," he bluffed. Outrageously.

"Of course. You missed it." At the realization that Casey *obviously* loved her baked goods, even if he didn't want to say so, Kristen couldn't hold back a wider smile. That was *almost* as good as him loving her. At least it was a fine first step. "Yeah, I'm always not seeing things that are right in front of my face," she told him wryly. "Sometimes, it's a real problem."

"Mmm-hmm." Confusingly, Casey's knowing tone suddenly matched hers. So did his smile, as he lowered his gaze to her chest. "Maybe that's why you didn't notice that you're hugging my shirt."

"Hugging your . . . huh?" Caught now herself, Kristen froze. Dumbly, she looked down at her arms—which were, just then, blatantly cuddling Casey's shirt like a teddy bear. "Oh!" Snared in the act of openly *embracing* Casey's shirt, as though it were a part of him instead of merely a memento from their weekend together, she searched for an excuse. "*This?* I'm just tidying up."

"That's funny." With utter confidence, Casey forked up more pie. Overtly, he savored it. "Because there are clothes strewn from one end of this place to the other"—at that, he gave her a wicked eyebrow waggle and a thigh-warmingly suggestive look—"yet you chose to wander around with my shirt in your arms."

Kristen lifted her chin. "It was within reach, that's all."

Casey's pointed gaze swerved to the small pile of gloves, scarves, and knit caps that had wound up on the peninsula after their ongoing adventures. Those misplaced items definitely needed tidying. They were, literally, well within arm's reach. Both of them knew it, too. Kristen felt her cheeks warming up.

"I'll forget the pie if you'll forget the shirt hugging," she offered hastily, giving him a canny look. "Deal?"

Casey considered it. "Maybe."

Argh. "Maybe what?"

"Maybe I'll want to sweeten the deal before agreeing."

Aha. "I'll throw in more pie. With my eyes closed."

At her flippant offer to support his secret pie habit—while simultaneously pretending not to know about it—Casey shook his head. "I don't want you doing anything with your eyes closed. Not when I love the way you look at me so much."

Deliberately, Kristen gave him a goofy, goggle-eyed look.

He laughed. "Although, speaking of your baked goods . . ."

Kristen waited, expecting him to request ketchup, just to make a point. Instead, Casey hesitated. He drew in a breath. He darted a glance at her, then rubbed the back of his neck.

Spying that gesture, Kristen froze. That neck rub was Casey's "tell." It was what he did when dealing with the cast and crew members from Heather's *Live! from the Heartland* holiday TV special, for instance. She'd seen him do it many times. But since that movement was so slight and seemed so natural, Kristen doubted most people noticed it. What in the world was he up to?

Probably he was conjuring up a custom pie-in-a-jar request, she decided as Casey's easygoing demeanor returned. That's what most people wanted from her—that or recipes. Most likely, Casey had been considering which items he could request in a personalized pie-in-a-jar that would best improve the deal she'd proposed. It would be just like him to push for bonus sprinkles.

Instead, to her surprise, he asked, "Have you ever thought of marketing your pies-in-a-jar? Maybe on a national scale?"

It was exactly what Shane Maresca had pressured her to do, Kristen realized. The idea had more appeal coming from Casey—from someone she trusted. But she still didn't want to do it.

She didn't want to risk grabbing for that brass ring—being the "*second* big success story" to come out of her hometown "burg"—because that was Heather's territory. Kristen couldn't possibly compete. She liked her life the way it was. Mostly.

Although having Repo Man/bankers stalking her over her mistakenly "in default" business mortgage wasn't ideal . . .

"I've thought about it," Kristen admitted. "I could use the money, if I could ever find any investors. And I do like the idea of more people being able to try my baked goods. I have that much ego. But . . ." Then she realized what Casey must *really* be doing: distracting her from her offer that they mutually agree to ignore their shirt-hugging, pie-loving, *hooray-I'm-in-love!* tics. "But what about my offer?" she pressed him, unwilling to give up on the idea so easily. She was stubborn that way. "No shirt-hugging noticing? No pie-loving mentioning? Is it a deal?"

"I don't know." Idly, Casey swirled his fork through his pie-in-a-jar's mocha-whipped-cream topping, giving up on his baked-goods-marketing idea much more readily than Shane Maresca had. He glanced up at her. "I still might want more."

"More? Well, I *do* have more pie in the fridge."

"And I have more shirts available for nonstop hugging." His eyes gleamed mischievously at her. "That's not what I mean."

"Okay." Kristen tried not to feel like a freak for holding on to his laundry. She couldn't relent now. "I'm listening."

"Well, what I want isn't a big deal," Casey said casually. "The thing is, we've spent a few really great days together—"

"Yes." Kristen nodded. Her thighs practically tingled in agreement as she considered everything that had gone on between them during the past few days—and nights. "We sure have."

"—and I've been thinking that I might want to duck out of The Christmas House earlier than I'd originally planned," Casey went on. "Because despite my interest in keeping an eye on Shane, and despite the B&B's friendly management and staff, I'm not really into all that holiday atmosphere."

At that preposterous understatement, Kristen smiled.

"So, if your offer to stay here for a while still stands," Casey said in a musing tone, "I'd like to accept."

Kristen blinked. She'd tossed out that invitation on a whim. But now . . . "You want to escape Christmas by staying *here?*"

Casey nodded. As though proving it, he looked around Kristen's apartment. Prompted by his example, she did, too—only to realize immediately that *no one* could ever realistically hope to escape Christmas in her apartment. Because pretty much, it appeared as though a supersize Christmas cracker had exploded inside. There were holiday lights and festive tchotchkes in every corner, plus a lighted Christmas tree in the other room. From its holly-and-poinsettia welcome mat to its wreath made of starlight mints glued to a Styrofoam circle—a handmade gift from the fifth graders at Kismet Elementary School—Kristen's apartment was decked out like Christmas Central. While it was *possible* that her place was a smidge less Christmassy than The Christmas House B&B was, it was certainly was no Grinchy haven.

But there was no payout in calling his bluff. Casey wanted to stay. And that made Kristen want to whoop. And maybe do a little happy dance. And maybe hug *him*, too. But she didn't.

Nonchalantly, she said, "Sure. I'll need *someone* to help me eat all those pies-in-a-jar. They're demo pies. Samples."

"They're delicious. Not that I'm admitting I ate any."

His grin captivated her, just the way it always did.

"I've never laid eyes on any of your shirts, either. Just FYI," Kristen told him, still cuddling the one she held. "As far as I'm concerned, you might as well be permanently shirtless."

It was an idea that had merit, she decided as she swept her gaze longingly over Casey's ultrabuff bod. He really was amazing to look at. Especially now, all shirtless and muscular and wearing yesterday's pants. They dipped dangerously low on his hip bones, encouraging her to look at Casey's bare rippled abs, consider his taut thighs, and remember all of the *very* impressive rest of him that was currently hidden from view.

If Kristen had her way, none of him would stay hidden for long. She liked the idea of meandering over to Casey's bar stool, dolloping some whipped cream on his chest, then licking it off. Slowly. She liked the idea of unbuckling his belt, unzipping his pants, and making sure Casey found something else to sound blissed-out about besides breakfast-time Black Forest pie-in-a-jar. Absolutely. She liked the idea of making Casey beg for her to love him, because he'd already done that at least once during their time together—in a husky, *urgent* tone that had thrilled her then and still thrilled her now—and Kristen suddenly wanted more. She wanted all of him. She wanted to give him all of her.

Including her heart. She'd kept it to herself long enough.

"Well, my part's done." Casey pushed away his mason jar, then rubbed his flat belly. "I guess we have a deal."

"I guess we do." Kristen tossed aside his shirt. Arms empty—but not for long—she sashayed over to him. She draped her arms around his neck, then gave him a provocative look. "We should probably do something to commemorate the occasion."

"Mmm." Looking interested, Casey swiveled on his bar stool. Appearing dubiously guileless, he reached for her. "That's a good idea. I wouldn't want our agreement to go uncelebrated."

"Me either," Kristen said, meeting his sham sincerity with an artless look of her own. "It's an important alliance."

"A monumental coming together."

"A party in the making."

"A party?" Casey raised his eyebrows in that sexy, playful way she loved so well. "Let's get the party started, then."

His new position placed her squarely in the V of his legs, and Casey took advantage of Kristen's nearness by bringing his hands to her waist. He slid his palms higher, caressing her through her short silky robe, making her feel lightheaded and needy and swamped with desire, all over again. With Casey, being touched was like a drug. She couldn't get enough of it.

His hands quit moving with his thumbs mere inches from her breasts. Breathlessly, Kristen resisted an urge to push herself all the way into his hands—to take what he was *almost* giving and show him how well she knew how to party. But then he kissed her, and his tongue slid against hers in an especially knee-weakening way, and a passionate moan rumbled from his chest to hers, communicating all the same yearning they'd shared for days, and it was all Kristen could do to hold on to him and kiss him back and remember to stay upright at the same time.

When their kiss finally ended, she gazed at him in wonder.

"If you could bottle your expertise at kissing me," Kristen said, "you'd be a millionaire. You could retire early from your troubleshooting job—"

"And take up kissing you full-time." Casey looked as though he approved of the idea. He also seemed just as moved by their kiss as she'd been. His jaw was stony, his eyes were compelling, and his mouth . . . Well, his mouth was *fabulous*. "Let's do it."

"Let's kiss some more?" Giddily, Kristen agreed. Among all the things she loved about Casey, his willingness to *not* be deadly serious about sex (at least not all the time) was at the top of the list. She lowered her hands to his fly. "Yes. Let's."

But just as she was getting to the good part—just as Casey was gazing at her through those dark eyes of his with caring and kindness and a gratifying amount of lust, just as Kristen was feeling herself becoming more and more liquid and languid and heated beneath his continuing touch—an irritating noise sounded.

Kristen started. She had the impression, somehow, that the sound had been going on a while. Casey didn't seem to care, but—

"I think that's your cell phone," she said, stroking him.

"It's probably yours," Casey insisted huskily, "with another 'something-in-a-jar' suggestion from your favorite 'consultant.'" He nuzzled her neck. "I silenced my phone."

"This time of year, my phone plays 'Here Comes Santa Claus,'" Kristen disagreed, panting. "That's definitely yours."

Casey frowned at her. "I keep my phone segregated with call lists for whatever job I'm on, and I don't let calls come through when I'm not on duty. I already made some calls and checked in with my agency in L.A. while you were in the shower earlier. The only way my phone could be ringing now is if—"

The unwanted reality hit them both at the same time.

"—if something's gone wrong with Heather's TV special," they said in unison.

At their synchronized hypotheses, Kristen and Casey both swiveled their gazes toward the source of that sound. As Kristen had predicted, Casey's cell phone skittered atop the peninsula near the pile of discarded hats and mufflers, chattering for attention with a decidedly non-Christmassy ringtone.

"Sorry." Casey gave her a beleaguered look. "That means there's an emergency on set. I've got to take this."

Kristen tried to be understanding. Truly, she did. But as much as her rational mind tried to communicate to her hot-and-bothered body that (for now) sexy-fun-time with Casey was on hold, the message did not get through. The pulsing sensation between her thighs only continued. So did the yearning in her hips, the breathlessness in her chest, and the achiness in her breasts. Her nipples felt hard enough to cut glass; her fingers couldn't resist trailing along Casey's thigh as he spoke on his phone to whomever was on the other end of the line.

Mmm. His thigh was tight and warm and muscular, and it led conveniently to a very intriguing Y-junction in his pants. Just when Kristen was approaching nirvana, Casey covered her hand with his. His quelling gesture effectively shut down her explorations. Kristen pouted up at him. *Buzzkill,* she mouthed.

"All right. Yes. I understand," he said into his phone.

Commiseratingly, Casey caught her eye. He squeezed her hand, too. But most of his attention was directed toward the apparent crisis he was being rudely interrupted to deal with.

Kristen didn't like it. She'd been hoping the "emergency" call was anything but—just an overeager gaffer who needed Casey to give him investment advice or a Galaxy Diner regular who wanted to invite Casey to yet another holiday party.

"I'll be there as soon as I can," he said authoritatively.

Impatiently, Kristen waited, hoping there was still a chance that *as soon as I can* would translate to *after I make love to Kristen on a bar stool and drive her wild with desire.* But to her dismay, when Casey disconnected the call and set down his cell phone, he did not pull her nearer and resume what they'd already started. Instead, he shot her an apologetic look.

"I'm sorry," Casey said again, already looking around for the rest of his clothes. After days of intermittent nudity, they wouldn't be easy to find. "I have to be on set right away."

"What's the matter?" Kristen asked. "Did a fight break out between the grips and the set decorators? Did someone find drip coffee in their espresso cup? What's the catastrophe this time?"

Not answering immediately, Casey grabbed his wrinkled shirt. He dragged it on. Hastily, he tucked it in his pants with the air of someone who had no time to waste on niceties like ironing. He strode around her apartment with an efficiency that could only have come from having a photographic memory of where he'd dropped his socks, tie, vest, and suit coat. With all their former intimacy clearly forgotten, Casey stopped in front of Kristen as he pulled on his overcoat and adjusted his collar.

"Heather is back on set," he said, "and she's given the

crew twenty-four hours to finish filming the TV special before she gets on a plane and buggers off to God only knows where."

Kristen gawked. "Heather is *leaving* Kismet?"

"Apparently so."

"But she's been in quarantine!"

"Evidently, it's ended." Casey pocketed his cell phone. He put on his cherished, ultraexpensive watch, then double-checked his wallet. "But her quarantine did put the production even more behind than it was before. Hence her rush, I'd imagine."

"Heather actually gave the crew an *ultimatum?*"

That didn't sound right to Kristen. Ordinarily, her sister was not the world's most ambitious pop-star songstress. Heather was content to sail along with other people directing her career. For her to take charge now didn't quite make sense.

But Kristen was too annoyed, just then, to worry about it beyond her initial sense of confusion. Because Casey appeared to be getting ready to bolt from her apartment (aka their impromptu love nest) without so much as a backward glance. And that kind of behavior, given all they'd shared, kind of hurt a girl's feelings. Especially a girl who'd been overlooked and/or thrown over, time and time again, for her glamourpuss sister.

Kristen frowned at Casey. "Can't someone else handle it?"

"It's my job. This is what I'm here for."

"I know, but . . ." A brilliant, practical, sexy-time-saving idea hit her. Doggedly, Kristen pursued Casey as he searched for his keys amid her apartment's jolly Christmas décor. "What about Shane? He could take care of this, couldn't he?"

Casey gave a dark chuckle. "He'd like that. But no."

"Why not? He's practically your doppelganger!"

"He's more like my evil twin." Casey jangled his car keys. "And the fact that you're suggesting he could double for me means you haven't spent nearly enough time on set."

"Oh. So now I'm an insufficiently supportive sister?"

"Huh?" Appearing genuinely baffled by her aggrieved tone, Casey stopped. "What are you talking about?"

Kristen couldn't believe he didn't understand why this situation bothered her. "What if I asked you to stay here?"

What if I asked you to choose me? she added silently.

But Casey only smiled. "You wouldn't ask me to do that."

"Why not?"

Now he looked certain. "Because you don't need to."

His cryptic reply irked her. "Obviously I do," Kristen said, "since you've got one foot out the door already."

"Very funny." Smiling, Casey cradled her jaw in his hand. Then he kissed her. "Thanks for a great . . . *everything,*" he said.

Then he tossed her a wink and headed off at a near run to answer Heather's imperious beck and call, just the way everyone always did, leaving Kristen behind to be forgotten about . . . just the way everyone, inevitably, always did.

Chapter 20

South side of Kismet, Michigan
*14½ mixing, stirring, fudge-making, expertly garnished
days until Christmas*

It wouldn't have been Christmas in Kismet without holiday
lights, a big snowy parade, and jingle bells. And it wouldn't
have been Christmas at the Galaxy Diner, Walden had
learned, without marshmallow-filled, chocolate Bûche de
Noël mini-cupcakes, chubby gingerbread cookies in the
shape of teddy bears with buttercream details, and several
batches of traditional mincemeat pies-in-a-jar with brown
sugar hard sauce and candied cranberries for a garnish. Unfortunately, the plethora of specialized holiday goodies—and
the sheer volume of demand for those goodies—meant that
he and the rest of the diner's pastry department were under
constant pressure during the month of December. As the
days piled up and Christmas Day loomed ever closer on the
calendar, he felt increasingly frazzled.

Maybe that's why everything came to a head with Talia.

It started off innocently enough. Walden was working in
his apartment's cramped kitchen, spending his day off
deeply engrossed in testing different ways to sugarcoat

fresh cranberries—because he was kind of a workaholic that way—when Talia arrived. Walden didn't know that it was her at first. Because despite the fact that he'd given her a key shortly after their Heather-boy toy masquerade began, Talia never used it.

Instead, she knocked on his front door. Elbow deep in sugar, surrounded by bowls of cranberries coated with vanilla-bean-infused simple syrup and a variety of test sugars, Walden decided not to traipse all the way across the room to answer it.

"Come in," he called. "It's open."

"Walden? It's me! Talia!"

Then why was she bothering to knock? "Come in!"

She did come in, but not before opening the door and peering around its edge in a very tentative, very un-Talia-like way. Holding a bunch of shopping bags by their handles, she stepped inside, wearing the leopard-print coat she used to impersonate Heather Miller.

"I gave you your own key," Walden groused, unaccountably bothered by the fact that she refused to use it. And possibly by the fact that Talia was *still* pretending to be Heather, when she was awesome as herself. "Just use it already, will you?"

Talia looked startled. Then, defensive. Her gaze swept his messy work area. As usual, his kitchen counters stood littered with bowls of chocolate ganache, scraps of parchment paper, and other accoutrements of his ongoing baking experiments. For Walden, creating new baked goods wasn't just work; it was an art and a hobby. This time of year, it was also insanely demanding.

"Oh, am I *bugging* you, Mr. Grumpy Pants?" Talia asked archly. She dropped her shopping bags, then rummaged through one. "Hold on a sec. I can fix that. I can cheer you right up."

"No, you're not 'bugging' me." With a sigh, Walden

watched as Talia huffily pulled out something hairy-looking, blond, and about two feet long. Another wig. "But if that's a Heather wig, you can put it away right now. I'm not in the mood."

"But the Heather wig *puts* you 'in the mood'!"

"Not anymore, it doesn't," Walden grumbled.

Talia's eyes widened. "Yes, it does!" she insisted. "The Heather wig is the whole reason we're together right now."

She couldn't seriously still believe that. Could she?

It was true that Talia had hinted a time or two that she thought he only wanted her as Heather. But that was too ridiculous to take seriously. He'd wanted her all along. He just hadn't had the nerve to say so until the right opportunity—their Heather-and-her-bohemian-boy-toy charade—had come his way.

"Just put it away." Walden gestured irritably at the wig. Fully fed up with pussyfooting around this issue—and feeling more than time-pressed at that particular moment—he decided to get down to brass tacks. "Whatever you think that wig is doing for you, it's not."

"I . . . what?" Talia stared at him. "But I thought—"

"I know. I should have told you sooner," Walden interrupted regretfully, wiping off his sticky hands. "You, me, that wig . . . I can't hack it anymore, Talia. I'm sorry if that sounds mean, but it's the truth. I don't like it. I'm done pretending I do."

Looking inexplicably stricken, Talia clutched her mangy wig. Her chin wobbled. Watching that uncharacteristic movement, Walden wasn't sure what was happening. On another woman, he'd have thought some waterworks were imminent. But Talia was way too tough and too cool and too self-assured to cry. So why . . . ?

"Well. You should have told me that *before* I bought a new wig!" she said. "I thought you'd gotten tired of the old one. I thought maybe a newer, longer, *sexier* wig was what you wanted."

Huh? Obviously, he'd have to be clearer about this.

"No more goddamn wigs!" Walden yelled. "I'm *done*."

Talia flinched. She went on staring at him with those big, wounded-looking, indigo-colored eyes of hers. For the life of him, Walden couldn't figure out why she looked so hurt.

"I'm sorry I yelled about it," he told her, because that part was true, at least, and he really wasn't sure what else to do. All he knew was that he had to make Talia quit looking so sad. "I guess I've kept this bottled up for too long. I should have said something sooner, but I didn't know how you'd react."

"How I'd 'react'?" Her acerbic tone bit into him.

Talia advanced toward him as she said it. Menacingly.

Warily, Walden held up both hands. "Yeah. I know it sounds crazy, but I thought you might be upset or something."

His blundering attempt at humor didn't fly.

"'Upset'? Of course I'm upset!" Talia waggled the wig at him. "Do you think I *like* putting gross fake hair on my head? Do you think I *like* prancing around in this skanky, ridiculous coat? Wearing sunglasses in wintertime? Making out in alleyways?"

"Well, that last part was pretty nice," Walden murmured, remembering it. He chanced a nostalgic glance at Talia, but she was obviously not on the same those-were-the-days kick he was.

"I'm doing all this for *you,* you lunkhead!" she shouted. "And now you're telling me you don't *like* it?"

"We're both doing it for Kristen," Walden clarified. "We're doing it to keep the paparazzi away from the diner."

"We are."

It wasn't *quite* a question. But it sounded too sarcastic to be a genuine statement of agreement. Fraught with the unwanted sensation that he was somehow making things worse, Walden frowned. "That's what I just said."

"I heard you! I'm not an idiot." Talia shook the wig. "This only makes me a *temporary* dumb blonde!"

"If you heard me, then why—" Feeling frustrated, Walden broke off to give Talia a shake of his dreadlocks. Maybe if he started over from the beginning . . . "Look, all I'm saying is that I hate your wearing that wig," he said in a gentler tone. "That's it. I don't know why you're making a big deal out of it."

"'Making a big deal out of it'?" Talia's eyes overflowed with tears. Angrily, she hurled down her Heather wig. "It's *already* a big deal! It's a big, fat, hairy, stinking deal!"

"Ew." Tentatively, Walden made a funny face. Usually Talia liked when he did that. This time she didn't so much as crack a smile. "That doesn't sound very nice," he joked anyway.

But Talia only stared at him. Exasperated. And hurt.

"You're joking now." Again, she gave him a supersize dose of sarcasm. Pacing, she added, "You're making jokes. Now."

"And you're asking questions that sound like statements!"

"Because we're having a fight! This is how I fight!"

"I'm not fighting with you!" Walden yelled, waving his arms and feeling confused. "I don't want to fight with you!"

In the crashing silence that followed his shouting (which sounded a lot like fighting, he supposed, if he were being brutally honest with himself), they both stared at one another.

"Maybe I should just leave," Talia said quietly.

"Maybe you should," Walden said, because she obviously didn't want to be there with him. She'd probably been looking for an excuse to end their let's-help-Kristen charade. Talia probably wanted to pretend it had never happened and maybe wash out her brain with amnesia shampoo so she could forget kissing him—so she could forget acting as though she loved him.

Walden knew he ought to accept that. He did. The trouble was, he'd honestly believed things had gotten real between them.

All those long, intimate nights that he and Talia had shared. All those funny, heartfelt conversations. All those kisses and hugs and . . . and, well, all that X-rated other stuff that would only live on in his dreams now. They were all over with.

This was it, Walden realized miserably. This was the moment when Talia realized she'd been hanging around with *him,* on purpose, for days now. This was the moment when she realized that the weird new guy at work had become—at least temporarily and for all intents and purposes—her de facto boyfriend.

"I never meant for this to happen, you know," she said, accidentally confirming his innermost fears. "It was so easy at first. Putting on that wig, making out with you, pretending we were a couple . . . I didn't realize how out of hand it would get."

"I know." Manfully trying to behave like an adult about this, Walden squared his shoulders. "You didn't even like me."

"I mean, Gareth and I kind of drafted you into this in the first place," Talia was saying, distractedly talking over him, "even though it was obvious that subterfuge didn't come naturally to you. I'm lucky it lasted as long as it did."

"Me too," Walden had to admit. Because . . . why not?

Then he realized exactly what Talia had said. "Did you just say you're 'lucky it lasted as long as it did'?" he asked.

"Didn't 'like' you?" she asked in a tone of equal (if belated) amazement. "You thought I didn't like you?"

They stared at one another. Again, silence fell between them. And that was when Walden realized *this* was a monumental moment, too. Because this was the moment when he had a chance to make it or break it with Talia. This was the moment when he could go for broke—or just go back to sugaring cranberries.

"You *didn't* like me," he said bluntly, opting to go for it.

After all, he had nothing left to lose. "We've worked together for months. All I ever heard from you were stories about this guy or that guy or some other loser you were going out with."

Talia gawked at him. "I was *trying* to seem in demand! I was *trying* to make you think I was a hot commodity! But you never even looked twice at me—not until I put on that stupid wig."

"Oh, I looked at you, all right," Walden said, liberated by the fact that she was leaving anyway. At least he could finally play it straight with her. "I looked at you plenty!"

"Well, I never saw you!"

"I did it! Okay? I couldn't help myself!"

Seeming almost pleased by his admission of helplessness in the face of her incredible allure, Talia touched her close-cropped lavender hair. Then, "You're still shouting at me!"

"You're shouting at me!"

"That's because you're being an idiot!"

"I am not! I'm being honest!" Realizing he was still yelling, Walden deliberately lowered his voice. "I don't like that wig because I'd rather be with the *real* you." Bravely, he stepped close enough to touch Talia's face. Because she hadn't left yet, and maybe that meant he still had a chance. "The real you is a million times more beautiful than that. Putting on anything that obscures who you really are ought to be a crime."

Talia gazed up at him. She sniffled. "Really?"

Somberly, Walden nodded. "Every time I saw you wearing those ginormous sunglasses, I wanted to rip them off your face and stomp on them. Because they hid your beautiful eyes."

"Aw. That's so Neanderthal of you. So sweet."

"*And,*" Walden added, high on honesty and bravado, "because they made it impossible for me to see what you were thinking."

"You can't do that anyway," Talia joked, "if you thought

I didn't like you. I thought *you* didn't like *me*—not until I put on that Heather wig, at least."

"That's crazy talk," he blurted, because he couldn't stop himself. "Nothing could be further from the truth."

"I thought you were mad because I came over without wearing the wig today," Talia confided further. "You looked at me with such disappointment on your face. It kind of broke my heart."

Oh. That explained why she'd come into his apartment with such a tentative demeanor at first, Walden realized. Because for the first time, Talia had arrived at his place *without* wearing her Heather wig. He'd been too engrossed in sugaring cranberries—and feeling exasperated at the wig—to notice that at first, but obviously, Talia had been worried about his reaction to the real her. Which explained why she'd rushed to grab that damn wig when he'd groused at her, too.

They were having their first colossal misunderstanding.

He decided to consider it a landmark moment—and a positive development, too. After all, at least they were both still there talking. That was something to be glad about, wasn't it?

"I was grumpy because you didn't use the key I gave you," Walden explained, beginning to feel maybe things *weren't* as dark as they seemed. "Again. You never use it! Why do you think I—"

"I lost it," Talia said sheepishly. "I didn't want to say so. And anyway, I thought you only gave me that key so we could conspire to be Heather and her bohemian boy toy more easily."

Walden shook his head. Her face felt warm and familiar and beloved beneath his palm, and he never wanted to stop touching her. Talia meant everything to him. "All I ever wanted was to be you and me, together. That's the whole reason I did all this crazy Heather-and-Heather's-boyfriend impersonation stuff."

"Well, you wanted to help Kristen, too."

"A little." Walden smiled. "Mostly, I wanted *you*."

"*I* wanted *you*." Talia reached up to cover his hand with her palm. She squeezed his hand, giving him a look so adoring that it nearly stole away his breath. "I'm not as fearless as I seem, Walden. Not one hundred percent of the time. Not about things that really matter." She inhaled a deep breath, then gazed into his eyes. "*You* really matter. You're kind and funny and sexy and strong, and I really like you, and when it started looking like we might actually have a chance together, I got so freaked-out thinking I might blow it that I . . ." Talia shrugged. She offered him a sardonic grin. "Well, I guess I blew it. Ironic, right?"

Her sarcastic tone was back. It was there, Walden realized in that moment, to cover up her vulnerability. Her sarcastic tone was there, if he paid attention, to alert him that Talia needed something from him.

This time, he did a better job of rising to the occasion.

"Nobody's blown anything," he said. "All that's happened is we had a fight. We cleared the air. Then we kept talking until we understood each other. That's how it's supposed to be." He gave her a long look. "We just survived our first fight! That's kind of great, right?"

"No. I hated every minute of it." Talia shuddered. "I hate fighting with you. I never want to do it ever again. Okay?"

"Not okay." Regretfully, Walden shook his head. "Because we're going to have misunderstandings sometimes. We're going to disagree about things once in a while."

"Oh no, we're not," Talia shot back.

Her eyes sparkled at him. It took him a second to realize why. She was disagreeing with him about disagreeing with him.

"Funny." Walden smiled at her. "All I mean is, you don't have to act like you're bulletproof. Not with me. I'm not here because you're cool and tough and amazing—"

"You're not? My illusions are shattered!"

"Well, not *just* because you're cool and tough and amazing," Walden amended. "I'm also here because I love you. No matter how goofily I might express it. So let's start over. Okay?"

"Okay, but . . . wait." She frowned. "You *love* me?"

Talia's awestruck tone—and her frown—nearly made him quaver. Because Walden had been too busy speaking from the heart to realize exactly how vulnerable he was making himself just then. Now it was too late to take it back—too late to be safe.

"I love you more than bittersweet chocolate," he told Talia ardently, going all-in now. "More than kouign amann or pâte feuilletée and brown butter tarte tatin or croquembouche with pâte à choux and fleur de sel caramel and crème pâtissière. More than all the best viennoiserie in the whole wide world—"

"Um, translation for *non*-pastry chefs, please?"

Walden smiled. "I love you with all my heart and soul, Talia. I love everything about you, from your purple hair to your tattooed left foot to your smile and your laugh and your obsession with drawing hearts on every frosty window you pass."

She blushed. "You noticed that?"

"I notice everything when it comes to you. You're fascinating to me. Why do you think I'm here?"

"Well, for the sex, of course." Talia counted that off on her fingers. "Also, *Pinky and the Brain* trivia. Sex. Joint subterfuge perpetuated on the paparazzi. Sex." A wide, beautiful grin broke over her face. "Oh, and frequent sex."

"Mmm-hmm. While I'm not denying that I love the sex," Walden said, taking her into his arms, "because I definitely *do* love that, there's a lot more going on here between us."

"Like the way I love having your arms around me?"

"Yes, there's that."

"And the way I love hearing your voice when I come in to work, and seeing you creating something amazing, and knowing that no matter what it is, you can always make it sweeter?"

"Um, maybe that." Walden frowned in dawning confusion. "Are you giving me a pastry chef recommendation or—"

"I'm saying I love you, too, dummy!" Laughing, Talia shook him. Or at least she tried to. Given the discrepancy between his big body and her smaller one, she mostly accomplished a sort of wobbly shove. "You're the most impressive man I've ever met."

"It's the dreadlocks. They make me look cool."

"It's *you*," Talia disagreed, tipping upward to kiss him. She stroked his face. "You have integrity, Walden. You have the ability to make the whole world brighter, just by being in it. So if you think you can put up with a wisecracking sidekick—"

"Yes." Emphatically, he nodded. Then he reconsidered. "That's *you*, right? You're not sneakily nominating someone else for the job of wisecracking Walden sidekick?"

"It's me," Talia said. "It's definitely me."

"It's always been you."

"It's always been *you*. Took you long enough to notice."

"Took *you* long enough to notice."

For a single wholehearted minute, they gazed at each other.

Then, "Maybe we ought to have a moratorium on discussing how long we were both too clueless and scared to approach one another," Walden suggested. "What matters is we're here now."

"We're here *forever*," Talia agreed, snuggling closer.

As though punctuating their agreement, a knock sounded at the door. This time, Walden had no interest in answering it.

"Go away!" he yelled merrily. "We're busy."

The knock only sounded again, louder this time.

Talia made a face. "I don't think they're going away."

"Whoever it is, I'll make them go away," Walden announced. Gently, he disentangled himself from Talia. With his heart full of happiness and his mind full of provocative thoughts of how they could best commemorate their newly declared love, he strode to his front door. He cast Talia a loving backward glance. "I'll be right with you. This is just a short break in the action."

"Not if I come over there with you!" Talia said gaily.

So she did. And that's how they were both standing there in Walden's doorway, full of sentimentality and flirtatiousness, when Walden opened the door and unleashed the full-bore media ambush that was waiting for them on the other side.

Cameras flashed at them. Camcorders focused on them. Portable boom mikes hovered overhead. Multiple voices spoke up at the same time as the paparazzi crowded onto the doorstep.

At their head, a smarmy-looking "reporter" shoved a microphone into Walden's face. "Walden! *Access Hollywood* here. How about an exclusive? Why did you pretend to be—"

Then the *Access Hollywood* guy suddenly glimpsed Talia. A rapacious expression crossed over his face. He abandoned Walden in a heartbeat, instead thrusting his microphone at Talia.

"Talia! *Access Hollywood* here. Why did you impersonate Heather Miller?" he asked aggressively. "Are you a deranged fan, or just a bored yokel with nothing better to do?"

As though that were a reasonable question, he angled his head expectantly to the side. Beaming an obnoxious grin, he held his microphone-wielding hand outstretched to await her answer.

Surprised and flustered, Talia stepped back. She boggled at the sea of journalists and photographers—and at the satellite vans parked across the street in the snow. More questions were shouted. More photographs were snapped. Flashes blinded them.

Their hoax had obviously been discovered.

But how? Walden wondered. Had one of the paparazzi followed him and Talia back to his place? It had to have been that. They'd been too giddy to be ultracareful. It wasn't as though they were professional-caliber celebrity impersonators.

Once someone tailed him and Talia home, Walden realized belatedly, they would have had an easy time learning exactly who they were, what they were up to, where they worked. . . .

Uh-oh. If things were this crazy here at his apartment, what might they be like downtown at the Galaxy Diner?

Most likely, the media had swarmed the diner, too. Just in case the Heather-and-her-bohemian-boy-toy impersonators they wanted to waylay for gossipy "comments" and jittery video footage weren't at home during their regular stalking hours.

Somehow, he and Talia had to warn Kristen.

"No comment." Shielding Talia with his body, Walden held up his hand. He tried to shut the door, but the *Access Hollywood* guy had wedged himself in the entryway. There were too many other journalists behind him, holding up the media onslaught, for him to back up now—not that he showed any signs of wanting to relent. "Everyone, please just leave us alone," Walden tried.

That only incited them further. "Talia!" someone else shouted. "What happened to your hair? Are you impersonating someone else now? Are you a serial impersonator or just crazy?"

Looking panic-stricken, Talia shook her head.

Still wearing her incriminating leopard-print coat, she tried to help Walden push the door closed. Even between the two of them, they were no match for the journalists, though, who seemed perfectly willing to be crushed, if necessary—to sacrifice any one of their number for the sake of a juicy story.

"We've got to warn Kristen," Talia said to Walden in an undertone, holding up her arm to ward off photographs. "She won't know *what's* going on if these guys head for the diner."

Despite everything, Walden felt weirdly pleased they were on the same wavelength, thinking the same thoughts. He knew that Talia was right about the dangers to Kristen. He also knew that, as the one who'd actively pretended to be Heather, Talia was in for a much worse backlash than he was. He wanted to protect her.

"I'll distract them," he told Talia privately. "You go for the phone. There's no other way out of here except the windows—"

"And they've probably got those covered, too."

"—but at least you can call Kristen and get yourself out of the line of photo fire." Giving Talia a heartfelt look, he squeezed her hand. "I won't let anyone hurt you, Talia."

"No." She shook her head. "I won't leave you here alone."

"I won't be alone," Walden said above the din. "I'll know you're waiting for me. Everything else is temporary."

"Everything except my love for you," Talia pledged. Then, as Walden nodded at her, she gave him a smile and ducked inside.

Fortified by her affection, Walden straightened. Heroically, he scoured the assembled media with a determined look. "All right. One question at a time, please," he announced.

In a furor of shouted inquiries and busy cameras, he was officially on his way—saving Talia and (he hoped) allowing just enough time for Talia to give Kristen a heads-up before the media caught her off guard and ruined her Christmas completely.

Chapter 21

ZUGZWANG (TSOOK-tsvahng) *noun*: a position where one is forced to make an undesirable move

On set in Kismet, Michigan
December 11

"You drive a hard bargain, Mr. Jackson." After shaking hands with Casey, Heather leaned back in her on-set dressing room's make-up chair. The lighted mirrors nearby offered a funhouse version of her own image—woebegone and faintly tear-streaked—along with an annoyingly perfect version of The Terminator's image—handsome and capable. Deliberately, Heather looked away from both of them. "I'll give the crew more time to wrap up my holiday TV special."

"And I'll surprise Kristen with this distribution deal for her baked goods." Looking pleased, Casey tapped the paperwork on the dressing room's table. "I had no idea you were going to be representing the new ad campaign for Torrance Chocolate's luxury cafés and chocolate boutiques, Heather. That was the missing link in this deal. Once Torrance Chocolates adds Kristen's pies-in-a-jar to their lineup of custom chocolates and Bandini Espresso drinks, their business ought to go through the roof."

"Right." Heather didn't care about Torrance Chocolates' business success. She didn't care about much of anything, frankly, since Alex had walked out on her. All she wanted now was to finish her disastrous TV special and go home to L.A.

She'd already spoken with her parents about her plan. While they'd been a little disappointed that she wouldn't be in Kismet for Christmas, their outlook had improved once Heather had offered them a New Year's Eve jaunt to Cabo.

"Don't get me wrong," Casey continued. "I'm impressed with how much you've accomplished since you came back to work this morning—"

"Being heartbroken will do that to you, I guess," Heather muttered. *Stupid Alex*. Why had he had to betray her? Why?

"—but I'm just not sure that pushing the crew this hard will lead to the kind of results you're hoping for."

"Mmm-hmm." *Whatever,* Heather thought privately. "That's why we made the deal, isn't it? So everyone's happy, happy, happy?"

Casey looked closely at her. "Are you all right?"

No. I'm heartbroken. "I'm fine!" Brightly, Heather picked up a make-up brush. She swabbed on some bronzer. It didn't help. She still looked wan and unhappy. Now she looked fake, too.

If you ever decide to get real, look me up.

Ha. Alex had been barking up the wrong tree with that line. If Heather Miller ever dared to "get real," her fans would revolt. They would desert her. They would not watch her special.

Speaking of that . . . The on-set hubbub picked up outside, in the spruced-up bungalow that the production had rented— and then totally redecorated and sprayed with fake "stunt" snow—as a stand-in for Heather's supposedly cozy home-town "homestead."

Heather sighed. Even her televised "homecoming" was

bogus. Nothing around her was real anymore. Except heartbreak.

She just wanted to get this over with. But first . . .

"Don't forget to tell Kristen about the ad campaign!" Heather trilled. She wanted *Casey* to do that part, not her. She added even more bronzer, hoping she might at least look awake on camera. "You don't know how long I've been trying to get her to do a project like this with me. Like, *forever,* it seems."

For the first time, Casey Jackson appeared uncertain.

"Don't worry. She'll be *thrilled,*" Heather assured him—and herself—mustering what she hoped looked like an impressive amount of cheerfulness. This deal was her consolation prize to herself for losing Alex. She deserved it. She was determined to feel happy about it. "Me and Kristen, together in commercials to promote her baked goods being available at TC cafés? Fab!"

"Fab!" echoed several members of her entourage, who'd been standing faithfully nearby. "You're fab, Heather! Good idea!"

Unnervingly, it occurred to Heather that maybe—just maybe—her glam posse wasn't entirely sincere in their admiration of her. But she felt too hopeless and too miserable to worry about that right now. She eyed Casey. He wasn't as cute as Alex was (who was?), but he was still pretty easy on the eyes. He wasn't as scary as his reputation had led her to believe, either. It was almost enough to make Heather feel sorry for misdirecting him—for making him break the ad-campaign news to Kristen *and* for making him "babysit" her little sister when they'd first met.

On the other hand, her impulsive plan had inadvertently led to this "fab" new project between her and Kristen, so that was good. At least it would be good for Heather. She'd been wanting to include Kristen in her celebrity life for a long time now. She'd been wanting to feel closer to Kristen, despite their different lives. But why did Casey Jackson look so concerned?

"Are you sure you're all right?" he asked kindly, letting her know *that's* why he looked concerned. He was worried about her. "Because you're putting bronzer on top of your lip gloss."

"Bronzer on lip gloss is fab, Heather!" her friends enthused robotically from the peanut gallery. "We love it!"

Casey ignored them. "And it looks like you've been crying." All but emanating caring, he took the make-up chair beside hers. He took away her make-up brush. He held her hand. "What's wrong?"

Heather gazed into his compassionate eyes and practically burst into tears on the spot. *This* was why Casey Jackson was called The Terminator, she realized too late. Because he was devastatingly good at recognizing when things were hopeless.

Worse, he was devastatingly good at making it seem as though those things could be fixed, when Heather knew darn well that the situation between her and Alex was insurmountable.

Insurmountable. She was going to have to take a Brillo Pad to her brain to try to scrub out all those Words of the Day.

"It doesn't matter." She straightened, searching her muddled memory for the posture-improving Pilates move she'd learned last year. She waved her free hand. "I'll be fine."

"You'll be more than fine, Heather!" chorused her glam posse. "You'll be better than ever! You'll be an Emmy winner!"

At that, Heather briefly perked up. She *could* win an Emmy for her holiday TV special, it occurred to her. But then she realized that if she did, she would not have Alex to accompany her to the awards ceremony at the Nokia Theatre. All the tentative hopefulness she'd felt drained away in an instant.

Beside her, Casey looked squarely at her friends.

"You know what?" he said nonchalantly to her parrotlike posse. "I think Heather could really use a nice decaf matcha latte right now. Will one of you fetch that for her, please?"

Her cadre of hangers-on and sometime friends all but stomped over one another to be first to the dressing-room door.

Left alone with Casey, Heather shook her head. "That was a nifty way of clearing the room just now—and thanks for that, too—but I really don't need anything." *Except Alex,* she wanted to wail. "Besides, I don't think matcha comes in a decaf version. Since it's a shade-grown Japanese konomi tea, destemmed and deveined by hand and not aged like black or oolong tea, matcha can't tolerate the usual decaffeination processes."

Casey blinked. Whoops. She'd accidentally said something knowledgeable. To compensate, Heather giggled inanely.

"Also, it's, like, Incredible Hulk green, so it's totally radioactive or something. I think. That's what I heard once."

But it was too late. Casey had already glimpsed the truth.

"You're smarter than all this, Heather." Illustratively, he waved at her improvised "down-home" dressing room with its lighted mirrors and excess of bronzing powder. "You're capable of more than this. I know you are. You're a good person."

She snorted. "Not everyone thinks so."

He seemed unconvinced. "Who doesn't think so?"

"My parents. My sister." *Alex,* she was about to say. *He thinks I'm awful!* But Casey broke in before she could.

"I haven't met your parents yet, so I can't speak for them," Casey told her, "but Kristen loves you. She thinks the world of you. She's rearranged her whole Christmas for you."

Surprised, Heather withdrew her hand from his. "No, she hasn't. I've barely made a dent in Kristen's Christmas. I made sure my homecoming special would hardly affect her."

Defensively, she informed Casey of the deal she'd made

with the paparazzi to leave Kristen alone at her diner and at home. It didn't seem necessary to Heather to mention that she'd only done that at the urging of Kristen's busybody Super Friends quartet, Gareth, Talia, Avery, and Walden. He didn't need to know that.

Besides, the truth was, she'd have done it on her own anyway. If it had occurred to her. Which, initially, it hadn't.

"That was a good idea," Casey said, smiling to give Heather proper credit, "but it didn't stop everything else from snowballing out of control. It didn't stop your fans from camping out at the diner, hoping for a glimpse of you. It didn't stop the town from declaring the second day of every December an annual 'Heather Miller Day' holiday, with banners and billboards and posters of your face everywhere. It didn't stop the animatronic reindeer or the artificial snow or the gossip. It didn't stop your parents from canceling their plans with Kristen so they could maintain their @Heather_Hotline Twitter account."

Gob-smacked, Heather stared at him. "Their what?"

Briefly, Casey told her about everything that had been going on while she'd been busy with her Christmas TV special—busy (fruitlessly) trying to make Alex fall in love with her.

"You know," Heather mused when he'd finished, "this doesn't sound like random interest in your assignment's little sister."

"That's because it's not random interest," Casey said.

He let loose a dazzling grin. It was . . . *captivating*.

It also told Heather everything she needed to know. The Terminator—no, *Casey*—and Kristen were an item. They were in love! And just because *she'd* failed at love—here, Heather stifled a self-pitying sob—that didn't mean her sister couldn't win big.

"I'm happy for you," Heather said sincerely. Because she was. Also, she was pleased to have brought Casey and Kristen together in the first place. Props to her! "But I'm afraid this means that you should probably cancel that distribution deal." She cast a reluctant glance at the paperwork she'd signed earlier. "And the advertising campaign. And all the rest of it."

"Why?" Casey frowned at her. "It's already in motion."

"Well, *un*-motion it, then!" Impatiently, Heather waved her arms at him. Unfortunately, he was not a spineless sycophant. So her gestures had little effect on him. "Kristen will hate it!"

At her abrupt change of heart, Casey looked understandably confused. "You said she'd be thrilled."

"I might have been fibbing."

"But if she'll hate it, why did you agree to it?"

Heather exhaled. She didn't want to admit this, but . . . "I'm kind of selfish sometimes. It's true. Plus, when I did that"—*fifteen minutes ago*—"I didn't really know you yet."

"We met more than a week ago."

"Right," Heather agreed, "but I didn't know *you*. I didn't know you loved Kristen! To me, you were just the guy who was here to crush my TV special. I was willing to push through the deal if The Terminator was going to be the fall guy in the end—"

"I really hate that nickname," Casey grumbled.

"—because I knew *I* would come out looking blameless. I knew I could always play dumb. I knew I could convince Kristen. After all, it's better to ask forgiveness than permission, right?"

"No. That's an idiotic saying."

"But I didn't have a smart enough accomplice to help me make the deal happen," Heather finished, "until now."

"Until me." Casey gave a disbelieving chuckle—a chuckle that said he couldn't believe he'd been outmaneuvered by a brainless pop star with a world-famous shoe collection.

"Yes. But now that it's *you* who'll take the fall and not The Terminator . . ." Heather sighed. "I just can't do it."

Casey's expression turned grave. "Kristen will really hate it? But you two have been talking about collaborating—"

"She's humoring me." Heather waved off his "proof" that Kristen might be anything less than unhappy about the prospect of teaming up on a project. "It's what she does to avoid hurting my feelings. Kristen likes keeping things low-key."

"But she needs the money," Casey insisted, jutting his jaw in a stubborn gesture. He didn't seem accustomed to encountering obstacles. Probably, he wasn't. "She has bank representatives hounding her. I've seen them. Hell, I've *talked* to them—"

"You talked to them?" Heather widened her eyes.

"—and while I didn't get very much information," Casey admitted, "I do know that running a small business is no picnic. It's a low-margin endeavor with every possibility of failure—"

"Kristen's not going to fail. She's very talented!"

"—and it can't hurt to have a safety net," Casey went on doggedly. "Like a lucrative partnership with a chain of international luxury cafés and high-end chocolate boutiques that's three thousand outlets strong. *That's* the security Kristen needs."

Heather shook her head. "Good luck convincing her of that."

"I don't need luck to convince her of that," Casey insisted with typical confidence. "The facts will do it for me."

"If 'the facts' could work that kind of magic, I'd have a boyfriend right now." *A boyfriend who didn't have suspiciously nonexistent "chicken pox" and questionably horrible photos of me on his cell phone.* Intently, Heather leaned toward Casey. "I'm serious about this. It's one thing for me to finagle a deal for Kristen and strong-arm her into doing ads with me. *That's* just life. That's just sisters being sisters." Feebly, she grinned. "But if the man she *loves* does that to her—"

"You think Kristen loves me?"

At his adorably hopeful expression, Heather felt her heart turn over. She was glad she'd spoken up before it was too late.

"Well, I can't know for sure, since all we've been doing lately is trading texts and voice mails," Heather told Casey. "But I can say that if Kristen ever invites you to spend the night at her place, you'll know you're in. Because Kristen *never* invites—"

"She *already* invited me to stay over. All weekend!"

Casey's eyes were big, his voice was raspy, and his hands . . . Well, his hands were actually shaking. Heather laughed with joy.

She wished she had a man who loved her so much that his hands literally shook at the thought that she might love him back.

"You'd better start looking for another Kismet-based troubleshooting job," she advised him with a gleeful poke to his arm, "because I think you might be here for a while."

"I *might* be here! Even for Christmas." Casey seemed astounded by the idea. "Even with all this snow and ice and holiday hoo-ha, and not a single margarita in sight." Suddenly, his cheery demeanor vanished. His stricken glance met hers. "Except I've already put out feelers about the Galaxy Diner pie-distribution deal. I've already spoken with people at Torrance Chocolates. I've already gotten the rumor mill cranking, made potential investors aware that a deal might be in the works—"

"I guess you were pretty sure you could convince me to go along with this," Heather put in. Casey didn't need to agree with her. The truth was obvious. She'd only thought she was in the driver's seat today. "Can't you just call it off?"

"I'm not sure," Casey admitted, his handsome brow furrowed. "This whole town is crawling with media. I took advantage of that and slipped out a few hints when I arrived on set today. Plus, I made a few additional phone calls this morning."

"That . . . doesn't sound so bad?" Heather tried encouragingly.

But Casey only shook his head. "Part of what makes this deal so perfect is its tie-in to your holiday TV special. That sponsorship—and the associated advertising—could single-handedly make up for all the budget overruns. I can't undo all that."

"You can try!" Heather jostled him. "You've got to try!"

Appearing conflicted, Casey bit his lip. From outside the dressing room came the sounds of Heather's prerecorded version of "All I Want for Christmas Is You." Everyone must be gearing up for another take of her "live" finale number. Her record label insisted it had to be Auto-Tuned to within an inch of its life for "consistency's sake." Remembering that, Heather sighed.

This . . . *phoniness* was not why she'd become a performer.

Looking at Casey Jackson's anguished expression was not why she'd just sacrificed her longed-for advertising gig with Kristen, either. She could have made it work. Heather knew she could have.

She'd be darned if she'd make a rarer-than-natural-blondes personal sacrifice, just to see her efforts to go waste on a man who didn't justify them. On a man who wasn't worthy of Kristen.

So, even though Heather knew that what she was about to do was a little questionable in the morality department, she decided it was for the greater good. It was for Kristen's sake.

"Well, do whatever you have to do." Dredging up every ounce of acting ability she possessed, Heather stood. She tried to seem as divalicious as possible. "But I'm afraid you can't have it both ways. I'm not here to be taken advantage of."

"Huh?" Distractedly, Casey looked at her.

"If you call off the distribution deal and the joint ad campaign with me and Kristen," Heather clarified, nodding toward the paperwork between them, "I'll cut my crew's available hours. I'll revert to my original twenty-four-hour timetable."

Casey frowned. "That won't be enough time."

"That's not my problem. It's yours." Holding up her chin, Heather took herself regally toward the door. "Because I'm pretty sure that if my TV special doesn't get done, neither does the job your agency sent you to Kismet to accomplish. And even if my special does get done somehow, without the additional sponsorship the budget overruns will crush it before it airs."

Casey caught her meaning quickly enough. "You're offering me a choice: my career or my relationship with Kristen."

Heather shrugged. It wasn't easy. But if Casey couldn't bring himself to work a little harder to make Kristen happy, then maybe he didn't deserve her. "Call it what you like," she said flippantly. "If someone comes back with my matcha latte, I'll be on set . . . *maybe* considering working before leaving town."

Then she held her breath, breezed out of her dressing room, and left Casey behind—hopefully to do the right thing for Kristen. Because at least one of the Miller sisters ought to be happy at any given moment, Heather reasoned . . . and right now, it looked as though Kristen had the best possible chance of that.

Striding through the disorganized downtown bungalow that served as the primary on-set location for Heather Miller's holiday TV special, Casey felt a new solidarity with the beleaguered-looking crew, extras, and catering staff who were milling around. Because he felt pretty sure—now that he'd spent more time with her—that Heather Miller was certifiably crazy.

She went through moods like a chocoholic through Hershey's. She was up one minute and down the next. She was kind, then haughty, then helpless. She was demanding and illogical, loyal and naïve, peculiarly smart and infuriatingly imperious, all at the same time. She was unfathomable. She'd set him up for a two-in-one deal that would simultaneously salvage Casey's assignment in Kismet *and* give him something wonderful to give Kristen for Christmas . . . then she'd cruelly and irrationally snatched it away.

Even more than Casey resented all the holiday lights, all the dancers ho-ho-ho-ing in Santa Claus suits, all the decorated Christmas trees and the wreaths and the candles and the candy canes he stalked by in those few minutes, he resented Heather Miller. Because she'd stuck him with an unthinkable choice.

Worse, she'd actually seemed to relish doing it.

Feeling ambushed and confused, Casey hurried past a few backup singers dressed as giant tin soldiers from Tchaikovsky's *The Nutcracker*. He nodded at some crew members he knew. He pushed past the garland-wrapped foyer, stepped onto the bungalow's snowy front porch while pulling on his coat . . .

. . . and almost ran smack into Shane Maresca.

"Casey!" His arch nemesis brightened. "I've been looking all over for you. Something's happening. Some crazy Heather-impersonation scandal just broke, and I think you ought to—"

"I don't have time for this, Shane."

Preoccupied, Casey glanced at his watch, then brushed past Shane. He didn't know if he could trust Heather or her take on Kristen's feelings about the Galaxy Diner–Torrance Chocolates deal. He didn't know if he was doing the right thing or even approaching the ballpark.

But he *did* know that he'd never failed to successfully complete an assignment. Being the man who completed assignments, every single time, on time, was his entire identity. And he knew that seeing Shane gave him even more reason to go forward with the deal. Because after all, his former friend had *also* advised him that Kristen wanted to put a baked-goods-distribution deal in motion. *Especially* if it involved Heather.

Casey had done that. So it looked like he won.

Or at least he might have won, depending on which version of Heather's story was true. She'd already admitted lying to him once. Was she actually lying about lying? Would Kristen appreciate the deal or not? If she was reasonable, she would. But reason didn't always trump feelings. Damn. This was a mess.

If he could get to Kristen, Casey knew, he could find out the truth. Maybe she would like the idea. Maybe the sponsorship deal could go forward and erase the budget overruns. Maybe he could do something nice for Kristen this Christmas. The deal was already put together, exactly the way Casey specialized in, awaiting only Kristen's signature to make it happen.

Maybe he could still win on all counts and emerge a hero. Just the way he always did. This situation was still manageable.

"But the press is going crazy!" Shane followed him down the bungalow's front walk, sliding as he maneuvered on the layer of SnoFoam the crew had put down to match the acrylic icicles on the eaves. "The story's already hit the Internet—"

"Seriously." Feeling beleaguered, Casey stopped. Wearing his most intimidating expression, he faced Shane. "I'm busy."

"You should be 'busy' crisis-managing this impostor situation." Shane shot an interested glance toward the bungalow, where Heather's crew were still hard at work trying to make her holiday TV special happen. "Hey, is it true what I heard about Heather's 'twenty-four-hours or bust' ultimatum? My sources say she's already booked a private charter flight back to L.A."

Casey wasn't sure who Shane's sources were, but they were uncannily accurate. "Heather won't be leaving Kismet anytime soon"—*he hoped*—"whereas *I* have someplace else to be."

"You're leaving all this in chaos?" Shane spread his arms, indicating the bungalow set. "*Now?* Is that a smart move?"

Exasperated, Casey stared at him. It was just like Shane to taunt him with his looming potential on-the-job failure. But in that moment, Casey realized, he wasn't worried about his job. He wasn't worried about his reputation. Or winning. He was worried about Kristen and how she would react to the deal he'd made.

"Yeah. I'm leaving," he said, and the decision felt weirdly easy. Weirdly right. "It looks like it's your lucky day."

"Lucky day?" With his usual disingenuousness, Shane frowned. "I wouldn't say that. The fact is, I'm not here to—"

Screw up Heather's production, Casey could almost hear him saying, in defiance of every shady thing he'd ever done. At that moment, Casey just didn't have the patience for it.

"If you want to try derailing Heather's TV special, have at it." Casey gave a belligerent gesture toward the set. "I won't be here to stop you. There's someplace else I have to be."

"You're giving up?" Shane's frown deepened. "But I—"

"I'm not giving up," Casey told him. "I'm reprioritizing." Then he turned his back on Shane and headed to his car.

Hunched in her favorite leopard-print coat and oversize designer sunglasses, Heather hid behind a light scrim on the bungalow's front porch, listening to Casey and Shane Maresca argue. The minute Casey resolutely announced, "I'm not giving up. I'm reprioritizing!" she heaved a tremendous sigh of relief.

Her gamble had paid off. She'd given Casey an opportunity to prove himself worthy of Kristen, and he'd triumphed. So far.

Obviously, Casey was headed to work some of his deal-*un*making magic with the investors and businesspeople he'd contacted. What would happen after that was anyone's guess.

Technically, that meant Heather should have cut her

crew's working hours again, the way she'd threatened to do. But that had been just that: a threat. Now that Casey had decided to reprioritize, there wasn't any need to go through with that. She and her crew could have all the time they needed to finish her special. Not that Casey needed to know that.

Feeling a little better about herself in light of that dual success—and in spite of losing her longed-for joint ad campaign with her sister—Heather looked up at the holiday lights strung along the bungalow's eaves next to the artificial icicles. Casey had told her she was capable of more than just a fake, crummy holiday TV special and all the ridiculousness that went along with it, and he'd been right.

She *was* capable of more. What she'd just accomplished with Casey proved it. She was capable of reconsidering her actions, evaluating the consequences . . . and changing her mind.

Biting her lip, Heather glanced over her shoulder to the bungalow's interior. Alex was there, busy at work on the latest iteration of the finale set. He looked sexy and stalwart and full of all the qualities she'd ever wanted in a man (except a true Luddite's loathing of picture-taking technology). For the umpteenth time, she wished things were different between them.

If you ever decide to get real, look me up.

Maybe, if The Terminator could grow a heart and turn into a real, loving man who put the woman he cared about ahead of his career prospects, Heather Miller could change, too. But first . . .

Jerking her chin in the air, Heather flounced down the bungalow's front porch steps. She approached Shane Maresca.

He wasn't quite as brilliant as Casey. Or as appealing as Alex. But Shane was certainly an arresting man in his own right. And his function on her holiday TV special's set was similar to Casey's. Shane was a consultant. He was trained to solve problems. And because Heather had foolishly sent away her assigned on-set troubleshooter, she needed a replacement. Stat.

She'd learned to trust Casey. She could trust Shane, too.

"Yoo-hoo! Shane!" Heather waved at him. "Hi!"

In the midst of watching Casey's car driving away, Shane turned. His eyes widened at the sight of her. "Heather. Hi!"

Was it just her imagination, or did Shane seem positively *eager* to get down to work with her? Well . . . who wouldn't be?

"I couldn't help overhearing what you said a minute ago—about the Heather impersonator?" she began. She was definitely curious about that development—and the answers it might yield about her supposed secret pregnancy, discount-toilet-paper shopping, and unknown bohemian boy toy. "I've obviously got to know more about that, even if Casey didn't." Confidingly, she smiled at Shane. Then she chanced another longing glance at Alex. She gathered her courage. "But first, I need your help."

"My help?" Shane seemed surprised. And maybe a little bit amused, too. "When I got here, you said you already had one too many—and I quote—'interfering know-it-alls' on set."

Heather waved that off. "Well, now I have one too few."

He raised his eyebrows. "Casey was serious about quitting?"

"He wasn't quitting," Heather reminded Shane. Loyally. After all, her sister loved Casey. "He was reprioritizing."

Now Shane seemed doubly surprised. "You heard that, huh?" He gave her an appraising look. "You're smarter than you seem."

God, I hope so, Heather thought. But Shane's comment proved he was more similar to Casey than she'd realized. It proved he was prepared to see Heather differently than the rest of the world did. Right now, that was exactly what she needed.

"Come inside," she told Shane, "and I'll prove it."

Then, with Alex undoubtedly looking on, Heather linked arms with Shane Maresca—miracle substitute consultant to the stars—and headed back on set to make holiday TV special history.

Chapter 22

Seated in Casey's usual reserved booth at the Galaxy Diner, across from a journalist from the local *Kismet Comet* newspaper, Kristen paused to consider her answer to the next question.

Ordinarily, she wasn't crazy about doing interviews. But she *did* need the publicity for her diner. And it *was* to support her own small-town daily. And it *would* (she'd reasoned) probably take her mind off feeling abandoned by Casey when he'd hotfooted it out of her apartment so abruptly after being summoned by her sister. So Kristen had agreed to meet the reporter and take part in her story about "Kismet's downtown small businesses successes."

"Well, what really inspires me are the people around me," Kristen finally answered. She shot a contented glance at her diner's customers, at the people waiting for a just-before-afternoon-closing-time table, and then at Avery, who was waiting tables. "All my baked goods are inspired by someone in particular. They're not described that way on the menu. I don't serve 'Grandma Miller's Dutch apple pie' or 'Walden

Farr's chocolate chip pretzel cookies.' But when I'm creating a new pie-in-a-jar or a variation on a favorite recipe, I'm always thinking of the person who will ultimately enjoy it most."

"It sounds like your recipes are really gifts." The journalist smiled at her. "Would you say that's true?"

"Definitely." Kristen nodded. "In fact, just before lunch, I started working on a new creation with someone special in mind." It was Casey, of course. She wanted to surprise him with a pie-in-a-jar that was custom made for him—and maybe, while she was at it, use that gift to segue into another, more forthright *I love you* declaration. "I think it's going to be my best yet."

"Any hints about who it's for?"

"Mmm. None I want to share." Kristen gave an enigmatic smile. "I'm not even sure it will be a menu item. It's . . . private."

"But you seemed so excited about it, just mentioning it!" the journalist said. "Surely you can dish out a hint or two."

Kristen shook her head. "Sorry. I'd rather not." From the corner of her eye, she glimpsed her cell phone lighting up. Although she'd silenced its ringer for her interview, she'd seen a number of phone calls coming in. "Any more questions?"

The journalist shifted her gaze from Kristen's cell phone. Efficiently, she consulted her notes. "Just one more question."

"Okay." Eager to be finished, Kristen sat back. "Shoot."

"All right." With a glance around the busy diner, the journalist gathered her thoughts. Holiday music played over the sound system. Customers laughed and enjoyed their pies-in-a-jar. The journalist fixed Kristen with a keen look. "How excited are you about your new association with Torrance Chocolates?"

"Hmm?" Distracted by an unusual pileup of customers at the diner's entrance, Kristen glanced at her. "I'm sorry. My what?"

"Your pending deal to have your baked goods distributed worldwide in Torrance Chocolates' thousands of luxury cafés?"

Kristen tilted her head in confusion. While she was familiar with Torrance Chocolates—anyone with a pulse and an appreciation for sweets knew about their famous chocolate boutiques and accompanying cafés—she certainly wasn't in any position to partner with them. It was unthinkable. She owned a typical mom-and-pop diner. They were the Starbucks of chocolate.

"You must be mistaken," Kristen said assuredly.

"No, I have the details right here." The journalist reviewed her notes. "Galaxy Diner, pies-in-a-jar, Bandini Espresso, Torrance Chocolates, ads with Heather Miller—"

That's when Kristen *knew* there'd been a mistake.

She almost laughed. "You're confusing me with my sister!" she said, relieved to have an explanation for all this. "Heather has so many endorsement deals, it's hard to keep them straight."

"No, my source is impeccable." The journalist didn't seem amused by Kristen's laughter. "This deal *is* happening." She gave Kristen another shrewd look. As though settling the matter, she added, "The Galaxy Diner is a trending topic on Twitter."

"It's a mistake," Kristen insisted doggedly.

"The @Heather_Hotline account confirmed it."

Frozen in surprise, Kristen stared at her. That was her parents' Twitter account—the one they used to brag to the world about Heather's accomplishments. If the news had been broadcast there, then Heather clearly believed it was happening.

Just as clearly, Heather had gone behind Kristen's back—not for the first time—and engineered a plan to "save" Kristen's "cute little diner" from the big, bad bank. Kristen wished she'd never confided in Heather about that mortgage mix-up. Her sister could be condescending sometimes—especially when it came to the small-town life she'd left behind and seemed to want no further part of—but this was a new level of audacity, even for her.

She could have at least *asked* Kristen first.

Kristen could easily imagine Heather calling in a favor with one of her famous friends, though—friends like hotshot playboy chocolatier Damon Torrance. At the thought of Heather's likely approach—which would have probably involved something about her "unsuccessful . . . but trying really hard!" little sister—Kristen deepened her frown. She didn't want anyone's pity.

She also didn't want this deal. After all, this wasn't about her baked goods. This wasn't some long-awaited validation of her small-town diner and her baking expertise. This was about her accidental association-by-birth with a celebrity. Because there was no way an opportunity like this would have come her way if she *wasn't* Heather's sister. Kristen knew that for sure.

"I guess Heather is surprising me with a big-time distribution deal for Christmas," Kristen said, still trying to make sense of it all. "You say there's supposed to be an ad campaign, too?"

Despite the undeniably sarcastic edge to Kristen's voice, the journalist appeared vindicated. And maybe a little self-righteous, too. "According to all the buzz"—here, she broke off to refer to her hand-scribbled notes again—"the ad agency reps 'can't wait' to meet Heather Miller's 'glam little sister' and get started on the ad campaign." The journalist glanced up, having made air quotes with her fingers in all the appropriate places. "'Glam little sister,'" she repeated in a withering tone. "Hmm. Obviously, they're making a few unfounded assumptions about you."

Speechless, Kristen stared at her. This was exactly what she'd feared—that people would compare her with Heather . . . and then inevitably decide that Kristen (obviously) came up short.

Well, Kristen wanted no part of it. Not now or ever.

"This interview is over." She stood. "Enjoy your pie."

But the journalist wasn't finished with her. "Is this the pie inspired by your famous sister?" she wanted to know, calling after Kristen. "There *must* be a pie inspired by Heather!"

At that, Kristen stopped in her tracks, midway to the back of the house. A pie inspired by Heather? A pie inspired by the same person who'd blatantly ignored all of Kristen's wishes, gone behind her back to wrangle a deal she didn't want, and made sure the whole world knew about it so that *Kristen* would look like the churlish one if it didn't pan out? That kind of pie?

"No." Kristen stalked back to the reserved booth where the journalist sat complacently waiting for her. "I don't have a pie inspired by Heather," she said. "Funny thing is, I don't find people who ignore everything I want in life 'inspiring.'"

The journalist gawked. The nearby customers did, too.

Avery stared at Kristen apprehensively. So did Gareth.

But as much as she knew she ought to, Kristen couldn't stop to reassure them right now. Right now, she had a bigger problem to deal with. And while she wasn't naming names, that problem's initials were H.M. and rhymed with Feather Diller.

Casey arrived at the Galaxy Diner and pushed through the crowded entryway just in time to glimpse Kristen seated in his regular rented-and-reserved booth. Catching sight of that familiar RESERVED sign, Casey felt the usual sense of belonging kick in. He felt the usual sense of welcome wash over him. He felt . . . *right*. As Gareth and Avery spotted him and waved, Casey realized that this place really was like home to him.

The Galaxy Diner—and Kismet—were the homes he'd never had.

At the heart of them both was Kristen. Always Kristen.

Kristen, who—if Heather was right—actually *loved* him.

That was remarkable all by itself. It was something to be treasured and protected. So when Casey overheard the tail end of Kristen's conversation with the smug-looking, legal-pad-toting woman who'd assumed Casey's place in his booth, he felt instantly concerned. And worried. And relieved. All at once.

Because somehow, Kristen had found out about the baked-goods deal that Casey had brokered. And somehow, she'd (erroneously) assumed that Heather was behind it. So even though Kristen didn't seem happy about the news—just as Heather had predicted—Casey realized that *he* could be off the hook. At least temporarily. At least long enough to make Kristen understand *why* he'd done what he'd done.

He had no doubt he could make her understand why he'd done what he'd done. That was his specialty, right? And he wanted to make sure that nothing threatened her feelings for him—at least not before they could grow stronger. So as Casey waited for Kristen to finish her conversation, as he listened to her saying, *I guess Heather is surprising me with a big-time distribution deal for Christmas,* the temptation to let Heather take the fall almost overwhelmed him.

Casey didn't owe anything to Heather. After all, the pop diva had entered into that deal while knowing (according to her) that her sister would hate it. Casey could just . . . let Kristen go on believing it was all Heather's fault. At least temporarily.

Because Heather had all but admitted steamrolling her sister into doing whatever she wanted. She'd probably never paid for those particular incidents. Casey could let Heather take the blame for this one screwup, and the cosmic scales would be balanced again. It was nothing less than Heather deserved.

The Terminator, Casey knew, would have done exactly that.

Funny thing is, I don't find people who ignore everything I want in life "inspiring," Casey heard Kristen say next, having missed the intervening bits of conversation, and he knew that now was the time to act—for better or worse. Clearly, Kristen wasn't feeling especially tolerant just at that moment.

Casting the woman in his booth a formidable look, Casey decided that she could be dealt with later. Right now, Kristen was striding toward her office in the back of her retro-gas-station-turned-diner with the sort of lean-hipped, purposeful motions that foretold—at least in her—a showdown in the offing. Casey didn't want to miss his chance to be her hero . . . his chance to be there to comfort her and promise her he'd make it okay.

Trying to get into full-on Terminator mode, Casey followed her. As he did, he couldn't help taking in Kristen's posture and demeanor and even her long blond hair with a new sense of appreciation. *This* was the woman who loved him, he marveled.

This was the woman *he* loved in return, even if he'd never admitted it to her. It was probably long past time to admit it.

He wasn't at all sure he could.

With that troubling thought in mind, Casey kept going, past the familiar stainless-steel bedecked kitchen with its familiar cooks and bakers and waitstaff. He kept going while the familiar Christmas music serenaded him and while the blinking holiday lights tried their best to blind him. He kept going, feeling proud of Kristen's fortitude and courage and gumption.

Even though she (apparently) hadn't wanted this deal to happen, she seemed fully prepared to handle it straightforwardly now. On her own. Paradoxically, Casey admired her for that.

She was exactly the kind of woman he needed.

Now *he* had to be the kind of man she needed.

Which *wasn't* the kind of man, Casey realized dimly and unhappily, who shirked responsibility for the things he'd done.

He managed to set aside that inconvenient fact long enough to duck inside Kristen's office right behind her. When she turned around with her cell phone in her hand and storm clouds on her face, clearly intending to call her sister, he was there.

"Casey!" Kristen's face cleared. "You came back!"

He couldn't think why she'd believed he might not.

"Of course I did." He shut the door behind them both. Then he took her in his arms and hugged her.

"Is everything all right?" She looked at him closely and lovingly, fueling his desire to make things work. She stepped back. "Are you okay? You look . . . kind of weird, at the moment."

That's because I love you, Casey wanted to say. But his voice stuck on the words. His mind refused to free them.

"Everything's fine," he managed to say. "I'm fine."

Thanks to her distracted state of mind, that was enough.

"Well, at least one of us is," Kristen said, obviously still upset. "You won't *believe* what my sister has done now."

Then, as Casey gazed in wonder at her familiar and beloved face, he heard himself say something astonishing.

"It wasn't your sister," he said. "It was me."

Kristen scoffed. "Very funny." She looked down at her cell phone, already scrolling through menus. "It's nice of you to try to work some troubleshooting magic between me and my sister, but I'm not falling for it. If there's one thing I've learned about Heather, it's that she never fails to surprise me. No matter how many times she does something inconsiderate, she—"

"It was me," Casey repeated, deliberately ignoring this tailor-made opportunity to blame the whole thing on her annoying pop diva sister. Hoping like hell that his charm would remain intact (and his heart and mind would properly sync up with his voice) while making a love declaration later—because he'd never done it before—he moved nearer.

He took a deep breath. "I thought you'd like it," he said. "I thought you needed it."

Kristen quit dialing. She frowned. "Needed what?"

"Needed a deal with Torrance Chocolates. To solve your financial problems," Casey said. "Hell, I spotted both of those bank reps outside the diner just now. It didn't look like they were here to tell you your mortgage mix-up had been forgotten about."

Her gaze skittered to her office door, then swerved back to him. "I didn't tell you about my financial problems."

"You didn't have to. Everyone else did, almost from day one," Casey said. "Not all at once, of course." He offered a tentative grin, imagining her cadre of quirky friends stampeding to Casey's special booth in the diner with stories of Kristen's mistakenly "in-default" business mortgage. "Garth and Talia and Avery and Walden all came to me separately about it. They confided in me. You should have, too. I could have helped. I know people. Lawyers. Bankers. I have connections—"

"Connections that make deals with Torrance Chocolates?"

Her sharp tone almost made Casey's heart stop. Maybe this wasn't going to go as well as he'd expected. Maybe love *wasn't* the cure-all his secretly hopeful heart believed it could be.

"I've already begun undoing it," Casey said hastily in his own defense, holding up his hands. "Obviously, I can't make a deal on your behalf without your cooperation—"

"Oh, *obviously,*" Kristen said sarcastically.

"—which means all I *really* did," Casey went on, "is float a few rumors to a few of the right people. Get the ball rolling. Make inquiries. I've known Damon Torrance a long time, so he—"

Kristen's expression changed. "You really *did* do this." Her astonished gaze met his. She clenched her cell phone. "I thought you were just trying to calm me down, so I wouldn't call Heather and say something I'd regret. But you weren't, were you?"

The hurt in her voice nearly gutted him. So did the wounded look on her face. Even more concerned now, Casey stepped nearer.

"Like I said, I'm undoing it! Shane said you wanted it—"

"Right." She narrowed her eyes. "You *totally* trust Shane."

Casey didn't know what to say to that. In retrospect, it sounded like lunacy. Should he tell Kristen that he'd been caught up in competing with his former best friend? That he'd wanted to win at all costs? That he'd sucked at gingerbread house building and paper snowflake cutting, and he just wanted to impress Kristen with the one thing he *could* do—make deals?

"I didn't have anything else to give you," Casey said. Because all he had left was the truth. And that was it. "On my own, I—" *I'm not enough,* he started to say, but the explanation got caught in his throat next to the *I love you* wedged there, and Casey found himself utterly unable to say anything more.

For the second time in his life, he was mute.

For the second disastrous time in his life, he couldn't say anything that might save him. The first time, he'd been a kid, trying to get from his latest foster home to a *real* home. He'd been competing with Shane, trying to be chosen for adoption as one of two "hard-to-place" fifteen-year-olds, muffing the interview with a prospective family. When the big moment had come—when his original plan had unexpectedly dissolved—Casey hadn't been able to find the right words to make it happen. Under pressure to cement his longed-for place in the world, he'd choked. He'd regretted it ever since.

But Kristen was too upset to listen anyway.

"Well, it looks like you were packing a hell of an attempt

to turn me into Heather's half-assed clone," she interrupted, "complete with glitzy ads and a big-money bank account."

Her aggrieved tone confused him. Casey shook his head. "You will *never* be your sister, Kristen," he said impatiently. "Everyone else knows it. No one else expects it. So why can't *you* see it? Why can't you just stop trying so damn hard to—"

At the anguished expression on her face, he quit talking. He didn't know what he'd said that was wrong, but he didn't want to add to it. Determinedly, Casey clenched his jaw.

"Stop trying so hard to do what?" she broke in, waving her arm in obvious despair. "Be happy? Be successful? Be pretty and talented and beloved? Is it so unthinkable that I could do all those things without turning into Heather?"

"No." He shook his head. "It's not unthinkable."

"Just unlikely. Right?" With all the bravado typically at her command, Kristen stomped toward him. She put her hands on her hips in a confident pose, but her eyes were awash in misery. "Just admit it, Casey. You, of all people, can be straight with me. You were hoping you could make me more like Heather."

"That's not what I meant." He pulled her into his arms. Holding her felt like cuddling with granite. "I've never wanted you to be like Heather." The idea baffled him. "Why would I—"

"You could've fooled me," Kristen interrupted coldly.

"I'm sorry," Casey said. When in doubt, an apology was always a good idea. "This is all a big mistake. I should never—"

"You're right. It *was* a mistake." Kristen wrenched away from him. She looked up at him with teary eyes. "I thought you were different, Casey. I thought you wanted me for *me*."

"I *do* want you for you!" Knowing how deeply that was true, Casey caught hold of her hand. He squeezed it, remembering all the times he'd touched her—all the times they'd laughed. "How did this get so out of control? I blew off work to come here—"

"Oh, that's rich. Everyone knows Heather's special is practically finished already. Tell me another one."

"I'm unraveling a million-dollar deal for you—"

At that impressive figure, Kristen didn't even blink. She took away her hand from his. "How much of that was your cut?"

"Huh?"

"You must have been owed a percentage for brokering the deal with Torrance Chocolates," she went on with a stubborn jut of her chin. "For setting up ads with Heather and all the rest. If it had gone through like you planned, how much was your cut?"

He shook his head. "It wasn't constructed that way."

"Wow. I guess I have *everything* wrong, don't I?"

Wary of her sarcastic-sounding statement, Casey nodded.

"You just wanted to do me a *favor*, didn't you?"

Even more cautiously, Casey nodded again.

"And you really just *loved* me all along. Right?"

This time, Kristen's words nearly leveled him.

For the third time, Casey nodded. His throat ached. His heart felt hollowed out and useless. "Yeah," he said. "I do."

Kristen actually scoffed. "You can't even say it," she marveled. "I thought you were better than that. Given your reputation and charisma. Given how much you stood to gain."

Casey had never regretted his reputation more than he did then. Desperate, this time, to somehow speak the truth, he looked at her squarely. "All I ever wanted was you." He gave her the ghost of a smile. "And maybe a real Christmas."

Because now he knew what magic could be found in that stupid holiday. Before, as a kid, he'd only dreamed of it. Now Casey had tried a taste of the real thing. He wanted more.

He wanted more with Kristen. But now, after this . . .

"Am I supposed to believe that?" she burst out, gawking

at him in evident incredulity. "From *you?* The twenty-first century Scrooge?"

Casey shrugged. He couldn't blame her for being skeptical.

"I don't usually let myself really want something," he told her. Wanting something gave other people leverage. It gave them the ability to hurt you—to take things from you. Growing up, he'd learned that the hard way. He'd learned never to yearn for anything, like a Christmas present or a family. At least not openly. "But with you, I couldn't help it. I really wanted you."

It had made him vulnerable, Casey knew. Too vulnerable.

As though protecting herself from him, Kristen crossed her arms. "Right. You wanted me to help you get a lucrative deal. You wanted me to help you get in on the inside with Heather."

Feeling frustrated, Casey stepped nearer. From outside her office, the holiday music and general diner hubbub continued, adding an incongruously jolly undercurrent to their argument. He'd tried getting through to Kristen. It hadn't worked. Tough and guarded to the end, she'd done everything except accuse him of stealing candy canes from babies. What else could he do?

You can't even say it, he heard her jibing at him again, unknowingly cutting him to the quick—unknowingly making him feel more hopeless than ever. *I thought you were better than that.*

"Yeah. I was just using you to get to Heather," Casey lied. Darkly, he looked at her. She wasn't the only one who could cut deeply. He'd just proved it. "Is that what you want to hear?"

Motionless, Kristen stared at him. With more tears welling in her eyes, she gulped back a sob. "No. I wanted to hear that you want me, Casey. I wanted to hear that you love me."

Her vulnerability was palpable. It nearly broke his heart.

Unfortunately, Casey's inability to say those words was just as real. No matter how true they were, he just couldn't risk it.

He couldn't risk it then, and he probably never would. He'd been kidding himself to think he could.

"Come with me to California," Casey said instead, trying desperately to regroup. Maybe if Kristen committed first—maybe if she *showed* him she cared—he would be able to find the words he needed. He would be able to tell her how he felt about her. "Have Christmas with me in L.A.," he said in his most persuasive tone. "We'll surf and shop and eat sushi in the sunshine, and if you really want tradition, I'll throw some Christmas lights on a palm tree for you. Come on, Kristen. Please."

Please forgive me. Please rescue me again, the way you've already rescued me from hating the holidays. Please be with me.

But Kristen only looked at him through tear-filled eyes. "I could do that," she said, "if you loved me. If you loved me, I could take that chance. If you loved me, I could blow off Christmas for you. But since you obviously *don't* love me—"

She broke off, watching him as though hoping to be proved wrong. Casey couldn't oblige. His heart felt just as inert as before. His mind refused to make him any more vulnerable than he already was. Why wouldn't Kristen just come and be with him?

Everything would have been easier then. There would have been no risk. No chance of being left alone and unwanted.

"—or if you *do* really love me, you could just say so, right now." She cracked a faint smile. "Christmas is the time for miracles, you know. Maybe this is a misunderstanding. Maybe we can start over. One good Christmas miracle and we'll be—"

"There's no miracle big enough for this," Casey said.

With evident disbelief, Kristen stared at him. "But I—"

"There's no miracle big enough for me," he added roughly. "I only wish I hadn't started believing there might be."

Kristen went on looking at him, probably wondering—like he was—how things between them had gone so wrong, so fast. It felt as though they'd spent years arriving at this moment. Casey knew he would need years to get over it, once he got back to L.A.

"Yeah." Bleakly, Kristen nodded. "Me, too."

For a long moment, she gazed at him—almost as if she was memorizing his features. Then, sadly, she walked to the door.

"I think you should leave," she said.

Knowing she was right, Casey nodded. There was nothing else he could do. No action he could take. No fixing he could manage.

With Kristen, he'd finally met his match. But the matchup between them wasn't—as he'd expected—one hundred percent good.

Miserably, he followed her to her office door. He couldn't quit looking at her hand on the doorknob, knowing—surreally and unwantedly—that this good-bye wouldn't mean "see you later," the way it usually did between them. This good-bye would be forever.

It would be the end of his hopes for the holidays.

Casey hadn't realized until just then that he'd *had* hopes for the holidays. But at that moment, looking down at Kristen's bowed head and forlorn shoulders, he realized that he'd been hoping he and Kristen would spend Christmas together in Kismet. He'd been taking for granted this Christmas would be a merry one for him . . . because Kristen would be there with him.

Now, she wouldn't be there. That meant that Christmas could never be merry. Not for him.

He should have been used to that, Casey knew. But somehow, the reality of it hurt twice as much this time.

"You were right about Christmas in Kismet," he told Kristen. "It really gets to you. Right here." Casey thumped his hand on his heart. Then he gave her a lingering, regretful look. "Have a merry Christmas, Kristen," he said. "I hope you get everything you want this year."

Then Casey squared his shoulders and took himself away from her office before he did something he might regret . . . before he forgot how strong he was supposed to be and just broke down completely.

Chapter 23

Once the news broke about Heather's "hipster impostor" (aka Talia) and her dreadlocked "bohemian boy toy" (aka Walden) and everything her friends had done to save her Christmas, Kristen should have had a pretty hard time feeling sorry for herself.

The only trouble was, she still did. Feeling woebegone and bereft, she sleepwalked through her days and wept through her nights. At home, she ripped off her snowman-print flannel sheets because they reminded her of Casey. At work, she suspended all production on her top-secret custom pie-in-a-jar (ditto).

Instead of thinking about Casey, missing Casey, and wondering why (oh why?) Casey couldn't love her back, Kristen immersed herself in every Christmas activity she could find, hoping that caroling and sleigh-riding and eggnog-quaffing would make her forget. She invited over all the fifth graders from Kismet Elementary School and redid the Galaxy Diner's windows with a tableau featuring the Abominable Snow Monster and Hermey—the nonconformist elf from

Santa's workshop who wanted to be a dentist—because those characters' misfit qualities suited her self-pitying state of mind. She wallowed in snow and icicles and naturally growing Midwestern evergreen trees. She gloried in Christmas lights and Kismet's frozen-over lake. If someone had offered her a plate of California-style sushi, Kristen figured belligerently, she might have kicked them in the face. *That's* how much she didn't want to think about what she was missing.

Unfortunately, her full-Christmas-immersion techniques didn't work. Because every time she smelled gingerbread, she thought of Casey and his toppling-over gingerbread skyscraper. Every time she saw a paper snowflake, she remembered Casey's scissors-wielding joy at his first-time creation. Every time she passed by her desk at the diner and glimpsed the RESERVED sign she'd snatched from Casey's designated booth on the fateful day he'd left, she felt her heart turn over with grief and knew that forgetting Casey was as impossible as ignoring Christmas.

Both were in her heart. Probably for good.

But knowing that didn't help. Not when the situation felt so hopeless. Not when *days* had gone by and she still felt as though she'd never be happy again. That's probably why, a few days before Christmas, when Kristen felt another one of those *I-miss-Casey* pangs, she actually gave in and picked up that RESERVED sign. Because it reminded her of him. She imagined she could almost *feel* Casey's fingertips touching hers, transmitting warmth through the injection-molded plastic table tent that held that handwritten sign, and for an instant, she felt better.

Then Gareth wandered in. He cast a knowing glance at the RESERVED sign she was hugging to her heart. "Do you want me to take that?" he asked. "We could use another sign holder to post the rules for the Yuletide Drunk Yahtzee tournament tonight."

Aghast at the thought of ripping out Casey's RESERVED

sign and replacing it, Kristen hugged the sign even harder. "No!"

She was all in favor of carrying on their pre-Christmas tradition of bringing together all their family and friends—especially those, like Walden, who didn't have anyone else locally to spend the holidays with except their Galaxy Diner pals—for a night of togetherness, games, gift-exchanging, and raucous holiday music. But there had to be limits. Right?

"Right," Gareth said, echoing her thoughts. Her friend grinned. "I didn't think you'd want to part with that."

"Not because of any . . . special reason!" Kristen hastily assured him. "I just think there are plenty of rules posted already. We don't want people to feel constrained or anything."

"Mmm-hmm." Wearing a compassionate look—and the diner's designated Santa hat, because they all rotated wearing it—Gareth came closer. He hugged her. "Things will get better. I promise. Eventually, you'll quit missing Casey, and life will go on."

"It's going on already!" Emphatically, Kristen plunked down the sign. "I'm fine! I mean, I should be proud of myself, right? I stood up for myself by turning down that deal with Torrance Chocolates. I protected my diner, and I made sure the whole world knew I didn't want to be like Heather by saying 'no' to doing those ads with her. I made *sure* Casey wasn't taking advantage of me by making him leave."

Gareth peered at her. "Do you *feel* proud of yourself?"

Grumpily, Kristen frowned at him. This was what she got for having such caring and intuitive friends. She couldn't hide anything from them—not even her own private heartache.

"No," she groused. "I don't feel proud of myself. Not *yet!* But I'm pretty sure it will kick in soon, and then—"

"If you don't feel it," Gareth said gently, "then maybe it's not happening. Maybe you're not proud of yourself for making those decisions. Maybe there's more going on here."

Kristen scoffed.

"I wonder what that might be?" Giving her a warmhearted look, Gareth pulled off the red felt Santa hat. He tickled her cheek with its white fluffy tassel. Then he plopped the hat on Kristen's head. "Don't you?"

"No." Annoyed, Kristen infused that single syllable with all the sarcastic world-weariness she could muster. "Anyway, it doesn't matter. All I ever wanted was for my Christmas to be back on track, and that's happening now. Heather has apologized for her part in everything—"

"That's *all* you wanted?" Gareth interrupted skeptically. "A nice Christmas?"

Kristen crossed her arms. "Yes."

"That's *all* you wanted," her friend prodded. "All."

"Fine. *Maybe* I wanted more, but that doesn't matter, either," Kristen told him. "Casey left town, remember? Evidently, once his big chance at cashing in vanished"—with both thumbs, she pointed at herself—"he didn't see any reason not to get the hell out of Christmastown."

Gareth grinned. "'Christmastown'? You sound just like him."

"I do not." Kristen made a face at Gareth. She put her hands on her hips. "For that to happen, Casey would have had to have had a long-term effect on me. And *that's* impossible." She rubbed the back of her neck. "You know, it sure would be nice if somebody burly would haul those kegs of mulled cider out front."

This time, Gareth laughed. "You *do* know that you just did Casey's 'tell,' don't you?" He mimed rubbing the back of his neck in apparent thought. "Are you *troubleshooting* me?"

"No," Kristen said defensively. His idea that she'd copied Casey's "tell" was preposterous. "But everybody *will* be getting pretty thirsty later." Promisingly, she added, "There's nothing quite so thirst-quenching as a nice hot cup of mulled cider."

Gareth shook his head. He eyed the kegs, which were standing at the ready in the hallway near Kristen's office.

"I'll take them out front," he said.

"Thanks." Kristen felt like whooping. She'd won!

Maybe she *was* getting to be a little like Casey after all.

"But before I do," Gareth said, "I'm going to tell you something that somebody once told me. Maybe it'll help."

"Hmm. Store Christmas lights on a reel so they don't get tangled?" Pretty soon it would be time to dismantle the displays. And Gareth *had* been looking at her office lights . . .

"No. That's not it."

"Um, keep your wrapping paper tidy with a slit-open paper-towel tube on it for storage?" she guessed. She was kind of an expert at Christmas tips and tricks. "It's like a cardboard bracelet for your giftwrap—a bracelet that prevents rumpling, but doesn't tear like tape or a rubber band."

"No." Somberly, Gareth stepped closer. "Somebody once told me that—despite what everybody always says—it doesn't take 'work' to make a relationship flourish. It takes trust. And it takes courage—courage enough to show yourself to someone else, then stand beside them while they do the same. Even when it's hard." Gareth nodded. "And believe me, it's *always* hard."

"Ha. If that were true, I'd have the most rock-solid relationships in the world," Kristen joked. "Because I have *no* trouble getting naked in front of people." She offered a lascivious wink. "Especially when it's 'hard.'"

Her ribald humor went right past her longtime friend.

"I'm not talking about getting naked," Gareth said. "I'm talking about being yourself with no barriers. Just being you."

"If you're telling me I should get all defenseless with the next guy I date . . ." Kristen shuddered. "No thanks. Not me."

"Not the 'next guy.' Just Casey." Gareth gave her one of his most easygoing smiles. "It won't be easy, but it'll be worth it. Because if Casey's the one, he'll do the same for you." Gareth nodded. "You can't get real closeness any other way."

But Kristen already knew better. "I asked Casey to tell me he loved me!" she said. "He couldn't do it. He *wouldn't* do it."

"Did you tell him you loved him?"

Uncomfortably, Kristen squirmed. "Only when showering," she mumbled. "Only when Casey couldn't hear me."

"What's that?" Gareth cupped his ear. "You did what?"

"I was the injured party!" Kristen informed him defensively. "Casey inveigled that deal with Heather and Torrance Chocolates. He went behind my back! He *used me* to get to my celebrity sister. It was enough that I was giving him a chance to say it at all." She raised her chin. "On top of all that, *I* shouldn't have had to go first."

"Somebody has to go first. If you had, that would have been the kind of courage I'm talking about." Gareth tweaked her Santa hat, then saluted. "Just sayin'. See you out front."

Alone in her office after Gareth had left, Kristen glanced at the RESERVED sign on her desk. She frowned at it.

Then she whacked it.

It flew through the air, bounced against her office wall, and landed on the floor with a satisfyingly loud clatter.

That's what she thought about "going first" with the I-love-yous. *That's* what she thought about Casey and romance and the possibility of having a happy Christmas ever again.

That's what she thought about being vulnerable and stupid.

Because she'd already shown herself to Casey, Kristen assured herself, just as she was. Exactly the way Gareth had suggested, she'd been open and trusting and honest . . .

. . . and full of all her usual defenses about not being Heather, her conscience prodded unnervingly.

Well, there was that.

But she couldn't just undo all those defenses overnight, could she? What if she couldn't get by without them?

Spooked by the very thought, Kristen frowned. Nope, *she* was the beleaguered one here, she reminded herself. She was the one who'd been hurt. She didn't plan to waste any more time second-guessing herself. So she gathered her courage, slapped on a smile, and went to finish preparing for her Yule-tide party.

Because ever since Heather had been forced to own up to her part in Casey's sneaky "deal," her sister had been going out of her way to make sure Kristen's Christmas was stellar. Heather had even footed the bill for tonight's Drunk Yahtzee party.

Everyone was going to be there—sans paparazzi—including their parents. All the usual traditions were going to be observed, just a little bit belatedly. At long last, Kristen was going to have the Christmas she'd dreamed of this year.

Too bad she'd never wanted all those traditional trimmings less . . . and wanted a certain troubleshooting Scrooge more.

But that was in the past. Kristen was done with it.

Because sure, it was *possible* she hadn't given Casey a fair chance to explain himself, because of the hurt she'd felt. It was *possible* she'd made a demand he couldn't fulfill, based on who he was and what was happening and the fact that she'd been ready to blow steam from her ears and/or bawl uncontrollably.

It was also *possible* that her Christmas tree might morph into the Jolly Green Giant and ho-ho-ho all the way to the North Pole. Right? But that didn't mean she intended to hold her breath waiting for it to happen.

Feeling more certain now, Kristen opened her office door.

Then, at the last minute, she paused. She glanced at the dejected-looking RESERVED sign, still lying there atop her industrial flooring. She scurried over to it. She scowled at it. She waited to feel vindicated, or at least proud of herself.

It didn't happen. So she picked up the sign, brushed it off, and put it back in its place of honor on her desk.

On her way out, Kristen rubbed the back of her neck. "It sure would be nice if someone would reserve that table again," she mused to no one in particular. Then she caught herself, gave a halfhearted, hopeless-feeling smile, and went to make merry.

Casey wasn't sure when his Los Angeles neighborhood had installed municipal Christmas decorations. He'd have sworn on his life that those swags of plastic evergreens, enormous red "velvet" bows, bright fake holly berries, and lights strung over practically every intersection had never been there before.

Frowning at a particularly egregious red-and-green example while waiting at a stoplight, Casey gunned his convertible's engine. If he'd still been in Kismet, he wouldn't have been driving a kick-ass convertible, that was for sure. He was *lucky*.

He was lucky to have escaped the madness of Christmastown. He was lucky to be back in the sunshine where he belonged.

Except for those damn Christmas decorations, of course.

Casey had half a mind to lodge a complaint with the city. Didn't they know that not every Los Angelino celebrated Christmas? Surely at least some of the people who came upon those seasonal decorations—*people like him*—felt excluded. What about Jewish people? Scientologists? Buddhists? Nonbelievers?

What about people who were allergic to tinsel and mandatory jolliness? What about them? Didn't anyone care about them? Didn't holiday-time Christian kindness extend to them?

Feeling indignant, Casey waited for the traffic light to change. Then he flipped his middle finger at the fake jingle bells dangling overhead and sped off toward his destination.

He'd be damned if he'd be forced into *liking* Christmas or feeling goodwill toward his fellow human beings. Screw that.

That's why he blasted non-Christmassy metal music from his car's stereo, to drown out the incessant, syrupy Christmas carols wafting from other vehicles. That's why he churlishly stalked to his luxury apartment building's elevator every day, ignoring any stray "Merry Christmases" that came his way by staring at his cell phone in apparent engrossment. That's why he was heading, right now, to his favorite frozen yogurt place.

Because *fro-yo* was *not* a holiday food.

You couldn't get fro-yo in Kismet in December. To do so would have been madness. Plus, all the seasonal fro-yo shops were meant for summer tourists and were sensibly closed in the winter. But here in California, where it was a balmy seventy-two degrees in December and flip-flops were year-round footwear?

Hell, yeah, you could get fro-yo. As a bonus, there was zero chance that fro-yo would remind him of Kristen.

Unlike every other damn thing Casey encountered.

Because somehow, Kristen had gotten under his skin . . . and so had Christmas. Holiday lights reminded him of Kristen's bedroom, where they'd made love in that sparkly lighted glow. Iced sugar cookies reminded him of the Galaxy Diner, where Kristen tended to everyone with sprinkles and pies-in-a-jar and abundant TLC. Christmas carols reminded him of Kristen singing—tunelessly but enthusiastically—along with them; wrapping paper and ribbons reminded him of an especially saucy erotic move she'd shown him.

No matter where Casey looked, he couldn't escape.

He needed Kristen the same way he now needed Christmas, unstoppably and unexpectedly, but if he couldn't have one, Casey was determined, he would be damned if he'd have the other. So he whipped his convertible into the shopping center's parking lot, stomped over to the fro-yo shop, and went inside.

The first thing that assaulted him was the holiday music. Next came the jingle bells that jangled as the door shut behind him. Then the Christmassy décor and the helpful-looking employee behind the counter, wearing a smile, a red-and-white striped stocking cap, and a HAPPY HOLIDAYS! badge pinned to her uniform.

"Hi! Welcome to Fro-Yo! Fro-Yo! What would you like?"

"Less Christmas," Casey muttered, scanning the favors.

"I'm sorry?" A wider smile. "What flavor do you like?"

He couldn't believe the holidays had even invaded here, at his favorite fro-yo shop. Was nothing sacred anymore?

"A chocolate-vanilla swirl, please." Casey pointed.

The teenage employee looked confused. "Which flavor?"

"Chocolate-vanilla swirl." He pointed again. Emphatically.

"Um, that's our special limited-edition holiday flavor combination. Candy-cane eggnog swirlaganza."

Casey frowned. "I asked for chocolate-vanilla swirl."

"Yes. But you *pointed* at candy-cane eggnog swirlaganza."

"No, I didn't. I always get chocolate-vanilla swirl."

The employee caught his disgruntled look. With a paper fro-yo cup in hand, she leaned nearer. Confidingly, she asked, "Is it just that you don't want to say it aloud? Is that why you're pointing to it instead? Some of our customers feel silly saying candy-cane eggnog swirlaganza, but I promise it's delicious."

Befuddled, Casey stared at his pointing finger. To his surprise, he was, indeed, pointing at the only Christmas-themed flavor in the entire fro-yo shop. What the hell?

"Chocolate-vanilla swirl," he repeated, pointing again.

The employee rolled her eyes. "Sir, you just pointed to candy-cane eggnog swirlaganza again. But you *said* chocolate-vanilla swirl. If you're just messing with me—"

"I'm sorry." This was ridiculous. Casey girded himself for another try. "I want chocolate-vanilla swirl, please."

As he pointed again, the employee shook her head. "Maybe you need a little more time to decide what you want."

Casey clenched his jaw. "I know *exactly* what I want." He pointed with increasing certainty. "Chocolate-vanilla swirl."

He watched in disbelief as his finger swerved straight to the Christmassy candy-cane eggnog swirlaganza flavor.

"I need a manager over here!" The employee flung up her hands in exasperation. She rang a bell. "Code purple!"

By the time the mild-mannered manager emerged from the back, Casey felt doubly determined to be served his usual order.

"Hi. I'm not sure what the confusion is," he told the manager, "but I'm asking for chocolate-vanilla swirl."

"You're pointing at candy-cane eggnog swirlaganza."

Argh. He was! Casey couldn't seem to do anything else.

"I *always* get chocolate-vanilla swirl," he explained. "It's what I like. It's my favorite flavor. *It's who I am.*"

The manager shrugged. "Maybe your tastes have changed." He signaled the stocking-cap-wearing employee. "Get him one of each flavor, on the house." He looked at Casey. "Merry Christmas."

And that's how, improbably, Casey found himself holding two cups of fro-yo and being forced to confront the impossible.

Maybe he *had* changed somehow. Maybe Kristen had had some undeniable effect on him. But even if she had . . . what came next?

Given everything that had happened between her and Kristen this Christmas, Heather knew she probably should just lay low and try not to cause any more trouble at her sister's annual Yuletide Drunk Yahtzee party. But the inescapable fact was, Heather still had a few things to wrap up in Kismet, and Kristen's holiday party at the Galaxy Diner was the perfect place to do that. All the important players were going to be there, including their parents *and* the crew of Heather's holiday TV special, whom Kristen had generously invited to come along this year before they all headed back home to L.A. Kristen would be there, of course. Also, Talia and Walden, Heather's impersonator/doppelganger and her boyfriend.

Heather *loved* Talia and Walden. Shortly after the news of their impostor "scandal" had broken, Heather had gone to meet them. Frankly, they'd inspired her with their love and their loyalty and—most of all—their oddball authenticity. Along with Casey and Shane Maresca, Talia and Walden had inspired Heather's newfound fresh attitude and her determination to turn over a new leaf.

Parking her car outside the diner, Heather nervously reviewed her outfit—a plain flannel shirt, cable-knit sweater, jeans, and boots under a toasty-warm puffer coat. She pulled out her newly created to-do list. She read over all the items. Then, nervously, Heather stepped out of her car into the snow.

Doing so felt weird. Because ordinarily, she had "people" to usher her in and out of places—not to mention drive her to them. Ordinarily, she had a red carpet to protect her toes from the muck and a wall of camera-wielding press to protect her from being forgotten. Today, though, all Heather had was herself. She hoped, as she clutched her list, that that would be enough.

Partway across the parking lot, she glimpsed a man hunched furtively near the diner's window. He appeared to be trying to peer inside. Under other circumstances, Heather would have given him a wide berth or maybe called 911. But because he didn't appear dangerous—and because, even if he was dangerous, there was a diner full of partygoers just feet away ready to rescue her—she didn't even slow her steps as she approached him.

"Hi! Merry Christmas!" she said.

The man startled. He blinked at her through his eyeglasses. The usual expression of amazement struck him. "Hey! Aren't you . . ."

Magnanimously, Heather waited for him to identify her. This happened a lot. Thanks to her music videos, her appearances on TV and the Internet, her cosmetics endorsement deals and awards-show wins and new-perfume-launch activities, she'd cast a pretty wide net, media-wise. Sometimes it took people a while to pin down exactly where they'd seen her world-famous face.

"You're *Kristen's* sister!" the man said. "Helga Miller."

Now it was Heather's turn to be startled. This was the first time anyone had identified Heather as *Kristen's sister!*

He couldn't be serious.

An instant reply rose to her lips—something along the lines of: *Have you been stranded on Mars? How can you not recognize me?*—but then Heather realized that this must be a test of her turning-over-a-new-leaf commitment. So she only smiled.

"That's me! Helga." She looked at the fat manila envelope in the man's hand. "You're not a process server, are you?"

"Me? No." The man smiled back at her. "I'm a banker."

"Oh. Well. Good for you!" Heather glanced at her to-do list. *Chat up bankers* was not on it. "Well, have a nice night."

She began flouncing away, then belatedly realized that *flouncing* places was no longer her M.O. She turned back to him.

"Can I help you with something?" she asked kindly.

"Actually, Helga," he said. "I think you can."

Chapter 24

Kismet, Michigan
4½ smooching, hugging, memory-making, love-filled days
until Christmas

Even though Walden would have liked to have spent the holidays with his family, he had to admit—as he lifted a beer to his lips and looked around the festively decorated Galaxy Diner—that Yuletide Drunk Yahtzee night was turning out to be pretty memorable. Already, he'd seen Avery perform karaoke Christmas carols, Gareth perform a dance routine to go along with Avery's karaoke Christmas carols, and Talia cheering them on with a suspiciously expert routine that turned out to have been the result of her hidden past as a high-school cheerleader.

Looking at her elfin-punk demeanor, piercings, and lavender hair, Walden had been disbelieving. Talia had way too much indie street cred to have taken part in something as traditional as cheerleading. Then she gave him a pert smile and executed a perfect Herkie jump, and Walden became a believer.

"I'm totally bangin' a hot cheerleader!" he exclaimed.

"Wait." Talia squinted at him. "You recognize that move?"

"Former band geek." Jauntily, he pointed at himself. "I saw a lot of the sideline cheerleaders during football season."

"Ah." Smiling, Talia kissed him. "I love you, band geek!"

"I love you, too, hot cheerleader!" Walden said. Sobering, he added, "Then you're not disappointed in my dorktastic past?"

"Are you kidding? I love it. Being musical is cool," Talia assured him. "Are you disappointed in my ultratraditional past?"

Walden shook his head. "It's part of you. So I love it."

They kissed again. Someone nearby groaned theatrically.

"*Come on!* At least find some mistletoe first, willya?"

As Walden turned to see who'd spoken, he saw a tall, lanky, very ordinary-looking dude wearing glasses and swilling beer. Tipsily, the man weaved toward him and Talia.

"You two," he said, using his beer to point at them, "are ruining it for all the rest of us with your overt *happiness*."

Talia frowned at him. "What's wrong with happiness?"

"What's right with happiness is more like it," the man complained. "Love doesn't work out. *I* faked chicken pox to get close to the girl *I* loved, and she *still* didn't want me!"

Chicken pox. Walden exchanged a glance with Talia. They knew two people who'd had chicken pox lately. Only one of them had been a man. The other, of course, had been Heather.

"You must be Alex Taylor," Walden said. "Heather's guy."

"You were *faking?*" Talia asked him at the same time.

A nod. "For all the good it did me," Alex said. "Heather started spying on me. She thought I was up to something."

Walden and Talia traded another glance.

"Dude," Walden said, "you *were* up to something."

"You were faking chicken pox," Talia added, reasonably. "Maybe Heather detected an undercurrent of subterfuge?"

Alex scowled at them both. "So? I *loved* her!"

Unsteadily, he put down his beer bottle. He whipped out his cell phone. He poked at the menus. He waved his phone in their faces. "Look. That's her. She's beautiful. See?"

Walden and Talia both looked at the photos he'd offered. After the first three, Talia recoiled. "Yikes!"

But Walden only nodded knowingly. "Nice! I especially like that one where Heather's wearing a bathrobe and pink calamine lotion on her face." Appreciatively, he took another look. "And that one, where she's laughing at the TV and dribbling popcorn."

Fondly, Alex looked at the photo. "Yep. I love it. It's so 'her,' you know what I mean? It just makes me smile."

He and Walden both nodded. Talia crossed her arms.

"You two are *nuts,* you know that?" She chanced another glance at the photo Alex was brandishing. "If you had pictures of me looking like that," she warned Walden, "I'd ditch you."

"Uh-oh." Alex elbowed Walden, giving him a mischievous look. "Better not show her your cell phone, dude."

"Or my computer. That's where I archive the videos."

"Yeah. I'm pretty sure every guy has a stash like that."

"What?" Talia shrieked, looking appalled. "I thought men's 'stashes' were porn! You mean you're secretly archiving all those 'impromptu' videos you take of me? But I don't wear make-up or strike a cool pose or even look *normal* in some of them."

"That's what makes you look real and lovable, baby."

Even as Walden said it, Alex was nodding in agreement.

Talia shook her head. Then she glanced sideways, spied someone else in the party crowd, and hauled her over.

"Heather, back me up," Talia said to her newly grabbed compatriot. "Candid photos are the worst, right?"

Caught in the midst of their conversation, Heather went still. She blinked at Talia, glanced at Walden . . . then saw Alex.

While Heather gazed longingly at Alex, Walden hastily filled her in on the discussion so far. He ended with, ". . . but it's all from a place of love, of course. Every guy knows that."

Eagerly, Alex nodded. His gaze never left Heather's face.

"I *do* love you, Heather!" he said. "I was scared you wouldn't love me back, because I'm not famous or anything."

"Fame is overrated." Looking giddy, Heather took his hand. "I'm planning to throw away mine, in fact. That's item number three on my new to-do list." She glanced at Alex's cell phone photos. Admirably, she didn't even flinch. "Do you think I can use some of those snapshots, now that I know what they're for?"

"Everything I have is yours," Alex swore. "I love you."

Heather beamed. "I love you, too, *amore mio*."

Alex looked at her in confusion. "You speak Italian?"

"I had to learn something new once I mastered all those Words of the Day," Heather said with a shrug. "It turns out, I *love* knowing stuff! I can be smart. Thanks to you, I learned *that* about myself. Also," she added, "'learn Italian' is number twelve on my new to-do list. I'm turning over a new leaf."

Happily, Alex kissed her. "Any way I can help with that?"

"Only by being you," Heather assured him fondly. "And by forgiving me for doubting you. Also, you could help me track down my sister. Because someone from the bank is here to give Kristen her new paperwork showing that her diner mortgage is in the clear." She nodded toward a bespectacled man standing near the mulled cider bowl. "That's Ernesto. He's a very nice man."

As Walden, Talia, Alex, and Heather glanced toward him, Ernesto the Banker spotted them. He waved a big manila envelope.

"Kristen will definitely want that paperwork," Walden said.

Talia agreed. Then she looked at Heather. "What did you mean, you're going to throw away your fame?" she asked.

"Oh, that." Joyfully linking arms with Alex, Heather nodded. "Well, it turns out that my holiday TV special was so overbudget and behind schedule that there was just no way to make it work. So Shane and I talked about it, and we came up with a whole new plan!" She leaned conspiratorially nearer. "We're breaking the news tomorrow. We're going to broadcast an entirely new live performance—a *real* home-coming performance—streaming online, independent of the TV network and the production company and all the traditional media. I've already given back the money they gave me for my TV special to pay for the overages we ran up, because that's item number four on my to-do list," she went on. "I've decided it's time to just have a little faith in myself—without all the fake stuff my management insisted on. Also, we're going to sell DVDs ourselves afterward from my Website, for five dollars each."

Walden was surprised. "Five dollars? That's pretty cheap."

"Yeah, I guess so," Heather agreed. "But I remember what it was like to be struggling financially. That was my *real* down-home background, growing up. I want to help out my fans. I want to restart my career in an *authentic* way, with no Auto-Tune, no lavish sets, and no fake outs. Just me singing."

While they all stared in amazement at her—having never heard anything quite so down-to-earth come from Heather's mouth—the former diva herself spotted someone else in the crowd.

"Whoops! There's my mom and dad, talking to Kristen," Heather said. "I have to go ask them something about their @Heather_Hotline Twitter account." She stopped and looked at Alex. Then she kissed him. "Don't go away, cutie. I'll be back."

While Heather left, Alex mooned after her. Then he turned back to Walden and Talia with a sheepish grin. "She'll be back!"

"Yep," Talia confirmed wryly. "That's usually how love works. It's hard to keep a relationship going otherwise."

"Aw, don't be so hard on him," Walden said, making his dreadlocks sway as he nudged his chin toward Alex. "He doesn't know what's hit him yet. I haven't even told him about the secret guy code of always letting your girl win at board games."

"Hey." Talia gave Walden a censorious look. "I *totally* smoked your butt at Scrabble the other night."

"Whatever you need to believe, baby," Walden said. "Next you'll be telling me that KATIPO really *is* a real word."

"It is!" Talia insisted. "It's a poisonous spider native to New Zealand. I heard a comedian making a joke about it."

"Well, everybody knows all the best educations come from watching YouTube comedy videos," Walden joked. "I stand corrected."

Then, because Walden knew he *did* stand corrected—and was only preserving his pride, which Talia generously allowed him to do—Walden gave his favorite Scrabble expert a wink, slapped Alex on the back, and went back to enjoying his first-ever Christmas in Kismet. And he couldn't have been happier to be doing it.

Kristen knew that something unusual was up when she glimpsed Heather barging over to where Kristen was talking with her parents at her Yuletide party at the diner. Because instead of just jumping in and dominating the conversation in the divalike way she usually would have done, Heather actually hung back for a second—with respect and consideration and absolutely *no* glam squad—and waited for a natural lull in the dialogue.

Then Heather jumped in with both feet. But only to say . . .

"Did you just tell Kristen you're *proud* of me?" Heather blurted, gazing in apparent astonishment from their mom to their dad and back again. "I could have sworn I just heard—"

"Of course we did," their mom said. "We always do."

"We do always do that," their dad agreed, nodding.

"They *really* always do that," Kristen added morosely. "Seriously. They cannot stop talking about how incredible you are. Have you not seen their bragtastic Twitter account?"

"Yes, but—" Heather shook her head, clearly skeptical. "I thought that Twitter account was to repay me for all the trips and things I give you," she said. "And I want you to shut it down, by the way, because thanks for helping me and everything, but you deserve to enjoy your retirement. And the important thing is," she went on breathlessly, "that all you ever say to *me* is how Kristen did *this* clever, amazing thing or *that* ingenious, talented thing, and how superproud you are of *her!*"

Kristen gawked, not believing a word of it. "They do not."

"Oh, they do, too!" her sister said with a vehement nod. "They won't shut up about their 'smart, accomplished' daughter."

Their parents shrugged. "You are smart and accomplished, Kristen," their mom said. "So are you, Heather."

"We're proud of both of you," their dad added with another shrug. "And we'll shut down that Tweety account tomorrow."

Kristen stared, dumbfounded. She'd been moping around all day, missing Casey, but frankly, this incredible news cheered her up. "Mom! Dad! You could have told *me* this! I thought you were only proud of Heather. You can't shut up about her."

"Really?" Heather appeared strangely pleased. "They can't?"

"We're proud! So what?" Their parents seemed befuddled. And a little bit harassed. "What's wrong with that?"

Kristen exchanged an awestruck look with Heather. She could tell that her sister was as stunned by this as she was.

"I thought Kristen was your favorite," Heather said.

"I thought Heather was your favorite!" Kristen disagreed.

But their parents only shook their heads. "Nobody is our favorite. But there's no point giving you both big egos."

"You're sisters," their dad said with a definitive air. "You should get along. We didn't want to make you feel competitive by comparing you with each other all the time."

"That's how sibling rivalry takes root," their mom explained with a knowledgeable tone. "I read it in a book."

In a book. Kristen had never wanted to host a book-burning bonfire more than she did in that moment. "So you just never mentioned to *us,* individually, how you felt about us?"

"Well, not per se." Their mom shot a baffled look at their dad. Then she shrugged, too. "You know we love you both."

In increasing astonishment, Kristen looked at Heather.

"So you never did anything except praise the *other* one of us?" Heather echoed. "Whichever one of us wasn't there?"

Their dad frowned. "It got tricky sometimes, too, believe me! Times like now, when you're both here . . . it's *impossible* to know what to say." He looked around. "When's the Yahtzee start?"

"When everyone is too blitzed to add up the die rolls," Kristen said in a distracted tone, still astounded by this life-altering news. "Sketchy counting skills make Yahtzee more fun."

Heather nodded in agreement. For the first time in a long time, Kristen felt a groundswell of solidarity with her sister.

Who knew that Heather had been struggling with feeling overlooked, too? Who knew that their parents *hadn't* been ignoring Kristen's accomplishments (if only to her face) not because they weren't proud of her (as she'd feared) or wanted her to be more like their more celebrated daughter (as she'd *really* feared), but because they didn't want to kindle sibling rivalry? As a strategy, Kristen thought, it was a major bust.

For her entire life, she'd believed everyone wanted her to be like Heather. Because if even her own parents wanted that . . . who wouldn't? If even the two people who knew and loved Kristen best didn't accept her as she was . . . who would? she'd reasoned.

But now all those doubts were reversed in an instant.

Because Kristen didn't care whether random newspaper reporters or paparazzi or strangers on the Internet thought she possessed an insufficient amount of "Heather-like awesomeness" (an actual quote she'd gleaned from reading reports of her one-and-only adventure accompanying Heather to the Grammys). She cared if the people she loved thought she was awesome. She cared if *she* thought she was awesome. And in most ways, she did.

Feeling liberated, Kristen smiled.

Then she gave her mom and dad two big hugs. "I sure wish we'd talked about this sooner!" she said with a laugh. "I could have saved myself a lot of heartache."

"Me too!" Heather exclaimed. Then she turned to Kristen with an intent look. "And speaking of heartache . . ."

Oh no. This could be trouble. Kristen had confided in Heather about what had happened with Casey, of course, but so far, she'd avoided the inevitable pep talk and/or "snap out of it!" conversation that usually followed in the aftermath of a breakup. She had a feeling her luck had just run out.

For all of Heather's positive qualities, being reassuring was not among them. Frankly, she hadn't faced enough obstacles in her life to be truly capable of empathy and encouragement.

All but proving it, Heather's eyes gleamed with zeal as she said, "There's something I have to tell you about Casey!"

Kristen held up her hands to ward off her sister's dubious "sympathy." "That's okay. I'm fine with things now."

"You're *not* fine," her sister insisted, "and I know the reason. First of all"—inexplicably, she broke off to consult a handwritten list—"there's the question of my sex tape."

Their dad blanched. "Let's get more pie-in-a-jar!"

"Yes, let's!" their mom agreed, and they hurried away.

Left alone with Heather amid the whirl of the party, Kristen eyed her sister. "You don't have to do this."

"I want to. It's item number nine on my to-do list."

"*You* have a to-do list?"

"Don't look so surprised. It's efficient." With a brisk motion, Heather consulted it again. Then, "As I was saying, about my sex tape—Casey hasn't seen it. I tested him."

Kristen crossed her arms. "You tested him?"

Her sister nodded. "Yes. I gave him my accidental catch-phrase from that dumb video, and he didn't even blink."

Given Heather's triumphant tone, Kristen could tell she was supposed to be impressed. But she was a little distracted by wondering . . . If she'd been so wrong about her parents, was she *also* wrong about Casey? Was she wrong about why he'd wanted to spend time with her? About how he truly felt about her?

It was possible, Kristen realized, that she'd jumped to all the wrong conclusions about Casey. Worried now, she gazed longingly toward the diner's exit. If she left right this minute and drove to the regional airport in Grand Rapids, Kristen calculated, she could be on a plane to California by midnight.

"Okay, good," she told Heather. "I guess that means Casey passes my boyfriend litmus test with flying colors. Now I've—"

"You don't believe me," Heather judged correctly, surprising her. "I get it. Fair enough. Watch this."

She turned to the closest male, a friend of Avery's. In a breathless, seductive tone, Heather said, "Giddy up, cowboy!"

To Kristen's further surprise, the man reacted by opening his mouth in an O, turning bright pink, then scurrying away.

"Sorry!" he blurted. "I've got to be somewhere private!"

Kristen watched him leave in bafflement. But Heather wasn't confused at all. "He has a boner," she confided to Kristen. "So many men have watched that sex tape so many times that it has an immediate Pavlovian effect on them. They can't help it."

"Oh, come on!" Kristen gestured. "Maybe he was thirsty!"

"*Casey* didn't even bat an eyelash. He hasn't seen it."

Well. That kind of made Casey her dream man, Kristen realized, for an altogether unexpected reason. "Okay. Fine," she said with a wave. "Not that it matters anymore, since—"

Since I'm potentially flying to California to be with Casey right now, Kristen was about to say, *to apologize for unfairly accusing him of things he probably never intended and maybe to try reconciling with him* (if she was lucky) *and maybe even to try kissing him,* but her sister interrupted her before she could.

"It does matter! And there's more." Eagerly and seriously, Heather checked her to-do list again. "Did you know that Shane Maresca and Casey grew up in the same foster home? At least part of the time, until Shane was adopted by this family who—"

"Yes, Casey told me about that," Kristen said, beginning to feel impatient with Heather's impromptu Oprah impression. She half expected her sister to thrust a microphone in her face and ask her to "share." "Casey told me that Shane got what *he* wanted for Christmas one year, and he had a hard time getting over it. I guess that's what caused the rift between them."

"*That's* putting it mildly!" Heather exclaimed. "Do you know what it was that Casey wanted—and Shane got—for Christmas?"

"Actually, I could just ask him." Kristen hooked her thumb toward the diner's exit. "I'm thinking of heading out to—"

"*A family!*" Heather burst out in a sympathetic tone. "When Casey was fifteen, he wanted a *family* for Christmas. Apparently, he had it all planned out. When the adoption interviews came, Casey was going to say that all he wanted for Christmas was a home and family of his own—because it was true, and because I guess he was quite a charming, scrappy little bugger, even then, and he knew he could pull it off—but then during the interviews, Shane went first, and he stole Casey's line."

Poor Casey. Kristen could just imagine him as a scrawny, needy, determined and inventive kid, believing and hoping he could ace an interview like that. After all, he *was* good with people. Breathlessly, she waited. "And? Then what happened?"

"Oh, I thought you were on your way out someplace."

"Heather!"

"Hey, transformation doesn't happen overnight." As though demonstrating that fact, Heather gave an impudent grin. Then she continued her story. "So then Shane got adopted into this superrich, ultra-swanky family and left the foster home forever, and Casey stayed behind—being teased by the other kids for choking at his interview. When the right moment came with his potential adoptive family, Casey couldn't say a single word."

Aghast, Kristen stared at her. "That's awful!"

"Yeah. Supposedly, Casey didn't ever admit wanting much of anything, so once the other kids realized he desperately wanted a family, they were pretty merciless about it. Little jerks."

I don't usually let myself really want something, Kristen remembered Casey saying, looking troubled and alone. *But with you, I couldn't help it. I really wanted you.*

She'd wanted him, too. But she hadn't been able to stand there, scared and defenseless, and admit it. Not then, she hadn't. What she *had* been able to do, Kristen realized to her horror, was accidentally goad Casey in the worst possible way.

You can't even say it, she'd remarked, too full of sadness and suspicion and hopelessness to hold it in. In contrast to Gareth's trust-and-courage philosophy, Kristen had held up her fearfulness like a shield . . . then she'd bludgeoned Casey with it.

"I've got to get to Casey," she said, gazing around her crowded diner with a new sense of urgency. "I've got to go!"

"But your party is happening here," Heather said with wide, disingenuous eyes. "Your ideal Christmas is happening *here*."

At that, Kristen shook her head.

"Christmas doesn't happen at a big party full of people,"

she said, finally realizing why immersing herself headlong in Christmas hadn't made her feel better. "It doesn't happen beside a cut Douglas fir—or three—or atop a big pile of wrapped gifts. It doesn't happen in a church. It only happens when at least two people who love each other come together to celebrate. And that means, this year, my Christmas can't happen here in Kismet."

"Right-o." Busily, Heather scratched off an item on her to-do list. She gave Kristen a satisfied glance. "That was item number one on my list. Making you realize that."

"It was not!"

"Yes, it was!"

"Let me see." Making a quick sideways move, Kristen grabbed for her sister's to-do list. She missed. "You are *not* this good at helping people," she said in exasperation. "Despite introducing me to Ernesto, letting me know my bank troubles were sorted, getting the fraud charges dropped against Talia and Walden, footing the bill for this party, getting Mom and Dad to admit their non-sibling-rivalry tactics—" Kristen broke off.

She gave her sister a suspicious frown.

Heather only rocked on her heels, looking tickled. "Yes?"

"Wow. I guess people really can change."

And if *Heather* could become generous and helpful . . . the sky really was the limit, Kristen realized. Next, she'd be making everyone declare month-old fruitcake as their favorite food.

Speaking of which . . .

"I don't know if *you* can change that much," Heather declared contrarily before Kristen could complete that thought. "After all, you *love* Christmas. You love snow and evergreens and icicles and decorations. You love Burl Ives ditties and tinsel and mistletoe and even those gross ribbon-shaped hard candies that Grandma Noble used to have every Christmas."

For a second, they both stopped to fondly recall their much-missed maternal grandmother.

"My point is," Heather went on doggedly, "I don't think you can survive Christmas in the sunshine, near the beach, without everything that makes Christmas Christmas. It's antithetical to everything you've ever wanted out of life."

"Antithetical?"

Heather shrugged. "I've been learning a few new words."

"Aha." Kristen nodded, feeling oddly proud of her sister—and unusually close to her, too. "But the thing you're missing is that *Casey* is my Christmas now. Without him," she said, "everything else just . . . loses its magic."

All at once, Kristen became aware of a stunning silence in her diner. The holiday jingles had quit playing. The boisterous crowd had quieted. Even the clanking of glasses had stopped.

Uncertainly, Kristen looked around. As one, her family and friends gazed back at her, beaming as if they'd just won the lottery. Which was silly, because Kristen knew *she'd* just won the lottery—if she could earn herself another chance with Casey.

"Go get 'em, Kristen!" Avery cheered, her fist in the air.

Everyone else joined in. Too late, Kristen realized that she'd pretty much just made a public love declaration to a man who wasn't even there, didn't like Christmas . . . and could make her forget to breathe or think or understand basic arithmetic with one of his dazzling smiles. Casey was just that amazing.

He was also just that far away, too. Disheartened, Kristen considered the journey ahead. "Thanks, everyone. But I'm not even sure I can get a flight to California this close to Christmas. The airport's going to be crazy."

"Oh yeah." Heather made a regretful face. "That's true. And I gave my place on my chartered private jet to Shane. He left for L.A. this morning." As an aside, she added, "He was item number five on my to-do list. I'm pretty sure I re-formed him."

At this point, Kristen would put nothing past her sister, in-cluding reforming a notorious "anti-fixer" with a mile-wide competitive streak and a dangerous excess of charisma.

Not Casey-level charisma, of course, but still . . .

"Congrats," Kristen told her sister, feeling increasingly urgent. And impatient. "But I still can't get to L.A.!"

"Not with that attitude, you can't." From her diner's door-way, someone else spoke up. "But I think I can help."

Everyone turned. Heather squealed. "*Damon!* You're here!"

While Kristen watched, her sister ran with both arms out-stretched, her to-do list fluttering, toward the handsome man with dark, curly hair who stood in Kristen's diner doorway.

Somehow, he made the whole place feel twice as glam-orous, just with his presence. Beside him stood a bubbly looking blonde and a towheaded boy, probably seven or eight years old. The kid smiled, gazing in wonder at the Galaxy Diner's decorations.

Damon greeted Heather. Heather greeted his compan-ions. As they all exchanged exuberant embraces and air kisses, the truth struck Kristen with a jolt. *This* must be Damon Torrance—playboy chocolatier, CEO of Torrance Chocolates, Kristen's erstwhile "business partner" in their cancelled deal, and all-around scandal-starter. The woman beside him had to be Natasha Jennings, Kristen realized, Damon's hyperefficient "gal Friday." Which meant that the child must be . . .

Well, Kristen wasn't sure who the kid was.

She *might* have done a little Googling to find out more about the deal she'd so hastily refused (so shoot her for being curious!), but there hadn't been any mention online of Damon having children. Surprised, yet still impatient to leave, Kristen was standing there frowning when they ap-proached her.

With a grin, Damon introduced Natasha Jennings, little Milo Jennings, and then himself. Kristen couldn't help liking the three of them immediately. Doing so felt . . . inevitable. If she'd been having second thoughts about having refused Casey's million-dollar deal, they would have been zooming around in her head like a sugared-up kid on Christmas morning with a bunch of new toys and a fresh pack of batteries.

"Kristen. I'm pleased to finally meet you." Damon shook her hand. Then he shook his head. "And I'm impressed! As far as I know, no one has *ever* turned down one of the deals Casey put together. I just had to meet the woman who finally did."

"Yes, I did turn it down." Now that Kristen had given the matter some thought—some *real* thought, based on the truth instead of her fears—she realized her decision hadn't changed. She was happy with her diner and her life, just the way they were. Not in defiance of Heather. Just . . . because. Her life wasn't fancy, but it was hers. She liked it. "So you might as well save your breath, if you're here to convince me to take the deal."

"Oh, Damon doesn't *convince* anybody," Natasha told her with a laugh. "He just magically makes them want to cooperate."

Kristen nodded. "Hmm. Sounds a lot like Casey."

She and Natasha exchanged knowing, curious glances.

"Well, I don't know about *magic,*" Damon said, casting a mischievous glance at Natasha, "but I do know about people, and looking at *you,* Kristen," he added with a self-deprecating grin, "I can tell you're less than awed by my infamous presence."

"He means you're itching to leave," the kid, Milo, piped up, watching astutely as Kristen edged toward the coatrack.

Damon and Natasha laughed. Heather ruffled Milo's hair.

Evidently, along with a mile-long to-do list, her sister had discovered a tolerance for children, Kristen realized. And a *boyfriend,* she saw further, if the goo-goo eyes Heather was trading with her nice—if surprisingly ordinary-looking—glasses-wearing construction manager from her *Live! from the Heartland* holiday TV special were any indication.

"Yes. I'm sorry if you came all this way just for me," Kristen said, "but I'm afraid my answer is still no. I'd rather not get into all the rigmarole of a partnership right now."

"Okay." Damon nodded. "Mind if we try some of your pie-in-a-jar anyway? The way Casey talked about it, I half expect it to tie my shoes, give me a massage, and make me shout its name."

"Damon!" Natasha covered Milo's ears. "Ahem."

"Sorry." Appearing wholly unabashed, Damon looked at Kristen again. "If you change your mind, I'm here to talk. In the meantime, don't worry about a thing. I have family in the area. We're visiting for Christmas and decided to drop by here."

"We've made a bunch of stops along the way," Natasha explained. "A private jet makes trips like that easy."

"I'll bet." Kristen nodded. "My sister travels that way, too." She smiled at Heather. "I'm really proud of her success."

"Aw!" For a minute, Heather actually looked teary-eyed. "I'm proud of you, too! You really *are* fab, Kristen!"

Then *they* hugged, and the whole diner got bored with the proceedings. Gareth jumped on a chair, clanged a cup of mulled cider with a spoon, then cleared his throat. "Everybody who wants Kristen to get to California to see Casey," he said loudly, "put some money in the Santa hat that Avery's holding."

Helpfully, Avery held out the diner's designated red-felt Santa hat. With a game-show-hostess-worthy flourish, she waved it, signaling for everyone to come near and start contributing.

"If we all pitch in," Gareth went on, "we can probably raise enough money for one of those overpriced last-minute airfares!"

Everyone rushed forward while digging for their wallets or handbags, but Damon held up his hands to stop them.

"Good idea!" he said. "Do that. *Or* Kristen could just take my private jet. It's parked at the Kismet air field. Natasha, Milo, and I can drive the rest of the way to where we're going."

Talia blinked. "Kismet has a private air field?"

Walden made a goofy face. "I guess so. Who knew?"

And that's how, with the blessing of all her family and friends—and the holiday help of one very persuasive Yuletide stranger—Kristen found herself bundled up with nothing but an overnight bag, directions to Casey's apartment building, and a whole heart full of hopes as she jetted her way westward . . . looking forward to finding Christmas, improbably, in the golden state.

Chapter 25

Los Angeles, California
T-minus 4 days until Christmas

Casey was busy making his way across the beautifully landscaped courtyard of his luxury apartment building in L.A. when he felt the first stirrings of . . . *something*. It was like déjà vu, but different. It was like being watched, only stronger. It was . . .

Hell. It was probably just his imagination heading into overdrive, Casey decided as he moved past the courtyard's stone-bordered flower beds and its palm trees with their tastefully subtle strings of tiny white lights. Those lights were the building's only nod to seasonal festivity. Casey had always liked that.

Until today. Today those subtle lights just didn't seem sufficient. But before Casey could consider the matter any further, he experienced that eerie sensation again. Self-consciously, he stopped. He frowned. He looked around.

Shane Maresca stepped out from around the corner.

Casey swore. "We've got to quit meeting like this."

His former best friend and current arch nemesis laughed.

"There's no other way for us to meet. You won't take my calls."

"There's a reason for that." Casey girded himself for another confrontation. "Look, Shane. I don't want to do this."

"And I don't want to stalk you. Yet here we are."

Despite the impatient, intimidating, get-lost look Casey gave him, Shane remained stubbornly standing there. He still had the same cocky, "what's it to you?" attitude he'd had as a kid, Casey noticed. Now there was a veneer of urbanity and politeness on top of it, but underneath it all, Casey could still see the same scrappy teenager with holey jeans and beat-up Nikes and (usually) a black eye or a bruise or a scrape from a fight.

He and Shane had always been alike in that way. That's how Casey realized, looking at Shane then, that his unwanted arch nemesis was not going to give up. He was just going to keep coming. After all, that's what Casey would have done.

Except when it came to Kristen, his conscience niggled. *You gave up on her.* But Casey managed to ignore that. For now.

"Fine." Casey plunked down the object he'd been carrying. Irritably, he addressed Shane. "What do you want?"

Looking amused, his former best friend nodded at the thing Casey had been carrying. "First, I want to know what the hell that's supposed to be."

Caught, Casey lifted his chin. He wished he wasn't doing this. With dignity, he said, "That is a Christmas tree."

Shane burst out laughing. "It's a twig!"

"It's not that bad." *It makes me feel closer to Kristen. So it's worth it.* "It just needs a few decorations."

"Whatever you say, Charlie Brown."

"Oh yeah?" Casey frowned at him twice as hard. "I hope you bust a gut laughing like that."

"I hope you claim that thing as a dependent for tax purposes," Shane said, "because it sure as hell couldn't survive on its own. That 'tree' would snap if a dog peed on it."

"I'll keep an eye out for incontinent Chihuahuas." Casey

put one hand on his hip, unhappy to have his just-discovered holiday sentimentality exposed—by Shane, of all people. Deciding he'd better steer this conversation himself, he said, "I heard about Heather's live-stream Internet broadcast." Grudgingly, he added, "Good idea. Heather has more talent than people realize."

"It wasn't my idea," Shane told him. "It was—"

Hers, Casey expected him to say, miraculously sharing the credit for that unexpected success, but then . . .

"—*yours,* according to Heather," Shane went on. "Apparently, you told Heather she was smarter than she was letting on, and capable of more than she was doing. She decided to prove you right." Admiringly, Shane shook his head. "Just goes to show, you never know the kind of impact you're having on someone."

Morosely, Casey had to agree with that. Because Kristen would never know the impact she'd had on *him*—so much so that he'd actually rescued a weedy-looking, pathetic Christmas tree.

Worse, Casey planned to erect that tree in his apartment, decorate it as best he could, and try to enjoy it.

If he couldn't have Kristen for Christmas, he'd decided, at least maybe he could have Christmas for Christmas. Somehow.

Hoping to draw attention away from that outrageously sappy plan, Casey looked at Shane. "I handed you a perfect opportunity to wreck Heather's TV special. I thought you'd take it."

Bleakly, Shane nodded. "I know you did."

"I guess I was wrong," Casey admitted. "Your bosses can't be happy about that, though. You never told me who hired you."

Shane shrugged. "I wasn't in Kismet for a job."

Casey guffawed. "Nobody goes to Christmastown for fun."

"It wasn't for fun, either." Looking aggrieved for the first time, his former best friend stared at him. "Come on, Casey. You're not this dense. Are you really telling me you don't know why I was in Kismet? Why I kept popping up wherever you were? Why I'm here, right now, worrying that your little stick of a Christmas tree is going to wilt in the sunlight?"

Defensively, Casey clutched his tree. "It's fine. I just have to keep it away from rogue birds," he informed Shane tersely. "A crow landed on it on the lot and nearly bent it in half. I'm going to tie the tree to a stake for support."

Dubiously, Shane eyed it. "Do you even have a tree stand?"

Surprised, Casey looked at the tree's base. It was bare.

He swore. "Damn, this Christmas stuff is complicated."

"Yeah. You need some serious help," Shane agreed. "And unless I'm mistaken, you're going to get it. But first—"

Instantly and hopelessly, Casey wondered if Shane meant that *Kristen* would be offering him some *serious help*—if Shane meant that she'd forgiven him and wanted him and had decided to accept his invitation and was on her way to L.A. right now. Because Kristen knew everything about Christmas. But that was ridiculous, he reminded himself. He'd messed up with Kristen.

He might have made enough progress that he could pay for a scrawny Christmas tree and lug it home. Casey didn't know if he'd reached the point where he could declare his love for her.

"I was in Kismet to try to make up with you, you jackass!" Shane exclaimed. "I knew you'd be trapped there, working on Heather's disastrous special. Everybody knew," he said, pacing now. "I gave you credit with your agency for the live-stream Internet broadcast idea, by the way," he added, "along with Heather, so your brilliant career wouldn't be destroyed."

Surprised, Casey stared at him. He wouldn't have credited his former best friend with that much generosity. Not even at Christmastime. Not that Casey had checked in with

his agency yet. Since leaving Kismet, he'd been feeling too
despondent to bother. He might be unemployed already. He
had walked out on his latest assignment, after all. That was
a dismissible offense. For all he knew, Shane was lying
through his teeth.

Although he didn't seem to be. And Casey was pretty
good at reading people. Reluctantly, he nodded in thanks.

"Anyway," Shane said, casting Casey an uncertain, determined look as he went on pacing, "I knew you'd be trapped
in Kismet a while. I knew you'd be weakened and extra-
susceptible, because Christmas is like your kryptonite—"

Casey scoffed, still reeling at the idea that Shane wanted
to mend the rift between them. It had gone on for so long . . .

"—and I knew I could get to you," Shane continued. "I
knew that was my make-it-or-break-it chance. But then you
hooked up with Kristen, and I couldn't get through to you no
matter what I did, and I was getting pretty pissed off and
frustrated by your stonewalling me by then, so I tried to
break up the two of you—"

"You *what?*" Casey felt his fists clench.

"—by telling you that Kristen wanted a baked-goods deal
that included Heather, because anyone but a *moron* could tell
there are some sibling-rivalry issues between them—which
I could tell you a *lot* about, by the way—"

"Not interested," Casey broke in, his frown deepening.

"—and a deal would be disastrous for them both, but even
after *that* I couldn't get through to you," Shane went on, "and
I was starting to lose faith in things working out until
Heather encouraged me to follow you back here. She even
lent me her chartered private jet. And then, well . . ." With
mingled ferociousness and hope, Shane finished up with a
disarming shrug. "Here I am."

Unreasonably, Casey felt a little bit moved by Shane's
efforts to reach him. *A little bit.* Not a lot. It was a ballsy move
for Shane to be so honest. Casey respected that. Still . . .

The truth was, he hadn't dealt well with Kristen. Partly

that had been because of his issues with Shane. So Casey stood there alone. He faced down his onetime friend. He dredged up all the patience and generosity he could, given the situation.

"Fine. You're here, dumbass." As he said it, Casey held tight to his Christmas tree for strength. He imagined, in a stupid and fanciful and un–Casey-like way, that its inherent Christmassy qualities brought him one step closer to Kristen—one step closer to being a man who deserved Kristen. "Now what?"

For a long moment, Shane only looked at him. Then he bowed his head. He looked at the courtyard, around which the luxury apartment building's exclusive living units nestled like jewels.

"I came to say I'm sorry," Shane finally said. In a blunt voice, he said, "I'm sorry I screwed you in that interview—"

Whoa. Casey didn't want to hear any of *this*.

He held up his free hand to ward off Shane's next words, but his former friend just kept talking. As though he'd stored up those sentences for years, he doggedly said his piece.

"I'm sorry I stole your big line," Shane said. "It was a crusher, dude. I *knew* it would work. It would melt that family's hearts like puppies on parade. So I just . . . did it. It only took a minute, but the effects of it . . ." Swerving his gaze to Casey at last, Shane shook his head. He swore. "They lasted a lifetime."

"Yeah. It must be hell, getting lucky like that."

"It was!" Pacing again now, Shane cast him a beleaguered look. "I didn't deserve to get that family. I *did* get fucking *lucky,* and I knew it. I was never able to forget it, either."

For a second, Shane seemed almost . . . *haunted* by that. Casey wondered if there was more he wasn't telling him. But then . . .

"Good," Casey said. "You shouldn't forget it, you heartless bastard. You stole something from me. I can never get it back."

At that, Shane looked straight at him. He didn't so much as

wince, not even as Casey's pain and raw enmity radiated from him. "I didn't steal it. You never had it," Shane said, head-on. "Even if you hadn't choked in that adoption interview—"

Casey went still. The bark of his first-ever Christmas tree felt suddenly cold and rough and sticky in his fist. He'd thought Shane hadn't heard about that. He'd thought Shane had left the foster home they'd practically been brothers in and had never looked back. It couldn't be possible that he'd thought wrong. Not about something as important as that. Could it?

"—you can never know what would have happened," Shane persisted calmly. "You like thinking you can, because then it feels like you can control it. It feels like you're less helpless. But the truth is, we were both two lost, unwanted little kids. We couldn't have saved ourselves. Not even with the best freaking interview line in the world. We couldn't do it."

Casey refused to believe that. After all, Shane had done exactly that. He seemed all right. Stonily, Casey stared at his apartment building. The sun was beginning to set. In his neighbors' windows, he expected to see Christmas decorations.

To his surprise, he didn't. It threw him.

Had he lost his ability to see them again? Like the municipal decorations he'd been hating all week—but had honestly never noticed before—had his neighbors' holiday stuff vanished?

Had his ability to see Christmas deserted him too?

"*I* could have done it," Casey insisted. "I was good at talking to people, even then. I was good at making sure everyone got along." It had been either that, he knew, or slug his way through even more fights and black eyes. "I was so good at it that I made it my goddamn career! So don't tell me I couldn't."

"You couldn't," Shane said quietly. "It wasn't your fault."

But Casey had heard enough. "That's it. We're done here."

"Ah." Shane nodded. "Cutting your losses?"

"The way out is over there." Casey pointed. "I suggest you take it. I could help you find the way, but that might hurt."

Incredibly, Shane laughed. "Same old Casey. I'd heard the stories about you, but I thought they were exaggerated. You're still an all-or-nothing guy. If you can't win, you want out."

"You don't know what you're talking about."

"Then let's stay here until I do," Shane volunteered with an open gesture. "Go ahead. Make me understand."

"You're not worth it. Besides, that's—" *Not what I do*, Casey was about to say, but then he stopped himself.

"That's not what you do?" Shane guessed. "Yeah, I heard that about you, too. If you can't 'fix' it, you abandon it. That's the only way anyone ever gets an all-star, all-home-run record like yours, you know. By not keeping track of the strikeouts. How's that working out for you, anyway?"

Casey glowered at him. "I already told you to leave."

"And I told you I'm staying. Nobody ever solved anything by *not* talking. Silence has screwed us up for twenty years." Seeming relieved to have everything off his chest, Shane offered Casey an overconfident grin. "Besides, I'm not scared of you."

"You should be."

Shane scoffed. "You're holding a threadbare twig of a Christmas tree. Right now, you're less than intimidating."

"I just want you to leave!"

"And I want you to say we're square," Shane said patiently. "I'm willing to stay here until you do."

Casey wished, just then, that Kristen had shown the same kind of stubbornness that Shane was. He wished that she'd insisted on sticking with him—on making him face the truth.

The truth that he loved her. Wanted her. Needed her.

But it wasn't Kristen's job to do that, Casey realized as he met Shane's obstinate frown with a scowl of his own. It wasn't up to Kristen to make him feel safe or whole or wanted.

It was *his* job to do that, whether he wanted to or not.

Casey inhaled a deep breath. "If you hadn't stolen my line," he began, but Shane cut him off with a gesture. Annoyed, Casey regrouped. "If I hadn't choked during that interview—"

But again, his friend stopped him. He shook his head.

"You can't know what would have happened," Shane said. "Believe me, I've given it a lot of thought. *Maybe* you could have done better. *Maybe* things would have worked out the way you wanted for Christmas that year." Shane gave him a rueful look. "Face it. You were a lonely little kid with no leverage. You've fixed that problem—in spades, I'd say—with all your success."

Damn right, he had, Casey thought belligerently. But he knew it wasn't the truth. He was still cracking under pressure. He was still unable to say the words that would save him.

Even more, he was unable to say the words that would make the woman he loved happy. Because during that last fateful afternoon, all Kristen had really wanted—all she'd asked for—was for Casey to love her. For him to say it out loud.

"Now all you can do," Shane went on, "is forgive that poor helpless kid you used to be for screwing up, and just go on."

"Right." Cynically, Casey looked at him. "I guess that's what *you're* doing? Just 'going on' after past mistakes?"

"I'm trying to," Shane disarmed him by saying, seriously and directly. "But you're making it pretty fucking hard to do."

For the first time, Casey actually felt sorry for him.

Maybe things hadn't been as easy for Shane as he'd thought.

"But it's been pretty awesome overall, right?" Casey asked Shane reluctantly, making an offhanded gesture with his non-tree-holding hand. "I mean, that family who adopted you—they were really loaded. And they really wanted you. So—"

"So you never know. Life's funny like that." Shane gave him a cryptic look. "Let's just say I didn't get as lucky as you thought I did, and leave it at that."

"You've *got* to tell me more than that!" Casey burst out. "You've seen me smuggling in this tragic Christmas tree!" In demonstration, he thunked it on the courtyard. A shower of brown-tinged pine needles fell off. "After this traumatic experience, we're practically brothers again."

Shane laughed. Then, "Does that mean you forgive me?"

Casey thought about it. "It means I'll let you buy me a beer sometime while I harass you about your favorite sports team."

It wasn't much, but it was a start. They both knew it.

"Fair enough." Shane nodded. "Thanks, asshole, for making this twice as hard as it had to be. Man, you had me sweating."

Nodding back at him, Casey couldn't help wondering . . .

If it had been this difficult for a tough, experienced, hard-knock guy like Shane to face down Casey for their conversation—to make him *have* that conversation—how much harder must it have been for Kristen to stand by him that afternoon? How much harder must it have been for someone as softhearted as she was to see all his stony defenses and still hang in there?

Neither of them had managed it for long, Casey admitted to himself. But *he* hadn't had to face down his own silence.

At least he could have reassured Kristen about some of those things they'd talked about, Casey realized. He could have told her—a *lot* more articulately—that he hadn't been seeing her just to get close to Heather. That he hadn't expected her to be like Heather. That he loved Kristen just the way she was and couldn't imagine why anyone would ever compare Kristen to her sister when she was so unmistakably wonderful in her own right.

Maybe, if he left right this minute and drove to LAX, he could be on a plane back to Michigan within a few hours . . .

"You seem different," Shane broke into his musings to say. He angled his head. "Maybe it's the teensy Christmas tree."

But Casey knew it was Kristen. She'd changed him. She'd made him see that the only one preventing Casey from getting what he wanted for Christmas—at least this year—was him.

"Yeah, you do, too," Casey said. "Taller."

"Better," Shane corrected him. "But Heather gets all the credit for that. We spent some pretty intense time together while planning her live-stream Internet concert, and she really made me reconsider a few things." Proudly, Shane nodded. "Reforming me was number seven on Heather's to-do list."

Now Casey *knew* he was losing it. "Heather has a to-do list?"

"Yep. And I'd better hurry up and get out of here, too," Shane added, "because if Heather accomplished what she said she would, then Kristen ought to be here any minute now."

At that, the whole world stopped. "*Kristen? Kristen's coming here?* To L.A.? But why? How? When? For how long?"

Shane smiled. "Yes, Kristen. To L.A. To see you," he said, ticking off items on his big, dumb fingers. "On an aero plane, I'd guess. Any second now. And as for how long . . ." Breaking off, Shane gave him a wiseass look. "I'd say *that's* up to you."

Filled with equal amounts of instant panic and white-hot joy, Casey gawked at him. Then he realized . . . "You're screwing with me. Right? Because there's no way in hell *Heather* could have reformed *you,* much less convinced Kristen to come here. She might be smarter than she seems, but that's miracle territory."

"Getting Kristen to come here for Christmas was item number one on Heather's to-do list," Shane informed him. "I'm serious. You have no idea what Heather Miller is really capable of, once she's properly motivated. She's a freaking dynamo."

Casey considered all the ways that Kristen had turned him inside out, upside down, and head over heels for her. "I can believe it," he said, "if she's anything like her sister."

Shane looked wary. "*Don't* suggest that to Kristen!" he said. "I mentioned to her once that she might be able to follow in Heather's footsteps, and Kristen practically shot flames from her eyeballs. *Never* compare two sisters to each other. Never—"

Shane went on, but Casey didn't hear him. He was too busy realizing that he had a *lot* to do, if he was going to be ready for Kristen's arrival in L.A. He had to plan something romantic. He had to reassess his communication style and practice a few *I love you*s. He had to plan a persuasive speech that would bring Kristen back to him, devise a heartfelt apology for hurting her, vacuum his apartment and buy her some flowers and get some wine . . .

Totally overwhelmed, Casey clutched his Christmas tree. That jolted him even further. He had to get more holiday stuff! Because Kristen *loved* holiday stuff. She'd already be weirded out by experiencing sunshine and green grass in December, Casey figured. If he could somehow get a hold of some fake snow . . .

No. Wait. Kristen hated fake snow. What was he going to do?

Whatever it was, he'd better hurry.

"Yeah. Thanks, Shane." Distractedly, Casey gave him a semifriendly, one-handed slug to the shoulder, cutting him off in midspeech. "I'll talk to you later. I have a lot to do."

Beginning with the Christmas stuff, Casey decided. Because he could plan all the rest—all the words and the gestures and the romance—while he was stocking up on multicolored lights and ornaments and eggnog. This would be the biggest troubleshooting campaign of his entire life. He had to get it right. *He had to.*

Gearing up to get started, Casey looked decisively at his dejected-looking cast-off Christmas tree. He didn't know what had possessed him to buy it. Except he'd felt that doing so was the kind of thing Kristen would have done. He'd felt it was the kind of gesture that would have made her proud of him.

But now, actually studying that wretched tree through semiobjective eyes, Casey wasn't so sure. "Starting with . . . this."

"You need a bigger tree," Shane said with certainty. "Women are all about size and grandeur and making a big impression. But with *that* thing, you won't even make a dent."

Hell. Shane was probably right, Casey realized.

He stared at his friend through panicked eyes.

But then, from somewhere beyond him in the courtyard, Casey heard a familiar voice. "I wouldn't say that," Kristen said. Her footsteps came nearer. "That tree just needs a few decorations."

Casey turned, and she was there, looking bedraggled and nervous and beautiful, wearing jeans and boots and a god-awful spangled, eyeball-searing Christmas sweater and holding a carry-on bag and looking exactly like everything he'd ever wanted.

Just like that, a sense of calm certainty came over him.

Because all he really needed was Kristen, Casey realized in that moment—and she'd come there to be with him. She'd come there . . . for him. No one had ever done that before.

"I like your tree," she said, striding nearer.

Through expert eyes, Kristen looked at its scraggly branches. Then she raised her gaze to Casey's face. Even as he—dimly—registered Shane Maresca offering a salute to them both and then scampering away, Casey felt his heart fill almost to overflowing. He couldn't believe Kristen was really there.

"I can't believe you're really here," he said.

"I can't believe you're voluntarily holding a Christmas tree," she countered, smiling at him. "You look good."

"You look *great*." Shaking, Casey stepped nearer. He thumped his tree along the courtyard beside him. What else could he do?

"I look ridiculous." Kristen frowned down at her holiday-themed sweater. "I was looking for a little liquid courage on the plane, so I asked for a few drinks, but then I spilled them, and then I smelled like a holiday office party gone horribly wrong, and I couldn't come here like *that,* so I ducked into a gift shop to find something else, and . . . Well, this was the best I could do."

She spread her arms, showing him the appliqued ornaments, puffy paint, glitter, and actual jingle bells on her sweater.

"I was planning to turn it inside out, but all the stuff on the outside was too scratchy," Kristen said. "So here I am, the archetypal *non*-glamorous, *non*-fabulous, everyday regular gal."

"Here you are." Feeling a goofy smile edge onto his face, Casey stepped even nearer. He thumped his Charlie-Brown tree those additional few feet. "Right where you belong. With me."

"I didn't know if you'd want to see me," Kristen confessed, "given all the mean things I said to you." She hauled in a deep breath. "I'm sorry, Casey. I'm *so* sorry. I didn't know—"

"No, *I'm* sorry," Casey told her, feeling his heart hammering with need and urgency and what felt like unrestrained *love*. In the single bravest act of his life, he stepped all the way to where Kristen stood. He looked at her. He nodded. "I'm sorry I hurt you, and I'm sorry I left you, and I'm sorry I didn't stand my ground and tell you how I really felt. Because—"

"You don't have to," Kristen interrupted, shaking her head as tears sprang to her eyes. "You don't have to say or do any of that, Casey. You don't, because I—"

Because I don't feel the same way about you, Casey imagined her saying for one terrifying instant. *And I wanted to come here and tell you so in person.* But then he just forged onward.

"I do," he insisted. "I do need to tell you. Because I love you, Kristen. I really do." His voice felt rough, the words unfamiliar but unabashedly right. "I love your smile and your walk and your talent with a mason jar. I love your generosity and your spirit. I love your laugh and your courage, and the way you can't help singing along to all the Christmas carols—"

"You noticed that?" She blushed prettily. "Whoops."

"I even love your mania for Christmas!" Casey went on, feeling—as he continued talking and she didn't stop him— that maybe this was going to work out after all. "Because of *you,* I faced down my inner Scrooge—"

"It looks like you won." Kristen nodded at his tree.

"—and because of you, I kicked his sorry ass to the curb," Casey continued joyfully, "and because of you, I might actually have a chance at the kind of Christmas I've always wanted—"

"Oh, it's *happening,*" Kristen assured him. She came almost close enough to step on his toes. Sweetly and softly, she kissed him. "Because I love you, too, Casey. I love you, and I want you, and I don't know how I ever got along without you, because when you're not there, the tinsel loses its sparkle and all the lights look dim, and I can't *wait* to give you a real Christmas. Because I can promise you, it's going to blow your mind."

"Will it include you?"

She nodded, gazing happily at him.

"Then that's all I need," Casey said, knowing it was true. "Because I love you with every single breath I take, Kristen. I really do. I know it sounds cheesy, and I wish I'd had time to prepare, because this could have been *so* much more impressive—"

"It's *perfect* already." Kristen kissed him again, leaving him yearning for more. More more more. "I love you the same way, Casey! I love your laugh and your determination and your talent for bringing people together. I love your sexy bod and your intelligence and your strength, and I love the way you disco—"

"You saw that?" Casey blanched. "Uh-oh."

"—and I admire you, too," Kristen went on, her eyes still sparkling at him. She sniffled. "Because some people would break after all you've been through. But you've managed to take what happened to you—to take what life handed you—and use it to become a man who makes a difference. You're a man who *helps* everyone, Casey, whether you want to admit it or not—"

"Well, I've heard I hypnotize people," he joked.

"—and that *matters*. It matters more than you know, to more people than you know." Kristen drew in another deep breath, then nodded. "It matters to me."

"*You* matter to me," Casey swore. "I'm sorry I didn't say so before. I wanted to. I did! But I—"

"No more apologies." With another kiss, Kristen cut him off. "You're home now, Casey. Home with me. As long as we're together, you'll never have to wonder if you're getting what you want for Christmas," Kristen told him. "Because I'm going to dedicate myself to making sure you get it, every single year."

"I always did want a big family," Casey said, only half joking, even as he grinned at her. "Do you think everyone at the diner would let me hang around a while? Because I think I could wrangle another assignment in Kismet, and I know I didn't know them for long, but somehow I feel as though Gareth and Avery and Walden and Talia are just like family to me. Just like you are."

"They're all waiting in Kismet for you," Kristen assured him with a smile, "just in case you want a turn with the Galaxy Diner Santa hat. You never did try it. Which reminds me . . ." Briefly turning away, she rummaged through her carry-on bag. She emerged with something small and plastic. She handed it to him. "I think you forgot this. But I know that it's yours."

When Casey looked at his hand, his RESERVED sign was there.

Inexplicably, the sight of it made him feel like bawling.

"You'll be in my heart forever," Kristen told him solemnly. "But just in case you forget that . . . Well, just look at that sign and remember. We want you, Casey. It'll take more than a supersunny Christmas and a cross-country flight to scare me away."

Uncertainly, Casey brandished his substandard-but-lovable Christmas tree. "How about this thing? Does this scare you?"

Kristen peered at it. "Not a chance. Like I said, all it needs are a few decorations. Speaking of which . . ."

She delved in her bag again. A heartbeat later, she pulled out a tangled string of holiday lights. She grinned at him.

"I brought these for that palm tree you mentioned," Kristen said. "I'm pretty sure you promised to decorate it for me?"

"Anything you want. I'll make it happen," Casey vowed.

"Anything? Hmm. *That's* interesting." With authority, Kristen took away his Christmas tree. It was so skimpy that she could easily carry it to the nearest raised flower bed in the courtyard. She leaned the tree securely against the stone edging. "Will you give me . . . garland?"

Passionately, Casey nodded. As far as he was concerned, Kristen could just go on challenging him—go on going toe-to-toe with him and keeping him real—for as long as she cared to.

"Whatever you want," he said. "You've got it."

"Okay. Will you give me . . . gingerbread and Christmas carols?"

"Every day and every night," Casey promised. "Until you're sick of ginger and can't face another chorus of fa-la-las."

"Sweet!" Looking cheered, Kristen came back to him. With utter conviction and total sexiness, she wrapped her arms around his neck. "Will you give me . . . *you?* Because that's all *I* want for Christmas."

"Done and done." Freed now of his pine-needle-dropping burden, Casey swept her up in his arms. She whooped as he hoisted her a bit higher, then headed toward his apartment.

"Where are you going?" Kristen asked, twisting around to look at his spindly fir tree. "Your tree's back there. We're going to need that to celebrate Christmas properly."

"Oh, I promise you we'll celebrate Christmas properly," Casey said with a meaningful look. He walked a little faster. "When it comes to Christmas, you might be the expert. But when it comes to 'celebrating'"—here, he stopped to kiss her again—"I know all there is to know about doing it up right. And as soon as we get inside, I'm going to show you."

As he began striding onward again, Kristen gave him an impish look. "Will this celebration involve Christmas things?"

"Yes," Casey said with certainty. "It will involve me, and you, and love—and *that* is the most Christmassy thing of all."

Then he put Kristen down, opened his door, and took her inside, knowing that even if he needed from now until next Christmas to do it, he intended to prove that to her.

Because while it might be true that for most people, Christmas was commercialized and codified, overloaded and overdone, shrunk and stretched and started in September, for him and Kristen, Christmas was something *real*. It was something right and necessary and amazing.

Because somehow, unexpectedly, he and Kristen had found Christmas in Kismet and L.A and everyplace in between,

Casey realized as he smiled and kissed her again. Thanks to the woman in his arms, he knew that all you really needed to feel the magic of Christmas was someone else to feel it with you.

For him, that was Kristen—today, tomorrow, and forever.

"Ohmigod!" she cried, looking in amazement inside his apartment. "You must have a hundred paper snowflakes in here!"

Oh yeah. He'd forgotten about that, Casey realized. He'd been trying to feel closer to Kristen. He'd been folding and scissoring and folding and scissoring, trying to get it right. He'd hung all the lopsided, crumpled snowflakes he'd created all through his apartment, feeling a little better whenever he'd looked at them, knowing no one else would ever see them.

Now though, his secret was out.

"Aw." Kristen looked at him with her face alight. Casey had never glimpsed so much tenderness and love in anyone's eyes before. Only Kristen's. With a saucy smile, she jumped in his arms again. "You are *so* getting lucky right now."

"Too late," Casey informed her. "I got lucky the minute you turned up today. The minute you smiled at me."

Then he swung shut his apartment door, lost himself in another kiss . . . and got down to letting Kristen know exactly how much he cared about her—using words and deeds and whatever else it took to assure her that she was his and he was hers, for this Christmas to come and every single Christmas after that.

Chapter 26

"All right," Kristen announced as she emerged from her diner's kitchen on Christmas Eve. Carrying an enormous, multiserving version of her latest top-secret, personalized creation, she caught Casey's eye as she crossed the room. "Now you're *really* getting inducted into the Galaxy Diner family."

Seated in his usual reserved corner booth, surrounded by Walden, Avery, Talia, and Gareth, Casey smiled. It turned out that the Santa hat they all shared looked *really* good on him.

He rubbed his palms together. "Awesome. I can't wait."

Proudly, Kristen set down her dish. In size and composition, it most closely resembled a traditional British trifle, which would have ordinarily been composed of layers of cake cubes and fruit and pastry cream and whipped cream. But this, despite its proportions and appearance, was different.

"Wow!" Casey eyed it with trepidation. "That's, um . . . really *big*. I was expecting a pie-in-a-jar." He cupped his hands, approximating the typical dimensions of her most famous dessert. "I hope I'm not supposed to eat all of that all by myself."

"Why not?" Kristen smiled. "There's always ketchup."

At her teasing, Casey gave her an affectionate smile.

They'd spent a few days together in California, exploring all the ways they could "celebrate" their togetherness. To Kristen's surprise, it had turned out that T-shirts and shorts made very comfortable attire for tree-trimming parties and light-stringing shindigs. Eggnog still tasted delicious while being sipped beside the ocean. Christmas carols sounded good even when not juxtaposed with howling winter winds. And sunshine didn't dampen her enthusiasm for Christmas a single bit—not when Casey was there beside her to share the holidays with, now and forever.

All the same, they'd decided together to come back to Kismet for Christmas. Because Kristen hadn't forgotten what Casey had said about wanting a big family—even if he *had* meant a big family made up of quirky, unrelated oddballs, all with an excess of enthusiasm for renovated fifties gas stations, sugary sweets, and being together to celebrate the holidays.

"Didn't Kristen tell you?" Gareth looked up from her supersize creation. "All Kristen's pies-in-a-jar come in a Godzilla-size, I-dare-you-to-eat-all-this version first."

"That's right," Avery agreed. "Each of us has a pie-in-a-jar dedicated especially to us. It's a tradition."

"A tradition that only happens for really special people," Talia said, shooting a loving glance at Walden.

"A tradition that, in this case, seriously taxes the resources of the pastry department," Walden added, "since Kristen put everything except the kitchen sink in there."

Leaning against the booth beside Casey, Kristen put her arm around him. "Well, I had to do that," she said warmly. "Casey's got a lot of making up for lost time to do. So I had to fit *everything* Christmassy in there." She gestured at her multilayer extravaganza. "It's got several layers," she told him, "so as you go, you'll taste fruitcake, spritz cookies, gingerbread, peppermint bark, sugar cookies, plum pudding . . . the works. All topped with whipped cream. And sprinkles!"

Casey's eyes lit up, like . . . well, like a kid's at Christmas. A kid who'd finally, at long last, gotten his heart's desire.

Casey looked at his custom, gigantic pie-in-a-jar. "I'm going to share this, of course," he informed them all with a smile. "If this is some kind of hazing, I'm not doing it. I learned the hard way that *sharing* is where it's at."

Everyone nodded. "Go on! Dig in!" Gareth shouted.

Casey looked more closely. He seemed puzzled. "What's the lighted candle in the middle for? It's not my birthday."

"It's for you to make a wish." Contentedly, Kristen nudged Casey sideways with her hip, then snuggled up next to him in his designated booth. They'd had his RESERVED sign professionally laminated and affixed to the diner's wall nearby, so there would never be any confusion about who belonged there. She shrugged. "I can't remember how it started. It's just what we do. So go ahead," she urged Casey. "Make a wish."

"Make a wish!" Avery chanted. "Make a wish!"

Gareth, Talia, and Walden joined in, too, clanging their forks on the table with comical fervor. "Make a wish!"

"You'd better give in," Kristen advised Casey with a jostle from her shoulder to his. "They're not going to quit."

"Okay." With his face lit by the glow of his *welcome to the Galaxy Diner family* candle, Casey closed his eyes. He paused to make his wish. Then he blew out the candle.

Everyone cheered. Kristen squeezed his hand.

Casey opened his eyes. He gazed into her face.

"My wish just came true," he told her.

And she knew as he said it that hers had, too.

Because all she'd ever wanted for Christmas was to feel happy. With Casey, Kristen did. Now and forever and for every single crazy Kismet Christmas that would come next.

Because life was sweet. And so was love . . . especially when it came along at Christmastime!

Dear Reader,

Thank you for reading *Together for Christmas*!

I had so much fun writing about Kristen and Casey and the whole crew at the Galaxy Diner. They really found their way into my heart. I couldn't wait to dream up happy endings for them! If you spotted a few familiar faces in this story, that's because this is my third visit to Kismet, Michigan. It's my favorite place to visit for Christmas!

To learn more about my other Kismet Christmas books, *Home for the Holidays* and *Holiday Affair,* please visit my Website at www.lisaplumley.com. While you're there, you can also read free first-chapter excerpts from all my contemporary, historical, and paranormal romances, sign up for my new-book reminder service, catch sneak previews of my upcoming books, request special reader freebies, and more.

Are you curious about how to make Kristen's apple pie-in-a-jar? Interested in getting recipes for other Christmas goodies and helpful holiday hints? If so, please follow @Heather_Hotline on Twitter, where I'll be posting recipes and tips this holiday season!

Finally, I love hearing from readers, so I'd be thrilled if you would "friend" me on Facebook at www.facebook.com/lisaplumleybooks, follow me @LisaPlumley on Twitter, or e-mail me at lisa@lisaplumley.com.

Until next time . . . happy holidays!

Lisa Plumley

P.S. If you want to read about how Natasha and Damon got together before their surprise visit to Kismet, turn the page for a peek at *Melt Into You,* available in paperback and as an eBook wherever books are sold.

Chapter 1

La Jolla, California
September 2002

Damon Torrance believed in a lot of things.

He believed in perfect surf, unassailable integrity, and the ultimate Baja fish taco. He believed in making connections, making things happen, and making a never-fail margarita (it was all about the blue agave tequila). He believed that nudity was better than wearing . . . anything at all, no matter how pricey the clothes were or where you happened to be going.

He believed that rules were made to be broken and that whoever had said virtue was its own reward probably hadn't tried hard enough to be bad first. He believed that person shouldn't have made that decision so damn hastily. Or so publicly. Because that idiot had ruined it for everyone else who just wanted to have a good time.

When it came right down to it, more than anything else, Damon believed that life was too short to waste time with anything less than one hundred percent pleasure. Plain and simple.

That's why, when he found himself spending a week

with an attractive, capable, flirtatious, and ultra-available journalist (she made it bluntly, sexily, one-step-short-of-manhandling-him obvious that she was single) who was writing a profile of him and his family's company, Torrance Chocolates, for *Oceanside Living* magazine's "Getting to Know . . ." feature, Damon took the only reasonable action.

He let her seduce him. On his desk. In full view of the glittering Pacific Ocean outside. Right between his stapler and his office phone, with his brand-new, full-size desk calendar for a cushion. Not that Kimberly (the journalist) bothered to scout a prime location before she smiled, dropped her notepad, and lunged at him.

It would have been rude to say no, Damon reasoned. So he met her kiss with a sliding, seductive, nice-to-meet-you lip-lock of his own . . . and before he knew it, they were "Getting to Know . . ." each other pretty damn well. Kimberly's warmth was a sharp contrast to the brisk ocean breeze coming in off the Pacific. Her perfume added synthetic flowers and spice to the sugary smells of the confectionary shop downstairs. Her breath panted over him. Her I'm-a-professional suit jacket hit the floor. So did his I'm-supposed-to-be-working shirt. They kissed a little more. Then they kissed again, more passionately.

A discordant electronic jangle startled them both.

Kimberly quit kissing him. She frowned. "What was that?"

"Who cares?" Right on cue, it happened again. At the sound, Damon glanced sideways. "Oh. It's my father's BlackBerry."

At her mystified expression, Damon nodded at the device.

"It's used to get e-mails and appointments on the go. I gave it to my dad as a birthday present, but he didn't take to the technology the way I hoped he would. That's why it's in here and not with him." Damon smiled at her. Confidingly, he added, "I think he's afraid he's going to drop 'that expensive gadget' into a vat of bittersweet chocolate ganache or something."

It was semilikely. Jimmy Torrance spent most of his time

and all his creativity on the family business. That's how he'd turned a tiny seaside sweetshop into one of San Diego's favorite "hidden treasures" for thirty years running. That's how he'd earned himself the very office that he shared with Damon today.

"Aw. You gave your dad a birthday present?" Kimberly cooed, running her fingers over his bare chest. "That's *so* sweet!"

"It's not that unusual, actually. He *is* my dad, after all. I give my mom something on her birthday every year, too."

Kimberly shook her head, seeming inordinately impressed with his filial devotion. "I knew you were more than just a studly corporate hotshot." More stroking. "You're a nice guy, too! I have to say, when I heard I'd be profiling the company's head of Internet development, I was expecting to meet someone a lot more . . ." Here, she broke off. She gave him a thorough once-over. She shrugged. "Well . . . geekier."

Damon grinned. "You can't judge a book by its cover. Any second now, I might start talking about byte serving, hypertext transfer protocol, and compression scheme negotiation."

"I have a better idea." Kimberly slid her hands lower. She cupped his ass, then hauled him nearer. "Don't talk at all."

"Yes, ma'am." Agreeably, Damon concentrated on using his mouth for more diverting activities than talking. But even as he did, his dad's BlackBerry chimed again. Damon began remembering something—something he ought to have remembered earlier.

At the same time, a familiar voice floated down the corridor outside his office. "Damon? Well, I guess you'd say he's a genius," his father was telling someone proudly. "His official promotion was a long time coming. He resisted it, but—"

Whatever else Jimmy said was lost to Damon. He was too busy simultaneously enjoying the naughty way Kimberly was nibbling on his ear and trying to remember what his father had said earlier.

All that came to mind was his father saying, as he'd done

a million times a day since Damon had been old enough to outwit his first babysitter and go looking for adventure, "You've got to *focus,* Damon. Focus! Try to behave for once. All right?"

But all those requests were bona fide lost causes, and they both knew it. Who did his father think he'd been raising all this time? One of the Backstreet Boys? A new Disney teeny-bopper idol?

Hell, no. There was no fun to be had in being *good.* Damon knew that. There was no glory to be found in staying focused, either. All that mattered was looking ahead . . . and maybe finding out if Kimberly's freckles meandered all the way to her cleavage. Curiously, Damon started unbuttoning her shirt.

The voices outside grew louder. His father—and his un-known guest—were coming closer. Probably to this office. Damon swore.

With a mighty effort, he wrenched himself away from Kimberly. He peeked down at his desk calendar. It was rum-pled. It had slid pretty far sideways. But Damon could still make out something handwritten on the square representing today's date.

There, right next to Kimberly's delectable bare thigh, were the words *administrative assistant* and the time, *9:30.*

Having deciphered his father's unmistakable scrawl, Damon blinked in surprise. "You can *write* on these things?"

Kimberly laughed. "That's what they're for, silly."

"Oh. I thought it was decorative. But in my own defense, I don't spend much time in the office." Momentarily dis-tracted again, Damon lowered his gaze to the cleavage he'd revealed, framed now by Kimberly's silky unbuttoned shirt. He looked at the high, high slit on her *Ally McBeal*-style miniskirt (damn, he loved that trend), then stroked his fin-gers over her knee. "It made a really fine landing pad, though. You were clever enough to discover that for us."

"It was my pleasure. *Believe me.*" Kimberly gave him another sultry look. She seemed to specialize in them. "Now . . . where were we?"

"Right about . . . here." Damon squeezed her thigh. Another kiss kept him pinned atop her, even as he heard footsteps coming nearer. Just then, he didn't care. Life was all about enjoyment.

". . . and this is where you'll be spending most of your time," Jimmy Torrance said as he opened the office door. "I'm afraid you might be stuck inside a lot, but the view is awfully nice."

"Oh, yes, it *is* nice," his father's female guest said in an appreciative tone. Her footsteps preceded his into the office. "I love the ocean!" There was a pause. Then, in a wry voice, she added, "Will the guy who's humping like a bunny on the desk be here every day? Or is that a one-time-only thing?"

No one ever answered her question. Natasha Jennings would have been lying if she'd said she wasn't disappointed by that.

In the few minutes it took for Jimmy Torrance to hastily cross the room, shut off his dinging BlackBerry on the other unoccupied desk, and confer with the desktop Casanova and his nearly naked female partner, though, she did learn several interesting facts about her new workplace.

First of all, she learned that either today was Nooky Monday or Torrance Chocolates was a *lot* more freewheeling than she'd anticipated. Second, she learned that it was both busier and much more charming—given its location inside a two-story former surf shop in La Jolla—than she'd foreseen based on her initial interview. Third, she learned that although her official job title was *administrative assistant*, they might as well have had *miracle worker* printed on her business cards.

Because so far, all she'd done was tour the shop, the chocolate-making kitchen downstairs, and the several makeshift offices upstairs, and already Natasha could see that Torrance Chocolates needed help. They had plenty of drive, heart, and inspiration, that was true; but their transition from mom-and-pop shop to burgeoning corporate power player was clearly overwhelming them. At the moment, they were short of staff, space, and direction. To manage those things, they needed *her*.

Jimmy Torrance and the rest of his staff might not know it yet, but the smartest thing they'd ever done was choose Natasha from among the dozens of (curiously bodacious-looking) applicants she'd seen during the open interviews last month.

In fact, it occurred to her, most of those applicants had looked a lot like the woman who'd been doing the horizontal desktop tango a minute ago. They'd been made up, perfumed, and dressed to attract. They'd worn superhigh stilettos and trendily flat-ironed hair. Most inexplicably, they'd been unable to say the name of their potential future boss, Damon Torrance, without giggling and trading giddy, girlish glances with each other.

All in all, the experience had been a lot like interviewing for a job as head groupie for a rock band. Which, in retrospect, made Natasha wonder why Jimmy Torrance *had* chosen her. Because while she did have her share of vanity—and her very own flat iron, lip gloss, and high heels—what she didn't have was the kind of va-va-voom necessary to hold the attention of a rock star . . . or the corporate equivalent of one.

Not that she cared about that too much, Natasha reminded herself. She didn't need nonstop reinforcement of her own attractiveness. Especially not now and especially not at work.

As the daughter of parents who'd both held down more than one job on several occasions—just to make ends meet—Natasha understood the value of hard work. She'd made it through high school and graduated from community college and then UCSD, all while working full-time to pay her tuition.

This was her chance to kick off her career, and Natasha wanted to succeed. Admittedly, she was starting at the bottom, but still . . . she was only twenty-four. She was here. She was *in* at a growing company. Unlike her competition, she hadn't had to outfit herself in sexed-up "office attire" like a hot-to-trot fugitive Victoria's Secret model to make it happen, either.

Speaking of hot-to-trot . . .

Natasha gave the office-hopping Lothario a second look. He was probably only a couple of years older than she was, but he'd made her first day at Torrance Chocolates memorable, that's for sure. She wondered if he made the rounds of *all* the offices and *all* the different desks, or if he'd come in here solely for the spectacular view—which, in hindsight, had only been improved by the addition of *him*, looking all shirtless and muscular and dark-haired and intense, doing his thing in the middle of it.

Either way, she doubted this particular incident was his first time getting lucky at work. Whoever he was, he had that aura about him—a quality that made people want to be close to him. Looking at him more carefully now only confirmed Natasha's initial impression: this was a man for whom things came easily, whether those things were women, good times, or success.

Speaking of success . . .

Where was her *über*-impressive new wunderkind boss? She wasn't going to be working as a direct report to Jimmy Torrance, Natasha remembered as she watched Mr. Desktop considerately shield his paramour from view so she could get dressed. She was going to work for Jimmy's son, the famously titillating Damon Torrance, who'd been curiously absent from the hiring process.

He's pretty easygoing about these things, Jimmy had explained with a nonchalant wave. *He'll be happy with my choice.*

Natasha hoped Jimmy was right. As she watched the now-dressed woman scoop up a notepad, a pen, and several glossy issues of *Oceanside Living* from the credenza, she further hoped that whoever worked in this office wasn't too attached to their desktop calendar. Because although Mr. Desktop hastily gave it a sideways shove to straighten it, the calendar looked wrecked. The only way to extract any useful information from it would be to read and interpret the butt prints. Everybody knew that, in the Internet age, butt-based cryptanalysis was a dying art.

Finally, the door shut behind the woman. Silence descended on the office, emphasized by the low crash of the surf outside.

Jimmy cleared his throat. The mystery man didn't speak, leaving Natasha plenty of time to notice that in addition to behaving in an undeniably chivalrous manner toward the woman, he'd also tried to compose himself by dragging on his shirt. But that effort was largely ineffective. He'd buttoned his shirt crookedly, he still seemed . . . *distracted* somehow (probably by thoughts of all the workplace exhibitionist sex he was missing out on), and his dark wavy hair, while doing a very good job of framing his handsome, sharp-nosed, stubble-jawed face, looked all bedheady and messy, too. It was way too easy to imagine him actually lolling around sexily in bed, Natasha thought, which definitely spoiled the whole "I'm hard at work" effect.

Evidently he hadn't gotten the memo that, these days, all the cool guys gunked up their hair with gel. Even her husband, Paul, who'd been a hard-core flannel-and-grunge guy when they'd met, now looked like a runaway member of 'N Sync. It could have been worse, though. He could have developed a thing for those velour tracksuits or the loud shirts worn by TV poker players.

Natasha was sick to death of poker. If she never saw another green baize table with sunglasses-wearing card players around it—on TV, in a movie, or at a party—it would be too soon. In fact, she didn't even know why poker was so popular. *American Idol* she understood. Kelly Clarkson really was talented; she'd deserved her win. As current pop culture phenomena went, even the merging of J.Lo and Ben Affleck into "Bennifer" was easier to tolerate. As a matter of fact, Natasha was kind of rooting for them both. At heart, she was a die-hard romantic. She *wanted* true love to conquer all. So when it came right down to it . . .

Suddenly, she realized that Mr. Desktop was watching her. There was no question: He'd caught her daydreaming on the job. It was a good thing *he* wasn't her boss, Natasha told herself with a stalwart lift of her chin, because she didn't think she wanted a supervisor who could read her so easily. She definitely didn't want one who looked quite so . . . *fascinating* while he did it.

No wonder he'd successfully seduced a woman on a desktop. In broad daylight. With strangers wandering the halls outside. Mr. Desktop had some kind of remarkable give-it-to-me mojo—some kind of you-know-you-want-to appeal that would have softened even the hardest of hearts. Or opened even the most tightly crossed legs. Not that *she* wanted to open *her* legs, but still . . .

Vividly, Natasha imagined *herself* on that desk, crumpling the calendar with her own nearly naked booty, having her shirt unbuttoned and her neck kissed, with her breasts heaving and her thighs parting as she pulled Mr. Desktop closer and closer. . . .

Too late, she understood. "*You're* Damon Torrance."

Chapter 2

Damon's eyes gleamed, brown and full of mischief. "Guilty. And *you're* my new assistant." He held out his hand. "I'm sorry about . . . before. It was all my fault. Sometimes I get carried away." His smile looked unrepentant, full of blatant resolve to besmirch that very same desk ten minutes from now if he had the chance. Probably he would. Contritely, he put his free hand over his heart. "I promise I'll try to reform while you're here."

He made it sound so temporary. "While I'm here?"

He seemed abashed. "Your predecessors haven't lasted long."

"Oh." Wondering why that was, Natasha accepted his handshake. As she did, an unmistakable jolt crackled through her. It felt real. Electric. Her knees weakened. She wanted to stare. She *did* stare. Damon Torrance was different when his focus was centered on you, she realized. His eyes, his face, his shoulders, his mouth . . . even his nice white teeth all seemed ridiculously interesting. "Why is that?" she asked, striving not to steer his hand to her breast. Oh God. Had she really just thought that? What was the *matter* with her? She slapped on a casually inquisitive look. "Is the work difficult?"

"Not really." Damon shrugged. "I don't think so."

She couldn't quit gawking. Reluctantly, Natasha slipped

her hand from his grasp. Sex appeal rolled from him in dizzy waves. It broke along the shore of her determination not to be wooed, then crested again. It was a good thing she'd armored herself with a prim suit, worn her hair in a strict ponytail, and gotten used to tamping down her more . . . *inventive* side while at work.

Well, technically she'd gotten used to tamping down her inventive side everyplace these days, in every circumstance—mostly to make way for Paul's inventive side to flourish, since he needed it to make a living and she didn't—but still . . . she'd been smart to play it cool for her first day at work.

"The truth is, my assistants all leave because I sleep with them," Damon explained, appearing unbothered by admitting it. "Sometimes they fall in love with me. Sometimes I fall in love with them. It never lasts. I'm kind of fickle." Another grin. This one seemed thoughtful . . . and maybe 10 percent devilish, besides. "But that won't be a problem with you, Natasha." He turned. "Right, Dad?"

Jimmy Torrance frowned. "I hope not, son." Astutely, he glanced at Natasha. "He's right. He *is* fickle. This thing with the journalist was just the latest in a long line of—"

"Come on. I already explained that. All my fault." Damon held up his palm, good-naturedly diverting the conversation. "Anyway, I won't be having those problems with Natasha."

"You won't be?" Perversely, she felt stung. She also felt idiotically enamored of the way he said her name. *Natasha. Nataaasha.* She could have listened to him say it all day. All night. Over and over and—just in time, she got a grip on herself. She shook her head. "No," Natasha announced in her most forceful, definitive tone. "You won't be." A beat. "You won't be having any problems wanting to sleep with me because . . . ?"

"Because you're married." Damon raised his eyebrows, appearing surprised to have to explain himself. "A man's got to have his principles. Mine involve Pop-Tarts, kung fu, and not screwing around with married women."

At her undoubtedly openmouthed expression, he laughed.

"Especially *happily* married women," Damon added, "which *you* qualify as, if that enormous hickey on your neck is anything to go by." He leaned nearer. With a conspiratorial whisper—and a cheerful wink—he added, "Make-up never works to hide them. Especially on blondes, like you." He nodded at her shoulder-length blond hair, then gave the rest of her a swift, masculine, thrillingly appreciative perusal. Natasha had the unmistakable impression he'd seen *all* of her . . . and approved wholeheartedly, too. Damon's gaze whipped back to her hickey. "Just hold your head high and forget about it. That's all you can do."

That sounded like the voice of experience talking. Aghast, Natasha flung her palm over her neck. She'd forgotten about her hickey—and for one brief nanosecond, she'd forgotten about being married, too. But now that Damon had pointed it out, her marriage came rushing back to her. So did her ability to use her brainpower for more than swooning over her new boss.

Of course she didn't want Damon to want to sleep with her. *She* had principles, too! While they didn't involve junk food or martial arts, they did involve avoiding infidelity.

No matter what.

"Wait a minute. I didn't tell you Natasha was married." With endearing old-school politeness, Jimmy swerved his gaze away from her telltale hickey. "I didn't even give you her personnel file—not that you would have read it if I had."

"You didn't have to tell me. I guessed." Damon gave her a speculative look. "You're a newlywed, right? Just back from your honeymoon? I'd say you went to . . . someplace sunny. Acapulco? No, wait." He snapped his fingers. "Cancun, right along the coast."

This time, Natasha *knew* she was staring openmouthed. "I haven't even unpacked yet. How did you . . . ?"

"Your wedding ring. And your glow. You're glowing."

At that, she beamed. She probably *was* glowing. Because of *Paul,* Natasha reminded herself. Because of her *husband.*

"My husband is an artist. A painter," she felt compelled to say. "He's very talented. He was especially inspired by Mexico."

"Mmm." Obviously, Damon was too busy practicing his Twenty Questions-style guessing game to give too much thought to trivialities like husbands. Or their unique artistic inspirations. "The pattern of your sunburn was a dead give-away." Damon nodded at the neckline of her suit. "If you weren't so buttoned up, it would be even more obvious."

It was a good thing she was "buttoned up." Otherwise, Damon's apparent X-ray vision would have left her feeling even more exposed than she already did. As though the imprint of her teeny honeymoon bikini was imprinted on her skin—and technically it was, only in reverse—Natasha crossed her arms over her chest.

"Besides, you didn't have to give me Natasha's personnel file, Dad," Damon went on blithely . . . the same way he appeared to do everything. "Brittney in HR was *dying* to do me a favor."

Jimmy sniffed. "I'll just bet she was." He shook his finger at his son. "This is why I hired a new assistant for you!"

"Right. And your insistence on doing that is why I went along with it." Damon tossed his father a plaintive look—one the elder Torrance seemed to miss. "I want to make you proud, Dad."

"That's easy. *Don't* sleep with this one! Hear me?"

"I hear you." All the same, Damon appeared wounded. "Don't I get any credit for doing my due diligence this time? I read the personnel file! It was boring!" He stared out the window, possibly hungering for a turn in the lineup of surfers. "That's more than I did when the last four assistants came on board."

"Four?" Natasha blurted. "You slept with *four* of them?"

Her new boss was a man slut. This job was going to be tricky. She was going to have her hands full of him. *With* him!

Damon had the grace to appear embarrassed. "Except for one instance, it wasn't my idea, I swear." He gave her a humble look. "Was I supposed to say no? Feelings would have been hurt."

"Right." She scoffed. "Women just leap into your arms."

Unfazed, Damon and Jimmy gazed at her. They both nodded.

"Yeah. Pretty much," Damon said, rubbing his stubbled jaw.

"Since he was a teenager," Jimmy agreed with a long-suffering sigh. "It's the damnedest thing. But when *you* interviewed with me, Natasha, and said you were about to get married, I knew—"

"You knew you'd found your son's kryptonite. Me."

It was all right there in Damon Torrance's philosophies for living: Pop-Tarts, kung fu, and not screwing around with married women. Simultaneously relieved and incredulous, Natasha frowned.

"My qualifications for this job go way beyond being married," she argued. "I'm smart, I'm capable, I'm passionate—"

"I'm listening," Damon said, perking up.

"—and I'm not going to put up with any bullshit. Get it?"

Both men widened their eyes. It was almost as though they'd never heard a blue-eyed, blond-haired, bubbly California girl talk frankly before. Jimmy rallied first. Soberly, he nodded.

"Based on my research"—and Natasha had, indeed, done plenty of research, because while you could take the girl out of UCSD, you couldn't take the UCSD out of the girl—"I think you're headed for the top of your field, Damon. And I intend to go straight to the top with you. If that's not what you want, tell me right now, because I don't have time to waste. I've done a lot of work to get my foot in the door at a good company. Now that I'm here, I plan to take full advantage of it."

She might have downgraded her ambitions to the assistant level in order to help support her husband, Natasha knew, but she'd be damned if she'd tamp them down completely.

Gratifyingly, this time Damon was the one staring at her.

Solemnly, he took her hand in his. "You're not kryptonite. You're incredible. You're like . . ." Seeming at a loss for words, he swore. "You're like a badass cheerleader who makes straight A's. Like a fast-talking Goody Two-shoes who just shot her first *Playboy* centerfold. Like the world's sexiest, strictest, most nurturing CPA-turned-supermodel." Seeming on the verge of coming up with several more unlikely alter egos for her, Damon stopped. He smiled. "You're unique, is what I'm trying so say. I *do* want what you want. In fact, I think I just fell in love with you."

For a heartbeat, Natasha was almost sucked in by that. His deep brown eyes lured her. His happy-go-lucky grin beckoned her. Even his body, all tall and strong and masculine as he stood there before her, seemed somehow magnetized to pull her nearer.

She wondered, incredibly and nonsensically, what it would be like to be truly loved by a man like Damon Torrance. Then she gave herself a mental pinch and came to her senses for good.

"Don't tell me that again." Natasha pulled away. Doing so required far more effort than she would have liked or intended ever to admit. This . . . *attraction* she felt toward Damon would have to be squashed, plain and simple. It was wrong and foolhardy and just . . . *wrong*. She loved Paul! She truly did. "Don't tell me you love me. Don't flirt. Don't inform me of your sexual conquests or expect me to bail you out of them. I'm your assistant, not your nanny. If you remember that, we'll get along fine."

"You're my assistant, not my nanny," Damon repeated.

Even as he dutifully said those words, though, he just kept on grinning at her. It was as though she were a ray of sunshine warming him, an adorable puppy cheering him, a plate of Pop-Tarts . . . well, she didn't know *what* the Pop-Tarts were for, only that he seemed to have an ideology constructed around them.

Someday, she'd have to ask him about that.

"Right. And if you don't remember that—if you try to take advantage of me—I won't hesitate to take my talents elsewhere. Got it?" Natasha held out her hand. "Do we have a deal?"

Curiously, Damon considered her. "Do you always set up so many boundaries before doing things?"

"Usually they're necessary."

To her relief, Damon didn't ask *why* they were necessary. Instead, he made a rueful face. "Why do I feel, all of a sudden, that *you're* the one who's hiring *me?*"

At the other desk, Jimmy laughed. "You'd better agree, son. If you try to stall, she'll talk you into a ten percent raise."

"Good idea." Natasha nodded. "But now that I've sized up the job, I'd say fifteen percent sounds more appropriate."

"Done." Jimmy agreed. "It'll be worth every penny just to see how this turns out—for however long it lasts, at least."

Natasha couldn't let his skepticism affect her. Now that she knew *they* needed her as much as *she* needed them, she had a little bit of leverage. It felt unfamiliar—but kind of good, too. Despite its newness, she couldn't help liking it.

And Paul had said she *wouldn't* be good at business. . . .

Damon gave her a forthright look. "Do you mean it?" he asked soberly. "Do you really think you can handle me?"

At that moment, Natasha could think of several scintillating ways to *handle him*. But since she was trying to focus on staying true to her wedding vows—and since Damon actually seemed concerned and hopeful and boyishly earnest—she turned her thoughts in a less bawdy direction. She nodded.

"Together, I think we can take on the world and win."

With that, Damon clasped her hand. Natasha felt another inner tremor rock her from her heels on up. As she and her new boss sealed their reckless deal, she hoped with all her might that the words she'd just said would be prophetic.

Together, I think we can take on the world and win.

She didn't know what that would look like or how it

would feel. But now that she'd met Damon Torrance in person, Natasha had the sudden, unmistakable sensation that for the first time in her life, winning big was possible. She would have been a fool to let that go . . . no matter how stupidly giddy she felt when Damon smiled at her. She could handle that. Easy-peasy.

All she had to do was get started.

Oh, and stay married.

That way, she'd qualify as Damon's kryptonite for the long haul. After all, that's what seemed to have nabbed her the job over all the competition in the first place.

But since Natasha intended to do both those things anyway—get started *and* stay married—there was no problem here.

No problem at all . . .